THE BE

ALSO BY PENNY FEENY

That Summer in Ischia
The Apartment in Rome
Secrets in Sicily

THE BEACH AT DOONSHEAN

and a reminder of south
Liverpool .....
To Morph
      with lots of love,
            Penny

PENNY FEENY XX

ⓐ

Prologue

9th July 1981

They called it the secret beach – their secret, because it felt so private and undiscovered. Yesterday they had it entirely to themselves, on a squally unpredictable afternoon when clouds chased the sun and a wild wind whipped eddies of fine sand along the shoreline. They spun in its powerful gusts and fell over laughing, breathless and exhilarated. In a lull they built a magnificent castle, only for it to be beaten down by the tide. This thundered in so quickly they had to scramble to reach the cliff top.

He stands on the ledge now, looking down, shading the light from his eyes, trying to make out the handful of silhouettes paddling in the shallows, foraging in the rock pools. No one is swimming. Today is different. Although the sun is bright enough to dazzle there's a chill in the air – similar to the chill that's settled around his heart. The fear he knows he'd be unwise to dismiss.

He's been looking for them everywhere. At first he pounded Dingle's pavements, past the brightly coloured pubs with their Guinness-dark interiors, then along the harbour and the pier, as if they might be hiding under a tarpaulin or behind a stack of lobster pots. Although his hunt was fruitless, the rhythm of walking calmed him. He wouldn't let the situation get the better of him: forbearance is his default setting. He climbed into the car and slowly cruised the back roads, eyes swivelling from side to side. When he swung towards the beach it was his last resort.

Perfectly secluded, Doonshean is a gift for those in the know. It's much closer to Dingle than Ventry or Inch Strand – that long finger pointing across the bay where campers squat among the dunes. In the distance, he can make out the curious rock formation named The Foal, like an enchanted seahorse rising from the waves, another instance of the magic that haunts this spot. He takes in the drama of the scene: the folds of land like arms embracing the series of coves and the deceptive surface of the water, a deep twinkling blue. The sand has a silver sheen; the sky is a bolt of silk unfurled. The beauty of it draws him down the steep cobbled incline.

The cries of a child skim across the beach towards him. He can't tell if they are cries of excitement or alarm. The breeze lifts the sounds into the air where they swirl in competition with the gulls. He's not sure if the voice is familiar, but suddenly he is alert to danger and a sense of panic returns. He begins to move faster towards the slippery outcrop with its trove of shrimps and limpets and sea anemones, where the small figure is perched. He's not close enough to make out facial features, but he can recognise a little boy in trouble. He curses the distance as he sees the boy lose his footing, windmill his arms and then, in appalling slow motion, topple from the rocks. There's a splash, followed by a moment's fraught silence.

He tugs off his shoes and runs. The sand is so firm his feet make no sound. He's pulling his arms out of his jacket and abandoning that also. He's aware of a frenzied yelling, voices wailing for help, figures jumping up and down in distress. Nobody else has gone after the child and there's no head breaking through the foaming water, no sign of movement below the swell of the waves slapping the boulders. He increases his pace, fixated on rescue. This is his job: to save lives. This is a life he will save.

He plunges into the freezing ocean.

PART ONE

APRIL 2010

WEDNESDAY THURSDAY FRIDAY

I

The House

Rachael was stacking meringue nests into ivory towers. The radio was burbling in the background. Meringues were fragile and liable to crumble into dust at rough treatment, but they required little effort and would keep forever. She produced them regularly at her catering functions and liked to organise advance supplies. Checking her nests were wedged firm, she slotted lids onto containers and arranged them on the slate shelves of the old pantry. Wiping away the sticky residue of spilled egg whites, dumping the used equipment in the deep butler's sink, she felt a satisfying sense of accomplishment. Then she glanced into the garden and saw the boy.

He was crouched in the middle of the lawn by the pear tree that had, until this instant, delighted her with its frilly white blossom. He was about nine or ten, a scrawny body muffled in a tracksuit. She couldn't see his face or what he was doing but it looked suspicious. She thumped on the windowpane. The boy raised his head and then resumed his mysterious activity.

Rachael was nonplussed. She should challenge him, of course. The trouble was, she didn't feel properly established in this house; she had only a toehold. It was the home where her husband, Matt, had spent his teenage years and he'd been reluctant to move back. He said it carried too much baggage and he'd rather have a fresh start. But Rachael, who had long coveted it, had pointed out the obvious advantages: the leafy location, the space, the garden, which would all be wonderful for Danny. It was far too big for just one person and if his mother chose to be generous, Matt shouldn't be selfish.

No money had changed hands. Julia, newly retired, had moved into the city centre apartment they'd vacated and gone to visit old friends in the Dordogne while it was being refurbished. Rachael had been so elated she didn't like to admit she was now having second thoughts: that perhaps she wasn't quite ready for suburbia, or that living with shades of her mother-in-law – with the strong dark colours and functional furnishings – was discomfiting. She longed to redecorate in a scheme that would be as light and airy and floral as her favourite perfume, but until they could afford to do this, she felt almost as much a trespasser as the boy outside.

The Victorian villa had been one of the first built in the street. Its exterior had a worn, comfortable air like a well-thumbed book, but its neighbours were a hash of different styles and periods. The bungalow next door had been empty since its elderly occupant moved into a nursing home and Rachael noticed there was a gap in the privet hedge dividing the two gardens, just large enough for a child to squeeze

4

through. She clattered down the short flight of steps from the kitchen and crossed the flagged patio.

The boy must have heard her but he didn't react. He was crouching over a piece of slate. Earthworms and slugs were squirming across the surface and he was chopping them into bits with the sharp edge of a stone.

'Whatever are you up to?' exclaimed Rachael.

He didn't stop. 'Feed the birds,' he said.

'That's not the way to do it!' It was macabre and repulsive and she couldn't bear to watch. 'Shouldn't you be at school?'

Danny was at school. It had been agonising at first to leave him drooping at the door of the reception class. But since Easter he'd rallied. He'd even let her say goodbye at the gate and watch him trot into the building with the staunch sense of duty he'd inherited from Matt.

The boy looked in her direction for the first time. His hair was shorn brutally close, his eyes rolled, wide apart. He had a scratch along his jaw and an outcrop of freckles that gave his face a rough innocence.

'Got the day off 'cos we're moving.'

Surely he wasn't coming to live next door? There was no sign of a removal van. 'Well, you shouldn't be in this garden, all the same.'

'She said I could.'

'Who did?'

The boy's lower lip jutted beyond the upper in an exaggerated pout. He scrambled up and with the toe of his trainer started pawing the ground. 'She what lives here.'

'*I* live here,' said Rachael – a phrase she repeated often in her head for reassurance. Then she realised he was referring to Bel.

Bel was currently installed in the attic recovering from a bout of malaria. She was an added complication because her life never ran smoothly. Other people didn't come back from a charitable stint in Africa to find their flatmate had re-let their room; other people managed to visit the tropics without getting bitten or infected with disease; other people didn't invite random scallies to invade their garden and sacrifice living creatures.

Rachael was fond of Bel, but she wouldn't have chosen her as a cohabitee. Their tastes and lifestyles were very different. And she had no concept of privacy. 'But you can borrow anything of mine!' she'd protested when Rachael tracked down her missing pashmina. 'Only I find it so *cold* here.' And Rachael couldn't argue, although she'd never been in the least tempted to borrow any of her sister-in-law's clothes.

'She probably thought you wanted to get your ball back or something,' she told him, giving Bel the benefit of the doubt.

'I weren't playing ball.'

'Okay, but you have to go anyway. And stop that… massacre.'

The worms weren't writhing any more, they were slowly desiccating in the warm spring sun. 'Worms eat dead people,' he said. He kicked at the slate so that sections of invertebrates leapt and scattered. 'Feed the birds.'

Rachael shuddered.

She watched his feet disappear through the hedge and once she was certain he'd gone, she went back indoors. The radio was informing her that although the Icelandic volcano, Eyjafjallajökull, was still active – how the newsreaders loved to twist their tongues around its name – the ban on flights had been lifted and stranded travellers would be able to resume their journeys. The sky had been empty of planes for almost a week: a blue distilled silence. It seemed incredible that billions of invisible rock fragments were tainting the atmosphere, disrupting whole continents, when superficially everything looked so normal.

To Rachael, the day no longer felt normal. The incident with the boy had unnerved her. She hoped the birds would snaffle the evidence of his visit; she didn't want Danny to see what he'd been up to. Dan was only five, far too young for inappropriate influences, though there was no telling whether he'd be as disgusted as she was or just that little bit excited. Child-rearing was a minefield. The fact that her mother-in-law was a paediatrician should have been useful, but actually made her feel an extra obligation to get it right.

She switched off the radio, worried she'd be late fetching Danny from school. She knew he'd emerge with his shirt askew, his bag trailing and his mood vulnerable. She usually brought a snack to revive him but because she'd been delayed they'd have to call in at the sweet shop. He regarded this as a treat to be savoured and would spend a long time making up his mind while louder, bigger children jostled in front of him at the counter.

It was another half hour before she returned home. Danny had chosen chocolate buttons and was letting them melt one by one on his tongue. When she turned into their street she was shocked to see a patrol car waiting outside the house. She braked sharply and the last few buttons scattered.

It will be about the boy, she reasoned. He'll have got into trouble with some other, less tolerant neighbour who's summoned the police to deal with him. Nothing to do with us. She parked in the drive and opened the passenger door. She was rescuing the schoolbag and the torn chocolate wrapper when she heard a footfall. Danny was gazing upwards with a thrilled expression on his face.

'Mrs Wentworth?' said the policewoman.

Rachael wasn't often addressed by her married name so she hesitated before straightening up and turning around. 'Yes?' she said. Instinctively she clasped Danny's hand. The appearance of two police officers with their peaked caps and their walkie-talkies did not bode well.

'Can we come inside a moment?'

'What is it? What's happened? Is Matt all right?'

She couldn't help it: it was always the first question that sprang to mind. Matt's father had died while on holiday in Ireland, saving a child from drowning. Matt had been four at the time, too young to comprehend the tragedy, but for Rachael this stranger cast a long shadow, the sort of shadow that could taint a future. Every now and again she'd have to crush the notion that, despite his apparent good health, Matt might suffer from some kind of jinx. And this irrational part of her prayed that the jinx was watered down from one generation to the next, otherwise Danny would be affected too, which would simply be more than she could bear.

'We're just making inquiries at this stage,' said the policewoman, going on to introduce herself and her colleague and indicate their identity badges. 'Can we come in?'

Rachael didn't want to let them into the house, their heavy shoes clumping through the hall. She wouldn't be able to despatch Danny to his room because he'd be eager to know what was happening and who had done something they shouldn't. Then she saw the boy – the garden invader – sloping past, staring with interest at the police car, the bright flash along its sides. The officers watched him too, perhaps waiting to see if he was going to gouge the paintwork or stab the tyres, but he moved on.

'Okay,' she said, fumbling through her keys for the one to the front door and then leading them into the sitting room. She switched on the television for Dan, who ignored it.

'I'm sorry for disturbing you, Mrs Wentworth,' the policewoman said, 'but we're following up an investigation in France.'

'France?'

'Yes. It seems a car you hired when you were over there, a red Citroën, was found abandoned in Bordeaux. It should have been returned to the airport in Limoges on Wednesday. There were concerns initially that it had been stolen and something had befallen you… so we just need to clear up a few issues…'

'But I haven't been in France,' said Rachael.

'This house is number 21? You are Mrs Wentworth?'

'Well yes, but—'

'Mrs Julia Wentworth?'

Rachael had been standing, half aware of their reflections – three puzzled faces – in the mirror on the wall. She sat down suddenly. At least the soft, opulent sofa was her own. The one Julia had taken with her wasn't nearly so comfortable.

'Actually it's Dr Wentworth and she's my mother-in-law. I'm Rachael.'

'This is her address?'

'It used to be, till she moved out a couple of months ago. But she has gone to France. Staying with some friends who run a gîte or something.'

The policewoman looked at her notebook. 'Yes. She gave their address when she collected the car, but they don't know her whereabouts. Apparently she didn't tell them where she was going.'

'That's odd,' said Rachael.

The policewoman sighed. 'There's been a lot of confusion lately – well, it's still going on – because so many flights are grounded. To tell the truth, we thought this was an over-reaction. Cars are being dumped all over the place because there's no room for them on the ferries.'

'Because of the volcanic eruption you mean?'

'Yes.'

'I saw the news reports,' said Rachael. 'But we weren't bothered because we knew Julia had planned to be away for two weeks... We didn't expect to hear from her.'

'As far as you're concerned, she's not a missing person?'

Rachael threw a shocked glance at Dan who had his thumb in his mouth. 'No of course not! Why would we think that?'

'Quite. We wouldn't want to alarm you. Perhaps we should speak to her next of kin.'

Rachael wasn't feeling well disposed towards Bel. She didn't even know whether she was in, beached on her bed in the attic playing the invalid card, or whether she'd gone out again to engage with undesirable youth. And what use would she be?

'You mean my husband?' she said. 'Right, I'll ring the office.' But Reception told her Matt was in a conference, which meant his phone would be switched to silent. 'I'm sorry,' she said helplessly to the police. 'I can't get hold of him until he's finished work.'

'Will you ask him to contact us when he gets in?'

'Yes of course... I suppose I could also try Julia's mobile myself.'

'The friends she was staying with have already done that, but they couldn't get through. You may have more luck.'

'She probably ran out of charge or something,' said Rachael. 'Though she's quite an efficient person usually.' She scrolled through her contact numbers under what felt like intense scrutiny. Her call went straight to answerphone.

2

The Alarm

Matt's spirits rose as he approached his home. His spirits always rose at the prospect of his wife – not only at the sight of her lithe limbs, the feel of her silky hair, but at the scents she carried with her too. These ranged from the sharp pungency of garlic and rosemary to a pleasant wafting (like today) of vanilla sugar and hazelnut. It was as if she glided around in a personal fragrance factory. In a matter of weeks she had transformed the kitchen that he'd only ever known as a perfunctory fuelling stop.

When he was growing up, food was never foremost in anyone's mind but his own. There was no pleasure in raiding fridge or pantry to be met with frozen pizzas and bland packs of yogurt. Pocket money went on chocolate bars and chips after school but, by God, he'd spent most of his adolescence hungry. Not now. Rachael's shelves were full of unusual pickles and elaborate pies; there'd be gravadlax curing in the fridge, stock simmering on the stove. Most of these treats were labelled and spoken for, but to come home to view the feast and sample a few leftovers could put a gloss on the most frustrating of days.

He shrugged off his jacket as he mounted the steps to the front door. His stomach growled a little in anticipation. It came as a surprise to find Rachael's demeanour didn't match the vision of milk and honey he'd conjured up. She was in the sitting room, hovering in front of the six o'clock news as if expecting a fearful announcement. He dropped his briefcase beside the oak bureau his mother had left behind. The television screen was filled with a fleet of planes lined up on airport tarmac. He leaned his arm across Rachael's shoulder and kissed her cheek. 'Crazy isn't it,' he observed. 'Half the world grounded in this day and age.'

'They're changing the guidelines,' she said 'They're going to let the airlines fly after all. They've decided the ash isn't as much of a threat as they thought.'

'They're losing too much money, that's why.' He patted her arm. 'Is Danny in his room? I'll go and find him. Can I smell custard?'

'No, meringues. Listen, Matt...'

'What?'

'No, you go and change. I'll tell you later.'

'Rach, what is it?'

Her head swayed and she chewed her bottom lip. 'The police were here, looking for you. I'm sorry, I was trying not to tell you till after you'd set yourself up with a drink. It's about your mother.'

'My mother!' He nearly said: what's he done this time? Julia had spent much of Matt's youth rescuing his stepfather, Leo, from irate publicans, taxi drivers and – more than once – a police station. But she wasn't married to Leo any more. 'Why?'

'She seems to have vanished.'

'Vanished!'

'Stop repeating everything I say, Matt.'

'But you're talking bollocks,' he protested. 'She's on holiday in France.'

Rachael, much as he loved her, had a disconcerting ability to freeze into an ice maiden. One moment she'd be warm and luscious as a ripe melon and the next an invisible sheet would solidify between them and she'd cast him one of her *noli me tangere* looks. She did this now and his homecoming fantasy of a welcoming kiss and a delicious snack evaporated.

'Don't you realise this is serious? The police turned up HERE. They were waiting for me and Danny. I thought something had happened to YOU.'

'What did they say?'

'They'd been contacted by the French authorities because her hire car had been found abandoned. That's true of lots of other cars too but mostly the drivers have been traced. And that's the odd thing about Julia. She's not at the Culshaws and her phone's switched off.'

'Have you rung the flat?'

'I left a message on the answering machine. Even if the builders were there, I don't suppose they'd know anything.'

'She's probably just lost in the travel chaos, people rerouting their journeys and trying to get on ferries and so on. What does Bel reckon?'

'I haven't told her yet.'

He'd been loosening his tie. His hand curled around the knot and tugged it. 'Why ever not?'

'Because she wouldn't know what to do. You will.'

'Will I?' he wondered, touched by the trust placed in him, but as much at sea as the next person. They were interrupted by a skidding on the stairs and across the floor. Dan hurtled into the room and ambushed his father's knees; Matt nearly lost his balance. 'Hey, big boy, how goes it?' He swept up the child until their faces were level and they rubbed noses. Dan giggled.

'The police came here, Daddy!'

'Yes, I heard.'

'I think you should ring the Culshaws,' said Rachael.

Peter and Dorothy Culshaw were long-standing family friends who'd recently restored an old farmhouse in the Dordogne and turned it into a B&B. This was the first year they had opened for business and Julia was an early visitor. It was as good a place to start as any. Reluctantly Matt set down his son, pulled out his phone and tapped on their number.

After a pause there came a long foreign trill. Another pause. Then: '*Bonsoir. La Maison Verte.*'

'Dorothy? It's Matthew Wentworth.'

'Matt. Oh, goodness!' Dorothy's voice had never lost its breathy girlish pitch. She always looked the same too: like a gawky overgrown elf, with ears poking through flyaway hair she maintained at a shade between rhubarb and carrot. (Though Matt, being colour-blind, had to take this on trust.) 'How is she?'

'Bel? Oh, she's recovering. But our concern now is my mother.'

'I was talking about Julia,' said Dorothy. 'Is she not back yet?'

'No. And you heard about the abandoned car?'

'Yes… we didn't know what to think.'

'When did you last see her?'

'Saturday. I mean, we expected her to stay until Wednesday but she just upped and left four days early. To be honest, her behaviour was a little odd while she was here. A little *distrait*. I couldn't put my finger on it exactly… But I do recognise that sense of anti-climax you get when your working life comes to an end and you don't have the same status any more and you're at a bit of a loss.' Dorothy was known for her tendency to gush, to skirt around issues without ever getting to the point. Julia was the opposite. Matt was surprised to hear her described as 'at a bit of a loss'.

'Did she say something to you? Drop any hints?'

'Not specifically. It was entirely her choice to leave so we didn't want to make an issue of it.' She paused, lurched onto a different track. 'I hadn't realised, Matt, that she'd given away her house!'

Matt looked around the large room with its assortment of artefacts from two quite different lifestyles: was this to become his albatross? To Dorothy he said, 'She was finding it too big, so we swapped. There's nothing sinister in that.'

He wandered into the kitchen and took a beer from the fridge. Evening light slanted through the back door, open because Dan had run into the garden.

'It wasn't only us,' Dorothy said. 'Leo was bothered too.'

'Leo? Why?'

'Well he's here and he thinks—'

'*Leo* is with you?'

Rachael returned his surprised glance with a grimace. Matt knew she didn't much care for his stepfather. When they'd first met, Leo had greeted Rachael with 'All hail the domestic goddess!' which she found patronising. Later, on their wedding day, he hadn't improved his reputation by getting disgracefully drunk.

'Yes,' said Dorothy a little sheepishly. 'We're planning to run courses, you see, as added value for our guests. And painting's one of the most popular. We had another artist lined up actually, but he got gallstones and had to drop out at very short notice. Leo has been such a dream, came for Easter and stepped into the last-minute breach...'

'Did Julia know he was going to be there?'

Dorothy was defensive. 'We'd been trying to persuade her to come out here for ages and we didn't want her to change her plans. One never quite knows how to play these things and, I confess, we may have made a misjudgement on this occasion.'

The mystery was beginning to make more sense. Typical Dorothy, he thought. Soft-centred as a marshmallow. Probably trying to get them back together again. 'So Leo's the reason she left ahead of time?'

'If you want to put it like that.'

How else could he put it? Rachael was peeling an onion, prising off the golden papery skin with her fingernails. He was tempted to lift her hair and kiss the hollow of her collarbone. Then the onion fell to her knife. He loved watching her chop and slice, the speed with which she flashed the blade through the white flesh. The house had been noisy when Julia and Leo lived in it, alight with recriminations. Now, in contrast, it was blissfully calm: the sizzle of oil in the frying pan, the murmur of music from the radio, and outside his son playing with his truck, the clatter of its wheels on the paving.

Dorothy was saying. 'It's true they had a slight disagreement, and you know he likes to be provocative: he made some reference to *King Lear*. But all Julia told us was that she wanted to go touring by herself for a bit. Explore more of France. Only…'

'What?'

'I've known Julia for twenty-five years, Matt. She's always been so organised. And I think she's behaving out of character. Like a cat.'

He snapped the top off his bottle of San Miguel. Through the doorway he saw a ginger tom squirm through a hole in the hedge. 'A *cat*?'

'Or any mammal,' said Dorothy. 'When they're ill they crawl away, don't they, craving solitude.'

Matt was confused. Bel was the person who'd been sick and his sister had never in her life craved solitude.

'My mother's ill?' he said now. 'With what?'

'Nothing that she *told* us about, but goodness, Matt, she's a doctor! She'd know, wouldn't she?'

'Know what?'

'Well, if her blood count was down or something.'

'You think she's got leukaemia and is keeping it to herself?'

Rachael's head jerked up; the onions were sweating gently, becoming soft and transparent.

'I didn't want to worry you,' said Dorothy as firmly as her high girlish voice would allow. 'Obviously one would expect a person to give their family important news – good

18

or bad – before they'd let on to a friend. It's just that, coupled with everything else…'

'What else?'

'I mean giving away her home and now this disappearing act. It makes you think, doesn't it?'

Matt thought Dorothy was being decidedly fanciful. 'Perhaps I ought to speak to Leo.'

'Actually I'm not sure he's here. He's been a bit elusive.'

'Him too?'

'I think he only went down to the village. Do you want me to get him to call you?'

Matt sensed his shirt sticking to his back, even though the weather was no more than mild. He needed to rip off his clothes and stand under a pounding, purifying shower. 'Yes, please. Urgently.'

3

The Visitor

When the phone blasted into her sleep Bel was dreaming she was back in Sudan, caught in a sudden storm: raindrops bursting like shot on her head and shoulders, making a terrifying rattle on corrugated roofs, driving the squealing shiny-faced children she was teaching to seek cover. Afterwards, with the earth fizzing yet dry as a bone, she wouldn't have believed it had rained at all if her hair hadn't been plastered, sopping wet, to her skull.

The clamour persisted, drilling into the effects of the Temazepam (hospital turned you into a pill popper, she'd found). Her hand floundered on the bedside table, seeking the off button. She pressed answer instead and nearly tumbled onto the floor.

'Hiya, sweet.'

Bel righted herself, clutched the phone to her ear, adjusted her pillows. She shivered and wondered if she would ever be warm again. She recognised now that she was under the eaves, in the cool white attic. These rooms, opened up years before to create a studio space for her father, had been deemed her quarters. Her quarter. The rest of the property was Matt and Rachael's.

'Bel?' said the voice, a touch impatiently.

'Dad! I've been trying to get hold of you for ages.'

'You have?'

'Since last night, anyway. You didn't pick up!' Frustratingly, Leo wasn't as attached to his phone as she was to hers. He could forget where he'd put it or forget to switch it on or, worse, ignore it altogether, claiming it sapped the creative impulse.

'So how are you?'

She shifted position, trying to get comfortable. 'How I am is not the point. Everybody here is in a total state about Mum.'

'Ah… yes.'

Matt had stalked up and down, rumpling his hair, as he'd told her about the visit from the police. No cause to jump to conclusions, he'd said. Since half the continent was in travel chaos they didn't yet need a manhunt. But an image of the abandoned car had hooked into Bel's brain, though she tried to dismiss it. 'Good grief! Aren't you worried too?'

'I'm sure Julia knows what she's doing,' said Leo.

Bel recognised his tone of withdrawal. 'What's been going on? Why did she leave the Culshaws' early? Was it because she was pissed off to find you there too? Or was it something you said? You do goad her sometimes.'

'You know Julia,' said Leo. 'That tendency to seethe below the surface.'

'So you did have a row?'

'Darling, she just blew up.'

'Are you going to tell me what it was about?'

There was a long silence, then a snort. She imagined him putting the mobile down, staring at the screen for a few moments before picking it up again. He refused to conform to other people's expectations. Another snort. Then a bark. 'You.'

When Bel was growing up, her mother used to be exasperated by her knack of finding trouble (or rather, trouble finding her). Matt was pretty good about helping her get out of it, but her father's sense of fun sometimes made it worse. One time, giggling together, he'd painted her all over with red spots so she could pretend to have measles and stay off school. Although Julia couldn't have been taken in for a minute, she was furious. She'd exploded at Leo, castigated him for being so juvenile, for getting acrylic paint on Bel's tunic, which would never come out, for turning a deadly disease into a joke. 'Lighten up, woman, for God's sake,' Leo had shouted. And then he'd slammed out of the house and Bel had to endure having the spots rubbed crossly from her skin.

When she'd arrived back from Sudan to find her room occupied, she'd carted her possessions to her father's flat and settled there to look for work. As a freelance graphic designer most of her contacts were in London and they needed to be reminded she was available again. Except she wasn't, because within days she'd collapsed with a high temperature. Leo had sent her home to Liverpool, to her mother. Real illness was alien to him and he preferred not to deal with it.

'Me!' she exclaimed now. 'This is my fault?'

'I was keeping out of her way,' said Leo. 'I mean, why wouldn't I? I had a job to do. I'd been busy over Easter. But

Julia let rip. She certainly knows how to lay into a person when she thinks they haven't done their duty. She accused me of not caring for you properly, claimed you cramped my style so I stuck you on the train and left her to pick up the pieces.'

'But, Dad, that's what you did.'

'Because I thought it was the best course of action! I wasn't in a position to look after you and she was. I mean, Christ, malaria. What a fucking wild card that was. Why didn't you take the fucking tablets?'

'I *did* but they had these horrible side effects, remember? I was hallucinating and everything. I didn't have any *choice*. I had to change to another sort.'

It had been a sly undercover assault, the mosquito bite – literally, for she had used a mosquito net. There was no single occasion to which she could pinpoint the infection. She'd been told, too often in her view, how lucky she was to be treated in England; how lucky she wasn't holed up in some base camp clinic on the edge of the desert. Well that was true, and she *was* grateful. But what people didn't realise was that being ill stank. Being ill was a complete, utter, unbearable, depressing, grinding pain in the arse. It knocked the spontaneity as well as the stuffing out of you.

'Anyway, we've been through all that. Have I got this right? You're saying it's because of me that you and Mum fell out?'

Leo grunted.

'And she left the Culshaws' to get away from you? And it's because she's pissed off in general that she's ignoring our calls? You don't think she's had her phone robbed or there's anything suspicious going on?'

'I doubt it very much,' said Leo. 'I'd let her go her own sweet way.'

Of course he would. Thunder, tempest, followed by an eerie calm: this was a familiar pattern in her parents' relationship. 'That's not very helpful.'

Matt hadn't been much use either. 'I refuse to speculate,' he'd said as if it indicated a triumph of will rather than sheer stubbornness. That was Matt all over: a pleasant, affable exterior and a bullish obstinacy Bel could seldom conquer.

'Unfortunately,' drawled Leo, 'Julia seems to like keeping people in the dark.' This was a dig; he was clearly sore about something not necessarily connected with her mother's disappearance.

Bel shifted on the bed. She felt as if she were on a raft, barely afloat in the austere expanse of the attic. This impression was reinforced by the sight of her belongings dotted about on lonely islets of furniture. 'So where are we supposed to go from here?'

'Where are you now?'

'I'm back at home. Squatting in your old studio.'

'Then stay there,' he advised. 'Dig your heels in. Julia will turn up.'

It was a grim day. Bel and Rachael tuned in to the twenty-four-hour news channel and fed each other's fears until they were both wildly on edge. They jumped at every ring on landline and mobile, hoping Matt would have something to report. They took turns to text him for information but there was no news. He was late home too.

'Where have you been?' demanded Rachael as soon as he came through the door.

'I went to the flat.'

'You mean our old one? In Canning Street?'

'Yes, I wanted to try and catch the builders, see if they'd heard from Julia.'

'And had they?'

'They'd gone, unfortunately. But there's still a lot of work to be done. The kitchen's all loose cables and carcasses and there's no bath. She couldn't live in it yet.'

Bel had curled herself up on the sofa, wrapped in the borrowed pashmina. (She'd brought scarcely anything with her, which was why she had to raid Rachael's wardrobe.) Rachael perched on the arm of a chair but leapt up every now and again to check on Danny who was playing in the garden.

Bel said: 'Haven't you been able to get through to *anyone*?'

Matt stood, arms folded, legs braced, a solid figure of authority. 'I've spent most of the day on the phone to those bloody hire car people. They as good as admitted their paperwork was all over the place because there've been so many stranded passengers trying to get home. Carjacking's been rife. They're going to check the documentation again and get back to me.'

'Soon?'

'Well I hope so. I also rang Mum's bank and asked them to look into the dates of her credit card transactions. That should flag up where she's been using them. But I've cancelled them anyway, to be on the safe side.'

'Why?'

He took off his glasses and polished them on the sleeve of his shirt. 'Because it's a sensible precaution to take. Because if they've been stolen along with her phone—'

Theft, hijack, kidnap. Or worse... Bel really didn't want to go there – that ghastly tabloid hinterland peopled by victims of violent crime. She sought an alternative. 'What if they haven't?'

'Then she can get them activated again, can't she? They'll run a security check and it means we can flush her out. I don't see what else we can do.'

Could her mother have *chosen* to go into hiding? Could she really have the mysterious illness Dorothy Culshaw had suggested? Beneath her layers, Bel's flesh erupted into goose pimples. She could do without another calamity. She caressed the mobile on her lap, willing it to burst into a jingle of good news.

When the ring came on the doorbell the sound was both a shock and a relief. For a moment the three of them stared at each other, stunned. Then Matt went to answer it.

They heard a murmur of voices and he came back, not with any official messenger, but with a teenage girl none of them seen before. Her hair was scraped into a tight band, exposing a face that looked sharp and wary. She was wearing a skimpy vest and a strip of skirt. A stud glittered in her navel and a snake tattoo coiled around her ankle. Her mouth was making rapid chewing movements; she pushed the gum into the corner of her cheek. 'I've come for our Nathan,' she said.

'Who?'

'Our Nath.'

'I think you've got the wrong house,' said Rachael.

'Nah. He's playing out with your little lad.'

Matt said, 'Oh, then they'll be in the garden.'

'What's going on?' said Rachael. 'Who are you?'

'I'm Nath's sister. It's time he came home for his tea.' The girl was looking with interest around the room and at the darker patches on the walls, which marked the outlines of Leo's absent canvases. They'd been taken down and stored at the back of the garage until Julia decided their fate.

'But Danny's on his own.' Rachael stumbled as she made her way to the window and peered out. 'Oh God, it's that boy again.'

'What boy?'

'The one who was here yesterday. You met him too, Bel. And did you see what he was doing?

'Yeah! Gross, wasn't it?' She'd gone outside for an illicit smoke (which had tasted foul) and found him in the midst of operations. 'But he was only trying to help. I told him he didn't need to. Birds can manage on their own. That's how they're programmed. And that if he fed the birds, he'd encourage the cats.'

'Why did you say he could come in the first place?'

'I didn't. I don't know what it is with children, they just seem to latch on to me. I guess they think I'm non-threatening. What's it matter anyway?'

'Because he's much older than Danny. It really isn't a good idea.'

Bel thought Danny might be lonely; he could do with more friends to play with. She didn't see the harm in his getting to know new neighbours. 'What's your name?' she asked the girl.

'Kelly.'

'And you've moved nearby, is that right?'

'It's only temporary like. We had to find somewhere quick 'cos our house burned down.'

'No? Really?'

'Yeah, it's totally wrecked, all our stuff melted to bits or up in smoke, the lot.'

Bel wanted to hear more – was it a gas explosion? An electrical fault? A firework through the letter box? An arson attack? – but Rachael said, 'He must have come through the hedge again. We need to fix it, Matt. I mean, suppose Danny escaped? We don't want anyone else to go missing.'

'Who's missing?' asked Kelly, scratching the back of her thigh.

Nobody answered. Rachael flung open the French doors and Kelly clumped across the room. 'Hey, Nath!' she yelled from the top of the steps. 'Move it.'

Danny came up sulkily and tugged at the hem of Rachael's top. 'Why does Nathan have to go now? We were in the middle of our game. It's not fair.'

'His sister wants to take him home.' To Kelly, she added: 'Can you tell your mother to keep a better eye on Nathan so he doesn't go round being a nuisance?'

'We live with me nan.'

Bel twirled her collection of bracelets. The knob of her wrist bone gleamed palely through the coloured beads. 'Does your mother live somewhere else then?'

Kelly said, 'Me nan looks after us because me mum's dead.'

There was a moment's silence.

Matt said, 'God, I'm sorry.' It was a knee-jerk reaction and Bel could see he was annoyed with himself. It used to happen a lot when they were younger. People would apologise to him when they heard about his father and afterwards he'd mutter: 'Why do they always say that? It wasn't their fault!' What they meant, of course, was that they were sorry they'd asked. They wished the question had never left their lips.

4

The Office

Matt's desk was heaped with stacks of bulging files – he was resisting the campaign for the paperless workplace – but he always knew where to find what he wanted; he drew a case folder towards him. He was acting for a client whose siblings were contesting their father's will. It was an ugly squabble, the sense of injustice so acute all perspective was lost. Blood ties could be so fraught. Thank God he didn't have that problem with Bel.

He'd been seven when she was born: a curious alien creature with big eyes and scaly skin like ET. Leo was nominally in charge after Julia returned to work, but he tended to be absent-minded, forgetting to change nappies or sterilise bottle teats unless Matt reminded him. He had never lost his sense of obligation towards his sister, the feeling that *someone* had to be responsible for her. (Her love life was turbulent, her relationships short-lived.) So, naturally, she should stay in the house until she was well again.

Unfortunately this didn't seem to be going down well with Rachael. She hadn't voiced any direct objection, but he reckoned she'd been on edge for about two weeks, coinciding with Bel's arrival. And last night in bed she'd observed: 'It's hard to feel this is really our home. It's more like we're just camping.'

'You know that isn't true. It takes time to settle in properly. And Bel won't be here forever. Eventually we'll be able to buy her out and make the place our own.' A colleague in the conveyancing department had drawn up the deeds; the division between brother and sister was fair, everything was watertight.

'You don't understand,' said Rachael with a heavy sigh.

'Understand what? Well of course it's worrying, not knowing what's happening – with Julia and so on. But we will resolve things, I promise. Come here...'

Matt had wanted to make love; he *always* wanted to make love to his wife. Even when he was tired, or he'd had a bad day, or there was a looming question mark over the whereabouts of his mother or the health of his sister, Rachael's touch could arouse and appease him. In addition, she had agreed to stop her contraceptive injections and try for a second baby – although she had taken some persuading. That was another conversation he'd mishandled.

'I don't know if I could go through it again,' she'd said when he'd made the suggestion. Her first pregnancy had been difficult and it had knocked her confidence. 'I'm not ready yet.'

'Darling, it's been five years.'

'But Danny's only just started school. And how would I cope with the catering business when the baby came?'

'If we get some extra help you can fit it in, can't you? Isn't that the whole point of running the outfit from home?'

'I can't believe you're being so condescending! When your own mother worked full time.'

'Ah,' said Matt. 'But she was the breadwinner.' This was not entirely true (though Julia's income was the steadier) but it was the worst possible remark he could have made, apart from: Look, Rachael, your earnings are hardly significant enough to make a difference. She'd given him an anguished look and he'd had to embark on a copious programme of tender reconciliation.

Their move to the perfect family house was one of its elements. Now it was looking as though it hadn't been such a good idea after all. When they'd lived in the Canning Street flat, they'd both loved being in the heart of things. And in the early days of their marriage Rachael had been more carefree – wild enough to dance on the table when she wanted to celebrate. But she'd given up alcohol during pregnancy and never really gone back to it. She found it hard to relax and he wished he could help her unwind.

He had reached across the bed to embrace her, running his hand along the smooth curve of her hip. And she had pushed him away, presenting him with her eloquent back. He blocked this image of rejection and opened the file in front of him. He would focus on his work. He'd lost precious time yesterday and he had targets to meet.

The switchboard buzzed the phone on his desk. 'Your mother's on the line,' said Lucy from Reception.

He thought he'd misheard her. 'My mother?'

'That's what she said.' Lucy had blonde hair extensions, violet nail extensions and false eyelashes. Even her voice, her permanently chirpy tone, had an artificial twang to it. 'Do you want me to tell her you're busy?'

'What?' Matt rubbed his temples. 'No, no. Put her on.'

There was a click, a pause, then: 'Matt?'

He should have been relieved; he *was* relieved. A small suspicious part of him had feared someone might have been impersonating her. Why stop at identity theft? 'Julia. Is it you?'

'Of course it's me.' The crackle in her voice was so familiar he couldn't doubt it, yet there was something else too, something he couldn't place – or maybe it was the poor quality of the line.

'Where are you? And where've you been up till now? I tell you it's been panic stations around here. Dorothy Culshaw—'

'Did you cancel my bank cards?'

'What? Yes.'

'Why?'

'I had to. In case they'd been stolen.'

'Stolen! Oh my God, why would you think that?'

'Because Rachael had the police calling to the house, thinking she was you.'

'The police! Why on earth would they be involved?'

'You'd gone missing, your phone was dead and no one could get hold of you.'

'I wasn't missing! I'd just run out of battery. I'd lost my adaptor so I wasn't able to charge it up again till now.'

'Have our messages come through?'

'My inbox is completely jammed! What's the fuss about?'

Matt relaxed, tumbled a pencil between his fingers, nudged a ball of paper on the floor with his toe. There you go: yet another storm in a teacup. Nothing to fret over. His mother was perfectly well and in perfect control of her faculties and her possessions. He said, 'The police came because the car you'd hired was found abandoned. When you weren't answering your phone we didn't know what to think. Dorothy had some wild theories.'

'I'll bet she did,' said Julia. 'But I don't understand about the car. I took it back – not to where I hired it from, obviously, but I'd cleared it with them first.'

'Looks like the message didn't get through. Anyway, it was found outside Bordeaux.'

'Bordeaux! But I dropped it off in Cherbourg.'

The point of Matt's pencil snapped. This confirmed the general inefficiency of car hire companies: a licence to print money. 'Then it's just as well I cancelled the cards,' he said. 'Or they might have carried on charging you.'

'There was a man...' He thought again that the line sounded muffled, but Julia was speaking slowly as if retrieving the experience. 'When I got to the drop-off he was inspecting some of the other cars. He had a clipboard. He wore a boiler suit. I mean, he was dressed as a mechanic. He took the keys from me and the paperwork. I didn't think anything of it. I'd picked up this couple who were hitching...'

'Mum!' Matt was aghast. She was letting herself in for disaster: hitchhikers and unidentified con men.

'Oh they were just kids, English kids. One of them had a job interview the next day he was frantic to get back for. Everybody was doing it, giving people lifts. Everybody was trying to get the next ferry home. I was grateful the man was there so I could hand in the car. How could I know he was a trickster, taking advantage of the situation?

'Well that's how they operate,' he said. 'Con men wouldn't get far if they weren't totally plausible. It could happen to anyone.'

Julia said, 'Please don't patronise me, Matt. My problem now is I've got no money.'

Here's a turnaround, he thought. More than once, as a student, he'd had to ring home towards the end of term, unable to afford a train ticket. 'Can you or Leo come and fetch me?' he'd mumble. 'Only it's like, I've, um, got no dosh left.' (Though his cash-flow dilemmas had paled in comparison with Bel's. Leo joked that her signature tune was 'Buddy, can you spare a dime?')

'Where exactly are you?' he said.

'I'm in Ireland.'

'Ireland!'

'The trouble is, everything's become rather difficult. I had enough euros to start with but without access to any more cash I'm completely stuck.'

'Do you want me to call the bank again? They can ring you and go through the verification process?'

'I've already spoken to them. Once a card's been cancelled, that's the end of it. They have to send me new ones and it'll take seven days.'

'Look, I'm sorry, but really I was acting in your best interests.'

Julia continued. 'I've decided to stay here another week anyhow. They're running behind schedule in the flat. The bathtub was delivered with a crack in it and they're having to hang on for a replacement. I've found a cottage to rent and I want you to ring the owners, Matt, and pay for it. I'll reimburse you.'

'Oh. Okay.' He reached for a biro and a Post-it note. 'Go ahead and I'll make a note of the details. Where is it?'

'It's in Dingle.'

The thought had crept into his head as soon as Julia had said she was in Ireland. Over the years she'd taken trips to Dublin and Belfast for occasional conferences, but she'd never delved into rural Ireland or returned to the Dingle peninsula. So why had she gone there now? He blurted out the question before considering how it might sound.

'Ah, well... Because the terminal in Cherbourg was in total chaos. Because people were so desperate to take the Poole route there were horrendous queues. Because I wasn't in a hurry to get back to England and the Irish ferry looked like a good opportunity. Because when we got to Rosslare coming here seemed a natural progression. And about time, I thought, that I grasped the nettle.'

He detected a quiver along the surface of her voice. He recalled nothing of their Irish holiday before the accident and afterwards there had been such confusion. He knew his father, William, had been hailed as a hero, but he couldn't understand where he had gone. He remembered being stuck in a hotel lounge with a chambermaid trying to entertain him, her freckles like grains of coarse sand, her hand stretching under the table where he was hiding, her Kerry lilt promising him extra helpings of ice cream. When a child doesn't know what's going on around him, when even the adults are bewildered, it helps to focus on the simple things, on what you know you want: three scoops of vanilla ice cream or a Tiffin bar of chocolate; the immediate sensation of sugar on the tongue sweetens everything else.

'I see,' he said, although he wasn't sure that he did.

'So anyway,' said Julia. 'Here's the number. When you ring it you'll speak to a woman called Teresa Hogan and you'll tell her you're paying for a week's rental of Dolphin Cottage. Oh, and if you'd settle up with her for the nights I've spent in her B&B.'

He made a note of the number and tried to calculate whether he would need a temporary overdraft. 'You should ring Bel too, you know.' He glanced at the wall clock. 'I might not have time this afternoon and she needs to know you're okay.'

'Fine, I'll do that. I'll speak to you later. Bye, darling.'

Strolling home from the station, Matt was looking forward to the restoration of normality and devoting time to his son. He wanted Danny to have more than he'd had as a child, so he lavished him with praise and attention, with small toys he'd pick up from the corner shop. He worried that Danny's sense of satisfaction was shaky: there was a yearning in his wide brown eyes that never cleared for long. He seemed uncertain of his place in the world – beyond the sphere of his parents, at any rate – and he was shy with other children, which was why Matt was pretty sure he needed a brother or sister.

There was no reason why they shouldn't have *one* more child, even if not the large brood he'd envisaged in his mind's eye: a gaggle of little Wentworths jostling for his favour. Then, as he turned into his street, he was surprised to see them materialise in actuality: five children sitting on the low sandstone wall at the front of the house. He quickened his pace.

They couldn't all be described as children, he realised as he drew nearer. The first two were adolescent girls, rhythmically chomping gum. One was Kelly, who'd come calling yesterday; the other was presumably a friend, wearing, if possible, an even shorter skirt. Her glowing coppery skin accentuated Kelly's pastiness. Next in line, the brother, Nathan, was gripping the handle of a round bat attached to a ball on a length of elastic. Matt recognised it as one he'd recently bought for Danny. Nathan was hitting the ball with a regular staccato action and Dan was watching in admiration. The fifth person was not a child at all, but Bel. She was the only one who left her spot on the wall to greet him.

She slipped her arm through his and upturned her face. 'I knew you were right,' she said joyfully. 'About Mum I mean.'

'Well,' he said, pleased with himself. 'No need for the doom-laden scenario after all. She rang you then?'

'Yes, and that's what I wanted to talk to you about.'

'Fire away,' said Matt. Then, seeing the four pairs of eyes staring at him: 'Is something going on? Where's Rachael?'

'Oh...' Bel squeezed his arm a fraction tighter. 'She had to nip out. Some crisis over a christening that's been moved to a venue that doesn't allow outside caterers and she's trying to talk them into a deal. I've been left in charge.'

'But what are you doing here?'

Flicking her ponytail, Kelly spoke up. 'She says we can't go in the house.'

'She doesn't want to be responsible for other people's children,' said Bel. 'It's quite reasonable really.' Though the way she arched her eyebrows indicated that she thought Rachael was over-reacting.

Matt looked at the teenagers. '*Are* you children?' he asked.

'No way!' said Kelly in indignation. 'Me and Sheba, we're nearly fourteen.'

Sheba crossed one lean leg over the other friskily. Both girls – and the boy too, come to that – had an edgy tension about them, a smouldering that might leap unexpectedly into life. Matt had had a long day and although buoyed up with relief that the Julia situation had been resolved, he didn't want to deal with any more demands. He wanted a shower and a shot of alcohol and maybe a silly mindless game with his son who was, unusually, ignoring him.

'Hey there, Danny boy,' he said. 'Time to come in.'

Dan hesitated, but his new friends made no attempt to hold him back so he jumped off the wall and let his father ruffle his hair. Kelly, Nathan and Sheba stayed on their perches.

'Don't you want your bat and ball back?' Matt said.

Danny rubbed his foot along the back of his calf and looked wistfully at Nathan. The boy carried on batting without a break in the rhythm.

Dan said, 'No, Daddy, it's all right. I've given it to Nathan. He likes it.' He slipped his hand into Matt's. Bel took the other. The two girls waved cheerfully and showed no signs of moving on.

Once they were indoors and settled on the sofa with a good view of the back of Dan's head and a patchwork of cartoon characters hurtling across the television screen, Bel began, 'Did Mum tell you she's renting a holiday cottage in Kerry?'

'Yes.'

'D'you know why?'

'Because her kitchen and bathroom aren't finished.'

'But... Kerry! Didn't that surprise you?'

'Yes it did. God knows what happened in France but there must have been a cock-up somewhere along the line. Shall we blame Leo?'

'It's like she's doing a sort of stock-taking of the past, don't you think?'

'It's a possibility.'

'Anyway, here's the thing. She's asked me to join her. She doesn't want to be alone and she thinks it will be good for me. Help me get better.'

He grinned. 'She probably wants you to be her courier, take her some more spending money.' He couldn't help finding it amusing, the notion of his efficient parent stranded and destitute.

'Do you think I should go?'

'Why not? Don't you want to?'

'I'm not sure, to be honest...'

In Matt's view the opportunity for himself and Rachael to have some privacy was too good to miss. He said encouragingly, 'It'll be a break for you. What else are you going to do next week?'

'Well, actually there's Dad.'

'What do you mean? Has he been in touch?'

'We had this weird exchange of texts. I told him that Mum was okay. And he said he was planning to make a flying visit. Could he tempt me with quality time or a few drinks.'

'He's feeling guilty, isn't he?'

'Yeah, I reckon. That's what they rowed about apparently, him neglecting me. He made out he was coming to my rescue.'

'Bit late for that, isn't it?'

Bel scrolled through the messages on her phone and read the screen: '*No worries, pet. I'll have it out with them, fight your corner.* Any idea what that means?'

'Not a clue. Just tell him you aren't going to be here.'

'He says he's setting up some meeting with the Tate too.'

It was typical of Leo to talk about a flying visit when half of Europe was trying to work through a backlog of cancelled flights and postponements – though he did have a feline knack of falling on his feet. Could he really slip ahead of the queue and into an aeroplane seat that other people had spent days trying to negotiate? It was a chance Matt was prepared to take. 'Look, Bel, if he shows, he shows.'

'You'll handle him?'

'Sure we will. Anyway, it's more important to find out what Mum's doing. You can play detective.'

'Then tell me, how am I going to get there?'

'Ireland?'

'Yes. See, I'm skint.'

So this was the crux of it: another subsidy. But it was worth it. 'Guess I could lend you a few quid. I'm already bailing out Julia. You can get one of those cheap rail/sail deals. It'll be a long journey, but time's something you've got at your disposal isn't it?'

She beamed at him: the wide smile that hadn't changed since she was a little girl, tugging at his sleeve, begging for his complicity in one of her schemes. 'Thanks, Matt. I knew you'd come up trumps.'

PART TWO

SATURDAY SUNDAY

5

The Crossing

The rail track passed so close to the sea Bel could have felt its spray on her face (if she'd been able to open the train window). She loved travelling. She loved the thrill of stations and airports, the notion of so many different destinations, so many different destinies. She liked to strike up conversation with fellow voyagers, people she would never meet again. And if they turned out to be dull, she would enliven the journey by creating an exotic persona for herself: investigative journalist, solitary yachtswoman, prima ballerina.

She had mixed feelings about the enterprise she'd embarked on, but it beat sitting around getting bored. Winkling a subsidy from Matt hadn't been as difficult as she'd feared. He was so relieved at the low cost of the fare and so mortified about cancelling Julia's credit cards that he'd given her a wodge of notes. 'Whatever you don't spend on the journey, you're to give to Mum,' he'd said. 'And she can pay me back. It's not carte blanche to drink yourself silly on the boat.'

'Fuck off, Matt. I already told you I'm not supposed to drink at *all*.' (Although Guinness was such a healthy iron-rich product it was almost medicinal. She thought even Julia might allow her to make an exception for Guinness.)

She'd stashed the money in her wallet, which had bells on it so no thieving hand could slip into her bag and withdraw it without her noticing. That was another aspect of frequent travelling: you could pick up some useful tips. Rachael had lent her a suitcase on wheels. It was a very Rachael suitcase, an expensive and floral Cath Kidston. Nobody could look at Bel and the suitcase and think they belonged together. Nevertheless, the combination of its bright pattern and Bel's purple jacket and red leggings offered a splash of colour to the dismal docks of Holyhead. North Wales was absurdly tame compared to Sudan, its palette restrained to half a dozen shades of grey: slate, graphite, pewter, gunmetal, steel, dove. It was quiet and thinly populated and no one was walking around with a rifle slung casually over their khakis.

She trundled through the terminal and onto the high-speed hydrofoil. When the engines started churning and the ferry nudged into the Irish Sea, she prowled its corridors in search of something to spark her interest. Unrewarded, she joined the queue at the sandwich bar and bought a hummus wrap, which tasted like paste rolled in wallpaper, and a mug of green tea.

She sat down at a table. Around her, fruit machines juddered and flashed; war escalated between two toddlers; an old couple struggled with a crossword. She couldn't pick out anyone interesting to talk to. She'd deliberately stowed her headphones away so people wouldn't think she was trying to shut the world out. Bel was keen to engage.

A small black face popped above the rim of the seat in front of her and rested its chin on the padded red plastic. The child's hair was braided in neat cornrows, her eyes were round as toffees and she reminded Bel of the kids she'd been working with, who'd been so cute and enthusiastic, so eager to improve their English. When the little girl's tongue flickered through the gap in her teeth, Bel's tongue flickered too, licking her lips with brio. The child was delighted. For several minutes they held each other's gaze and played the copycat game, mimicking every dart and quiver until, abruptly, the head disappeared.

Bel waited for a few moments to see if this were a new phase of the game. Then she rose to tip the debris from her lunch tray into a disposal bin and check the neighbouring booth. It was empty. If even a six-year-old kid had been bored by her company, how could she expect to keep herself entertained? She loitered by the pulsing games machines to absorb some of their warm energy. She fished in her purse for change, pulled the lever and rang up three lemons. A shower of coins toppled into the tray. It took her about ten minutes to lose them again, but there was still nearly an hour to kill.

Beyond the bar at the back of the boat she noticed outdoor access to a limited deck area. She pushed through the doors and leant against the rail, letting the wind lift her hair from her face, inhaling the salt tang of the sea. A man in a leather jacket was also leaning out, gulping air. He had his back to her, his collar was turned up and his knee was bent, raising his foot so she could see the sole of his trainer worn thin. He turned his head as if he'd felt her stare piercing him. It would be too awkward to look away, to pretend to be fascinated by the horizon or the creamy wake of their progress, so she met his eyes and smiled. He smiled back, but then left his spot to return inside, walking in an oddly rigid manner, as if he were in pain.

Before he reached the glass doors he stumbled, or else some motion of the hydrofoil caused him to lurch towards her. The collision took her by surprise. They reached out simultaneously to steady each other, hands on arms. Bel wasn't easily embarrassed. She laughed and apologised, joked about her feet – her red ankle boot inter-locking with his trainer. His face wore an expression of alarm.

'Are you okay?' They both stepped back, a little clumsily.

'Sure,' he said in a soft Irish whisper, but then bludgeoned away from her into the bar, leaving Bel with the feeling that she was toxic. He had dropped a cigarette lighter, as they tangled, an orange cylinder that fitted neatly into her palm when she picked it up. She wondered if there was something in the air to cause his bizarre behaviour. Causing other bizarre behaviours, come to that. Some chemical in the volcanic particles that encouraged a certain freakishness?

She began to spin a fantasy to herself, compelling enough to drive her back to her seat and take out the notebook she devoted to her graphic novel ideas. As she sketched she became aware of breathing at her elbow, the light quick breathing of a child. Bel's pencil halted; she looked up. It was the little girl again and this time she spoke, a faint twang of south London in her voice.

'What are you drawing?'

'I'm drawing a story.'

'Is it about me?'

And Bel saw that, inadvertently, she'd sketched a character with a headful of dainty plaits. 'Would you like it to be about you?' The child nodded. 'Then tell me your name.'

'Clementine Alice Beaumont.'

'Hey, cool! Is that Clementine after the fruit or the song?'

'It's for my granny, but you can call me Clemmie.'

'Okay, Clemmie. You can call me Bel.' She glanced around for a handy parent. 'Where's your mum?'

'She's not on this boat – she's not coming.'

'Oh… right. So who are you with then? Your granny? Your daddy?'

'He left me,' said Clemmie in a matter-of-fact way. She was a tidy well-dressed child, a vision of pink candyfloss; she didn't look the type to mislay parents. Nor was she rattled. 'My daddy was being sick,' she said.

'Ah,' said Bel. 'Yeah, I can see that would be tricky. Is he in that Gents over there? Does he know where to find you?'

'What's going to happen next in your story?'

'Well, everybody's been breathing magic dust,' Bel explained. 'And it's made short people grow very tall and it's given some people special powers while others have sprouted horns or started speaking in strange languages and—'

'Have I got special powers?'

'Sure. What would you like them to be?'

Clemmie considered. 'I want to fly,' she said at length. 'We was going to fly on an aeroplane. I never been on an aeroplane.'

'Well a boat can be fun too, you know. Let me draw you some wings. Do you want little fairy ones or big feathery wings like a bird or an angel?'

Naturally Clementine Alice Beaumont chose angel wings. She flapped her arms. 'Like, massive!'

They were both engrossed in watching the soft plumy strokes of the lead pencil, the cross-hatch shading of the sky, the little earthbound figure soaring like an eagle into flight. As Bel worked, they debated the content of the next frame: how would Clemmie use her magic powers? Gradually they became aware that the other passengers were gathering their belongings together, getting ready to disembark.

'Watcha know,' said Bel. 'I think we're nearly there.' She had assumed that at some point the child's parent would arrive in search of his daughter. It seemed preferable to keep her safe and occupied rather than hand her in like lost luggage. There was a risk that a monstrously irate father would come and bellow at her, but hey, he'd just been vomiting – how scary could he be?

What concerned her more, as families funnelled themselves towards the stairs to the car decks, was that no one appeared at all. Surely the guy couldn't have forgotten her? Was it possible that his illness wasn't seasickness but something more serious? Wouldn't the crew have noticed a body passed out in the toilets?

'I'm going to have to take you to the help desk,' she told Clemmie.

'Where's that?'

'It's near where you board if you're on foot. Or did you come in a car?'

'In a car.'

'Okay, well maybe we should go and find it then.' Curiously, the tannoy announcement she kept expecting never came. 'I can't think why he isn't looking for you. Can you remember what make of car it is?'

Clemmie shook her pigtails solemnly. 'No.'

'But you must know the colour,' persisted Bel. 'Haven't you ridden in it loads?'

'No. Just today.'

This was becoming troubling. 'He *is* your dad, isn't he? You do live with him?'

'No.' Then she added, 'It's my uncle's car.'

'What, is he like a real uncle?'

Clemmie cocked her head as if she were giving this some thought. 'I don't know. What d'you mean, real?'

'Oh Lord…' Bel took the child's hand and patted it. 'Well, you'd be related to him by blood. You might even look a bit like him. Whereas if he was your mum's boyfriend…'

'He isn't mum's boyfriend,' said Clemmie. 'He don't look like me neither.'

This was not helpful. 'Right then. We'll have to get them to put out a call and I'll stay with you till they find him. You're being a very brave girl.'

'I am!' said Clemmie with a huge smile, tracing the outline of the flowers on the wheelie case, while Bel packed her things away.

There was a crush of bodies to negotiate, an obstacle course of suitcases and golf clubs, backpacks and buggies. There also appeared to be a hold-up near the top of the steps but neither of them could see over the heads of the queue. After a slow shuffle forward, Bel spotted two men in the midst of exasperated argument. One was slumped against the wall with his hands on his knees, the other was stooping to admonish him. She stopped, for the jacket was familiar. She tapped his leather arm and pulled the cigarette lighter from her pocket. 'I think this might be yours,' she said.

Startled, he glanced at it in her palm. 'Ah yes… How did you know…? Where did you find it?'

'You dropped it when we bumped into each other.'

'When we what?' He raised his head to look at her and she was confused again. She'd been misled by the jacket. It wasn't this man she'd seen before, but the other. She recognised his mobile, finely chiselled face, although it was decidedly green at the moment, a pale glassy green like a slice of melon. 'Are you all right?' she said.

'Clemmie!' he croaked.

Clemmie was gripping the hem of Bel's coat. She regarded the sick man with a kind of dispassionate resignation.

'Is this your daughter?' Bel was fired with scorn. 'And you just abandoned her? Didn't even try to find her? Didn't you worry about what might have happened to her, whether she'd fallen overboard or… anything? The poor kid!'

The man she'd seen on the deck muttered, 'No fucking sea legs.' Then he put out a hand and patted the child's dark head. 'Were you worried, sweetheart?'

'No,' said Clemmie stoically, 'not a bit.' And Bel was reminded of the tactics and deals she had struck in her own childhood, with Leo.

'He gets seasick,' said the other man with a shrug. 'Not that he'll do anything to help himself.' He spun the wheel of the lighter. 'Like lay off the drink and fags. But it isn't as bad as it looks. We got separated and I thought Clem was with Tom and vice versa. It's only just now we've realised she was missing and I've been trying to get my bloody useless dickhead of a brother to come to his senses.'

Their resemblance was striking – the curling brown hair, the horizontal eyebrows, the truculent set of the chin – but the uncle had broader shoulders, the jacket was a better fit on his sturdier frame.

'I can't believe anyone would leave you two in charge of a postage stamp. Anyway, she's been good, really good...' She paused, reluctant to leave the little girl, yet wishing she hadn't got involved, that she could cut loose and walk away. A large family group flooded past, squashing the four of them into closer proximity.

Tom swept his hair off his forehead. His irises were an intense blue but the whites of his eyes were webbed with a fine tracery of blood vessels. 'Isn't this the trip from hell?'

'This!' said Bel, riled again. 'A little paddle across the Irish Sea? I'll give you a trip from hell. Try waiting in a corrugated shack in forty-five degrees centigrade for a tin-can aeroplane; then try flying in it. Or—'

'It's not just the boat,' he said with a sigh.

'Enough of that,' said his brother. 'We need to get moving. You should thank the girl, Tom, for rescuing Clem. You've had a lucky escape as usual. You know that.'

'Thank you darlin',' said Tom, making an effort to pull Clemmie close to him and showing the shadow of a smile that she imagined could dazzle on a better day.

'I don't want you to go, Bel. I want you to stay with me.'

'Bel, is that your name?'

'Yes.'

'I'm Kieran.' He shook her hand, although it seemed a little late for such formalities. 'What deck is your car on?'

'Actually I'm a foot passenger.' She indicated her decorative suitcase.

'Well maybe, if you want to come with us, we could give you a lift somewhere. Where are you off to?'

'Oh, the station in Dublin. I have to get a bus I think.'

'Let us drop you off there. It's the least we can do.'

'Well…' She became aware that Clemmie was watching her intently. 'Okay then, thanks.'

As they filed down the narrow metal staircase, a call was put out for the driver of a Renault Megane that was blocking the passage of other vehicles. Kieran cursed softly. 'Is that you?' said Bel, as the registration number was repeated.

He nodded. 'We've got off to a bad start, what with one thing and another.'

'She doesn't seem to know you very well,' observed Bel. Clemmie continued to clutch at her sleeve as if she didn't want to become separated.

'Ah, you see, it's a complicated situation.'

On the car deck a strong smell of petrol fumes assaulted them. Engines revved impatiently, as if noise alone could shift the green Renault that wasn't going anywhere. Kieran unlocked the boot and slung Bel's case inside.

'Will you sit in the back with me?' said Clemmie.

'Yeah, sure.'

The two brothers settled themselves in the front seats. They crawled off the boat onto dry land and were waved through the customs sheds. Kieran ground up a gear and they skimmed past the palm trees and pastel-painted terraces facing Dun Laoghaire marina. 'And where will you be going from Dublin?'

'I'm getting the train to Tralee. My mother's picking me up there tonight. She's renting a cottage near Dingle and I'm joining her for a week. I've been ill and she thinks your Irish air will help me get better.'

He slammed on the brakes for a red light. 'No kidding? Dingle?'

'Yes.'

'That's where we're headed ourselves.'

'Really?'

'It is, yes, would you believe. Though it's kind of a tense trip for us. That's what I meant about the complications. We're on our way home to see our father. It's his birthday this week. He's supposed to be in remission, but you know how it is with cancer...'

'Oh God, that's awful.' Bel could not imagine Leo as anything less than a vivid, thundering presence.

'And here's the thing.' Kieran lowered his voice. 'He's never met Clemmie before.'

The little girl was looking out of the window. Bel shot a glance at the reprobate parent dozing against his headrest, eyelids lowered, his hands – flexible long-fingered hands like a pianist – splayed limply on his jeans.

'Holy Moses.'

'So you see, we could take you all the way. Clem would appreciate the company. Of course, this may not be a set-up you bargained for...'

This was true enough, though Bel relished spontaneity. 'Well I do already have a train ticket...'

'I never take the train. I've no idea what they're like. It'll be a long journey though. One change or more.'

Clemmie bounced up and down on the seat. 'Please say yes! Please come with us.'

Another, sleepy, voice spoke: 'Come with us, Bel.' And then Tom turned and threw her a smile of such tremendous wattage the interior of the Renault felt alight.

'Well I guess if it's no hassle for you, it would save Mum having to fetch me.'

'And you'll get there sooner, so you will.'

6

The Farm

His wife had a habit of organising his day for him, which Vince Hogan did not necessarily appreciate. This Saturday he was to take the lady doctor to Dolphin Cottage and settle her in for the week. She was expecting her daughter to arrive and Teresa had seen to the preparations.

'I don't want to put you to any trouble,' Dr Wentworth had said. 'I can drive myself over there.'

'No trouble at all,' said Teresa. 'Vince will just check you have everything you need.'

She wanted him out from under her feet – that was the truth of it – while she finished her spring cleaning, poking her brush into every corner. Her cleaning was obsessive in any season, in his view. He stowed the lady doctor's bag in the boot of her hire car and went back for his keys.

'And another thing,' Teresa said, as she unhooked his jacket and gave the hook itself a rub with her duster. 'On the way back you should visit the Farrellys. Find out how Pat's getting on.'

Vince shuffled his feet. 'We'll be seeing them along with everybody else next week, at his birthday do.'

'All the more reason to get over there in advance. Show you're a true friend and not a hanger-on. Ronnie will appreciate it too.'

He couldn't argue when Teresa had her mind set, so he dutifully escorted the English visitor to Dolphin Cottage and showed her how to operate the heating and hot water. 'There's provisions in the fridge,' he said. 'To keep you going. But you'll be wanting to get some other shopping in, I daresay.'

'I'll pop out later. I'll probably need more petrol too, if I'm to get to Tralee.' She had a low husky laugh. 'I hope I can afford it.'

'Don't ye be worrying,' Vince assured her. 'Pay a visit to Jimmy at the pumps, tell him I sent you and he'll let you fill up on credit. No problem.'

At least he hoped it wouldn't be a problem. She seemed a trustworthy sort and had paid in advance for the cottage rental. She seemed anxious to be rid of him, too, and he toyed with the notion of going for a jar to set him up for the rest of the day. Why was he so bothered about a social visit to an old friend? Teresa would say, and Vince would find it hard to put into words. But what women didn't realise was the importance of being equal with your fellows. A man likes to keep his dignity: prefers to recall his prime, when his shoulders were wide and his gut tight and full with a good few pints. Pat, diminished by illness, might not want his weakness exposed.

So it was after a fortifying drink and a chat at the bar that Vince turned up the track to the Farrellys' farm. In the yard a black and white Border collie was napping beneath an unkempt rose bush. Whiskers of straw eddied and bobbed in a gust of wind, which brought also the warm comforting scent of cowhide. Beyond the sloping fields the ocean lay dimpled and burnished like beaten metal.

He pushed open the farmhouse door and called a greeting. In the scullery a large pair of Wellingtons flopped against the side of the freezer. They had a forlorn, redundant air, but soon enough he banished that piece of melancholy from his mind because weren't there half a dozen empty pairs of boots scattered over the quarry tiles, some so tiny they must belong to the grandchildren?

He went through to the kitchen which, unlike his own, had never been updated: a peat-fired range, an old electric cooker speckled with grease; a hectically patterned oil cloth crooked on the table. Ronnie was on the couch sorting through a heap of wool skeins. She was seldom without her needles or crochet hook these days, churning out little favours for the craft shops in Dingle. Knitted pouches for your spectacles or your loose change, covers for your photo album or your mobile phone, egg cosies in the shape of chicks – things you'd no idea you needed until you were a tourist sauntering the streets of a colourful small town in the south-west of Ireland. It kept her busy, she said.

Ronnie was wearing a lemon yellow jumper the moths had been at; there was a coffee stain too, but she hadn't noticed it. Years back she'd been such a fine-looking girl all the lads, Vince included, had the eye for her; Pat had won her with his chest-thumping bravado and the shining temptation of his motorbike. She'd since grown stout, as women do (even Teresa, despite the energy she put into running the holiday cottages now they'd sold the pub) but the extra flesh was beginning to hang loose on Ronnie. Her face, above the lemon, was haggard from the worry over Pat. Her hair was a dense steely grey; her eyebrows very black.

'Vince!' she exclaimed, jumping up.

'I don't want to intrude,' he said. 'I happened to be passing.'

'When I heard the car I thought you were Anna,' said Ronnie. 'She's bringing the kiddies over. But come in, won't you. Can I get you a cup of tea?'

'No thank you. I was wondering…' He cleared his throat. 'How is your man? Is he up to visitors?'

She moved away from the kettle and patted a fireside chair. 'Will you sit down? I know he'd be glad to see you, but he often has a little nap in the afternoon.' She was through the door – he could see the backs of her legs, still in fine shape, disappearing around the bend in the staircase – before he could make any excuses.

It wasn't that Vince felt threatened by mortality (at least no more than anyone of his age) and you'd evidence of it every minute in the country anyway. No, it was sick rooms that disagreed with him. He wanted to see his old friend in his right place, in the carver chair with the scratched wooden arms, erect and glowing with his fist curled around a shot of Bushmills. Not rotting as limp as the Wellington boots.

After a while Ronnie returned, settling herself on the couch beside her basket, picking up her needles and a ball of deep-dyed purple wool. 'He's just surfacing,' she said. 'He'll be down in a moment.'

'And how are the plans for the party?' Sixty-eight was not an age you'd make a song and dance about as a general rule but these were special circumstances.

The creases in Ronnie's face softened. 'Grand. Nuala's in charge of the catering of course and the boys are on their way over from England.'

'The both of them together? That's good.'

'They've not been home since Christmas,' she said. 'Kieran was planning a weekend but something came up. And Tom, well, he's hard to get hold of, you know…'

The one thing you could never do was predict Tom Farrelly's behaviour. The boy could be enchanting. Ronnie used to call him her angel, especially in the early days before his voice broke, when the sweetness of it soared above the rest of the choir, when the parishes were fighting over him to accompany their Masses. They were less pleased when money went missing from the collection plate or graffiti appeared behind the choir stalls. Tom might help you out one day, working like a Trojan, shifting barrels, stacking crates, replacing the filter in the fryer; the next he'd be popping at the lemonade bottles with his airgun.

Vince and Teresa had not been blessed with children although they were godparents to a dozen. It had never bothered him (and Teresa very little) and he was more often grateful than not. He could see the pain caused by an errant youngster and the disappointment leaching into a parent's life. It wasn't as if you were dealing with cattle where there were accepted procedures and you could always call in the vet. You couldn't control a human being in the same way at all. Pat Farrelly wasn't the type of father who beat his kids, but even if he had been, it wouldn't have made a blind bit of difference. If anything, those boys would have left sooner.

Ronnie smoothed the band of knitting over her knee and joined two pieces of wool together with a deft tug. Then she glanced up and gave him that look of hers, that green-eyed look that had broken hearts in dance halls from Tralee to Castlemaine. It almost made him envy Pat again, his way with machines, the way he had all the girls lining up to ride pillion. He had loved his bikes and his cars and his tractors more than his cows. Going off to work on those rigs in the North Sea, leaving his wife to manage the farm; if that was the example he set for his sons, how could anyone be surprised they'd upped and left? Although neither of them was an engineer exactly. Kieran, he thought, had something to do with computers and Tom was still waiting to find his vocation.

That was how Ronnie put it. 'The pity is that Tom hasn't reached his purpose yet. I worried Pat would die without knowing it.'

It was her belief that God had a plan for him. At first, with his beautiful soprano voice, the notes so clear they pierced the listener, she was convinced singing was his future; this was the way he could bring joy to the world. But puberty arrived to sabotage him and, though the boy could sing well enough, it wasn't the same; it lacked distinction. So then the lad's vocation was to be the priesthood itself.

Vince remembered this with some amusement, remembered Pat leaning across the bar over his pint and the racing pages of the *Kerryman*. 'There's not a priest around here who doesn't want to tan his hide,' he'd said with a grin. 'Dirty old perverts. But the lad's too quick for them. I've told her a million times they will never take him on. She's stubborn, Veronica. She won't give up on her Holy Grail.'

In the end it was Kieran who'd flirted with religion. As for Tom, no one rightly knew what he did over in London, but if he was searching for the Holy Grail he needed to put his nose outside of a bar once in a while and sniff some clean air.

From the backyard they heard a throaty roar and a crunch. Ronnie abandoned her knitting and jumped up. 'That'll be Anna, now. Her little ones are such a delight!'

Anna and her husband had built a house nearby in the boom years and taken over the day-to-day running of the farm. (Nuala, married but childless, managed one of the town's hotels.) Anna was the spit of Ronnie when she'd been younger, though her boys took after their father, with their pale lashes and their bushy ginger curls. Released from their mother's grip they careered around the room.

There came a shuffle overhead, a tentative step on the stairs, a shadow in the hall. Pat was gaunt, no doubt about it; his hair fizzed out at odd angles from his skull; his clothes hung baggy on him. He had to lean against the doorframe before he could step over the threshold. Ronnie moved as if to help him, but he gestured her away. Vince half-rose but Pat didn't look at him until his wife had settled him in the armchair with cushions stacked at his back and his stick in easy reach. Only then did he raise his eyes and although they were a little bleary, he was visibly there, Vince's old mate. He hadn't become a different person; his brain was sharp enough.

'I've been meaning to come over,' said Vince. 'For I don't know how long. Have you everything sorted for the party now?'

Pat's shoulders lifted. 'I'm leaving it to the women.'

Anna said, 'And we have it all in hand.'

'You're not letting that tiresome Rooney fellow bring his accordion? I value my hearing.'

'The music's under control, Dad. I told you. And Nuala's sorting the menu. It's going to be a grand night.'

'I hope so.'

Pat had not been so curmudgeonly before his illness, but Vince understood his reservations. You couldn't tell how a party would go. Sometimes there'd be too many vested interests, too many lads spoiling for a fight, too many girls upset at the state of their dresses. Or the buffet would get trodden into the floor and the music would be shite. In truth, a wake was often more enjoyable than your average wedding (or even a christening) because it had a spontaneity you couldn't drum up any other way. Not that he would mention such a thing to his old friend. Instead, he said, 'I hear the lads are coming home?'

One of Anna's sons clambered onto his grandfather's knee and reached up to stroke his face. Pat gave a melancholic smile. Anna said, 'Yes. We thought they might not make it, on account of the airports being closed, but Kieran has decided to drive so they'll be staying for the week.'

'When will they get here?'

Ronnie had her back to them, assembling cups while the tea brewed. She said, 'Oh later this evening. I have the lamb ready to go in the oven.'

Anna, swinging the child from Pat's lap onto her hip, mouthed at Vince: 'Fingers crossed.'

7

The Graveyard

This was the third week in which Julia was living out of her small suitcase. Vince Hogan had brought her round to Dolphin Cottage in the morning and hopped about in that sprightly way of his, showing her the ropes. But she'd wanted to be alone – she hoped she hadn't made it too obvious – and so he'd left her to unpack. She'd unfolded tops and trousers and hung them in what he called the press. She'd stored the case under the bed and tossed a batch of underwear into the washing machine.

Built in a traditional design with two bedrooms flanking a central living area, Dolphin Cottage was the perfect hideaway. It was picturesque from the outside, with a thatched roof and a clump of hollyhocks sprouting beside the door; snug within. The ceilings were low, the walls thick and the windows tiny – but the glimpse of lush green pasture with the mountains beyond was spectacular. Julia, gazing through the pane, could see a swirl of mist, light as chiffon, on the distant mountain peak. It brought to mind the ash cloud that had blown her here, into retreat. She'd almost confessed this to the Hogans on arrival – they had been so friendly and hospitable – only it sounded too whimsical, too *Wizard of Oz*. Finding it difficult enough to explain her actions, she'd made up some bland story, pretending she was reconnoitring for a healthy spot for her daughter to recuperate.

She checked the room where Bel would sleep. The sheets were scented with bergamot and there were towels at the end of the bed: a white one for the bath and a striped one for swimming. She hadn't commented on this, hadn't said to Vince, 'Swimming! In April?' She'd noticed the surfers in their wetsuits, like glossy black beetles riding the waves. The water wasn't cold if you were encased in rubber. The ocean wasn't dangerous if you knew the right places to go.

Most of the beaches along the peninsula were perfectly safe, but Doonshean was known for its riptide and each day so far Julia had paid a visit there, in memory of William. The first time, she had made her way down the ancient stone path in the lee of the cliff to find the waves pounding the rocks, casting spray in her face, swallowing every scrap of sand. If she hadn't known better, she might have thought the beach no longer existed. Subsequently she'd planned her visits more carefully. At its lowest ebb the full wild beauty of the strand was exposed: the glisten of seaweed at the shoreline, the frill of lacy foam, the scattering of shells. And all around her, the rocks rose like exotic hanging gardens, rich with jewelled clumps of sea thrift and mallow.

Today, however, she would concentrate on practicalities and buy some food with the last of her cash. She set off down the lane, rolling past high hedges lively with green shoots of fuchsia and the starry white petals of wild brambles. She often felt as if she'd spent half her life in the driving seat. Much of her job had involved travelling from school to school, cajoling reluctant children with her toy medical kit: the magic thermometer, the rattling pill boxes, the fake syringe. The stethoscope in particular had fascinated them. She used to explain she was listening to their heartbeats, and for any whistles or wheezes, skips or jumps. Their young bodies would writhe and twist like eels in a basket and she'd been glad she'd chosen a speciality so full of boundless life. Year after year she'd dispensed prescriptions, referrals, advice, tussled with red tape, drafted reports.

And now it was over.

For someone accustomed to discipline and structure, the infinity of time stretching ahead took some getting used to. She knew she should seize it, mould it, enjoy it – this lovely lazy future – but look at what happened in France! She'd been anticipating a relaxing fortnight with old friends, eating meals infused with garlic and drinking rich red wine, visiting chateaux and cathedrals and galleries, sipping strong coffee in tree-lined squares. Instead, she'd been shocked to have Leo sprung on her.

She'd made an effort to behave in the cool-but-civilised manner appropriate to an ex-wife, but then – it was such a silly little thing – a chance remark about the house-swap had kick-started one of their more spectacular rows. She cringed at the memory. She'd always had a fiery temper and Leo could get her going like no one else (which, long ago, had been part of his attraction).

The atmosphere in the farmhouse had become tense and hostile. Rather than embarrass the Culshaws any further,

Julia decided to remove herself. Dorothy protested, of course. She couldn't accept that Julia wasn't hiding some ulterior motive that she was choosing to be impulsive for once. Wasn't that the point of being retired: not having to cater to anyone's needs except your own? In retrospect, her early departure was cowardly, as if she were running scared. But she had turned things around. She would never have set out to revisit Dingle but, by taking the chance when it came, she could prove she had courage after all.

Her foot was depressing the clutch, her hand shifting the gearstick, but her mind was elsewhere. Perhaps this was the reason the car began to stray towards the ditch. Pulling the steering wheel sharply to the right, she attempted to accelerate out of trouble. She caught the flash of a swift scurrying creature and felt a thud. She stopped the car and got out. She had hit a rabbit, now quaking on the verge.

Julia knelt and laid her hand on its soft fur. Both back legs were smashed; blood was soaking into the ground. Oh hell, she thought, I'm going to have to break its neck. She had nothing sharp with her; she cast around for a heavy stone. Speed and accuracy were essential: the animal wouldn't feel a thing. She wouldn't lift the stone up afterwards. Even so, she hesitated and as she did the rabbit's eyes acquired a filmy glaze; the heart ceased to thump beneath her palm.

She was quite irrationally upset by this small death. After all, no one in the country would worry over roadkill and she had encountered far worse ends. But for a moment she could not lift her hand, detach it from the still-warm flesh. She had to force herself to rise on unsteady legs, dust her knees and return to the driving seat. She sat for a while, bent over the steering wheel, resting her forehead on her forearm. She knew it was only a release of suppressed tension in her nerve endings; even so, the stupid shaking wouldn't stop.

Then she heard a squeal and another car, its passenger wing dented, came out of nowhere. It juddered past, narrowly missing her. Julia felt for the keys. She was blocking the road – she had to move on. A little way beyond, she could see a cast-iron gateway leading to an old church in a walled graveyard. In front was a strip of shale big enough for a hearse to stop and unload. She started the engine and crawled towards it. This would do.

The church was derelict and abandoned, a romantic ruin, like hundreds of others strewn throughout the countryside. Most of the tower had tumbled inwards and crows flapped around its high remaining wall. The original wooden door was missing and trails of ivy festooned the entrance arch. Moss spread across the flags and the gravestones had a neglected air, as if the descendants who might have cared for them had long moved away. New populations worshipped in the grey stone churches built at the outskirts of towns and villages, with their electronic bells and their loudspeakers broadcasting Mass to latecomers in the car park.

Julia got out of the car again and trod through leafy docks and stinging nettles. The headstones were marled with lichen; the engraving was too faint to read. At the back of the churchyard were more recent plots, marked with slabs of shining granite and green marble chippings. They looked incongruous in this gothic Victorian setting, where you could so easily conjure up the ghosts of another era: generations of farmers and fishermen, mothers and milkmaids, babies wrapped tight in shawls.

She stooped to right a jar of plastic roses that had blown over. Straightening up again she saw a gate that led to an extension of the cemetery, to fresh mounds of soil awaiting recognition. A group of trees hovered at the far boundary, their crowns distorted by the wind, their branches straggling in the same direction as if trying to escape.

She continued on and found herself in a field that hadn't yet acquired the gravitas of an ancient burial ground. It was like the chiming electric bells: the notes were technically the same, but they lacked depth and resonance; they couldn't compare with sonorous brass. Nevertheless, the field was peaceful and her muscles had relaxed; she was no longer trembling. She decided to walk to the trees and back to stretch her legs and then she would complete her errands.

A path had been cut through the turf but the grass had regrown and damp soaked into her shoes. Coming back towards the gate she stepped aside to avoid a molehill and noticed a plaque set into the wall. Something about the shape of the letters caught her eye.

'William Langley,' she read. 'Drowned 9th July 1981. May he be Rewarded in Heaven with Everlasting Grace.'

Julia gasped, put her hand out to the dry stone wall, felt its sharp edge bite her palm, wondered if the silly business of the rabbit had affected her vision, if she were hallucinating.

She read the inscription again. It couldn't refer to a different William Langley. The date was correct. She would never forget that date.

She tried to think logically. This was a memorial plaque, not a gravestone. There was no grave. William hadn't been interred. His body had been flown back to England, to Bristol, where they had been living. Over two hundred people, colleagues from the Bristol Royal Infirmary, neighbours in Clifton, friends and relatives, had packed the crematorium. His heroism had been celebrated in style. And then afterwards, in the awful throes of anti-climax, Julia had been left with a container of ashes.

One evening after work, when the Avon was at high tide, she'd collected Matt from the childminder and brought him onto the suspension bridge. Dusk cloaked the gorge; lights began to spring alive on the rods and cables strung between the two towers. What else could she do but return William to the water? Matt seemed to understand the solemnity of the occasion. He hadn't fidgeted. He had watched with the steady unswerving gaze so reminiscent of his father as she'd taken the lid off the urn and let its contents drift down towards the river and ultimately out to sea.

Another thing she would never forget, nearly thirty years on, was the kindness of the locals here, their astonishing capacity for goodwill wherever she and Matt had fetched up. At the time she'd found it difficult to respond to their compassion, their friendly words and gestures. She presumed she'd thanked people, but her brain had frozen as a way of anaesthetising the pain and her thanks would have been as mechanical as the endless telling of a rosary.

But for someone else, it seemed, gratitude was a strong and deeply felt emotion, powerful enough for them to erect a memorial. Perhaps a parish collection had raised the funds? Or the family of the little boy William had saved? She'd forgotten their name: her recollection of that period was hazy, as if it had been filmed with a hand-held camera using the wrong exposure.

She traced the lettering gently with her finger. She had tried so hard to put the tragedy behind her and look for a new beginning, to bury her guilt at the role she had played, to kid herself that Matt was not the image of his father. How strange now, to find that somebody in this distant part of the world had wanted to make sure he was remembered.

8

The Hotel

It would have been easier to make conversation if she'd been in the front seat, but Bel was in the back of the car with Clemmie dozing on her shoulder. Tom dozed too and Kieran wasn't much of a talker, so she sat watching the ribbon of road unspool ahead through the rolling green landscape, while the radio churned out a slew of forgettable pop tunes. Two hours into the journey, a sudden blaring of horns roused Tom and he jerked awake. 'Fuck, are you trying to kill us!'

'There's no accounting for eejits,' said Kieran, accelerating away from danger. 'Still, we're nearly on the home stretch.'

Tom snorted with such derision that Bel said, 'What was it that made you leave? I mean, in the first place.'

Kieran said, 'Why does anybody leave?'

'The real question,' said Tom, now revived and re-energised, 'is why does anybody stay? When you're young you want adventure. You don't want to spend your life with your arm stuck up a cow's arse or tootling about on fishing trips. And yes, it's true, prospects were good for a bit, but there's nothing to come back for now. Our house of cards has collapsed and our country's drowning.'

'It was different for you, whatever,' said Kieran.

'Different?' said Bel. 'Why?'

'He had the voice, didn't he? He was going to be Jesus Christ Superstar.'

'Feck off!'

'Or Joseph and his Amazing Technicolor Dreamcoat, elevated above the rest of his family.' He clashed the gears and cursed. 'But he lost it. Lost that God-given gift, those dulcet tones, his meal ticket.'

'It wasn't a meal ticket I wanted. It was a one-way out of there ticket.'

'You see, where we come from, there's not much you can keep private. Some people like it – they have that sense of belonging. Whereas we got too big for the country, did we not?'

Tom adopted a falsetto: 'Wait until you hear the latest on those Farrelly boys! Shit, I could never have stayed in the one place.'

'So where does Clemmie live? Not with you, I'm guessing?'

'With her mother.'

'You aren't married to her?'

'Does either of us look like a married man, darlin'?'

The mention of her name had drawn Clemmie from sleep. She uncurled herself and stuck out her legs until her toes touched the back of her father's seat. 'I'm hungry.'

Over his shoulder, Kieran said, 'What about you, Bel?'

It was a long while since she'd felt a genuine hollow hunger, so the sensation surprised her. 'Yes, actually I am. I had some sort of wrap for lunch but I couldn't finish it.'

'Okay, then. I'll find somewhere to pull in for a bite. We're not far from Adare.'

Adare's wide central street was lined with quaint thatched cottages and generous grass verges, which gave it a peaceful civilised air. Bel sniffed the distinctive comforting peat smoke that told her she'd truly arrived in Ireland. Kieran turned into the car park of a gracious hotel, cloaked in Virginia creeper.

'We've a friend who works here. Maybe he'll give us a discount.'

He killed the engine and they got out. Tom loped round to the back of the car and tore off his T-shirt. 'This stinking thing!' he exclaimed, shoving it in the boot and rooting for a clean one in his holdall. 'I need to go for a decent wash.'

Clemmie was watching him with detachment. Although rumpled from the journey, she carried herself with prim composure. Her pink jeans had a blotch of ketchup on the thigh but the matching cardigan was buttoned neatly; her bouncing hair bobbles were still in place.

Tom seized her under the armpits and raised her high in the air. 'Hey, my gorgeous girl!' he cried. 'Do I smell better now?' She wrinkled her nose silently. He crushed her against his bare chest and then set her on the ground with a flourish. She took hold of Bel's hand.

'Will we start with a drink?' said Tom. 'You can have a Coke, Clem, and everyone will think you're on the Guinness, same as us.'

The friend they'd hoped to find behind the bar was on his day off so Bel, flush with the cash Matt had given her, offered to buy the round.

'We'll put it on a tab,' said Tom waving her money away. 'We can settle up later, no problem.'

He went off to scrub himself clean and Bel took Clemmie to the Ladies. She couldn't help asking, 'How often do you see your daddy?'

The little girl squirted a stream of lemon-scented soap onto her palms. 'I don't know.'

'Not very often then. Have you ever been away with him before?'

'I don't think so... Maybe when I was little.'

'But your mum knows where you are, doesn't she?' Her concern was crazy. How could this possibly be an abduction? Two white men travelling with one black child in rural Ireland – they'd be picked up in no time. But Bel couldn't rid herself of the suspicion that something wasn't quite right.

'Oh yes,' said Clemmie.

'Wasn't she invited too?'

'No, 'cos she's very busy.'

'At work?'

'She's on holiday with her friend.'

'Oh, I see.'

They joined the brothers at a table in the conservatory, overlooking tranquil well-tended gardens, pansies in the borders, roses in bud. Tom was reading down the menu and chuckling. 'Beats me why everything must come with a jus.' He exaggerated his Kerry accent. 'They do a magnificent roast chicken here, to be sure. Will you not have the roast, Bel? The chef will wring the bird's neck personally and serve you potatoes three different ways. Your English potatoes, you know, bear no comparison with ours. And...'

'Actually I'm vegetarian.'

'Would you believe it!' He slapped his thigh. 'Then you probably have a choice of salad, salad sandwiches or salad.'

'I was going to try the mushroom risotto. It'll be my first mushroom for a month.'

The young men were amused by the idea that anyone would compute their mushroom intake. Presumably they had been brought up on slabs of bloody meat: half a cow in the freezer and strings of home-made sausages dangling in the pantry.

'And what about you, my darling Clementine?'

'Burger and chips.'

'Isn't that what you had on the boat?'

'It wasn't very nice,' said Clemmie. 'That's why I want another one.'

'However did you manage it?' said Kieran. 'A daughter who knows her own mind. You could learn from her, you know.'

Clemmie sat up a little straighter, preening, but at the same time she glanced in her father's direction, as if unsure how he'd react. Tom didn't notice. He went to place the order and when he came back his demeanour had changed again. He ran his fingers down the smooth chilled side of his glass. 'Less than two hours from Tulsa,' he said.

Bel said curiously, 'Don't you *want* to go home?'

'Conflicted, I'd say. Wouldn't you, Kieran?'

His brother nodded. 'Our mother's strong on disappointment.'

When the food arrived, it came in enormous portions on enormous plates. The men both had steaks that were pooling blood, staining their chips. Bel tried to concentrate on her own dish but struggled to make headway. She poked her fork into the grains of rice, clumped together under a glistening veneer of cream, and it stood upright.

'Are you all right, Bel?' said Kieran. 'Is it not what you were expecting?'

'No, no, it's fine. It's just I've been ill – got bitten in Africa – and it's affected my appetite.'

Clemmie had been about to take a chunk from her bun. 'Was it a lion?' she asked, her round eyes popping with speculation.

'More like the opposite,' Bel said. 'An insect so tiny you can hardly see it.'

'Like fluke in cattle,' observed Tom, attacking his steak.

'Anyway,' said Bel, uncertain of the comparison. 'I'm better now.' She was reluctant to go into details. She approached the risotto again, but whether she nibbled into the sides or dented its centre the heap didn't seem to diminish much. She yearned for Rachael's dainty portions: small, tempting, easily digested.

Clemmie tugged at her father's sleeve. 'I'm bored.'

'Jaysus, Clem, we're eating our dinner.'

'Can I play on your phone again?'

'Are we not company enough for you?'

'It's been a long journey for a kid that age,' said Kieran. 'She's held up well.'

Tom laid his phone on the table top. 'Okay then. But don't drop it.'

Clemmie seized it with glee and in between mouthfuls of burger and snatches of fries her thumbs moved swiftly on the screen, which gave out a series of grunts and bleeps and satisfying trills.

Tom pushed aside his plate and said in an undertone to Kieran, 'We need to check up on things with Sean.'

'Well go on then.'

'Can I borrow your phone?' His head jerked towards Clemmie. 'Best if she stays occupied while we sort it out.'

Kieran delved into his pocket. 'I thought it was sorted.'

'It will be.' Tom took the mobile, and moved away to a quiet corner. Bel could see him beginning to speak, his expression animated. Then it became shuttered. She thought she heard him swear. Kieran was alert, half rising from his seat as if expecting Tom to beckon him over. Instead he turned his back and paced the length of the room, still talking, until he headed into the foyer and out of view. Clemmie, absorbed in her world of avatars, was unconcerned. Kieran fidgeted restlessly.

'Do you and your brother always swap everything?' said Bel after a while.

'You mean the phone?'

'And your jacket.'

'Oh that. He just borrowed it to go out on deck because he'd left his in the car.'

'You don't live together?'

'Christ no! I've been in Birmingham the past few years. Tom's in London mostly.'

'Because of Clemmie?'

'Partly. They've not long been back in touch.'

'You don't have any children?'

'No,' he said and they fell into silence again. He wasn't an easy man to draw out, Bel felt, although his brother's presence seemed to stir him up, get him going.

Eventually Tom returned and, shortly after, a waiter came over with a tumbler of Coke and three brimming pints.

'I thought we could do with another round,' Tom explained.

'A half would have done for me,' Kieran said. 'You know I'm driving.'

'Ah go on, you can hack another.'

'No I can't.'

Bel had scarcely touched her first drink and now had two in front of her. She thought she could recognise a manic determination in Tom's flouting of common sense.

'Right,' he said, pressing his fingertips together. 'Here's a thought for you. We'll stay the night.'

'What!'

'I know. I know.' He began to hum 'Twenty-four hours from Tulsa'. Then he said softly, 'Sean's not ready for her.'

Kieran, reclaiming his phone, frowned. 'I knew it! It was too much of a gamble. We should have broken the journey in Dublin. We could have stayed at Ned's.'

Tom said, 'You were the one who wanted to get it over with, insisted we could do the whole thing in a day.'

'Yeah, because I wasn't sure Ned's place would be fit for Clemmie. And because I thought if we don't stop then at least I have the chance to get you there in one piece. Those were my instructions. Not to lose you on the way.'

'It's only a minor delay,' said Tom. 'Sure, who will notice? We should make the best of it.' He plucked at his T-shirt. 'And the state I'm in, let's face it, is rank. You can't clean up in a washroom. I need a shower, a proper lathering. All we have to do is make a call home. We can be there dewy-eyed and sweet-smelling soon after breakfast. *And* you can enjoy your drink.'

The velvety black Guinness was sitting in front of Kieran like a reproof. 'You've blown it this time,' he said, lifting the glass.

Bel exclaimed, 'How can you let him manipulate you like this?'

Tom hummed another few bars, fixed her with his intense sky-blue eyes, so very different from his daughter's. 'Because underneath he's a great softie,' he said. 'Possessed with the notion of doing the right thing. For the grace of the Lord.'

'What's that supposed to mean?'

'He has a calling, darlin'. As a priest.'

'A what?'

'I'm not a priest,' said Kieran.

'Why did he say you were then? You don't look like one.'

'Of course I don't. He's winding you up.'

'It's, like, totally a lie?'

He shifted on his stool. 'Maybe not totally. I did think at one point I might have a vocation. There was a lot of talk of it around our house. I was wrong.'

'You were never a priest?'

'I was never ordained. I stuck about two years in the seminary. And then I came out the other side.'

'Came out!' crowed Tom. 'And wasn't it a bugger's delight while it lasted.'

'Feck off. Don't you believe a word he says.'

Tom's giggle had fished Clemmie away from her game and back into their world. 'Can I have an ice cream now?' she said.

'Sure you can. What flavour are you after?'

She leaned her head against his shoulder. 'Strawberry.'

Tom leapt to his feet, pulling her with him. 'I have a grand idea,' he said. 'We'll go and choose your ice cream and then we'll ask the lovely lady at the desk if they have rooms free. How would you like to stay tonight?'

'Stay in a hotel?'

'You'd enjoy that, wouldn't you?'

'What about your friend who makes the music?'

'Ah well, that'll be the night after. And maybe they'll be having some live music later on in the bar here. If you're good you can stay up to listen to it. This is a magical mystery tour, is it not? Full of surprises.'

'Aren't you forgetting something?' said Kieran. 'We have another passenger.'

Tom's eyebrows shot up. His expression was innocuous. Bel thought she had never seen anyone change character so often. 'It's not a problem for you, is it?'

Kieran didn't give her a chance to answer. 'Of course it is,' he said. 'Her mother's expecting to meet her and you're eating into her holiday. Ah Christ, but we have ourselves a mess.' He jiggled his knee, chewed at his lip. Then he said to Bel, 'If I drive you to Tralee you'll still arrive before the train and your mother can pick you up like you arranged.'

'How long would that take you?'

'An hour or so each way, I guess.'

'Then it'd be daft!'

'You could ring her, couldn't you?' said Tom. 'She won't have set off yet. Tell her we've some trouble with the car or something, but it'll be fixed in the morning.'

'Well… I guess I could. I mean, like, I don't *mind*. I'm not in a hurry. I just don't quite understand what the hold-up is. What exactly is going on?'

Tom sighed and went on to explain that Clemmie had been going to stay with their friends, Sean and Kath McCauley, for a day or two because her grandparents needed forewarning. It wasn't fair to spring a shock on a couple who were already beleaguered.

Bel could see the logic of this, though it vexed her the girl was being treated like a parcel – her mother handing her over to a distant father, the father handing her over to strangers. 'Does she know these people?'

'Sure she does! Kath's come to London many a time. It's only because she's unexpectedly away on family matters that we have to change our plans now. Maybe it's my fault for not firming up the date. Whatever. But Kath will be home tomorrow. And I might even stay there myself. The point is, we get a chance to prepare the ground.'

'You,' Kieran said. 'Nothing to do with me.'

'Look, I didn't even know Clem existed till recently when her ma came after me for the maintenance. We've all had a lot of catching up to do.' He clasped the child's hand. 'And don't worry about the cost. I'll put the rooms on my card, the bar tab and all. It's great that you're coming along with us for the ride, Bel.'

9

The Encounter

In Julia's eyes the town of Dingle wasn't much altered. There was more bustle perhaps, more hanging baskets and fresher paintwork, a rash of new bungalows in vibrant colours plonked down like little Lego homes, but people still came from their scattered smallholdings to drink and gossip, to get their hair cut or their shoes mended, to stock up on necessities; visitors still marvelled at its quaintness as they trundled the narrow streets. She remembered well the kink in the road, the sea wall spread with fishing nets, the boats bobbing in the harbour. As she parked the car and set off on foot she half expected to come face to face with her old self, the unscarred Julia.

The call last night hadn't surprised her – not a bit – though it had made her curious. 'Sorry, where did you say you are again?'

'Actually,' Bel had said. 'I'm not sure. A pretty place, dinky little thatched cottages and a wonderful scent of peat. I've forgotten its name.'

'Right, I see.'

'You're not upset, are you? You don't feel I've let you down? I'll be there tomorrow morning, promise. The hotel staff know a mechanic who can sort out the car. I couldn't get a train now anyway because we're miles from a railway line.'

'These people you're with…'

'They're sound, honestly. One of them even used to be a priest.'

'Used to be?'

'Like a trainee. Years ago. It doesn't mean he's crossed over and grown horns and a tail. Anyway, I can look after myself.'

That's what she'd said when she set off for Sudan. But there was no point in arguing; Bel had travelled widely and Julia preferred not to hear about her more dubious encounters. 'It might be tricky to find the cottage. It might be too remote for the satnav.'

'Oh but they know the whole area, the guys – they were brought up round there.'

'Even so, I think it will be easier to meet in the town, in one of the hotels. I'll be waiting for you.' Julia was too restless to spend the morning pottering in Dolphin Cottage. She'd enjoyed being on her own until the moment of finding the memorial stone. That had spooked her. 'Text me when you're half an hour away and I'll let you know where I am.'

Since she was down to her last few euros she delayed going for a cup of coffee. On her way up the hill she passed Dick Mack's pub and recalled with a flash of nostalgia the cobbler publican and the two wooden counters facing each other: one a working bench for shoe last, hammer and leather; the other fitted with hand pumps. She could picture Dick Mack laying down his tools and shuffling from one occupation to another as he crossed the aisle to pull two pints of Guinness (and a red lemonade for Matt). The old man must have died by now, but when she peered inside the bar looked exactly the same.

She continued in the direction of the church. Mass had just ended and the congregation was spilling out of the doors and into the road. She tried to turn back to avoid the knots of locals gathering, but found herself trapped in the surge. She also had the uncomfortable feeling she was being watched; not so much spied on as talked about. It wasn't her imagination: three women were staring directly at her, blinking and conferring. She couldn't think why until she realised one of them was Teresa Hogan.

Julia waved a tentative greeting. Teresa came towards her. 'Good morning,' she called out. 'And how are you? Have you everything you need?'

'The cottage is perfect, thank you,' said Julia. 'Very well equipped.'

'Dr Wentworth,' said Teresa. 'Let me introduce my friends, Mary O'Connor and Breda Malone.'

The women shook hands and Mary O'Connor twitched her head to one side like a bird. 'Is this your first trip to Kerry?' she asked.

'Well no, actually I came once before. Ages ago.' She didn't elaborate, but added, 'It's as lovely as ever.'

The women were in their Sunday best, their hair prettily coiffed. They were smiling and fiddling with the straps of their handbags. They didn't seem anxious to move on.

Julia said, 'I went exploring yesterday and came across an old church. A ruined one covered in ivy. Very atmospheric, but such a pity that it's fallen into disrepair. Though I noticed the graveyard's still in use.' She wondered how she might drop the memorial plaque into the conversation.

'Ah yes,' said Teresa. 'You'll be meaning St Silas. The gable end is quite dangerous you know, but no one does the least thing to stop it falling. You could get a mighty crack on the head just strolling past to tend a loved one's…'

A text pinged into Julia's phone and Teresa failed to finish her sentence. Julia apologised for the interruption but didn't feel she could pick up the thread again without making her question too obvious. The women were already darting enquiring looks at each other.

The message was from Bel:

Sorry, running late xx.

'My daughter,' Julia said with a mock sigh. 'Never gets anywhere on time.'

'She's coming today?'

'She was due yesterday! See what I mean?'

'Indeed she was,' said Teresa energetically as if she wanted to show her friends she was fully informed. 'There's no major problem I hope?'

Julia shrugged. 'I'm hoping the same thing.'

Her phone was lying flat in the palm of her hand. She had a picture of Danny, wide-eyed, as a screensaver. Leaning forward, Mary O'Connor said, 'What a little sweetheart. Your grandson?'

'Yes.'

'He's coming with your daughter?'

'Oh no. He's my son's child. That photo was taken over a year ago actually. He's just started school now – he's growing so fast!'

'Ah, he's at a lovely age, so. Do you have any other pictures?'

Which was how Julia, at their urging, found herself flicking through the photos of her family. The women studied them, cooed and clucked and nudged each other, and agreed that little Danny took after his father and what a fine pair they made.

Eventually Teresa passed the phone back. 'We mustn't keep you,' she said. 'But you will be sure to let me know if there's anything I can do for you during the week. We want you to...' she paused a moment '...think well of us.'

'And enjoy your holiday,' said Breda Malone, reaching out unexpectedly to pat Julia's shoulder.

Then the trio tottered away, heads as close as schoolgirls', and Julia decided to take her coffee break. She'd earmarked the hotel lounge: restful and old-fashioned with wood panelling and high-backed chairs, sepia photographs on the walls, a row of Sunday newspapers neatly folded. She settled herself in a spot where she had a partial view of the street entrance. A waitress took her order and she idly turned the pages of the *Irish Independent*.

She had no idea what 'running late' actually meant. It was anybody's guess – Bel's poor timekeeping was well documented. She could miss trains and appointments with ease. Even when she'd been dropped in front of the school gates, she could miss assembly or registration. There had been a single exception, twenty-six years ago, when she'd sallied down the birth canal three weeks early to great inconvenience. Julia had her case packed in readiness, but it was a shock to find her waters breaking as she collected Matt from Cubs.

It didn't help that Bel's premature arrival had induced a terrifying wave of grief that confounded her expectations. When you have been climbing out of a pit you don't expect the hopeful prospect ahead of you to be a mirage; that you will be knocked back down again. At least she had easy access to medication. She knew what to take; she'd learned to cope once before and she could do it again.

It was particularly ironic because the baby was supposed to be a turning point. She had moved to a different city and she was in love with a man – a few years younger and several degrees wilder – who continued to surprise and elate her. Leo, as she was to discover over years of unearthing him from squalid drinking holes, was attracted to what he called grit and she called grime. But back then, in the beginning, she had fallen for his ability to spin romance out of sawdust, to transform any place they might find themselves into somewhere poetic and life-enhancing.

Friends considered them an unlikely pairing, but Julia didn't *want* to replicate her former, traditional life. At medical school her future had seemed predictable: she and William pursuing their careers in tandem, bringing up their family. Once this had been thrown into disarray, why not embrace the opposite? That was the joy of Leo: he'd been able to sweep her out of herself in a way no one else could. She'd believed in his work as passionately as he did, and encouraging him as his career bloomed had been hugely exciting. The downward spiral less so.

She sipped her coffee and looked up expectantly each time the door swung open, but there was no sign of Bel. Another text message winged into her phone.

Where are you?

She frowned. She'd given Bel directions to the hotel. Surely this was the question *she* should be asking. Then, reading more closely, she saw that the message hadn't come from Bel at all, but from Leo. The nerve of him! It was bad enough that he'd driven her out of France; her present whereabouts were none of his business.

Julia had put up with the groupies Leo attracted for years. Art students mostly, in gothic make-up and swathes of black, in thrall (as she'd once been) to his combination of iconoclasm and authority; intense, ambitious young women who liked to drink late and didn't need to get up early. It had come to a head with the girl who'd wanted to be found out, who'd left cryptic phone messages and taunting mementoes of her visits. Julia finally acted when, plumping up the sofa cushions in the studio, she'd found an unfamiliar pair of earrings. She'd confronted Leo over supper.

'I would never wear these,' she'd said, dropping the two brazen Coptic crosses onto his plate as he was about to fork up a mouthful of chicken.

He laid down his cutlery and picked them out of his food, glancing at the neat enamel studs in Julia's ears. 'No,' he agreed.

'Whatever I need to be told, I'd rather it came from you. So go on.'

'What?'

'Why don't you tell me who they belong to?'

'Probably because I can't remember.' He produced the wry smile that he relied upon to extract himself from trouble, but Julia had become resistant to it.

'She's escaped your memory already? Nice one, Leo.' She rose from the table and scraped her own dinner into the bin; she wasn't feeling hungry.

'Look, Julia, your imagination's running away with you. Why the hell are you bothered about a pair of fucking earrings?' He'd cradled his arm around her waist and buried his face in her neck.

But the evidence had been cumulative and once you knew for certain, whatever the excuses, whatever crisis of career or ego he'd been trying to assuage, you couldn't back-pedal. She'd found out who the girl was – a young and pushy events organiser, with the sly eyes, plump buttocks and high round breasts of a seventeenth-century painting – but she'd made a point of forgetting her name.

She deleted Leo's text.

10

The Breakdown

Julia had given up watching the door. When a burst of spring air ruffled the pages of her newspaper, she wasn't looking in its direction. She felt a light tap on her shoulder, a kiss on her cheek. There was a whiff of smoke and alcohol too, though that could have been emanating from the coat – the purple coat that someone had thrown out once before, to Oxfam, and still lacked buttons.

'Bel! You got here at last!' She rose to embrace her and their bones clashed.

'Yeah, I'm sorry. It was, like, one thing after another, a whole catalogue…'

'Never mind that now, let me look at you.'

Bel had never been the kind of pliant, amenable daughter other mothers boasted of. She was scatty and unreliable, with a complicated attitude to food. But she had a generous nature and charm in abundance and Julia had nearly lost her. The memory of the frail body plugged into drips in the isolation ward still made her shiver. Bel wilted a little under her scrutiny, knowing she was looking for signs of good colour and plumpening cheeks.

'Oh, darling, you've bags under your eyes.'

'I didn't sleep very well...'

'Then we must get you back to the cottage so I can look after you.' Julia took the handle of Rachael's suitcase, stuffed carelessly with Bel's things. 'I'm in the car park at the side.'

'Can't I have a cup of tea first? I'm parched.'

'I'm afraid I've got no money left.'

'But I have.' Bel hailed the waitress and pulled out her purse with its jangling bells.

Julia glanced inside it. 'Gosh, is that all Matt gave you?'

'I had to pay for the room last night. Sorry.'

'Oh well, I suppose it's only until the banks open tomorrow morning. The transfer will have come through by then. Honestly, twenty-four-hour banking is a complete joke when what you need is cash in hand.'

Bel ordered her tea and sank into an adjacent chair. 'Mum, I hope you didn't just invite me to bring you cash?'

'Of course not!'

'So why? And why did you come here in the first place? What was that about?'

Julia said, 'Aren't you forever telling me to be more spontaneous? Especially now I don't have a job to go to. Like you, for example. Spontaneously leaping into a car with strangers. I was quite worried.'

'Not half as worried as we were about *you*,' said Bel, her face shining with self-righteousness. 'Me and Matt and Rachael, we thought you'd been abducted or murdered by a psycho in France. Dorothy Culshaw was doing her nut, convinced you had some terminal illness, and apparently the police were, like, chill out, it's probably nothing (which it *was*) but which was just the kind of false assurance that sets your cage rattling. So it's not me this time, it's you. You're up to something and you have to come clean.'

'I'd have thought it was obvious what I was up to.'

'What?'

But Julia couldn't answer. Something was squeezing her chest, hampering her breathing. A shaking began in her shoulders, beyond her control. She hunted for a tissue and pressed it to her mouth to stifle the gasps.

'Mum! What is it? What's the matter?' The tea arrived: a white pot on a tray, a jug of milk, a strainer. 'I can leave it,' Bel said. 'If you want to get back.'

Julia wished the wings of the chair would give her more cover to hide behind. Tears were tracking a course of their own; she couldn't quench them. Why, she thought, why is this happening to me when I've managed so well up to now?

'I'm going to the Ladies,' she said to Bel. 'There's no hurry. You drink your tea and by then I'll be fine to drive.'

'I'll come with you.'

'No. You should mind your case. I need to get a grip. We'll talk later.'

'But, Mum...'

Julia blundered past the other tables and into Reception, looking for the sign to the toilets. A woman at the desk asked if she was all right and she brushed her off. Speech had been replaced by a panic-stricken choking. The awful reckoning was finally catching up with her. That stupid incident yesterday with the rabbit had only been the beginning.

In her profession she'd often had to give bad news. And the reactions, especially from parents, whose expectations were so high, were almost always the same. She knew them well: stunned disbelief, denial, anger, guilt. She had experienced every single one herself. Disbelief and denial she'd been obliged to conquer, but in the depths of her subconscious, rarely brought up and examined, guilt and rage still battled. Perhaps if you are content in your life, you don't look back at what might have been, but she had forced herself to make this journey.

Two days ago, on her visit to Doonshean beach, she'd stood facing the sea, exposing herself to the salt-laden wind. She'd watched the rhythmic pull of the tide as it scooped away at the sand, showing no sign of the power beneath its surface. The swell of the encroaching waves was gentle, an occasional burst of white at the rim. A couple were walking their dog on the cliffs above. A lone man was bird-watching through binoculars. The scene was soothing and Julia, dry-eyed, had felt a sense of peace. She'd thought: I've done the right thing, coming back here, laying ghosts to rest. She blamed herself for what happened to William – if only she had been with him… But striding across the wet sand at sunset she'd felt she was conquering the past.

Which made it all the more distressing to find her emotions now ambushed. In the privacy of the Ladies she kept flushing the toilet to drown the sounds of her weeping, the noisy gulping of air. A knock came on the cubicle door, which she thought might be Bel until an Irish voice said: 'Are you all right in there?'

'Yes, yes. I just need a minute or two…' She should compose herself; she'd had plenty of practice. Balancing on the edge of the seat, she surveyed her face in her make-up mirror, wiping away the sooty trail of mascara. She kept waiting for the tap of retreating heels. After a while she supposed the woman must have left quietly, without her hearing. She unlocked the door and went to wash her hands in the basin, focusing on rubbing the liquid soap into every finger joint, every wrinkle of skin, as if she were preparing to examine a patient. The woman had not gone away, she was hovering just behind her.

'Are you sure you don't need anything? I could—'

'I'm not staying here,' Julia said.

'No, but if you've had some bad news, maybe a seat in the Residents' Lounge would give you some breathing space for a while.'

'Thank you, that's very kind but I'll be fine.' She put on a bright false smile that wouldn't fool anyone and stalked through the door and back to the bar.

Bel twisted in her seat and reddened as if she'd been caught misbehaving. 'Mum, what happened? Is it something I've done?'

'No, darling,' said Julia, seizing the suitcase. 'But can we go please? I've made enough of a fool of myself.'

'It's because you bottle things up,' said Bel, keeping a slightly breathless pace. 'You want to be in control the whole time and it doesn't work, you know. It's like trapped wind isn't it, it can be so painful, and you don't even know how you did it and then the release—'

'Isabel,' said Julia. 'Please stop it.'

In the car her mother's knuckles gleamed on the steering wheel. Bel snatched surreptitious glances at her profile. She didn't look troubled any more except for a twitch along her jaw as if she were clenching it too tight and the muscles were rebelling. Beyond her head was a view of the coastline, the long grass rippling in the fields, the sea sparkling and serene.

In true parental fashion, although Julia wouldn't answer Bel's questions, she had plenty of her own: 'I'm still confused about what happened last night,' she said. 'I mean, why didn't you stick to your original plan?'

'It seemed like a good idea, getting a lift,' said Bel. 'It should have been much quicker. How could I know the car was going to break down?'

'Lucky, I suppose, that you were near a hotel.'

'Actually we had to crawl the last few miles till we made it: crank, thump, clatter. It was quite scary.'

'What was it? Clutch? Gearbox? Oil pump?'

'Oh God!' exclaimed Bel. 'I don't know anything about engines!'

'But it got fixed easily enough?'

'Oh yes, no problem.'

'So what was it that held you up again this morning?'

'The guys had to stop off somewhere to see someone. It was only meant to take five minutes. I think Irish time must be different from ours, don't you?'

There was no reason to have lied to her mother, to have invented engine failure – when in fact what had happened was that she'd shared a hotel room with the mad Farrelly brothers and a six-year-old girl who'd subsequently been swapped for a violin. But the difficulty with lies was that once you'd started you felt you had to carry on, adding layers of embroidery. The difficulty with the truth, in this particular instance, was that it was so peculiar.

The hotel in Adare, a weekend retreat for Dubliners, had all the comforts of an old-fashioned country house: well-upholstered armchairs, walnut wardrobes, four-poster beds. It had also been busy, but there was a family room available and Tom had jumped at it. The night's reprieve had put him in roguish good humour, cracking jokes and telling stories so tall even Clemmie wouldn't believe them. She was finally persuaded to go to bed as long as Bel came up to give her a goodnight kiss.

Afterwards, Tom switched off the side lamp and followed Bel from the room. In the hushed corridor with its deep pile carpet and warm sense of seclusion he coiled his arm around her shoulders. 'Thank you. You've been fantastic with her.'

'No big deal. I like kids.'

'She thinks you're wonderful, you know. As do I.'

'Don't get ahead of yourself. We only just met.'

'Can I have a kiss too?' He didn't wait for an answer. She felt a light, friendly pressure on her lips and was startled by her own response. It seemed a long time since she had been kissed. Heck, she wanted a proper one even if she was going to regret it later. By the end she was literally breathless.

'Ah, Bel,' he said, enfolding her. 'You've been our saviour today.'

Partly because of this moment of intimacy (though how could she tell? They'd also stayed up late and too much unaccustomed alcohol was flooding her system) she'd slept badly, aware of every snuffle from her companions. Her dreams were rough and rampaging; despite the deep soft mattress and fine linen sheets, she wouldn't have been surprised to wake up black and blue like someone who'd been in a fight.

In the morning, when they went to settle up after breakfast, Tom's bold offer came to naught when his card was declined. Kieran stepped in, observing that he might have guessed it. Bel insisted on paying more than her share.

The mood, as they set off on their final leg, was not celebratory and they drove in silence. A few miles from their destination, the Megane had turned off the road and lumbered up a dirt track. A modern bungalow, with huge windows reflecting the ever-changing skies, stood amid a series of old barns and converted outbuildings. Clemmie clung to Bel and drummed her heels, reluctant to leave her.

'Why don't I give you my number?' said Bel. 'So you can call me whenever you want. I'm here all week same as you.'

'Promise?'

'Of course.'

Tom handed over his phone and she tapped it in.

Clemmie said, 'Will you come indoors with me?'

'Okay.' She thought they'd just be there long enough for the child to feel welcome but the McCauleys insisted on giving them a tour of the workshops where Sean repaired musical instruments. It was nearly an hour before they left again and Clemmie had been replaced with what Tom explained was his mother's old fiddle.

The violin sat beside Bel on the back seat. 'Is your mother very musical?'

'*She* doesn't think so,' said Kieran, 'but yes, she is. Though she says she never has time to play. This has been hanging around in Sean's workshop for months. I took it in when I was last over and she's not even tried to collect it. She's probably forgotten where it is. So this is by way of a sweetener for us being late.'

Were all families the same, Bel wondered: existing in a delicate state of checks and balances, compromise and negotiation? You didn't want your behaviour to hurt the people closest to you, but your interests were *never* going to coincide. Now, sitting beside Julia – who would probably ask awkward questions about Matt's money too – she gripped the phone in her pocket. She'd switched it to silent, but she was alert to vibrations.

11

The Violin

Ronnie had wanted to put on a feast. The lamb was one of
Bernie O'Connor's, so she knew the meat would be pale and
tender from a diet of new grass. Before roasting, she spiked
it with garlic as Nuala advised, though it seemed to her a
pity to drown its subtle flavour. Then she'd baked potatoes
and onions and boiled up spring greens. But the greens had
gone on wilting to death, the onions had blackened and the
potatoes had shrivelled inside jackets so crunchy they could
break your teeth. None of the meal was eaten; Anna said
to save it. She'd taken the kiddies back home to give them
spaghetti hoops.

The lamb joint, being a whole leg, was too big for
the fridge. Ronnie covered it in foil and stowed it in the
sideboard on her best meat platter. She could have predicted
this. Like dealing with a cow with a difficult labour: your
instinct tells you that delivery will be problematic, that
you'll need to call the vet, and yet you cling to foolish hopes
of a miracle.

They'd given a lift to an Englishwoman – that was their excuse. They weren't dumb, her boys, they knew how to string her along. A little bit of chivalry was pardonable, was it not? 'The girl didn't really know where she was going,' Tom explained. 'We've ended up making a magnificent detour.'

'There's time enough to get here tonight,' Ronnie had said. 'I've your beds made ready.' (She didn't mention the dinner.)

'But you shouldn't be waiting up for us. You should get your beauty sleep. We'll be with you right after breakfast.'

Beauty sleep. That made her laugh. Though in point of fact, she'd no idea what she looked like. The mirror never gave her a glance. It might as well have been a piece of slate. She didn't believe the promise about after breakfast anyhow.

When she took the lamb out of the cupboard and unwrapped it again, it had lost its attraction as the centrepiece of a laden table. She'd got in a few loaves of sliced pan so she'd make sandwiches instead. A sandwich would give them something to do with their hands, give a lining to their stomachs. She took a knife and began to hack at the meat. She preferred a generous chunky filling. But handling the cold grease of the leg made her palms slippery; the blade of the knife shot forward and skidded into her fingertips. The next thing she knew, she was hunting for plasters and trying to staunch the flow of blood so the bread didn't turn pink.

This was how she was fixed when her boys came marching in, ducking their heads beneath the lintel, filling the space between the table and the range. The room seemed to have trouble containing them. Were they so much bigger than her other visitors? Vince Hogan, for instance, was a little gnome of a man, shrinking as he aged. If he'd still been running the bar, he'd hardly have been able to reach the optics. At least, that was Ronnie's perception, but her perception was shot to pieces these days. She needed to get herself to the optician for an eye test – though there were some advantages to missing the cobwebs and the desiccated insects and the dust balling in the corners; dirt couldn't bug her.

'Will you look at this, Mam,' Tom greeted her. 'We've brought you a surprise.' He whipped an old fiddle case from behind his back and held it out like a votive offering.

'What's that?'

'It's your violin.'

'Ah.'

'Ah? Is that all? The wood had a crack in it, don't you remember? Kieran took it to Sean McCauley to be fixed only you never went to fetch it back. I don't know why Sean didn't drop it off but there you go...'

'I expect we both had other things on our minds. I didn't miss it. Lord, I haven't played a tune for years.'

'Then you can give us one for Dad's birthday bash and liven things up. We want to hear you play again.'

'Well I can't.' She held up her bandaged hand. 'This wouldn't have happened if you'd been on time.'

'That isn't fair, Mam. You know—'

'And don't think I can't see your game, the both of you. Trying to flatter me into forgetting you've arrived nearly a day late, that it hasn't been the greatest inconvenience to get everything ready and have you tell me you've been partying with some English girl.

'We never said we were partying.'

'How do you think your father felt?'

'Look,' said Kieran with a helpless shrugging of his shoulders. He might be a full-grown man with more than one failed relationship behind him, but as far as Ronnie was concerned, he remained the ungainly adolescent whose good intentions never quite came off. 'I've taken a whole week off work to make this trip for Dad. I'm not arsing about. We had a delay, that's all. You can ask Tom for details. But, if you recall, you told me not to turn up without him. So I got him here, didn't I? I deserve some congratulations, I reckon.'

Tom laid the violin case on the kitchen table beside the ragged leg of lamb. He put his arm around his mother's waist and laid his cheek against hers. 'It's great to see you,' he said.

'Tell me about the girl,' said Ronnie.

'There's nothing to tell.'

'Then what secret are you hiding from me now?'

'Always so suspicious,' he said lightly.

'Answer me. Why is it one girl after another? Are you never going to settle down?'

'You know you don't want me to. It'll make you feel old. You said so yourself.'

'That was years ago,' declared Ronnie. 'I *am* old now. So it's not a question of what I feel. It's more a question of not having enough grandchildren.'

Kieran nudged Tom; Tom said, 'Enough for what? A five-aside football team?'

'Every mother hopes to see her child established in the world. A good job. A happy family.'

'Is that so?' He was going through that routine he followed on a rare visit home, touching all the old things: the mantel clock, the framed photos, the Waterford glass vase that ought to be filled with flowers rather than string, scissors, pens and Sellotape. It was as if he were making sure the objects were three-dimensional and hadn't lost substance. He was moving around the room with his back to her. He'd always had a swagger to his stance, a cocky tilt to his shoulders, but she could see beyond that, couldn't she? To the wayward impulsive little boy.

She shouldn't spoil the homecoming. The dinner was ruined and her sons had let her down – but they were here now, weren't they. She should be drinking them in, their powerful masculine presence. Why would they unsettle each other with reproaches? 'Will you have a cup of tea?' she said. 'Or a bite to eat?' She indicated the sandwiches. 'Or will you see your father first? He's been waiting for you.'

'Where is he?'

'In the back room watching the television.' They could hear its murmur through the wall. Pat wouldn't get up to greet them, she knew. He didn't want his sons to see him leaning on his walking stick.

'We're not hungry,' said Tom. 'We had a massive breakfast.'

'What makes me think you don't look after yourself, I wonder?'

'Because you're not there to dose us with cod liver oil every bedtime? Actually, Mam, as I remember it, that was about your limit: a window of opportunity at nine o'clock of a night. All day long we'd to fend for ourselves.'

'Because I had my hands full with getting the milk to the creamery! And weren't you forever running off, hiding in the blanket box because you couldn't stand the oily taste?'

'It wasn't only the blanket box. I was way more imaginative than that.'

'Indeed you were. Hours I'd spend ferreting in ditches. And wasn't my heart in my mouth every five minutes in case you'd electrocuted yourself or fallen off the barn roof or—'

'Happy days.' Tom grinned.

She'd no more idea what he got up to now. She'd lost count of the job openings, the enticing deals from new contacts he generally seemed to meet in bars. London, which she seldom visited and didn't much like, must be a more convivial place than it appeared at first sight. She knew he'd given up on the music industry, or maybe it had given up on him. The band had been on the verge of a breakthrough that never came. Tom was the lead singer and he should have tried for a solo career, but off he went on a film-making course. He was going to get into TV: all these channels, he said, not enough ideas, not enough technical expertise. But he ran out of money so the course was never completed. He went back to pulling pints for a living – oh, and painting and decorating.

Ronnie didn't like to think of him stinking of turps and being ordered about by some rich banker's wife who never chipped a fingernail. 'It isn't like that,' he'd said when she'd once phoned him in the middle of a job. 'What is it like then?' she'd demanded. 'Put me in the picture, Tom. Describe it to me, where you are now.'

She was half-joking but he'd answered without a whiff of hesitation. 'Well,' he'd said. 'I'm in a fine big room on the first floor with long windows overlooking the street but you can't hear the traffic because they're double-glazed. I'm knee-deep in wet wallpaper because I've been stripping it off with the steamer and my next job is to fill in the cracks in the plaster and touch up the architrave and then...' And that was when she heard a giggle (fast suppressed but a giggle nonetheless). And the elegant room she'd been imagining, in a stuccoed town house, disappeared from her head. She didn't want to replace it with an image of a double bed and sweaty sheets and some randy unfulfilled banker's wife (or worse), so she pretended there was someone at the door. 'Call me back when you're on your next break,' she'd said, but he hadn't done so.

He'd had cards made up with Tom Farrelly Interior Design printed on them, but it seemed an awful waste of a talent to be choosing other people's wallpaper because they were too lazy to do it themselves. More honest to call yourself a decorator and earn a bit of respect. She would tell people he was running his own business; she didn't have to tell them he had no employees.

Kieran was a different proposition. He had a steady job and there was no point asking about it because she didn't know the first thing about computers. She and Pat had a slow old thing Kieran called the dinosaur, where she processed the accounts and emailed suppliers. They kept it in the boys' old bedroom, but it was Nuala who had to sort it out when anything went wrong.

'We'll go and say hello to Dad then,' Tom said, lifting the violin onto the table and leaving the case carelessly open. They jostled each other in the hall in a lively enough manner but she could hear their feet pausing before they stepped across the threshold, into the room where Pat was sitting. She wouldn't follow. Father and sons could get used to each other in private. She ran the fingers of her good hand down the shaft of the fiddle and plucked at some of the strings. It had been well tuned but she was too rusty to play.

When the phone shrilled it made her start. Anna or Nuala, she guessed as she raised the receiver, checking up on their brothers, but it was Teresa Hogan. 'Ronnie?'

'Yes?'

'I'm not long back from Mass and you know I have a lady doctor renting Dolphin Cottage for the week?'

'So?'

'Well we bumped into her again outside the church. I have a good memory for faces on me and I'd had a niggling suspicion from the start. Now Mary and Breda have seen her they agree with me; think it quite likely she's the same person.'

'I'm not following you, Teresa. Which person?'

'Wait till I tell ye!' Her voice rose in excitement. 'The widow.'

'Whose widow?'

'Why, *his* – your man's! Different surname now, which explains why I didn't make the connection sooner.'

Ronnie sat down on a chair; the telephone cord twisted under her arm. 'How can you be certain?'

'Maybe tis only a hunch, but really, in thirty years, she's changed remarkably little. Mary got her to show us the family pictures – just on her phone, mind. Her son is grown up now, happily married with a little one of his own. He's a lawyer, she told me. A proper professional. Done very well for himself. Isn't that extraordinary?'

Ronnie felt dizzy. She should have grabbed a sandwich for sustenance.

Teresa continued. 'I have the press cuttings somewhere. Vince had a mention in quite a few of them. So I thought I should root around, check the photographs. Then I can let you know for sure.'

'The newspaper reports? You kept them all?'

'You've a lot on your plate. You'll be out and about this week with the arrangements for the party and so forth, but I thought, if there's the possibility you might run into her…'

'Thank you, Teresa,' said Ronnie.

'It's best to be forewarned is it not?'

PART THREE

MONDAY TUESDAY

12

The Artist

Three headless chickens were lined up on the kitchen table, the stumps of their legs pointing at the ceiling, their plucked flesh a buttery gold from their corn-fed diet. This should have been a morning of pure pleasure, immersing herself in the sensuous process of cooking – chopping, stirring, assembling, garnishing. But Rachael couldn't find her boning knife.

She'd looked in every drawer, in the dishwasher basket and the utensils jar and both knife blocks. Boning a chicken was a delicate operation and the right tool was essential. She'd noticed recently that things were disappearing. Usually they were unremarkable: a pencil sharpener, a small screwdriver, a bottle opener, a box of matches. She'd assumed at first this was the result of Bel's inability to remember where she put anything, forever borrowing replacements. But Bel had left for Ireland and, anyway, what would she want with a boning knife? Rachael had found some of the missing objects scattered on the lawn and tried to have a conversation with Danny about them.

'You do know you shouldn't play with matches?' He'd rolled his eyes as if he couldn't believe she had such low expectations of him. 'So you promise you won't take them again?'

'But, Mummy, I didn't!' His lower lip trembled and she had to force herself not to throw her arms around him and squeeze him to death. This was the boy Nathan's doing. It had to be. He kept turning up like a bad penny, but Dan thought he was the most exciting companion on the planet. She hoped the phase would pass.

She went into the garden to scour the flowerbeds. Bluebells and lilies of the valley were beginning to open, their fragrance fresh and sweet. The pear tree was shedding petals like snowflakes, drifting beneath its trunk. The trunk itself looked scarred. She made out some kind of inscription but the carving hadn't been very successful. Pear bark didn't offer a smooth etchable surface like sycamore or beech – it was too rough. The missing screwdriver was sticking out at right angles, plunged like a dagger up to its shaft in the wood. That wretched boy!

Rachael wrenched it out, catching her knuckles as she did so. She licked the graze and spotted, at the foot of the tree, the knife she'd been searching for. She examined it closely to check the narrow blade wasn't damaged. She sprang the point against her thumb; it felt sharp but she couldn't be certain until she slipped it beneath the chicken's ribcage.

Sometimes her life seemed a constant series of tests. As soon as she'd completed one, another would demand her attention. She was never able to put her feet up and let the world flow around her, as Matt kept recommending. There was always something to worry about, like a power cut while her soufflé was rising, running out of a vital ingredient, or spilling red wine on her white table linen. She was pondering the unfairness of this when she heard the doorbell ring. There was no reason to assume Nathan was the caller – after all, he generally wriggled through the hedge – but when the ring came again, she stormed back into the house and along the hallway. She flung open the door with her left hand, the knife dancing and flashing in her right.

For a second she didn't recognise the figure leaning casually against the handrail. He looked, as he always did, a little the worse for wear. Behind him on the drive was a gleaming but, to her eyes, very dated sports car. 'Leo!'

He stepped back, took his hands from his pockets and held them up in mock surrender. 'I come in peace, you know.'

Rachael followed his gaze to the weapon in her fist. She dropped her arm to her side and said, embarrassed, 'Why didn't you phone?'

'Why don't you like surprises?'

She shuffled her feet. This was an odd situation. She'd only occupied the house for a couple of months, had barely begun the process of making it her home and getting to know the area. The man on the doorstep, awaiting admission, had lived here for well over a decade, far less of a stranger than she.

'Anyway,' he said. 'I *did* phone. Spoke to the delightful BT lady. Don't you ever listen to your messages, Raquel?'

She bridled. 'I use my mobile mostly. Landline calls still tend to be for Julia.'

'Ah… Well, I was passing anyway, saw the car, guessed you were in and thought I'd take a chance. I didn't expect a disembowelling.'

'The knife's not for you,' said Rachael, to match his levity, although he made her feel as if she were trying too hard. 'It's for the chickens.'

'Are you keeping livestock now?'

'No! I haven't killed them myself. They're for a client who's having a lunch reception tomorrow. You bone the birds, then you layer them with ham and a spicy stuffing and roll them up and truss them again for cooking. They carve nicely and look pretty on the plate. I know it's a bit retro but actually retro dishes are quite fashionable and my client...'

'Why don't you show me?'

'Oh, of course, come in.' He had a bag with him, she noticed as he followed her, slung by one strap from his shoulder. 'Are you, um, staying long?'

'I'm waiting for the wind to change in France,' he said. What did that mean exactly? 'Thought I'd see how Bel was doing.'

'But Bel's in Ireland, didn't you hear? You've just missed her. She's holidaying with Julia for a week.'

'Ireland?' said Leo. 'So that's where they are. And I'm out of the loop again.' She couldn't decide whether his tone was irked or ironic. 'Shall I pop over or hang on here? I'll think about it. I have a few plans anyway... galleries to visit.' He dumped the bag and accompanied her into the kitchen. 'Nice place you've got.'

Surely he was winding her up on purpose. 'Do you need somewhere to stay?'

'Well, I spent last night with Nick Roden. Sculptor. Did you ever meet him?'

'No, I don't think so.'

'The new wife's a bit of a cow.' Leo smothered a yawn. 'You don't expect a man to be under the thumb at Nick's age. So if you have room…'

'I suppose we have. I mean, the attic's empty since Bel's away.'

'My old stamping ground.'

He made her feel ill at ease. His ex-wife had thrown him out of this house, but now that she'd given it up he was wangling his way back in. Could he be trying to prove something? She inserted the tip of the knife beneath the chicken's backbone. Leo, restless, was pacing up and down, peering through the window, opening the door to the larder, inspecting the dishes and bowls that were hers and Matt's, that had nothing to do with him or his previous tenure.

'And how's the boy himself?'

Did he mean Matt? Or Danny? 'Oh… fine.' She began to tease back the poultry flesh. 'Look, I'm sorry, Leo, but I have to concentrate on this because if I don't do it right it gets into a shocking mess and…'

'No worries. I'll settle in. The attic, you said?'

Rachael cast him a doubtful look but his back was turned and he didn't register it.

By the time he returned she'd removed the carcasses and swept the frail ribcages and sturdy thigh bones into her stock pot. She was inserting the centrepiece stuffing into the cavity of the first chicken.

'Impressive handiwork,' said Leo. 'Can I help?'

'You can pass me the string.' He fetched it for her, then pulled out a chair and sat down. 'I don't really like being watched,' she said.

'I thought you used to give cookery classes.'

'That was different.'

'Why?'

'Because it was information for people who wanted to learn. This isn't the same as teaching. I feel I'm making an exhibition of myself.'

'You make a fine exhibition, Raquel.'

'Why do you call me that?'

'Oh...' He leaned his elbow on the table and his cheek on his hand, studying her. 'Too many Rachels in your generation, aren't there? It gets confusing. This way I can keep tally.'

She knotted the string with a deft tug and moved onto her second bird. 'Does Matt know you're here?'

'I spoke to him a couple of days ago. Told him I might pass by. He'll be home tonight though, won't he? I wouldn't want to disturb him at work.'

'You're disturbing me at work.'

'My dear!' He sprang up, nearly knocking the chair over. 'I'm sorry. Christ, that was thoughtless.'

'Well...' Now he was veering too far in the other direction. That was the problem with Leo. You could never be quite certain how sincere he was. And any flattery came hedged with qualifications.

'I'm so bad at that,' he continued. 'Putting myself in other people's shoes. But you're right. I *hate* being interrupted during the creative process. How could I forget that *you* are a creative too, an artist no less.'

'I don't know about that.' She concentrated on spreading the herb stuffing over the sheet of ham before rolling it up.

'Look at those colours,' said Leo. 'Green and pink and white. Visual harmony.'

'Well, flavour's paramount of course, but I like to co-ordinate too. Especially salads: I mix beetroot with red onion and cherry tomato, and chicory and fennel look good against the green of avocado and baby spinach. And then—' She broke off, suddenly suspicious that he'd been humouring her, that what was a passion to her was only dreary domesticity to him. Where was the intellectual stimulus in producing a decorative plate of food? How could it compare to someone who leapt around drenching six-foot canvases in acrylic paint – even if the average viewer was baffled by the image and had to buy an expensive catalogue to have it explained.

'You have a natural talent,' said Leo. 'Matt's a lucky guy.'

Other men had said this to her and she never knew how to react; whether it was because they were obsessed with their stomachs or because they fancied her. Once or twice she'd tried the response: 'I'm lucky too' and encountered blankness.

When she'd met Matt – while ladling pasta at a function for young solicitors – the first thing she'd noticed was his tie: the bold patterns and raging colours clutching at his collar like a cry for help. When he'd persuaded her to go for a drink with him, she'd challenged him to take the tie off and tell her what he liked about it.

Gladly he'd loosened the knot and placed it in her hands like a gift of silk ribbon. 'It's striking,' he'd offered. 'Makes a statement. I wouldn't want something wishy-washy.' And when she learnt that he couldn't distinguish one shade from another, she fell in love with his misplaced confidence.

This, along with his knack of reassurance, had drawn her to him. She'd no idea whether it was because tragedy had entered his life so early and forged his character or whether it was a trait inherited from the father he'd scarcely known. But she relied on his encouragement – and she envied his ability to see the positive in everything, because she was beleaguered by doubts. She'd been an ugly duckling as a child and still couldn't consider herself beautiful. She'd also struggled with dyslexia and become convinced she'd never be good at *anything*. And now, although she'd discovered she could cook, it was such an ephemeral skill: once a meal was demolished there was nothing to show for it.

'Look,' she said, ignoring Leo's comment. 'I need to get these birds roasted so they've time to chill overnight. I like to keep ahead of myself, but you have to achieve a balance between advance preparation and absolute freshness, so...'

'How do you wow them at the lunch?' said Leo. 'Chef's hat askew? Tight black T-shirt? Are you always to be found with a knife in your hand?'

'Actually I'm just delivering the buffet and setting it out. They don't want me to serve, which is just as well because...'

'Because then you can come out with me.'

'Oh, but...'

'No buts. We'll go for a spin and find a pub somewhere. Did you see my new toy?'

'Toy?'

'A 1975 Lotus Elan +2. One of the last to be produced. Nick wants – or rather his wife insists – that he sell and I'm trying to decide if I want to buy. Completely impractical, but that's the charm isn't it? And I quite like tinkering with engines. I've never minded getting my hands dirty.'

'I'd have to get back for Danny.'

'Absolutely. I'm looking forward to seeing him myself. He probably doesn't remember the last time, does he? When would it have been, two years ago perhaps? And he'd have been what, three? There you go. Three years old. He won't have a clue who I am.'

'You told him who you weren't,' said Rachael. 'You told him you weren't his grandfather.'

Leo was unrepentant. 'Well I'm not.' He gave her the smile he shared with Bel, the one that made people, however frosty, melt into forgiveness. She continued with her stringing.

He said, 'Look, I can see you're busy. I'll get out of your hair if you promise to come with me tomorrow.'

'Where?'

'Oh... I'll think about it.' He clasped his hands behind his neck and surveyed the ceiling.

Rachael looked up too, horrified that a cobweb might have materialised in a corner. One of her priorities was to put in decent lighting, clear bright halogen, so she could see exactly what she was doing. There was so much that needed updating in this house but she and Matt were on a tight budget. She wrapped the stuffed chickens in foil and stepped around Leo's sprawling legs to put them in the oven. 'Um, if you don't mind... Matt will be home around six.'

'Raquel, I believe you're dismissing me.' He rose and let his hand rest for a moment between her shoulder blades, an innocent fatherly touch. 'I shall see you later.'

As soon as he had gone she rang Matt. 'Did he tell you he was coming?'

'I think he said he might. Why the panic?'

'I'm not panicking. It's just the way he sauntered in like he owned the place. He's taken his stuff up to the attic.'

'I can see you might find that a bit tricky, but it's not for long surely?'

'I think he's after something, but I don't know what. He hinted at unfinished stuff with Bel. Or Julia. I didn't know whether to tell him where to find them.'

'Is that what he wants? Are they ignoring his calls?'

'How should I know?'

'It's not like they're in hiding,' said Matt. 'On the other hand he's already majorly pissed Julia off. Perhaps you'd better warn her.'

'Can't you?'

'Okay, but it will have to wait till I get home.'

Rachael added, 'He says he wants to take me out tomorrow afternoon.' There was a pause, as if Matt were considering the import of this. 'I don't want to go.'

'Why not?'

She struggled to put her reservation into words. 'There's no special reason. I just don't feel comfortable alone with him.'

'We haven't seen him for ages,' he said. 'You're not still bothered about his performance at the wedding, are you?'

'He was so rude, Matt. Nobody knew how to take him.'

'I know he can be a liability. Perhaps he wants to get back in favour.'

'Actually I think he wants to show off the car.'

'What car?'

'It isn't even his. He's borrowed it from a friend who's trying to sell it, but I bet he'll hammer it and then say he doesn't want to buy after all.'

'I'm sure you'll be a good influence, Rach.'

She hung up in defeat. Sometimes Matt's positivity could be wearing. Because he was so sure of himself he'd grind her down until she agreed with him, talk her out of her choices, into his. It was like being strapped into a runaway vehicle unable to reach the brakes. Which was why she was keeping her looming life-changing predicament to herself – even though she was feeling hopelessly ambivalent about it.

13

The Lotus

Leo insisted on driving Rachael to the client's house in Childwall, even managed to find space in the boot of the Lotus for her crates and boxes. The previous evening he'd put on a surprising performance as a children's entertainer: organising games in the garden for Dan and Nathan, the latter's sister Kelly and her friend Sheba. The girls were on the awkward cusp between puberty and womanhood, but they shrieked as loudly as the younger boys as they raced around the pear tree. Matt had watched them from the French windows. 'That's what this place needs,' he'd said. 'Lots of kids.'

The client, Mrs Dudley, chaired several committees and was raising funds to send the local amateur orchestra on a European tour. She was a squat, wide-hipped woman who seemed about to overbalance on her tiny feet. Her magenta skirt and jacket strained at the seams; her matching fingernails couldn't have withstood the intricacies of preparing a buffet lunch for fifty. She'd charged steeply for the lunch tickets, so none of the guests would have been under the illusion she'd cooked the food herself. Nevertheless, she was keen for Rachael to deliver and arrange her dishes and then disappear.

This suited Rachael too. Leo heaved the containers of food from the boot and carried them into the house. He was looking like a superannuated cowboy in his dusty denims and plaid shirt with the sleeves rolled up. Mrs Dudley found it hard to contain her curiosity. 'Don't I know you?' she said.

'No, love, afraid not.'

'You didn't put in Lynne Page's bathroom?'

'No.'

'Or Liz Everett's new windows.'

'Sorry, darling,' drawled Leo in his poshest accent.

'My father-in-law's a famous artist,' said Rachael, unveiling her green, pink and white circles of stuffed chicken and transferring them to her client's platters.

'Oh,' said Mrs Dudley. 'Well, that must be it. Are you on the telly much?'

'Frequently,' said Leo.

'Then I must look out for you, though music's more my thing actually. Hence this bash. You've done a very nice job, dear, thank you.'

'I wonder if you'd be able to settle the balance now,' said Rachael, adding a final scatter of pomegranate seeds to the salads. 'A cheque will be fine.'

'I know I should be more hard-faced,' confessed Mrs Dudley. 'But the fact is, the ladies haven't all paid up yet. They will of course. They know it's for charity. Why don't you pop an invoice in the post?'

'I did explain my terms,' Rachael said, aware that her voice was beginning to rise, 'when you gave me the deposit. I have to be strict because I've had problems in the past. Can you imagine what your house might smell like when you're left with several kilos of raw fish because somebody's cancelled at the last minute?'

'But I haven't cancelled,' Mrs Dudley pointed out.

'You did agree you'd pay the balance on delivery though.'

'I'm asking you to wait, that's all. This isn't for *my* benefit, remember. It's for a good cause.'

Leo stepped in. 'I think you're confusing the issue here,' he said. 'Because Mrs Wentworth is not herself a charity.'

Mrs Dudley flushed and teetered out of the room. Leo picked up the crate of empty plastic containers and held it against his chest. Rachael rearranged her tower of salmon beignets, adjusted the garnish of watercress.

Five minutes later they were back on the street and she was tucking a freshly written cheque into her wallet. The fact was, her business account had toppled into the red and she'd recently had to make purchases from the joint household account. Now she could pay the money back. Matt understood her cash flow was erratic, but it was important to her to be self-sufficient, to prove her business could be viable.

'Thank you for sticking up for me,' she said.

Leo shrugged. 'I've been there,' he said. 'You have a product. Wanker's supposed to pay for it, but he'll do any damn thing to weasel out of giving you the full whack. That's why you have a dealer – among other reasons. Simple self-protection. Now, are you ready?'

'Ready for what?'

'Well, there's the thing. Southport, I thought.'

'Southport!'

'It will be a good test. Especially the road through the dunes.'

'I have to be back by 3.30.'

'Christ, Raquel, that's hours yet.'

He rolled back the soft hood of the Lotus and secured it. 'All manual, you see,' he said. 'Nothing electronic to go wrong.' Then he leapt over the door and into the driver's seat like a much younger man and started the ignition.

Rachael fastened her seatbelt. They were very low down and close to the road, vulnerable to exhaust fumes and the bullying manoeuvres of 4x4s. Leo was making more noise than necessary, she thought, revving the car's engine at every traffic light and screeching around corners. They had to battle the drone of traffic as well as the onrush of wind so they scarcely spoke as they raced northwards.

'I used to come up here with Julia,' Leo shouted above the engine as they navigated Crosby. 'I had a bike in those days, a Triumph – that was vintage too – an old honker. Gave me endless trouble but I loved it.'

Rachael tried to imagine her mother-in-law, helmeted, on the back of a motorbike.

'Julia hated it,' he added.

'Was she scared?'

'Not exactly.' He threw back his head and laughed. 'But she got hopping mad when I lost it. The bike, I mean. I'd parked up and we'd gone for a frolic in the dunes. Sand dunes can be very disorientating and we completely lost our sense of direction. Took us hours to find it again. She was very chary of riding with me after that, but it wasn't so much a question of fear as of not being in control. She isn't good out of her comfort zone, Julia. You must have noticed – you're a bit the same, aren't you?'

Rachael gritted her teeth, didn't answer.

He continued, 'Though, when we first met, I managed to convince her a jolt was what she needed. She said being with me was like a fairground ride. Harrowing.'

'I'd have thought she'd want to avoid harrowing.'

'Well it's kill or cure, isn't it? Sometimes you need to take your mind off things. Unfortunately the treatment didn't work long-term. She's feisty, the first Mrs Wentworth, but we don't bring out the best in each other.'

'The first?' said Rachael. (She knew an affair had caused the divorce.) 'I didn't realise you'd remarried.'

His eyebrows rose. 'I haven't. The second Mrs Wentworth, Raquel, is you.'

'Oh...'

He took his hand off the steering wheel and for a frozen second she thought he was going to place it on her knee. The day was warm and her legs were bare. Instead he curled his palm smoothly around the knob of the gearstick and nudged the accelerator. As they sped along the Formby Bypass, Rachael thought of the other things she could have been doing: meeting friends, testing recipes, going to the gym. Or completing those tasks that nagged at her, like sorting Danny's outgrown clothes or tackling her accounts. Actually she was grateful to be spared the accounts: at present they didn't make positive reading. Forget all that; she was going to enjoy herself.

He suggested they look out for a pub. She said she wasn't thirsty.

'I won't drink and drive,' he said, 'if that's what's worrying you.'

It was, but she wouldn't admit it. 'No, I'm fine as I am, honestly.'

'Not hungry either?'

'I don't eat during the day. It's easier.'

'Exactly!' This time he did clap his hand on her leg, but in an extravagant comradely gesture. 'A woman after my own heart. You get absorbed in a project, the last thing you want to do is break off for a fucking sandwich.'

'My throat closes up,' said Rachael. 'If I'm tasting stuff a lot I just can't swallow. I think it's a useful reflex. It allows my tongue to get on with its work but it doesn't mess up my appetite.'

'When you're concentrating,' said Leo, surveying the road ahead, 'you don't *have* any appetite. That's why grazing's bad for you – Julia was right about that. It's part of the same malaise: superficiality, short attention spans. Nothing sticks for more than two minutes.'

'You mean like that boy.'

'What boy?'

'Nathan. Remember? He was round last night with his sister.'

'Ah… with the freckles? Interesting lad, isn't he?'

'Interesting? I think he's weird.'

'Well,' said Leo. 'Weird, wonderful, whatever. Biggest crime in the world is being boring.' He swung the car across the roundabout and onto the coast road, which was straight but narrow. 'Now this is more of a challenge. Are you ready for the full throttle?'

Rachael held on to the edges of her seat. Her hair stung her cheeks and her eyes were watering. The road ran through waving sheaves of marram grass; the sea was a blistering blue. The exhilaration she felt was not so much a novelty as a reawakening, stirring up fragments of adolescence: the excitement of a rollercoaster or a cantering horse. Or dancing – she used to love to dance – though this was more like flying.

They were soaring, as if windborne, towards a speck in the distance. The speck seemed to grow alarmingly, took on a box-like shape, mutated into a truck. The high-sided vehicle was straddling the road in front of them and showed no sign of yielding. Leo made no effort to brake and she was terrified there wouldn't be room to overtake. If he tried to pass it they'd end up veering off the road into the dunes. The Lotus would flip over on impact like some fragile boat meeting a cresting wave; they would land on their unprotected heads.

She opened her mouth to scream but the sound was snatched away from her. There was the rushing of a downdraught, the menacing tyres of the lorry, a strong odour of diesel and smouldering rubber, a black shadow cast. Then, suddenly, the horizon was clear again, bright and beckoning. She looked at her hands twisted together in her lap, and wondered how they had got into that position. She couldn't feel her legs; they'd been hijacked by an attack of numbness. And her brain was trying to work out how (and if) she had survived – or whether she was skating through the after-life in some kind of limbo. Wheezing, because the air had been sucked from her chest, she croaked out: 'What happened?'

Leo had finally relaxed his foot on the accelerator pedal. 'Road hog,' he said. 'But we had two inches. We only needed one.'

'There might have been something coming towards us.'

'I could see miles ahead. The view was fine.'

'You didn't slow down.'

'Well that would have been fatal. If you err and dither you lose direction. You're more likely to keep on track if you maintain velocity. Simple physics.'

'It wasn't simple,' she said. 'It was nerve-racking. I was absolutely petrified.'

'I'm sorry if I gave you a fright. I can be as sedate as the next man in a nice little VW Golf. But this is a *sports* car and needs to be treated as such. You don't use a racehorse to pull a cart.'

She crossed her legs and tugged down the hem of her skirt. Leo pulled into a lay-by and cut the engine. Now she could hear the murmur of the tide, the chirruping of grasshoppers in the dunes, the plaintive cries of gulls. The lorry they had overtaken trundled past. Leo leaned across her and she shrank against the back of the seat. There was a panther-like quality to his movements: swift, sinuous, unpredictable. *And* he'd nearly killed her.

He withdrew a hip flask from the glove box. 'Drink?'

'I thought you said you didn't drink and drive.'

'Which is precisely why I'm offering it to you, Raquel.'

'I shouldn't.'

'Go on, it's medicinal. It will settle your nerves.'

It was neat vodka and still early in the day. She gagged at first, but the powerful fiery spirit of it reclaimed her sooner than she'd expected. It scorched her throat and buzzed in her brain.

'Better now? Do you want to stretch your legs in the dunes? Get some air?'

'Not if there's any chance of getting lost,' she said. He didn't pick up on the reference initially, but then gave her a quizzical look that made her feel foolish. She clambered out of the car, a little unsteadily, and removed her ballet pumps, dangling them from her fingertips. She walked towards the sea, savouring its briny tang, the dry sand chilly beneath the soles of her feet.

She didn't check to see whether Leo was following her. She wouldn't have heard him in any case – the soft furrows absorbed both sound and vibration. But from the corner of her eye she caught a movement and turned. He'd got out of the car and was gesticulating, holding aloft some object in his hand. She would have ignored him, but she stubbed her toe and almost stumbled into a crater of debris: tin cans, plastic bottles, greasy paper and the charred remnants of a barbecue. She put her shoes on and started back to the car.

'That's enough fresh air for me,' she said when he was in earshot. 'This place is filthy.'

He held out her smart phone. 'I'm afraid they rang off,' he said. 'But it's okay, I took the message.'

'You answered my phone?' The presumption shocked her.

'Why not? Thought you might want to take the call. I wasn't stealing your soul.'

Something in his voice made her suspicious. 'Was it a client?'

'Clinic,' he said.

She snatched the phone and turned it off. She climbed into her seat and stuffed it into the bottom recess of her bag.

She gripped the bag's leather handles and stared through the windscreen at a red mist of outrage.

'They were just confirming the appointment. Friday.'

'It's only a consultation,' said Rachael.

'Sure.' Then he said, 'I recognised the number. Went there myself for the snip.'

When she didn't answer he added, 'Julia didn't want any more kids after Bel. I didn't feel emasculated. I'm not the type of artist who's as profligate with his seed as his canvases. My creative energy goes into my work. I know how you feel. The trouble with children is that they can take over your life. No time to call your own. You have to have a robust sense of self not to be swamped by them.' He unscrewed the top of the hip flask again. 'Here, have another draught.'

It gave her something to do with her hands, with her mouth. If she spoke, she was terrified she'd let out the wrong thing. She'd been told it could take a year for her fertility to return when she stopped the injections, so she'd expected to have plenty of time to adjust to the prospect of another baby. Instead she had been ambushed – and she was totally unprepared. Although she longed to confide in someone, she was wary of mentioning it to friends who might not understand her fears. Hence the clinic appointment. Leo seemed to have some sympathy, but she wasn't sure she could trust him. And it would give him a hold over her.

'You've been shaken up,' he said. 'I'd like to give you a treat, something restorative. Sure you won't change your mind about lunch?'

She savoured the final drops of the vodka on her tongue and shook her head. She did not want to sit opposite

Leo and meet his eye, risk him dropping hints or asking questions she couldn't answer.

'Nothing in Southport to tempt you?' he went on. 'And please don't say shopping. Okay, I'll amend that. Actually I don't mind shopping with women as long as it's not shoes. You'd be amazed how singular the average woman's feet are, how difficult it is to find the right style to support the arch or cup the heel or lengthen the leg, one that doesn't pinch the toe or thicken the ankle. Cobbling – that's where the money must be.'

Rachael, who possessed a fine and much-valued collection of footwear, had to smile at this. An idea came to her, a way of salvaging the trip. 'There's a place the other side of Southport that's supposed to have a good selection of cookers and I could do with a new one. Since we've got this far I wouldn't mind having a look.'

Leo was a practical man, after all. He liked machines, engines, good design. 'Right,' he said. 'Do you know the address?'

'I'll find it.'

As they cruised down Lord Street in the 1975 Lotus, they garnered glances of amusement from passers-by who presumed they were shooting a commercial. Rachael didn't enjoy being the centre of attention; she wasn't an exhibitionist, but the vodka was having its effect, mellowing her mood, and the stares bounced off her as she tracked the Google map to Kitchen Solutions.

'Wonderful nowadays,' muttered Leo as he glided into the car park, 'how the world has no problems that can't be sorted by White Van Man whizzing past with his promise of Total Solutions.'

'You can stay in the car if you want.'

'My dear, I wouldn't dream of it.' Gallantly he escorted her into the showroom.

Nothing could turn Rachael on, distract her from her worries, like a store of kitchen equipment: from tiny lemon zesters and cunning devices to take out cherry stones, through grinders, mincers and mixers, to full-scale appliances like the ones confronting her in splendid shiny rows. She walked up and down aisles of fridges, freezers, sink units, cookers and hobs, dazzling in enamel, chrome or stainless steel. She made her way to the display of expensive ranges, opening oven doors, inspecting warming drawers and grills. The most important piece of equipment in her life needed to be simple and functional. Not a flashy sports car, but a reliable tank that wouldn't break down.

A salesman hovered, eyeing the two of them, assessing their relationship. Rachael was beginning to feel light-headed, even audacious. 'You can be my architect,' she whispered to Leo. 'You're building me a new kitchen and getting rid of the crappy old one that was put in years ago. Fuck!'

'What?'

'*You* installed it, didn't you? You and Julia. A friend got you some knock-down cupboards and you put them up together, only you had to stop work because you bludgeoned your thumb and you had a triptych to finish for a commission for the foyer of some insurance firm and she tried to keep you going with painkillers and... oh shit...' She rubbed her hand across her face in mortification.

'Well recalled,' he said dryly. 'You might have been there.'

'It was Matt,' she said. 'Whenever I've complained, you know, about a drawer not shutting properly or something, he'll tell me I'd no idea of the blood, sweat and tears that went into whatever I'm dissing.'

'It was only a fraction,' he said, 'of the blood, sweat and tears spilt in other areas. Don't beat yourself up, Raquel. Time passes. Show me what you fancy.'

'This.' It was top of the range: lustrous steel, dual fuel, with three ovens, five gas burners, a griddle and rotisserie. 'It's as classic as your Lotus. It will go on forever.'

The salesman swooped. He was young and blustering, rocking on his heels and puffing out his chest so the stripes on his shirt appeared to widen. Andrew (according to his name badge) had clearly decided Leo was sugar daddy, not architect. He discussed the cooking properties of the Rangemaster with Rachael, but when cost was mentioned he gave Leo a full, frank man-to-man appraisal.

'What are your terms?' Leo asked. 'Would there be a discount for cash?'

'I'll have to check,' said Andrew. 'If you'd like to come over to my desk we can go through some figures.'

He started to lead the way. Rachael hung back. 'Perhaps this is a bit hasty.'

'Depends,' said Leo, 'on how much you want it.'

'Oh God!' she sighed. 'I've been *lusting* after it. But, you know, you have to be sensible.'

'You're talking to the wrong man then.'

'I could ring Matt.' But she felt awkward calling Matt at work in case he had a client with him and she came across as needy. Anyway, she knew how the conversation would go.

He'd advise caution and then if he sensed her regret he'd try to chivvy her up. He'd end by saying 'Of course, Rach, if it's what you *really* want...' which would make her feel worse – as if she'd overstepped some line and shouldn't have got away with it.

'You don't even know what the deal is yet,' said Leo. 'I'll get him down. Bastards are always trying it on with me so I'll enjoy getting my own back. I'm a good haggler.'

Rachael sat, as invited, but Leo stood over Andrew and his calculator, an intimidating presence. 'It's a display model, right?' he said. 'So you can knock a couple of hundred off for a start.'

'It's extremely high specification. It's what the professionals use.'

'She knows that. She *is* a professional. Ideal customer for you, I'd've thought.'

Andrew began, copying figures from his calculator onto a sheet of paper. Leo picked up the sheet and ripped it in two. 'Start again,' he advised. 'What's your turnover, Raquel? Healthy enough isn't it? She doesn't need a long repayment schedule. In fact...' He laid his hands flat on the desk; his fingernails, she'd noticed before, were rimed with paint, never completely clean. 'If she pays a decent deposit you could lower the interest rate significantly. Plus an option to pay the balance early. You'd still make on the deal.'

'I'd have to clear it with head office.'

Leo gestured towards the telephone. 'Be my guest.' He murmured to Rachael. 'You've got a deposit, right?'

'Well I suppose...'

'There's madam's cheque,' he reminded her.

Andrew kept his eyes fixed on them encouragingly as he spoke to his boss. Rachael had the sense of things running away from her, but she was jubilant, too, at the thought of her scoop. The price was good and rather than lose Mrs Dudley's cheque in the black hole of her overdraft, she could pay it into the joint household account.

Leo nudged her. 'It's in the bag.'

She beamed and allowed him a squeeze of triumph. Then, withdrawing, she saw the pitfalls. How would she reconfigure her working space? How would she manage her orders if there were any setback with installation? What if she had to wind down the business? What if... As she handed over the credit card it struck her, too late, that she had fallen into a trap, that Leo wasn't rooting for her at all. He was competing with Julia in a devious game of one-upmanship: delivery of the Rangemaster against donation of the house – only none of *his* money had been involved.

'I must get to a bank,' she said, when they outside on the forecourt again. 'I need to pay in this cheque right away.'

Why were there always queues at banks? And why was the person in front of her always the one with bags of change from the takings of some goddam car boot sale? She fidgeted impatiently behind the woman trawling through her coins. Leo was parked outside on a double yellow line, engaging admirers. She could see a portion of him nodding and gesticulating through the glass swing doors.

At last they were on their way back. They zipped down the by-pass but snarled with traffic when the road became single lane through the woods. That brief flash of euphoria, their shared camaraderie, was long gone. To top it all, Rachael realised, she was going to be late for the school run. She shivered a little.

'Cold?' he said.

'No, but could you put the roof up anyway? We're not going to make it, are we? I'll have to get someone else to collect Danny.' She pulled out her phone and scrolled to her friend Emma's number.

A pothole yawned in the road in front of them and Leo tried to dodge it.

Rachael paused in the middle of her text. 'What's that awful smell?'

There came a loud clang and what sounded like a ricochet of gunshots. A billowing black cloud settled over their heads.

Leo said, 'Fuck. Fuck. Fuck.'

14

The Barbecue

Drifting smoke; the scent of flesh charring over coals, redirected by a light breeze: at first Matt didn't realise the barbecue was taking place in his own back garden. He'd been delayed at work by a flurry of phone calls and the need to meet the deadline of an appeal hearing. The French doors stood open and he could see Leo waving a pair of long-handled tongs like a wand above sausages spitting on the grill, a young girl prancing on either side of him. Matt recognised Kelly chewing her gum and flicking her ponytail, sultry Sheba in a slick vest and snug denim shorts. The leaves of the pear tree rustled as if someone were in its branches, but he couldn't see either his wife or his son.

He withdrew before he was noticed, finding the sight disturbing. There was in it too vivid a reminder of the past: images of Bel objecting to the raw slabs of meat, of Julia pretending to be polite to unwanted guests – random hangers-on Leo had accumulated during his day – and Leo himself, in his element. Matt felt a rush of anger – not because he hadn't enjoyed Leo's ability to entertain or the presence of pretty young art students, which made him popular with his schoolfellows – but because those days were over. He was a fully grown adult for fuck's sake and he shouldn't have to revert to teenage self-consciousness because his stepfather had reappeared with his own mysterious agenda. Taking advantage of Julia's absence. And Rachael's. And where was Rachael anyway?

A loud guffaw from the garden almost drowned the whimper behind the sofa. Matt eased it away from the wall. He found Dan curled like a mouse against the skirting with his fingers in his mouth.

'Hey, Danny boy. What happened?'

Dan looked at him mournfully. 'No one will help me.'

'No one will help you what?'

'I can't climb the tree.'

'The tree isn't safe,' said Matt.

'Nathan's in it. He climbed high up, right inside.'

'Well he'd better come right out again.'

'And I hurt my hand.'

'How? Show me.'

Dan proffered the two fingers he had previously been sucking. A pair of tiny blisters had erupted on his fingertips.

'Did you touch something hot?'

'He shouted at me.'

'Right…' As a child, Leo's bellow had scared Matt too, but he'd soon realised it was just noise. Later, in adolescence, he'd sometimes pushed boundaries to see how Leo would react, but it was rarely satisfactory. Leo would either shut him out, his interest consumed elsewhere, or he would swerve suddenly into laughter and ridicule. You couldn't know where you were with mercurial types; you couldn't best them. So you gave up provoking. You took the easy way out. Anything for an uncomplicated life.

'Where's Mummy?' asked Matt, not comprehending why Leo had been left in charge.

'She's in bed.'

'In bed!'

'She doesn't feel well.'

'One of her headaches?'

Dan shrugged.

So now Leo was back as chief rooster, his wife had taken refuge in a darkened room and his son was, literally, licking his wounds in a corner. Matt pounded upstairs, Danny stumbling in his wake.

Rachael's family were not like the Wentworths. Her elderly parents and older siblings dwelt peaceably in Dorset, where they were scrupulously polite to one another and nobody ever raised their voice. She claimed she'd been grateful to escape to a livelier environment where people said what they meant and didn't care if you took offence. Nonetheless, she was easily hurt and Matt would do anything to protect her.

In the bedroom the curtains were drawn, shutting out the view of Leo cooking and the teenage girls with their burnished bare shoulders and tightly creased crotches, passing around cans of hooch they shouldn't have been drinking in the first place. Matt sat at the foot of the double bed and Rachael groaned. 'What's up?'

Her arm lay outside the duvet, pale and twitching. She dragged herself upright. Dan turned from the doorway with a little sigh.

'It's been a total mess,' she said.

She'd taken her jeans off but was otherwise fully clothed, he noticed. Her complexion had a faint glassy sheen. 'What has?'

'Well, today mostly. The stupid car broke down.'

'The Lotus?'

'We had such trouble on the way back.'

'From where?'

'Southport.'

'Southport!'

'He was just meant to be taking it out for a spin. But then the bloody exhaust fell off. That's what old cars do, isn't it – they fall apart. We tried to carry on but the noise and the fumes were just awful so we had to stop. He isn't a member of the AA so I had to ring them and we waited ages…'

He patted her arm to pacify her, but at the same time he found it odd that the incident had been so upsetting. 'What happened to the car?'

'Oh we got it to a garage in the end but it's so ancient it has to be fixed by a specialist and Leo will have to argue about the cost with his mate who owns it, but that's not my problem. And then we got the train home.' Her eyes were huge and watery, the pupils magnified in the gloom. 'I'm sorry. I shouldn't have agreed to the trip to start with.'

'Hey, stop worrying. You're back safely now.'

'There was a cock-up over Dan too. I'd asked Emma to pick him up when she collected Caleb but apparently she had to go on somewhere else so she brought him round here because I'd told her I'd be back, but when she rang me we were still on the train, so…'

He couldn't understand what the fuss was about. Faulty cars were a nuisance but they didn't compare to some of the human drama and hardship he dealt with on a daily basis. 'So?'

'Well I didn't know what to tell her to do. I hardly know the neighbours and I've had to rely on Emma too much already and *you* said he shouldn't go to the after-school club more than twice a week—'

'So this is my fault now?'

'And even if I'd contacted you, you wouldn't have got back to the house any earlier than I would.'

He frowned as he began to grasp what she was getting at. 'Are you saying she just left him on the doorstep? Christ, that's child neglect! It's a serious issue.'

'Don't be silly. Emma's not irresponsible.' Her voice was skittering from one register to another. 'Those two girls were hanging around so she left him with them. I said it was okay. I mean, they minded him once before. I don't like to encourage them, but I knew we wouldn't be long and I didn't really have any choice, did I?'

'So that's why they're here?'

'Leo invited them to stay. I couldn't... I don't know... He's a steamroller, isn't he? And it's difficult. I mean, he knows so much more about this house than I do. A fuse blew. I don't know why. I think it was something that boy, Nathan, did – whatever he touches seems to go wrong—' she was tearful now '—and I didn't even know where the fuse box was. Leo was able to fix it in seconds and then he said we ought to have a barbecue and the boys got wildly excited because it's the first this year. And I started feeling so ill.'

'Poor thing.' Matt wondered why a day spent with Leo should have this effect, making her so weak and emotional. Then a thought struck him. He reached forward to caress her. 'Hey, Rach, you don't think you might be…?'

She shook him off. 'It was because I hadn't eaten anything – and because of the broken exhaust I'd probably inhaled all sorts of petrol fumes.'

He said, 'Well why don't you come downstairs now? Let me fix you something. A cup of tea at least?'

'No, I couldn't.'

'Why not?'

'I can't face anyone. I don't feel like it's *our* house when those kids are hanging around. I just want it to be the three of us again. Can't you get rid of him?'

'Leo? How?'

'Can't we send him over to Ireland?'

'Not a good idea,' said Matt. 'I spoke to Bel last night, remember. She thinks Julia might be having some sort of breakdown. He's the last person she'd want to see. It's in everybody's interests to keep him here.'

He rose from the bed and went to the window, peering through the gap in the curtains. The scene below was playful. Dan was no longer sucking his fingers but chasing a cat around in circles. A couple more cats were sitting solemnly, the neat mounds of their paws pressed together, drawn by the meaty aroma and the expectation of off-cuts. 'And if we don't want the whole place taken over,' he said. 'We should join them. Come on. Let me brush your hair for you.' She usually enjoyed the sensation and he found satisfaction in it too: in the slow measured strokes of the brush and the silky spill of her hair.

'No!' She shied away as if she couldn't bear him to touch her. 'My head hurts and that would make it worse.'

'Have you taken a painkiller?'

'Yes, two.'

'Right.' What else could he do? She wasn't to be persuaded and there was something enticing about the prospect below, so different from the day spent in a stuffy office, drafting letters, mollifying clients, arguing over costs. The evening sun slanted through the leaves of the pear tree. Nathan leapt out of it with a whoop, landing on all fours beside Dan. The two girls had their arms entwined around each other's waists and their shoes kicked off; they were flirting shamelessly with Leo.

Kelly looked up at the window. At first she narrowed her eyes as if in concentration and then – had she spotted his face at the glass? – her mouth cracked into a wide joyous grin that transformed her otherwise sharp features into a bountiful invitation. Obviously it was ridiculous to be succumbing to invitations issued by strangers in his own home, but there was nothing to be gained from staying upstairs.

He showered and changed into his favourite long shorts – which he knew Rachael didn't care for, but which he thought were not unflattering – and a darkish polo shirt that was more likely to be green than red because he tried to avoid buying red. Then he sauntered back downstairs as master of *his* house. He took a beer from *his* fridge and wandered into *his* back garden. The interlopers greeted him heartily.

'Hungry yet?' said Leo, flipping a burger. 'Where's the rest of our dinner, girls? Ketchup? Mustard? Salad?' The burger, a brown wafer of latex, bounced and spat. At Leo's feet lay a crumpled welter of Cellophane and cardboard packaging.

'Salad?' Kelly wrinkled her nose. 'Me and Nath, we don't eat salad.'

'Not even tomatoes?'

'We're both, like, allergic to tomatoes.'

'You can't just help yourself to the stuff in the fridge, I'm afraid,' said Matt. 'Some of it will be supplies Rachael's ordered specially. But anything she puts in last week's organic veg box is fair game. That's why she keeps the two of them on the go so we know what needs to be used up first…' He tailed off. Kelly and Sheba were looking at him curiously.

'Fetch us some plates, girls, will you,' said Leo. 'And forks. And another couple of beers while you're at it.'

'I'll show you,' said Matt, suddenly galvanised on Rachael's behalf. He didn't like to think of her coming down and finding her store cupboard plundered and her kitchen wrecked. Wrecked was perhaps too strong a term, but there was something about these guests that made him wary, as if he should be on special alert.

Kelly was the one to accompany him, which was a relief. Sheba seemed impossibly cool and mature for a thirteen-year-old (a period he remembered as excruciatingly uncomfortable: braces and bum fluff and growing too fast; trousers too short and shoes that pinched; a painful hankering for well-endowed girls way out of his reach – like Sheba herself). Kelly was plainer, less threatening. She swayed her hips provocatively as they mounted the steps together but the action put him in mind of a duck's waddle and the cheeky curl of its tail feathers. When she let the strap of her orange vest slip from her shoulder he was amused, not aroused. Besides, he needed to concentrate on locating the everyday crockery that could be used outside.

He stacked plates and cutlery on a tray along with another pack of the cheap rolls that Leo must have bought at the corner shop. Kelly was leaning against the fridge with one knee raised, chafing her bare foot along the back of her calf. Her vest and bra straps still drooped. She was rolling a can of hooch between her palms as if anticipating the moment she would crush it. 'You're, like, a lawyer,' she said.

'Yes.' He added a pot of wholegrain mustard to his tray. His response was cautious because people often didn't understand how many different aspects of law there were to deal with. 'But I'm not a criminal lawyer. Do you know someone who's got into trouble?'

'It's me dad.'

'Has he been arrested?'

She squealed and he felt wrong-footed. 'Nah! But he's got to look after us, right? Take proper care. It's his job.'

'You don't live with him, do you?'

'Nah. He's with this new foreign bint, slap an inch deep on her face, talks like you have to wind her up with a key first. One of them names ending in ova. Vancouver me and Nath call her.'

'Vancouver?'

Her grin was almost too wide for her jaw. 'Near as we could get to wank-over.' She chortled with delight. 'D'you gerrit? Anyhow, he shouldn't be fucking off with her, should he? Miss Vancouver. Me nan won't talk to her because she reckons she's a tart. So me dad in't talking to me nan. They had a big row and that's how come we got dumped.'

'Well I'm not a family lawyer either, but I can tell you that as a parent he's likely to be legally responsible, unless your mother—' And then he remembered. He should have remembered before.

'Me mam's dead. Thirty-three. Just like Jesus.'

My father too, he thought.

'Overdose,' said Kelly casually. Then her eyes narrowed between their stubby lashes. 'She weren't a junkie. They was prescription drugs, but she got the dose wrong. Vomited. Drowned in it.'

A shadow must have crossed his face because she left the cool slab of the fridge door and came and tucked her arm through his. 'We need advice,' she went on. 'I mean, like, me nan's at her wits'. She's getting these asthma attacks. They keep sending her to see places that are so grim you wouldn't keep rats in them. And she can't get Nath back into school until he's seen the ed psych and whenever she rings the council, like, the person she needs to speak to is on leave. Or...' She screwed up her face. 'Or they're sick. Lots of sick people in social services.'

Matt was trying and failing to inch away from her. The two girls larking about with Leo had seemed carefree but now, with this warm, grubby, sweaty creature clinging on to him, he sensed an undertow of despair.

She let go of his arm so she could flail her hands in the air. 'It's a mess innit? Someone's got to sort it out.'

'Well,' he said. 'A lot of high street solicitors will give free advice, initially.'

'But not you?'

'I'm afraid it isn't my field.'

'That's what Sheba said, said you'd be useless.'

Poor kid. He felt sorry for her, the way her mouth wobbled – though her lips were her best feature, rosebud plump – but there was no point in building up false hopes. He carried the tray outside and searched for a spot to leave it, safe from the spinning, leaping game Nathan was devising.

'Don't you have no chairs?' said Sheba, lighting and inhaling deeply on a menthol cigarette.

Matt glanced up at the master bedroom and resolved that on no account would this barbecue supper be eaten indoors. 'No,' he said. 'We haven't had any use for garden furniture yet. But I could bring some out from the kitchen.'

Leo was moving the sausages to the edge of the grill. 'They'll be at the back of the garage,' he said.

'What will?'

'The table and chairs you need to fetch. Better get a move on. Food's just about ready. Apologies for the lack of choice but I'd delegated the shopping to Nathan and it seems this is his idea of a feast.'

Matt entered the garage through the side door, cursing himself. He should have remembered they'd be there: he'd helped his mother shift the slatted wooden table and chairs into storage every autumn.

The garage was large but ramshackle and in need of repair. Their Passat occupied the front area and at the back were a quantity of paint pots and a couple of redundant bicycles with flat tyres and rusted chains. He recognised his old Raleigh and a lilac one that must have belonged to Bel. There was also the new child's bike bought for Dan at

Christmas but not much ridden. He couldn't see the garden furniture at first because it was shrouded under a dust sheet. The fabric was heavy with distemper fallen from the ceiling; a furry spider's web garnished one corner.

'We should have a thorough clear-out,' Rachael had said when they'd arrived and tried to integrate their own furniture with the pieces Julia had left behind. 'This isn't going to work.'

And he had talked her out of it because of the expense. 'Why would we chuck a perfectly good sideboard we can keep stuff in? This place is going to cost us a fortune, Rach, to heat and decorate and maintain. We can't afford to rush at things.'

She'd insisted, however, on taking down Leo's paintings because she didn't like the fierce colours. She'd agreed Matt could move one of them into his study; the rest were blocking his way as he yanked at the cloth.

Kelly reappeared at his side with Nathan in tow. 'Leo sent us to help you.'

'Right.' This was probably not the time to draw attention to the abandoned canvases. He used the dust sheet to cover them more thoroughly and hoped they hadn't been spotted by Leo when he dug out the barbecue. 'It needs two to carry the table. Kelly, you take one of the chairs.'

She rubbed up against him again as she reached for the chair. 'Wish I had a dad like that.'

'Like what?'

'Like yours. He's cool.'

'Actually, he's my stepfather.'

'Yeah, right. Still sound though.'

'He's had Miss Vancouvers of his own, I can tell you,' said Matt. 'Here, Nathan, give me a hand with this will you.'

Nathan looked as though he were making up his mind, as though a more interesting activity might divert him at any minute. His hand strayed towards the tower of paint pots.

'You take that end,' said Matt firmly. 'I'll go backwards and you follow. We want to get this meal eaten, don't we?'

This was the way things had always been when Leo was left in charge: haphazard, random, out of sequence. Letting the dinner congeal or burn before having anything ready to eat it with/or off/or whatever; hunting for last-minute essentials. Despite its protective cover the table top was dusty and needed to be wiped down, as did the chairs. The contents of the tray had to be unloaded and more condiments fetched. Then, finally, they gathered around the selection of leathery burgers and overcooked sausages, inferior bread rolls, jars of gherkins and piccalilli, bottles of ketchup and brown sauce and several cans of lager. And they were all laughing.

'Go on,' Kelly prodded Matt. 'You can't tell the difference, can you?'

'What difference?'

'Between ketchup and HP.'

'Who says?'

'Him.' She pointed at Danny. 'Says they both look the same to you.'

'Doesn't mean I can't tell them apart.'

'Go on then. Show us.'

'Don't watch,' said Sheba picking up the two bottles. (Rachael made her own ketchup; the Heinz variety was bought for Dan's benefit.) 'Turn around while I squirt them out.'

Seconds later they presented him with two puddles of sauce. He knew perfectly well which was which. Although they were both muddy shades, they weren't the same muddy shade: the brown sauce was darker, the ketchup more mellow. He was planning to give them a run for their money, make them giggle by getting it wrong. He liked the way the girls giggled, open and unaffected. 'Can I taste them?'

'No, 'course not! That would be cheating.' Sheba pushed the plate towards him. He raised his eyes and met Leo's. Leo winked.

Well this is a shambles, reflected Matt: Dan with something smeared around his mouth and sticky in his hair; Nathan, cheeks bulging, teasing a cat with a stick; the tipsy teenagers fascinated by his handicap, but it was an enjoyable shambles. When women took charge there was no room for playfulness. Their determination to have everything well appointed (the Martha Stewart factor, Leo used to call it in baffled disgust); their need for co-ordination and harmony; the absurd distress caused by the wrong glassware or the absence of floral display – well, it missed the point didn't it? The point was to be able to relax, have a drink, a bite to eat, a laugh. He pointed, deliberately, at the wrong puddle. 'Tomato ketchup.' He finished his beer and snapped the ring-pull from a second can. The girls fell about in peals of laughter. Sheba was bending so far forward he could see right down the front of her T-shirt, her shapely breasts in their balconette bra.

Leo dug into his pocket and slapped a pound coin on the table. 'You proved me wrong, mate,' he said.

'Hell, I didn't know there was money on it.'

'These girls…' Leo's arm was draped across the back of Sheba's chair, his thumb a centimetre from the dark lustre of her skin. His eye held Matt's again, this time in a measure of defiance.

He's not stupid, Matt told himself. He's arrogant and provocative. He can be a prick. But he's not an idiot. He knows she's under age. He's just messing, like Nathan with the cats. 'I knew all along which was which,' he said. 'I can tease too. That's the thing when you have a party trick. You're the one in charge, not your audience.'

Kelly was sidling closer to him on what seemed to be the most rickety of the chairs. So it wasn't much of a surprise when the chair wobbled and capsized and she fell directly into his lap. Leo snorted. Dan and Nathan had already left the table. Because Matt had been distracted by the colour test, he'd failed to spot Nathan using the spatula to lift some glowing charcoal onto the grass and encouraging Dan to add a wigwam of kindling. And when he did see the beginning of a blaze he couldn't do anything about it because Kelly was spread-eagled heavily across him, refusing to right herself. Then some inkling made him turn his head, look past the debris to the top of the steps where Rachael stood, appalled.

She screamed and ran straight past him, knocking the boys aside and stamping out the embryo fire, even though she was only wearing slippers. Matt succeeded in pushing Kelly off his lap and got to his feet. 'Christ, be careful! You'll hurt yourself.'

'I can't believe you lot,' she raged back. 'How could you not *notice*?'

By now Danny was sobbing, upset by his mother's wrath and confused by the change in the mood of the party.

Rachael attempted to calm herself in order to comfort him, but he turned his face away.

In the lull, Kelly said to Sheba. 'Come back to ours, yeah?'

Sheba said, 'Nah, I'm cool here thanks.' She was still sitting disturbingly close to Leo.

Rachael mouthed at Matt: No!

Matt said mildly. 'Probably better if you get going, girls.'

Leo continued to smirk, but he moved his arm to reach for an empty beer can, which he crumpled in a quick clench of his fist. Kelly and Sheba put their heads together and whispered. 'S'all right,' said Kelly after a bit. 'We've got stuff to do anyhow.'

'Make sure you take him with you,' said Rachael, pointing at Nathan.

'Mummy,' said Danny. 'You're spoiling everything.'

Matt was about to intervene when Rachael said to Leo: 'You won't be staying much longer either, will you? Don't you have another friend you could go to?'

He ladled cream into his voice 'My dear girl. You only have to say the word.'

'It's just that it's been a bit much…'

'I know. We've had quite a day. Don't mention it. We understand each other.'

Matt was surprised to see Rachael blush and a curious look of complicity dart between them.

PART FOUR

TUESDAY WEDNESDAY

15

The Breakfast

As soon as she'd woken on Tuesday morning, Bel knew she was alone. Dolphin Cottage was small enough for her to be aware of another person's breathing. Or their absence. In her pyjamas she pottered around the living room. Last night's peat turves smouldered in the inglenook fireplace but they didn't stop her poking her head under the mantel. At the top of the chimney she could see a tiny square of blue sky. She wrapped herself in one of the crochet throws intended to give the armchairs rustic appeal and went outside.

There was a field at the back of the cottage, nothing so grand as a garden, hemmed by a tumble-down fence and cultivated with thistles and ragwort. The westerly wind, which so often contorted birch trees and fuchsia hedges and swept pastures into submission, had abated. Dew glistened on the grass; the air was cool and refreshing; the light soft and clear. Rising in the background, the spine of mountain peaks was a breath-taking violet. She spotted a clump of wild flowers and picked some stems of white stitchwort and red campion. She brought them indoors and put them in water but they looked spindly out of their habitat so she left them on the windowsill.

She took a long shower and dressed in one of her Oxfam-find shirts and a pair of skinny jeans. She sat by the hearth and switched on RTÉ One, which offered little of interest. An electronic beep startled her and she seized her phone, hoping for a text, a morsel of gossip, the news that someone was missing her, but its screen was blank. The only calls she'd taken recently had been from Matt and Rachael, separately warning her of Leo's descent. He hadn't bothered to get in touch himself. Anyway, there wasn't anything she could do. She hoped she'd made it clear that he should be prevented from hassling Julia.

The jingle had come from Julia's laptop, which was set up on a small drop-leaf table and plugged into the socket below. Bel raised the lid and clicked it into operation. She found herself looking at a series of photographs, recently uploaded. Some she recognised from yesterday, when they'd had, on the whole, a successful outing. They'd driven around the glorious Dingle peninsula and taken the corkscrew climb to the summit of Mount Brandon. After a dramatic descent they'd arrived at the tiny harbour where St Brendan set off for Paradise and allegedly found America.

Perched at the edge of the Atlantic, the sense of isolation and stillness made it feel like the last place in the world. Julia had carried her digital camera in her pocket and whipped it out frequently. She hadn't spoken much, but she'd squeezed Bel's hand once or twice and the lines had been smoothed from her face the way stains vanish from laundry in clear air.

Bel scrolled through the images on the computer: the mist eddying over the Conor Pass, the raspberry pink pub at the quayside, the black-tarred coracles (just like St Brendan's) upended on the shore. Then came photographs of a forbidding rock face, the sharp spikes of sea holly and a curving strand at dawn. The tide was low and there was no distinction between the sheen of the water and that of the wet rippling sand: both reflected the rising sun.

One snapshot followed another, so little difference between them Bel wondered if Julia had kept clicking the shutter by mistake. She realised, however, this was not a place they had visited on yesterday's excursion; this was not a beach she had seen.

When she heard a key in the lock, instinctively she closed the lid. She *would* ask about the photographs, the purpose of them, but she'd choose her moment.

Julia entered as if laden with heavy baggage, although she was only carrying a newspaper, a carton of milk and a loaf of soda bread. 'Slept well?' she said. 'You must have been tired.'

Bel inched back towards the fireplace. 'Yes, I did thanks. Where have you been?'

'Me, oh, I've been rambling about in the back lanes. And I've bought some breakfast.'

She set down her purchases and began to lay the table with plates, knives, butter and jam. She filled the kettle and fetched teapot and mugs. These actions were performed with a balletic poise that made it impossible for Bel to intercept or help. Eventually she sat down while her mother sawed through the loaf and poured out two cups of tea. Bel nibbled at the bread.

Julia said, 'I wish you'd eat properly, darling. You need to put on weight.'

As if Bel didn't know she was as spindly as the stitchwort. Why couldn't she have said something more endearing, as Leo might have done: Let's feed you up, my little chickadee. 'I'm doing my best,' she muttered.

'It will always be there,' said Julia. 'In your gut, you know that. You have to build up your strength against it.'

Bel sipped the tea, which was too hot and too strong, and wondered whether Julia was referring not to the malaria at all, but to the wound she herself had received. Is that what she was doing here: testing old scar tissue?

'Are you all right, Mum?'

'I'm fine.'

'I guess it ebbs and flows,' said Bel. 'Like you were okay yesterday, weren't you, but upset on Sunday. I wish you'd tell me a bit more about what you're going through. You must have been really really mad at Dad.'

'Yes,' said Julia. 'I was.'

'Why? I thought you'd got all that heavy stuff out of the way.' Her parents had divorced while she was at art college; she'd been taken aback by the speed of it.

'I suppose my patience had worn thin.'

Bel ventured, 'It's not because of how much he hurt you?'

'I know it doesn't sound very romantic, but you'll discover that love wears out too, like shoe leather.'

Except for first love, thought Bel. High on a pedestal. Love that didn't have time to disintegrate – love that nobody else can match. 'So are you going to explain why you came *here*?'

Julia's dark eyes were opaque. 'There isn't an explanation for everything in life, you know. Sometimes the subconscious simply takes over.' She added in a low whisper, 'Perhaps it was connected to the shock of nearly losing you.'

Bel pushed back her chair and went round to the other side of the table. She wrapped her arms around her mother's shoulders, which felt as tense as steel cable. She laid her cheek against Julia's hair. 'Well you didn't. I'm still here.'

'Yes, thank God, you are. And now I want to see you get better.' Julia buttered another piece of soda bread and slathered it with jam. 'You've been stuffed full of medication and I'm hoping, with a bit of luck, that fresh air and tranquillity will complete the process.' She held out the plate.

Bel took it and sat down again. She bit into the dense, moist slice. Okay, she thought. You win.

Julia watched her eat. 'Any idea what you'd like to do today?'

'Well...' Bel contemplated the glint of sunlight through the deep-set window. 'I think I fancy a boat trip, maybe go out to see the dolphins. People swim with them, don't they? It might be cool, you know, to watch them splashing around.'

A shadow of alarm crossed Julia's face. 'I'm not sure I'd fancy one of those tourist excursions,' she said. 'They cram you in and fleece you. And there's only one dolphin after all.'

Oh God, thought Bel, she doesn't want to be out on the water, does she? It's bound to rattle her. What an idiot I am!

Her phone was lying by her plate. It began to jiggle and, relieved by the interruption, she snatched it up without looking at caller display.

The Irish voice was at first unfamiliar. 'I have to pay you back the money.'

'Hello? Is that...?' Well, how many Irishmen did she know? 'What money?'

'Saturday night in the hotel,' said Tom. 'I promised, didn't I? And you shouldn't be out of pocket because of me. Well I've been to the bank now. I have cash for you.'

Julia had also been to the bank, yesterday morning before they set off for Brandon; she was flush again. 'It's okay,' said Bel. 'I said I wanted to pay for myself anyhow.'

'Ah, but it was our fault we made you stop over. You shouldn't have had to fork out.'

'It doesn't matter any more. Honestly. How was the prodigal's return?'

She could picture his quicksilver grin. 'Prodigal! Enough to eat for a week.'

'And Clemmie? How's she getting on?'

There was a pause as if he didn't quite know how much to tell her. 'Oh... grand. In fact she's wanting to see you too. Have you made any plans for the day?'

Bel shot a quick look at Julia who was wrapping the bread in cling film and replacing the lid on the jam jar. 'Not yet. I'm still having breakfast.' She wandered, as naturally as possible, across the room and through the front door, which gave on to an area of gravel and budding hollyhocks. She preferred to pace up and down during phone conversations.

'Breakfast!' he exclaimed. 'We've been up for hours.'

'Well I'm on holiday. I've been slow getting going, that's all.'

'Will you not meet us then? We could do with the distraction.'

'You and Clemmie?'

'I'm on my way to her now.'

'In the car?'

'Kieran doesn't need it. He's out helping my brother-in-law mend the fences on the lower pasture. He can bang a nail straight can Kieran.'

'Can't you?'

'I've lost the inclination. Come on, Bel, aren't you looking for a little distraction yourself?'

'Well…' She scuffed the gravel with the toe of her trainer. 'I wanted to see the dolphin, but my mother's not keen. She thinks it's a rip-off tourist scam.'

'She could be right. Fungi's a draw because he's so tame. But there are schools of wild dolphins in the bay and they're a marvellous sight if you can catch them following the fish. We may be able to borrow a boat from Gerry Lenane if I can sweeten him first.'

'That would be great. If you could…'

'I can fix anything,' he said.

'Even straight nails?'

'Anything I've an inclination for. Will I pick you up after I've fetched Clem?'

She glanced through the sliver of doorway. 'Let me get back to you in a few minutes.'

Julia had spread the *Irish Times* over the table and was studying it through her rimless reading glasses. She looked up as Bel re-entered.

'That was Tom.'

'Tom?'

'He's one of the brothers who gave me a lift. He asked if... if I was up for an outing. I think he probably just wants some help with his kid.'

'And do you want to go?'

'Well we were in the middle of talking about it, weren't we? What we might do. What do you think?'

Julia flattened the newspaper with the side of her hand. 'I'm perfectly happy to stay in and read. But if you're bored you should go out.'

She didn't know how to interpret this. Why had her mother dragged her across the Irish Sea if she didn't care whether she stuck around or not? Every time she reckoned she was making progress, getting to the heart of what was bothering Julia, she withdrew.

'Fine,' said Bel. 'Then I will.'

16

The Ladder

Tom waited at the end of the drive so he wouldn't have to negotiate the potholes in his brother's car. Clemmie jumped out of the passenger seat and threw her arms around Bel's knees. 'Have you been having fun?' Bel asked. The child nodded and began to talk about the new kittens she'd played with and the hens' eggs she'd collected, warm in the straw.

'Must be quite an experience for her,' said Bel, as they set off. 'Coming from the city, to see her grandparents' farm.'

'She's talking about Sean's place,' said Tom.

'You mean she hasn't yet...?'

'It's tricky, with my dad being the way he is.'

'Oh. But I thought... I mean, wasn't that the whole point of bringing her with you?'

'It's not as easy as you think,' said Tom. 'Dad's tired, still sleeping a lot. Mam's obsessed with keeping things uncontentious...' He overtook a milk lorry on a bend and cut in front of it so abruptly Clemmie would have skidded across the back seat if Bel hadn't strapped her in. 'And Sean and Kath have been taking good care of her. You just heard, she loves pottering around on their land.'

'She's not been anywhere else?'

'Ah, Bel, you should be grateful for the joys of anonymity! It hits me whenever I come back – from Dublin, London, wherever – the way you can't just stroll down a street teeming with strangers. Here every person you meet wants to know your business.' He looked at her mournfully, his eyes the colour of the sea. 'I find it hard adjusting.'

'What do they want to know?'

'What don't they! Where am I living, who am I courting, what work am I doing...'

'Is that a problem?'

'It is when you've had as many jobs as me.' He tapped out a list on the steering wheel. 'Farmhand, singer, songwriter, postie, barman, van driver, waiter, cook, salesman, TV runner, gardener, interior decorator...'

She interrupted. 'What did you cook?'

'Burgers.'

'What did you sell?'

'Swimming pools.'

'Seriously?'

'To ex-pats in Spain. And timeshares. Sunshine melts resistance you know.'

'D'you speak Spanish?'

'I didn't really need to, but I picked some up.'

'And the TV stuff?'

'Outright exploitation, and I'm not good at being told what to do. I have a temper on me, Bel; you wouldn't want to push me too far.'

Was that a warning? she wondered. And if a person had run through all those occupations by the time they were thirty and *still* didn't know what they wanted to do… For Bel the magic number was more than four years off but she could see the shape of it on the horizon. It loomed, it definitely loomed. How would it feel to be rudderless?

'Tell me about the singing.'

'Ah, The Voice – it was my best talent once; sadly I peaked too soon. Now you'd have to wait till I had a few pints inside of me.'

'My dad was very successful when he was younger,' said Bel. 'He's an artist, an abstract painter. Leo Wentworth. Have you heard of him? No? Well his work was very fashionable in the late eighties, early nineties. And then it wasn't, if you know what I mean. That Brit Art stuff took over. He kept plugging away of course but he found it quite hard to come to terms with. I think that's why he had the affair, the one that led to my parents' divorce. The ego takes a battering doesn't it, with the stress of…'

'Failure,' drawled Tom wryly. He turned into a narrow lane; high hedges rising on either side formed a long green tunnel, like an entrance to a mysterious world.

'So where are we going now?'

'Moment of truth. I can't put it off any longer. I need you, Bel, that's the nub of it, to help break the ice.'

'What ice?' Bel remembered how cordially Sean and Kath had welcomed them.

He was dismissive. 'Oh, it's just a manner of speaking. It'll be easier for Clem if you're with us. She asked for you, didn't you, darlin'?'

A family reunion in difficult circumstances – why would they want a stranger present? 'Better, surely, if her mother was there?'

'Ah, but that's never going to happen.'

Clemmie's brown legs stuck out in front of her, ending in pink Wellington boots studded with stars. She gave Bel her gap-toothed smile. How much of a secret was she? Bel wondered.

Tom added, 'I'm trying to make a good fist of things. You will help out, won't you?'

There was undoubtedly some magic in his voice, some quality that sent tremors up her spine and plucked at her emotions. Bel possessed an easy social poise, but it hadn't often led to romance. Tom Farrelly had the knack of making her feel special, her company desirable. A knack, that's all it was. 'Of course.'

She could see on a rise ahead of them the plain grey rendered farmhouse with its slate roof and blue painted window frames, blending into the sky. A Border collie barked and cavorted as they approached and seemed to disappear beneath the car wheels. Horrified, Bel waited for the crunch.

Tom said, 'He's a noisy bugger but he'll come to no harm.' He stopped the car and got out. 'Stay there, JP, stay. He's named after a feckin' pope, wouldn't you know.' He aimed a kick in the collie's direction; JP cringed and Bel gasped. 'Jaysus, I wouldn't hurt him! But he needs to know who's in charge.' He opened the passenger door and scooped Clemmie from the back seat. 'Don't you be afraid of him, Clem.' As she wriggled in his arms, he added, 'Or me. Or anyone. Now why don't I show you the hay byre? When I was your age it was my favourite spot in the world.'

'Your parents,' Bel began, 'I thought they were expecting you.' The house looked bleak. There were no lights on, no cat sunning itself on a doorstep, only a straggling rose bush to soften its austerity.

'There's time enough,' said Tom, leading them down a dung-spattered track. 'You'll have been expecting mud. You won't be disappointed.'

Clemmie's pink boots splashed into puddles and through the cowpats. And then they came upon it: a stack of dusty straw bales beneath a corrugated-tin roof, a ladder propped against them.

'It's bit depleted after the winter,' he said.

Clemmie craned her neck. 'It's very high.'

'It's wonderful up there. You can see all the way to America.'

'America!' she squealed.

'And you can spot anyone coming across the land, that's for sure. When I was a lad I used to lie low, make myself scarce. If I was really in deep shit...' his laugh was throaty, mischievous '...I'd bring the ladder up too. Anyway, as you know, priests wear skirts, they're not great at climbing.'

Bel said, 'Was it always the priest who was after you?'

'Well now.' His hand was resting on one of the rungs, stroking the wood. 'Children's memories are so exaggerated, aren't they? It certainly *felt* like I was always in trouble with Father this or Father that. They believe in putting the fear of God into you around here and the priest has a direct line. I was a terrible rascal, forever missing choir practice. And besides, there was the matter of the collection plate...'

'Can I go up?' begged Clemmie. 'Please. *Please.*'

'If you fell, my darlin', your mother would never let me take you out again.'

'I'll be careful. I won't fall.'

'That's what you're telling me now...'

'I won't,' insisted Clemmie, stamping her foot. 'Bel will look after me.'

'Well I don't know,' said Bel. 'I have a terrible head for heights.'

Clemmie wasn't going to be deterred. She took hold of the ladder's sides and put her foot on the first rung. Then the second. Tom watched, helpless and half admiring. 'I shouldn't be surprised,' he said. 'Somebody tells you no, you just want to prove them wrong. Right?' And he started nimbly after her.

At the top of the stack Clemmie's face appeared, dark and disembodied above the yellow straw. 'Come on, Bel, it's boss!' she called.

Well I'm not going to be shown up by a six-year-old, thought Bel. (Though when she got to the top the distance from the ground startled her.)

'Don't look down,' said Tom as she pulled back from the brink. 'Look out to sea.'

The view was impressive. The fields were the rich green of grass mixed with clover, a glorious quilt ruffling beneath a fast-moving sky. The cows stood about, stolid black and white chunks, like chess pieces waiting for a hand to move them. Beyond lay the Atlantic, its froth-capped waves mirroring the plumes of cloud. There wasn't a human figure to be seen.

Clemmie was crawling over the bales, picking up loose strands of straw. 'Can you make me a corn dolly?' she said.

Bel was amused. 'Where did you hear about corn dollies?'

'I saw it on the telly. Please!'

'Okay I'll try, if you find me some long pieces.' She began to braid the strands together.

Tom had been scouring the horizon, as if in search of something or someone. He said suddenly in a passionate undertone, 'I didn't want to come, you know. I didn't want to be part of this sentimental sanctimonious shite. God, I hope I die suddenly!'

He was upset, Bel told herself, by his father's condition. An angry, cynical reaction would not be unusual. Unsure how to respond, she gave his shoulder a tentative pat. He seized her hand and held it against the side of his face, drawing her closer. Conscious that they weren't alone, she looked for Clemmie. The child had crawled to the end of the barn and was burrowing into the hay, creating a little nest for herself. She had her back to them.

Yes please, thought Bel, I do want to repeat the experience of Saturday night. I want physical contact. I want to come alive again. She leaned towards him. She didn't say a word – nor did Tom – but their tongues combined with alacrity. He slipped his hand beneath her sweater, tapping his way up the xylophone of her ribs, caressing her breast until the nipple hardened. 'There's nothing of you, is there?' he murmured.

'It's because I've been ill. I told you before, I haven't been able to eat properly for weeks. It's *so* tedious.'

'Ah, that's a topic I know about. Endured many a time. Fucking unbelievable boredom. But not right now. Sweetheart, you've brightened my day.'

He sounded sincere, though it hardly mattered. She suspected they both wanted to find somewhere more private, a warm dark space where they could explore each other's bodies. He picked up a piece of straw and ran the end meditatively along the curve of her jaw. He reached for another kiss.

'Daddy!' called Clemmie.

He spun around, dislodging one of the straw bales. It rolled towards the child and she put out her foot to stop it. She in turn lost her balance and Tom lunged forward. He caught her by the arm and clutched her against his chest. The bale changed course and bowled into the prongs of the ladder, knocking them at a vulnerable angle. In slow motion the ladder slid sideways and fell to the ground.

Clemmie froze, but Tom laughed. Still holding her, he swept his other arm around Bel and said, 'Ah, girls, is this what you were planning all along, to be stranded with me on top of a haystack?' Clemmie, who might have been going to cry, giggled instead.

Bel said, 'So what are we going to do now?' The moment of sexual arousal had dissipated. The corn dolly was a few brittle twists of straw snapping between her fingers. A wind was getting up and the clouds were darkening.

'You'll be astonished,' he said. 'Tom Farrelly can get out of anything.'

'So astonish us.'

'It's not difficult, darlin'. What we need to do is toss down some bales so they mount up like a staircase. Then jump.'

'And break a leg?'

He grinned and cracked his knuckles. 'If you fell awkwardly you could break something, yeah. But it only needs one of us to get down and right the ladder again.'

'Go on then.'

He pushed the first bale over the edge and it landed in a cloud of dust. Bel thought she saw a creature scuttle away from it, a field mouse probably. Was Clemmie frightened? She took the child's hand to reassure her. She wouldn't allow herself to be bothered by a field mouse. After all, in Sudan she had encountered snakes and scorpions, a spider as big as her fist. The spider had terrified her but done her no harm. Instead she had been laid low by a vibrating speck scarcely visible to the naked eye. Danger doesn't necessarily come from the obvious source.

Tom's pile was growing, though it took time and looked dangerous. 'Oh, Daddy,' said Clemmie solemnly as he lowered himself on to it. 'Don't hurt yourself.'

He sneezed and rocked on top of the pile, which didn't seem stable at all. Bel held her breath as he slid from level to level until he finally reached the ground. He raised a fist in triumph and she and Clemmie both cheered. Tom hefted the ladder so the topmost prongs were once more within their grasp.

'Clem, you must go first,' said Bel. 'While we hold it steady, top and bottom.'

When Clemmie was safely down, it was her turn. But she was experiencing a crushing wave of vertigo. She used to be so fearless. What had happened? Having all the stuffing knocked out of her, that's what.

'Bel, what are you waiting for?'

She inched one foot onto a rung of the ladder, then another, scared it would peel away from the stack. Tom had angled it more steeply than before; it seemed vertical. And she wasn't small and agile like Clemmie. 'Oh God, I'm stuck.'

'If you think you're going to fall,' said Tom from below, 'then you almost surely will. Do you want me to help you?' He climbed a little way up and closed his hand around her ankle, guiding her descent. 'Don't panic,' he said. 'I'm right behind you.'

Bel, convinced the ladder was buckling under their double weight, kicked out.

'For fuck's sake,' said Tom, leaping off.

Unfortunately his jump destabilised the ladder, which swayed, bearing Bel with it. She slithered rapidly downwards and was ejected onto the concrete floor with a smash.

17

The Press Cuttings

Teresa had been polishing the taps again, an endeavour Vince found mystifying. If you wanted to look at your face – and really it was only a necessity for shaving – then you could use the mirror above the basin. He'd screwed it there himself. You'd not gain much from trying to peer at your reflection in the shine of a tap. Though there was no doubt about it: Teresa Hogan's taps shone. In the old days you'd have been lucky to have such bathroom facilities. When his bachelor uncle Seamus inhabited Dolphin Cottage he'd had to piss into a bucket outside the back door. Come spring he'd soak his winter blankets in the urine for twenty-four hours to kill off the bugs and stretch them on the bushes to dry. The whiff of ammonia when Teresa brought home the dry cleaning would remind Vince of his uncle's methods.

He emerged from the downstairs toilet drying his hands on the seat of his trousers. She would have reproved him for not using the fluffy apricot towel swinging from its hoop, but she was busy entertaining her friends, Breda Malone and Mary O'Connor. They were perched on easy chairs with their teacups; the three witches, was how he thought of them when they were together. Teresa had been doing more than a bit of unnecessary spit and polish, he could see now – she'd been ferreting through the press cuttings.

She kept them in an old box file: several years' worth of christenings, weddings and obituaries, accounts of local Field Days and Festivals and the Rose of Tralee snipped from the *Kerryman*. She'd had them out before, on Sunday, and he'd thought maybe she was after the date of an anniversary of some kind – though it would be unlike Teresa not to have such information written down. Hers was always the first card through the letter box; people said her goodwill was much appreciated.

She had the scissored ribbons spread on the table top – including the thirty-year-old photo of himself when he still had hair on the top of his head and could rise to the challenge of an arm wrestle. And win, mostly. But it wasn't her younger, fresh-faced husband's picture Teresa was passing across to Breda Malone; it was the reproduction of a family snapshot: a broad-chested man, a petite woman and a stocky little boy in dungarees.

'What do you think?' she was saying. 'Is there not an incredible likeness?'

Breda adjusted her glasses so she could look more closely at the grainy image. 'I believe you are right, so,' she said. 'The little boy here, he'd be a mite younger, would he not, than the grandson she showed us on Sunday?'

Teresa nodded agreement and lifted her chin in a mulish way as if waiting for Vince to join the discussion.

He said, 'Who are you talking about?'

'The lady doctor. The one who stayed here before she moved into Dolphin Cottage.'

'What about her?' He recalled the crisp accent, how she was polite but withdrawn as the English tended to be. They'd had a conversation about TB, about whether or not you were safe to drink green milk (which Vince had done all his life, in point of fact). She was very knowledgeable about the TB, which was only to be expected from the medical profession, but she came round in the end to his point of view. Indeed, she had poured the milk on her cereal in the mornings. Nothing else had struck him.

'You didn't recognise her?'

'Should I have done?'

Breda and Mary pursed their lips and continued to pass the press cuttings between them, studying the detail.

'We were first alerted,' said Teresa, 'when we bumped into her after Mass and she'd told us she'd been to the burial ground at St Silas.' The women nodded to confirm this. 'She didn't mention the memorial that Ronnie and Pat put up, but she must have seen it. And it got us thinking. Here—' She took the black and white photo from Breda and thrust it towards him. 'Take a good look. Is she not the wife of the man who drowned? Cast your mind back.'

'I don't know,' said Vince.

'But you saw more of her than any of the rest of us. You were a witness.'

The last person to speak to William Langley alive – what a responsibility that had been. He'd not felt easy about it. How could he have realised its significance at the time? And it was only because he was asked so often afterwards – while it was fresh in his mind – that he could still picture the scene.

It was back when they'd been running the bar, before he and Teresa sold it for redevelopment. The English couple had come in and taken a corner table in the snug with their drinks. The man, neutral, inoffensive: chestnut eyes, beige shirt, brown trousers, like he could blend into the landscape with no trouble at all; the woman's hair cut so short it cleaved to her skull. They were speaking quietly, but with an intense insistence: a quiet fierce argument. The bar was deserted. Vince didn't know why they were keeping their voices down, unless on account of the fluffy-haired child they had with them, blowing bubbles in his red lemonade.

He'd been shaking out his damp tea towel and checking the pressure on his barrel taps, when the woman pushed her chair back so it legs grated on the floor. She jumped up and swung a large canvas holdall over her shoulder, like a game bag loaded with duck or rabbit. Then she knocked the boy's thumb from his mouth and jerked him from his seat, tugging him out through the doors.

At this point Vince met the man's eyes. His smile was rueful. He was a big fellow, well-built but nimble with it. He leaned his elbow on the bar and glanced at his watch. 'Might as well have one for the road.' He took a punt note from his pocket. 'Bushmills please.'

'A large one?'

'Why not? A dose of Dutch courage.'

That was the remark they kept asking Vince about. But it was only an expression, he insisted, it wasn't significant. One thing he did remember, three decades later, was the hungry way the widow had watched him in the courtroom in Tralee when the Coroner asked: 'Did William Langley seem agitated at all?' At that moment Vince had glanced in her direction and seen her crane forward in her seat as if she couldn't afford to miss whatever he was going to say.

'No, not particularly.'

She'd relapsed then, slumped like a sack of Kerr's Pinks. She'd only mentioned the quarrel glancingly herself. They'd had a disagreement, she acknowledged, which was why she'd left the pub ahead of her husband; she'd needed to curb her temper. This fitted with Vince's view. She had steamed off at a gallop because that's what some women do, is it not? For a man, a drink can go a long way to soothe a hurt. There was no suggestion that William Langley might take his own life, nothing to indicate suicide. No reason for him to plunge into the sea again after the rescue. The riptide had claimed him. The verdict was accidental death.

Ronnie Farrelly hadn't brought her sons to the inquest – they were far too young for such proceedings – but she'd brought Anna. The older girls had been minding the little ones that day, beach-combing while the boys fished in the rock pools. Anna had pulled the child from the water and got him breathing again. She had acquitted herself very well, for it was a terrible ordeal and the Coroner had praised her.

Afterwards Vince had spoken to Ronnie and they'd been standing not a yard away from the widow, the pair of them building up the nerve to approach, to shake her hand and tell her how sorry they were for her loss. But she had given them a glittering black-eyed stare, her pupils so dilated Vince felt as if he was looking straight through them into her brain and the torment churning there. She didn't acknowledge him, or Ronnie.

And then the reporter from the *Kerryman* had talked him into going for a Guinness at the Grand. They'd sat on high stools at the mahogany counter and he'd repeated his story again – No, he hadn't been able to hear what they were saying and no, your man hadn't seemed agitated, although it was true he'd joked about Dutch courage. And Vince finished his jar and the photographer (who'd died since from a severe asthma attack, so there was another life cut short) took his photo, the one that Mary O'Connor was putting back in the box because it wasn't Vince in his younger days they were interested in.

'I don't know,' he said again. 'I can't be certain.'

'I've told Ronnie anyway,' Teresa said.

'Told her what?'

'That we think the widow's come back.'

'Isn't that a bit hasty?'

'She needed warning,' said Breda, peering at him over her spectacles like the schoolteacher she had once been. 'It could come as an awful shock otherwise.'

'Why put the wind up her? There's no need for their paths to cross.'

'It could be helpful for them to meet.'

'I don't see how.' He thought they should leave well alone, but it was hard to get this across to women: meddling was in their bones.

'Ah well…' Teresa paused. 'Because it's haunted her, has it not, that she was indirectly responsible for the death of a man? And since her own husband…' Her hand shook a little as she replaced her cup on its saucer, though the Lord knew why, because Vince was in tip-top condition, never a day's illness – apart from the osteoarthritis in his knee joints. *He* wasn't going to leave her anytime soon.

'And how can you tell what's inside another person's head?'

'She used to have nightmares,' said Teresa. 'She told me about them: a man striding out of the ocean dripping with seaweed, coming to claim her boy.'

'She told you once,' said Vince. 'I was there. It was after he'd fallen off the roof of Chrissie O'Grady's henhouse and concussed himself. There was fear of brain damage or a haemorrhage of some kind, was there not? But he was up and running within hours.'

'That doesn't stop a nightmare recurring,' chirped Mary in her birdlike way.

Vince was outnumbered. He'd known all three of them as girls (four if you counted Ronnie), hanging around the local bars and ballrooms, and they'd been no less terrifying then. Even so, he was not easily pushed around. They shouldn't have started the conversation if they didn't want his contribution. 'And what about *her*?' he said, recalling how reserved the lady doctor had been. 'The widow. If that's who she is. Do you think she will welcome a meeting?'

'If she's been to St Silas, she'll have realised how much the family cared, how grateful they were. I can't see that bringing the two of them together would do any harm. People get satisfaction, you know, from closure.'

When Teresa wasn't reading the romance sagas she borrowed from the library, she'd rummage through her collection of self-help books and read aloud what she considered to be plums and Vince regarded as nonsense. Closure was one of those expressions he was highly suspicious of. It only made sense to him in terms of shutting down: a shop for instance, or a factory producing goods people didn't need any more.

In the country you had to carry on as best you could – though they were struggling to keep their heads above water. He wouldn't get involved in the reasons why, but it was generally the wrong fellers lining their pockets and that was the truth of it. People used to oblige each other in return for the side of a cow. They were having to go back to that kind of bartering now to keep the banks at bay.

'Well,' he said, folding his arms to give himself a look of authority. 'I don't think you should interfere.'

'You have to ask yourself, don't you, why else is she here?'

Breda and Mary nodded.

'But, Teresa, all I'm suggesting—'

'You'll not understand, obviously.'

He understood he wasn't going to get her to change her mind.

'A simple phone call.' She collected the scraps of paper from her friends and returned them to the box file. 'Or rather, two. I shall broach the subject with each of them tactfully. I know how to handle these things.'

'Well,' said Vince who knew when he had lost. 'Let's hope you'll not be mistaken.'

18

The Introduction

Ronnie was knitting when Tom reappeared. Her needles were clicking an insistent rhythm – a sound that could be calming or irritating depending on your mood. Her grandsons, Eoin and Conor, were sorting through her ends of wool, dividing them into piles of red and green, blue and violet. Pat was in the back parlour, dozing in front of the television. There was an old set in the kitchen too, which she kept for the little ones, but they were more interested in her overflowing basket. She had to keep stopping what she was doing to help them untie knots or disentangle skeins – but there was no hurry. She'd more than fulfilled her orders. The craft shops of Dingle would have a glut of fingerless gloves, jaunty berets and stripy scarves to sell.

She was relieved when she heard Tom's footfall. She had always wished, helplessly, that she could keep him within her sights. He had this knack of walking out without telling anyone where he was going. And finding trouble. She couldn't count the number of times there'd been a phone call or an infuriated knock on the door.

She looked up from her knitting and was surprised to see he'd brought company. The young woman couldn't be local – Kerry girls were rosy-cheeked and dairy fed; they had bounce and energy. This was a waif-like creature with huge eyes in a hungry face, unsteady as a calf on her skinny legs. And there was a little girl with her, a little black girl who could hardly have sprung out of nowhere.

'This is Bel, Mam,' said Tom. 'From England. We met her on the ferry. And this is Clemmie.'

So this was the woman who'd delayed their arrival. Ronnie had expected someone more alluring. And there'd been no mention of a child tagging along. She wondered what had happened to the husband though she knew well enough how casually people treated their obligations these days. Bel was shivering, she noticed. She never felt the cold herself but she'd kept the range stoked up since Pat came back from the hospital. The room, in point of fact, was sweltering and the two little lads were playing in their cotton vests. They'd given up sorting the colours and were coiling the lengths of wool to create the shapes of trains and boats on the squares of lino. 'Are you cold?' she asked.

'The thing is,' Tom said. 'Bel has an injury.' He pushed up the sleeve of her jumper and she flinched. There was fierce bruising on her arm and grazing on her elbow, as if she'd been in a fight.

'What have you been doing with yourself!' exclaimed Ronnie. 'Get that blood rinsed off and I'll find you an ice pack. The little one can play with the boys. Go on, Eoin, make room for – what's your name again dear? Clemmie?' As she laid down her needles the little girl came to her side and kissed her. Ronnie was startled, but taken with the greeting nonetheless. 'What a sweet little thing,' she declared, patting the child's fuzzy plaits and heaving herself out of her chair. She was carrying too much weight and her joints creaked. She foraged in the freezer in the pantry and came back with a bag of ice.

'Are you sure there's nothing broken?'

Bel was holding her arm in front of her, bent at the elbow. 'I took a battering, but everything still moves. It was more the shock than anything.'

Clemmie said, 'She couldn't talk; she couldn't even cry.'

'I was winded for a bit. I'll get over it.'

'Then you'll be needing a cup of tea too,' said Ronnie. 'And, Tom, did you miss lunch again?'

'No one's hungry, Mam.'

Switching on the kettle, she said, 'So go on, tell me what happened.'

Tom shrugged. 'I was showing Bel around the place because she'd expressed an interest. She tripped over the ladder in the barn and went sprawling.'

Ronnie suspected she was being lied to, but it seemed to her she'd rather have some attempt at a story than nothing to go on at all. If you had a little hint, you could work out the rest for yourself. She poured the boiling water onto a teabag and added generous spoonfuls of sugar. She handed Bel the mug. 'Farms are dangerous places. You should have looked after your visitor better, Tom.'

'I'll be fine in a moment,' said Bel.

'You've no flesh to cushion you, that's the problem.' She had a narrow pointed chin and a flat chest; not Tom's type at all, Ronnie decided. 'Is this your first trip to Kerry?'

'Yes, I'm just here for a week.'

The child, Clemmie, had joined the little boys on the floor. She sat with her tongue poking through the gap in her teeth, teasing the strands of wool into shapes of her own: houses, trees, buses.

'We thought we might go fishing tomorrow,' Tom said. 'That is, if Bel's okay and you can spare me.'

Ronnie was indignant. 'It's not up to me! You're here to spend time with your father – isn't that the plan? You're home rarely enough, for the love of Jesus.' She shouldn't have let her anger out. It was the surest way to antagonise him. He was sweet as honey when he had what he wanted.

He said, 'Only while he's having his afternoon nap. The tides will be right and I reckon Gerry Lenane will lend us his boat. A couple of hours, that's all, depending on the weather.'

She knew that Pat would tell her to let him go. 'Sure, you're a devil for disaster,' she said, capitulating. 'First you nearly break the girl's arm, now you want to drown her.' She turned to Bel. 'You've discovered already the liability that's our Tom. You'll have to take your chances.'

There came a sharp yelp from Conor on the floor. Clemmie, in the manner of precocious little girls, had taken charge. She was explaining that you couldn't have a boat sailing down a main street along with the traffic and anyway she'd decided they were going to change the story and build a hospital. Or better: an operating theatre. Then they could use the red wool for dripping blood. Eoin warmed to this idea, but Conor, being younger, wanted to continue his own game. Ronnie could foresee tears but she was impressed with Clemmie's air of authority and the way she was taking control. Clemmie picked up a length of blue wool and coiled it into the shape of a person. 'This is my mummy,' she announced.

'Is your mummy a nurse?' said Ronnie.

'Yes.' Clemmie took the wool basket onto her lap and rifled through it for more colours. Squeezed out of the game, the boys moved back to their collection of toy fire engines, combine harvesters and dump trucks.

It seemed to Ronnie that Bel hadn't much of a clue when it came to first aid. 'I didn't realise you had medical training,' she said.

'Oh I don't – but my mother does. I'm staying with her here. Actually she's a doctor.'

Ronnie was thoroughly confused. Did that mean the child was talking about her granny? Or was she pretending? Letting her imagination run wild? That was the glory and freedom of childhood: you had no need to be shackled to the mundane. Further questions queued on the tip of her tongue, but were blocked by a commotion in the yard. The dog, JP, could make you think you were being savaged in a terrorist attack, when in point of fact it was merely Kieran strolling home and taking off his boots on the doorstep. He entered the kitchen soundlessly in his socks and glanced at the visitors in surprise.

'Have you met Tom's friend?' Ronnie began. 'Well to be sure you have, what am I saying!'

'Well,' said Kieran to Tom. 'How did it go?'

'I got your car back in one piece,' Tom said lightly. 'But Bel hasn't been so lucky. She's had rather a mishap.'

'That's me all over,' confessed Bel. 'I'm just accident prone.' She hugged the bag of ice to her chest.

'It was the ladder,' said Clemmie. 'It wasn't my fault.'

'Nobody's blaming you,' said Bel.

The child put aside the basket, got to her feet and crossed the room to Kieran. She tugged him down to her level so she could whisper in his ear.

Ronnie noted the confident way she approached him. 'She doesn't suffer from shyness at all,' she observed.

'And isn't that a good thing?' said Tom with one of his wicked smiles.

'Ah but you know how the English can be so reserved and the kiddies, they can just clam up when you talk to them. They often need a little drawing out.'

'Not me,' said Bel. 'Guess I'm a freak really. Forever in trouble for not holding back, putting my foot in it. Full-on honesty that's amusing in a child is seen as weird in a grown-up. My mother despairs because she's always had to be especially tactful. When you've bad news to give to people you can't go charging in like a bull in a china shop, can you?'

'Sure, she must take after you then,' said Ronnie.

'Who?'

'Herself.' Kieran had straightened up and Clemmie was standing beside him still; his hand was on her shoulder. Ronnie nodded towards her. 'She's a grand little thing, you should be proud of her.'

Bel blurted, 'Clemmie? You think she's mine? Oh Lord no! I'm only twenty-six.'

For goodness' sake, what did her age have to do with anything? 'Then who...?' In a moment of confusion and

190

chaos, it seemed to Ronnie that all the objects in her kitchen rose up and spun around as if in the vortex of a tornado. She saw the contents of her dresser dance; she saw the cushions on her window seat tumble and regroup; she saw the apples leap out of the fruit bowl and jostle back into a pile; she saw the features of her sons and grandsons and those of the Englishwoman dissolve and reassemble. And she saw the brown-skinned child grow into a monstrous giant filling her vision, and then shrink to a normal size again, with her dinky braids, her gold earrings, her round eyes. Where had she come from, this creature? Who did she belong to? Surely not one of her sons?

Since no one else was prepared to speak, Ronnie addressed her directly. 'Is your mummy not with you then, Clemmie?'

'No.'

'So, is she working in the hospital like you told us?'

'She's on holiday,' said the child in her high, precise voice. 'In another country. I come here with my daddy.'

'Did you now? And where are you staying?' To her relief a new thought had struck her. Tom and Kieran had arrived home two days ago. Unaccompanied. She was barking up the wrong tree. They were giving the child an outing while her father had some errand to run. There was no mystery to it.

'She's been staying with the McCauleys,' said Kieran, his eyes fixed on Tom.

'Ah well, they're a lovely couple,' said Ronnie. 'Very welcoming. So where did your daddy go today?'

Clemmie wrinkled her small blunt nose as if she didn't understand the question. Bel let the bag of ice slip and it thumped onto the floor. 'Gosh, sorry,' she said, picking it up again. 'I think my fingers are numb.'

Kieran said, 'It's not been easy for us, Mam, judging the moment to tell you. You've had so much to deal with.'

And then Tom began to whistle. The sound pierced her, the beauty of it, the way he could turn even a simple bout of whistling into a melody. He would use it to calm the animals when they were distressed, to lull them into doing what he wanted. She still mourned the voice he had lost at puberty, although occasionally, in the drift between sleep and wakefulness, she could hear it soaring in her head.

He came over to her chair and put his arm around her. She stiffened, for she was not a heifer to be easily placated. He stopped the whistling to murmur, 'She's a grand little thing. You said so yourself.'

Ronnie took a deep breath. She twined her fingers into his in a tight grip but she would not look at him. She stared at the child and the child stared back. 'How old are you?' she asked.

'I'm six and three quarters,' Clemmie said.

'Six whole years, Tom… And you never told me!'

'Well, Mam, it wasn't so clear-cut. I mean I didn't know myself.'

This time she did look at him. She tilted her chin and said sharply. 'And how is it then that you know now?'

'It's a long story. Do you need the gory details?'

Ronnie couldn't decide which was worse – having the child sprung upon her in such a way or being robbed of the excitement of her birth and the chance to watch her grow. It wasn't the poor mite's fault. She didn't care to contemplate the mother, for whom she only had disapproval (on a par with the rich banker's wife of her imagination). Besides, how could she be sure of anything? Where was the evidence? 'Yes,' she said. 'I believe I do. How many more are there to come out of the woodwork do you think?'

'It was time she met you,' said Tom. 'And Dad.'

'You haven't been thinking of him at all. This could break his heart.'

'Why?'

Why indeed? Tom had broken Ronnie's heart a thousand times into a million pieces, but Pat, she knew, found him resistible. 'Has she your name?' she demanded. 'Is she a Farrelly?'

'No she isn't, but what's that got to do with anything? He needs to see her. I've had to work myself up to this, Mam, so don't spoil it now. Give the kid a chance. Clem, come over here.'

Clemmie trotted towards them and Tom hunkered down to embrace her. There was nothing, thought Ronnie, examining the pair of them, that would give you the idea they were related. Her head was bursting with unwelcome information; she couldn't tell where her thoughts would go next.

She was aware of Kieran saying, 'Why don't I drive you back home, Bel?'

'Thank you. I think that would be a good idea.'

'Don't go yet.' Tom rose to his feet in a graceful leap. 'We've the boat trip to arrange.'

The girl was embarrassed – that was apparent. She said, 'You can ring me later.'

'Wait!' Tom turned back to Ronnie. 'Will we invite her to the do, d'you think?'

He certainly knew how to shift the conversation. And how could she refuse in a situation like this: a minefield when any utterance could take on another meaning? Tom had her on the back foot, all right. Ronnie glanced across at Kieran, but his expression was more than usually enigmatic. Well yes, anything to get the girl out of the way. 'Surely,' she said, thinking of the gossip Clemmie would cause and how she could counteract it. 'The more the merrier.'

19

The Rock

Bel insisted that Kieran stop at the end of the track to avoid the potholes, as Tom had done. 'Are you sure?' he said. 'I'd rather see you right to the door.' He had none of Tom's agitation, but a sort of measured calm that she supposed would be useful for a priest.

'I'll be okay. Honestly. You've got enough on your plate back home.'

He grinned. 'Not my plate, thank God.'

She smiled too and waved him off jauntily, although the cack-handed way Clemmie had been introduced to her grandmother had been hard to witness: the awkwardness and confusion that came from keeping a secret too long. Bel didn't really believe in secrets. She didn't see why people couldn't be upfront more often, but she was going to have to break one of her own rules because she was worried about her mother's state of mind. She didn't think she'd react well to hearing her daughter had fallen off a ladder. She breezed into the cottage, full of apologies.

'Hey, I'm sorry. Was I out for ages? Only Tom took me for a tour of the farm. The colours are fabulous when the sun's out. You should have lent me the camera.'

Julia was sitting in the window recess, chin propped on her palm, gazing absently into the distance, but she said: 'Are you all right?'

'Sure. Why?'

'You seem to be wincing.'

Bel longed to tell the truth. She'd had some challenging scrapes in her youth and had never been able to predict whether Julia would react briskly – You'll be well enough for school tomorrow – or melt into solicitude – My poor darling, let me see how bad it is. In any case, recent events had changed everything. 'I'm fine,' she said with the same conviction she'd offered to Ronnie and Kieran. 'Got a headache though. Have you any paracetamol?'

She knew the answer: Julia would rather travel with medicines than cosmetics. She took the capsules and gave an appreciative smile. 'Thanks. I feel bad that you've been stuck in all day, waiting for me to get back.'

'I've been reading mostly. It's a luxury for me.'

'Well do you want to come out now? We said we'd go for a walk, didn't we, and it's lovely and mild.'

'I suppose we should make the most of any good weather. You've given up on the dolphins?

'We might take a boat out tomorrow. In fact, I was wondering...' She hesitated.

'What?'

'Where's that beach?'

'Which beach?'

'The one you took the pictures of.'

'Oh...' Julia tugged at a clump of her hair until it stood up in a spike. 'You saw them.'

'Shouldn't I have looked? Is this what you've been doing every day? Going out and taking photos.'

'For the past three weeks actually. I took loads in France too.'

'Why?'

'Why? To keep a record. Isn't that why people take pictures?'

'A record of what?'

When Julia didn't answer, she said, 'Can we go there anyway? Is it far?'

'About ten minutes' drive.'

'Well then.'

'Fine, I'll put my boots on.'

Julia turned on the car radio so they wouldn't be driving in silence. Adverts blasted for carpets, fertiliser and home insurance; a caller to a quiz show was trying to identify the voice of a character in a television soap. She took a sharp corner and drove along a narrow lane, then pulled over and parked on the verge. They got out and Julia led the way down a steep cobbled path. On either side the cliffs towered, as majestic as castle walls. The strand was bracketed by jutting rock formations; it was beautiful, bleak and deserted.

Bel couldn't confine her curiosity any longer. 'Is this it?'

'The beach in the photos? Yes. We used to call it the secret beach because you could only access it when the tide was low. Bracing, isn't it?' The wind lifted Julia's hair and rouged her complexion as she took swift strides along the sand.

'And you keep coming here?' She found her mother's behaviour ghoulish as well as obsessive, but she attempted to phrase her question tactfully: 'Are you... trying to recapture something?'

Julia stopped short. Under the great expanse of sky Bel could see the creases around her eyes and mouth, but the quality of the light was such that it softened them, erased years. 'Like what? My youth, do you mean?'

'It's okay,' said Bel. 'I shouldn't have asked.'

'This is where it happened,' said Julia in a terse, matter-of-fact way. 'William's accident.'

'Oh, Mum, do you really think you should be doing this?'

'We had happy times here too. Only the day before, Matt had spent hours building a sandcastle by a rock pool. I thought I'd never forget, that I'd recognise it instantly but I can't seem to locate it... My memory's a blank.' She raised her camera and pointed it at the horizon, then replaced it in her pocket without depressing the button. 'In the old days, pre-digital, if you didn't change your film in the dark, if you exposed it too soon, you lost all your images...' Her voice began to crack.

'Mum, please don't!'

At Julia's feet lay a glutinous heap of seaweed. She turned it with her toe and bent to extricate a long stick. Then she started to draw letters in the sand. Because her bruised arm was throbbing painfully, it took Bel some time to work out what she was writing. At first she'd thought the marks were just nonsense hieroglyphics; eventually she understood them to represent chemical symbols and compounds. Julia muttered as she wrote, as if reciting an incantation; when she'd finished her list she ravaged it with the point of her stick.

'At medical school,' she said, 'you have to learn the names of so many things. Bones, body parts, diseases, pharmaceuticals. One damned inventory after another. You could memorise the lot, be the best student in your year and still cock up in practice. Basic human error. Will and I used to help each other revise, test ourselves until our ears were bleeding. Then we'd throw the books on the floor and go out and slaughter each other on the tennis court.'

Bel had no idea her mother played tennis. She'd never seen her with a racquet and it wasn't Leo's game. She tried to picture Julia hopping on the balls of her feet, the collar of her polo shirt turned up, and William (who she'd only ever seen flat and two dimensional in photo albums) poised to serve: a leaner version of Matt, in those tight shorts people wore in the seventies to play sport.

'Shouldn't you be telling Matt?' she said cautiously. 'This stuff about his dad...'

'Matt isn't here,' said Julia, throwing away the stick.

'I just meant in general... but of course I want to help too.' Bel wondered if she sounded like a complete prat. After all, Julia had been the stalwart of the family: the breadwinner, letter-writer, homework supervisor, problem solver, diviner of lost objects – she did everything except cook. 'Give moral support, I mean,' she said weakly.

Julia threw her arm around her and she had to bite her lip to stifle a yelp of pain.

'But you *are* a source of support! It's why I asked you. Truly. I'd had enough of being on my own.'

'Really? Only it seemed like you didn't need me. You were on some major one-woman mission.'

'A mission?'

'I don't know how else to put it.'

'In a way,' sighed Julia as two gulls began fighting overhead with angry cries, 'you're right. I have been looking for something. Stupid isn't it?'

Bel was intrigued. 'What?'

Julia set off again, as if it were easier to make a confession in motion. 'A rock,' she said.

'A what?'

'Not any old rock. There was one...' Julia still wouldn't look at her '...somewhere on the beach, where couples used to chisel their names. Hearts and arrows, that sort of thing. We laughed when we came across it, but it was impressive too. Like a memorial to long-lost love – not necessarily lost, I suppose. They're everywhere, aren't they – usually bus shelters and toilet walls – till they get scrubbed off. But I thought, well, a rock, you can't do away with that, can you, unless you're quarrying or something.

'Will teased me that he was going to add our names to the roll call. That was the night before, and we were full of Guinness and Paddy at the time. I'd forgotten all about it, like everything else I'd wiped out. But now I wonder if he ever did, if that was why he came down here, before the accident... I've been searching and searching, only I can't find it. I can't seem to remember where it was.'

'Someone must know,' said Bel. 'You only have to ask around.'

'I don't think I could,' said Julia. 'I'd feel too silly. It isn't important.'

'But if it's important to you—'

'Let it go, darling. I should never have mentioned it.'

It was just as Bel had feared: her mother was clawing her way back through the decades, seeking a love cut off in its prime. It couldn't be healthy. It shouldn't be encouraged. Was it really her father's fault, or was it that Julia had never had the leisure for self-reflection until now? What Bel needed to do was steer her mother away from past regrets and keep her positive.

The tide was encroaching and a sea mist began to wreathe up from the shoreline in billows and coils. At first, in Bel's fancy, the elegant dancing shapes could have been sea nymphs but they grew and thickened into a dense white blanket obliterating the squat boulders, the carpet of slippery seaweed, the furrows in the sand. The further end of the strand, the danger spot, could no longer be seen.

'Why don't we go into Dingle?' she suggested. 'It's getting damp out here.'

'Okay,' said Julia as the mist continued to roll towards them. 'If that's what you'd like.'

It was easier to behave normally, like any other tourists, if they idled around the little town, inspecting craft shops and picture galleries. Indeed the craft shops helped to lighten the atmosphere. They made them giggle with their eccentric assortment of novelties (although Bel found a sumptuous woven mohair shawl in shades of heather and persuaded Julia to buy it for her). The paintings appealed less: anodyne illustrations that captured nothing of the grandeur of the landscape. It was impossible not to hear the roar of Leo's scorn.

'God, wouldn't Dad hate this!' Bel burst out, in front of a slick acrylic: the sea a gaudy turquoise, the mountains purple and pink, not a single tint quite right.

'There's no accounting for taste,' agreed Julia. As they turned away, she added, 'You know he had the cheek to ask me where I was?'

'Dad? When?'

'The other day, while I was waiting for you. I didn't tell him.'

'He must have been on his way home,' said Bel cautiously.

'Home?'

'He's staying with Matt and Rachael.'

'What! When did this happen?'

'Only yesterday. He has stuff to do apparently.'

'Stirring up trouble is more like it.'

'He has a meeting with someone at the Tate. And maybe...' oh Christ, she should have kept her mouth shut '...he wants to make amends.'

Julia was silent a moment. '*That*'s what he wants?'

'I'm only guessing.'

'It hardly matters. I don't plan on seeing him.'

She stalked off and Bel hastened after her. 'Where are you going?'

'To buy some supper. Come on.'

Bel followed, hopping on and off the narrow pavement until they arrived at a fishmonger's. Julia was lured inside by the dressed crab in the window.

'The freshest sweetest crab this side of the peninsula,' the fishmonger assured them. 'A treat for two.'

'I'm sorry but I don't eat crab,' said Bel.

Julia took out her purse and said with a glint of mischief, 'That's tough. A treat for one then.'

20

The Tulips

On Wednesday there was no chance of going out to take more photographs; the weather was against her. Julia knew it could change rapidly, that if you stood in the right location you could see not only the blustery squall heading towards you across the Atlantic, but also the promise of blue sky beyond. Today, however, the rain skittered against the windowpanes as if someone were tossing fistfuls of shingle. Bel would not get her trip to see the dolphins.

Earlier she'd taken her a cup of coffee, which must now be cooling beside her bed. She'd said something about sleeping badly – the storm had got up in the early hours – so Julia had left her to rest. When she'd last peeked in, Bel had a book in her hand, but her head lolled on the pillow and her eyes were closed. She'd waited a few moments, watching the rise and fall of the feather duvet, her daughter's lips parted, her face in repose as smooth and creamy as in childhood.

Back in the living room she stoked up the fire. Then she returned to the computer, scrutinising the slide show as if a story were unfolding and a pattern might emerge. She knew perfectly well how much of life was random. She had seen it first hand: children with leukaemia or heart conditions or missing chromosomes; a volcano erupting as the wind changed, sending the world into a spin. It was crazy to think her efforts to capture the moods of the ocean, the formation of the clouds on the horizon, would tell her anything. What was striking about the photographs – even for a hopeless amateur – was the enormous breadth and power of the seascapes. How could a person not feel diminished?

She was startled from her reverie by a rap – which she thought at first was a sound from within the cottage – Bel's book slipping onto the floor perhaps, as she turned in her sleep. The second, sharper, she recognised as a knock on the door. She opened it to a large bunch of yellow tulips. The face behind the tulips belonged to a young man; his dark hair, sparkling with raindrops, was slicked behind slightly prominent ears.

'Goodness!' she exclaimed, trying to recall the last time she'd been presented with a bunch of flowers on her doorstep. And then realised it wasn't so long ago after all: Matt, eager and grateful, on the day they'd swapped houses and she'd moved into Canning Street, had produced a lavish bouquet. (Although she also knew, with ninety-nine per cent certainty, that the bouquet in question had been conceived and chosen by Rachael. Rachael had thoughtful, impeccable taste.)

'They're for Bel,' said the visitor in a mild Irish accent. 'This is where she's staying, I'm right in thinking?'

'Well yes, but she's not up, I'm afraid.'

She wondered whether to invite him inside. She could see that he'd left his car at the top of the lane and the wind and rain were still squabbling overhead. The bonnet of thatch above the door didn't offer much shelter. He could dry himself by the fire and hand the flowers to Bel in person. Except she might not want to be caught unawares. If she was keen on him she might need some time to make herself presentable. And if not…

'I can't stop,' he said. 'I just wanted to check she was okay after yesterday. No bad effects, is what I mean.'

'No bad effects?' echoed Julia.

'Her arm? It's not troubling her?'

Julia frowned. She recalled Bel wincing, her denial that anything was the matter. Walking along she'd held herself stiffly, it was true, but her movements had been jerky throughout her convalescence. It was bound to take her a while to get back to the elastic-jointed acrobat she'd been before illness struck. 'She didn't mention it,' she said. 'So I imagine it isn't. Troubling her, I mean.'

'Oh that's good!' His smile was lopsided but engaging. He thrust the tulips at her, in their soggy tissue-paper wrapping. As she took them their fingertips tangled.

'Do you want me to give her a message?'

'A message? Right, yes, if you will. You can tell her Kieran was asking after her.' He turned up the collar of his jacket against a rivulet of water shooting suddenly from the downspout. 'I'm afraid I have to make a run for it now. Got to get back to fixing the fences. If the cattle escape it's a hell of a trial herding them home again.'

Julia could believe this. She'd seen some errant cows lumbering along the road the day before. They were plundering new green shoots in the hedgerows and being chased by two teenagers in wellies waving sticks, like a scene from a child's picture book. 'I'll be sure to do that,' she said and watched him sprint up the lane, avoiding the puddles.

She carried the tulips over to the sink. Bel's posy on the windowsill was wilting and forlorn. Wild flowers never lasted indoors. She threw them into the bin and filled the vase with fresh water. The yellow blooms brought a bright splash of sunshine into the room. She was about to start arranging them when her phone rang.

'Dr Wentworth?'

'Yes?'

'It's Teresa Hogan here.'

'Oh... Teresa... Hello. Everything's fine actually. We've had no problems...'

'You've been sleeping well?'

Julia was perplexed. Surely she wasn't phoning merely to enquire after her sleeping habits? 'Almost twelve hours a night! I must have years of catching up to do.'

'I always say we have the best air in the world. It's a tonic in itself. I wanted to check that your daughter had arrived safely?'

'Oh yes, she got here in the end, thank goodness. All in one piece too.'

'That's grand.' Teresa cleared her throat and said in a casual tone, 'You remember, when we met the other day, you were discussing the old graveyard?'

'Yes?'

'Did you happen to notice a plaque for a man called William Langley?'

Julia didn't answer. She sat down on a hard wooden chair, welcoming its rigidity. She needed firm, unyielding support.

'Are you still there?'

'Yes.'

'It must have been a shock,' said the other woman gently.

'Yes.'

'You know I was certain I'd seen you before, only until you mentioned St Silas it quite eluded me – we have so many visitors. But then, when we saw the pictures of your grandson who is so like his daddy…'

What was she supposed to say to this? Was it foolish not to have realised she might set tongues wagging?

'You probably wondered how it came to be there, the plaque, I mean?'

'Yes.'

Teresa launched in. 'It was put up by the Farrellys, Patrick and Veronica. They used to own the land, you see. They've sold it since to the parish to extend the burial ground. They're old friends of ours. Ronnie's a good Catholic. Pat, well to be honest, for a long time he didn't go to Mass but just now he's been persuaded again. Illness concentrates the mind.'

The mobile slipped a little in Julia's hand, still wet from the tap. She tightened her grip, said again, 'Yes.'

There was a long interval. Had Teresa rung off? No; after more throat-clearing she was back. 'I didn't know what to do for the best. I've been turning it over and over. Will she want to know? Will I say something, will I not…'

Julia tried to compose herself. The woman was well meaning; she shouldn't leave her to flounder. 'I'm afraid that first visit was a total blur for me,' she said. 'People were very kind but I couldn't focus on anything. I don't remember who anyone was.'

'I couldn't leave you in ignorance,' said Teresa. 'I have to tell you that the Farrelly boys are home for their father's birthday.'

The wooden spindles of the chair were digging into Julia's back. She held herself erect and wondered whether this was a situation she had invited.

'The boys?'

'Tom Farrelly was the little lad your husband rescued.'

'Oh.'

Julia had observed that there was nothing harder to cope with than the death of a child. The mother's pain at the loss of her son would have been more profound than Matt's at the loss of the father he scarcely remembered – though how could pain be evaluated, parcelled up and weighed on scales to show whose was heavier?

'There's to be a party,' said Teresa. 'Celebrating Pat's recovery also. From the cancer. You should know that I've just spoken to Ronnie...' There was an edge of desperation in her voice. 'I told her you were here and she feels, in the circumstances, since you are visiting and so forth, that you should be a guest.'

'That's very kind,' said Julia. 'But it really isn't necessary...'

'It's tomorrow night,' said Teresa. 'His actual birthday. The way it goes is this. First the family have their dinner in the hotel and then they join their guests in the function room for a bit of a ceilidh. Music and dancing and so forth. It's not a formal occasion at all and they would be more than happy to see you. Give it a little thought, why don't you?'

'Yes. Thank you.' This was unfamiliar territory for Julia. *She* was usually the person giving patient explanation; the bewildered parents were the ones stunned into monosyllabic response. She had no intention of going to any party and there wasn't a single thing she could think to say to Teresa except, 'Goodbye.'

Which made it all the more ironic that Bel should totter sleepily into the living room with the purple shawl around her shoulders and ask: 'Whoever were you talking to?' as if she'd been having a raucous conversation.

She nestled her phone inside its cover. 'I had a call from the landlady, that's all.' She would explain later, when she'd been able to mull everything over. 'You look like a character out of Dickens, darling.'

Bel warmed herself by the fire, then raised her head and spotted the glow of yellow on the draining board. 'Hey, has someone been bringing you flowers?'

Julia was glad to steer away from Teresa's news. 'Actually they're for you.'

'Really?'

'That's what he said.'

'Who?' Bel seized the bunch and scrabbled amongst the stems in search of a card. She didn't find one, but Julia noticed the movements of her left arm were not as fluid as her right.

'You didn't tell me you'd hurt yourself.'

'Oh… it was nothing. I got my arm trapped in a door, bruised it a bit. I did ask you for painkillers, remember?'

'You said they were for a headache.'

Bel blushed. 'Yeah, I'm sorry. It wasn't exactly a lie. It's just… I feel as if I'm forever having to give an account of myself. And I know you've been worrying about me – and I've been worrying about you too, which I guess makes us quits – but anyway, I'm fine. There's no real damage.' In disappointment, she added, 'I can't find a note. Was there any message?'

'I'm to tell you that Kieran was asking after you.'

'Kieran!' Bel shook her head and laughed. 'What a tease.'

'Isn't he the man you went out with?'

'No Mum, that's his brother. Tom's, like, a total idiot, always winding people up. They look quite alike you see and when I first met them I got them muddled because Tom had borrowed Kieran's jacket.'

'I don't follow,' said Julia. 'How can you be so sure it wasn't Kieran?'

'Because he wasn't the one who called for me yesterday. And because he's gay, I think.' She cradled the sheaf of tulips and their heads drooped gracefully. 'Did you ask him in?'

'I didn't think you'd want me to.'

'No, I wouldn't. I don't know what he's playing at. I suppose these are, like, an apology.'

'For what? Did he trap your arm in the door?'

'He didn't mean to,' said Bel quickly. 'It was an accident. The thing is, it was quite tricky yesterday because Clemmie, his daughter, hadn't met her grandparents before and then there's the race issue. I'm not saying his mother's a racist but it was quite a shock for her. I think my role was to defuse things but I probably made them worse and then we ended with this embarrassing scene when he invited me – and she had to agree – to some kind of get-together tomorrow night. A birthday party and—'

'A birthday party?'

'Yeah. I'd pretty much decided not to go. Only he can be quite persistent, so perhaps this is an… inducement.'

The chill from the stone floor seeped through the thickly woven rug, through the rubber soles of her deck shoes and crept along Julia's veins. Flickers and snatches of information coalesced and multiplied in her brain. 'What did you say his name was?'

'Who? Tom?'

'Yes. Tom what?'

'Oh, Farrelly. Tom Farrelly.'

Another smattering of rain at the window, the sighing of peat in the hearth; otherwise the silence was thick and dense as fog. Julia had to fight it to speak.

'It *is* him. How extraordinary. We've actually met…' She shivered. 'I don't know how I feel about that.'

'Mum, what *are* you talking about?'

Unsteady on her feet, Julia jogged the laptop on the table and its screen sprang back into life. In a continuous loop, the slide show repeated its sequence of shots. Waves swelled and burst into foam, the sun rose and dipped, chains of seaweed glittered like necklaces bedecked with fat jewels, footprints in the sand disappeared from one frame to the next. Neither Bel nor Julia spoke as the images played out in front of them.

Eventually Julia sat down again. 'I have just learned from Teresa Hogan,' she said, 'that Tom Farrelly was the name of the boy who nearly drowned here thirty years ago.'

'The one Matt's dad…?'

'Yes.'

'And he's the same one I know?'

'It looks like it.'

Bel stepped back, sat in the chair nearest the fire and let the flowers spill across her chest. No longer Little Dorrit, but a dramatic Ophelia. She rubbed her eyes vigorously as if things might look different afterwards. The effect was to turn the whites pink and raw.

'I don't believe it! You're kidding me!'

'Bel,' said Julia quietly. 'Why would I do that?'

She looked anguished. 'He never said anything.'

'Why would he? People don't generally go around telling you they almost died.' (Well, Bel did, but only because it was so recent.)

'Don't you see how weird this is?'

'Yes of course I do! Though I suppose I must have realised it might be a possibility. Coming across the family, I mean. This is a small place where everyone knows their neighbours. Teresa Hogan especially.'

But Bel was on a different track. She played with the fringed ends of the shawl, plaiting and twisting the threads. 'The really freaky thing,' she said, 'is that if Matt's dad…' (could she not bring herself to say William's name?) '…hadn't come to Tom's rescue, then neither of us would be here today. Instead of which we've both met each other and…'

Julia didn't want to know about the 'and'. The facts were leaping ahead of her. She closed her eyes, pinched the bridge of her nose, trying to recapture the brief moment the young man's hand had touched hers.

Bel continued to burble. 'To think that I came across Tom on the boat when he could have been anybody! This has to be more than coincidence, doesn't it? It must be Fate or something.'

'I'm never surprised by coincidence,' said Julia. 'It's much more common than you imagine, but I don't believe in Fate.'

'Oh, Mum!' Bel came to stand over her, bent her head down until their cheeks were touching, a single tear (Julia's) squeezing into a gap below the bone. 'I'm sorry. Is this really traumatic for you?'

'I don't know,' said Julia truthfully. 'He seemed a pleasant young man. Sensitive. Considerate. It was nice of him to bring you the flowers.' Bel didn't respond so she went on, 'To be honest, it's hard to know how to react. It happened a long time ago and I've managed to work through the grief, but… it's not just the personal loss one has to deal with. There's the wasted potential. The waste of a life, I mean. What William could have gone on and achieved.'

'Like a cure for cancer or something?'

'You just cling to the hope that something good will come out of the sacrifice.'

'Oh God, Mum, you make it sound like everyone's duty-bound to fulfil their potential.'

'Well, yes I suppose… in an ideal world…'

'That's an awful obligation.' Bel was biting her lip and still twiddling the ends of the shawl. 'It doesn't necessarily work that way. I mean, we can't all of us live up to expectations.'

'Darling, whatever makes you think I'm getting at you?' Julia could remember, from her own distant past, when she and her friends had experimented with purloined substances from the chemistry labs and shocked the neighbours, the lament of an older generation: 'We fought a war for you lot, you know. Good men died.' And how, with the careless arrogance of youth, they had brushed this reproof aside, the war already an irrelevance.

Bel said, 'I wasn't talking about me.'

'Who then?'

'It doesn't matter. Nobody special. It's just… it makes you seem so unforgiving.'

Julia considered this. 'I don't see how anyone who spent twenty years married to Leo Wentworth could be described as unforgiving.'

Their eyes met and they both laughed. Bel reached to clasp her mother's hand. 'It's okay, I won't see Tom again. His life's complicated enough and I wouldn't want to do anything to upset you…'

'What about the party?'

'I don't even know why he suggested it. I'm not bothered. I'd rather do something with you.'

'As a matter of fact,' said Julia, 'I've been invited too.'

21

The Visit

Ronnie had scarcely slept; her mind was in such turmoil. She had found the child a candy-striped duvet and tucked her into Nuala's old bed because, however obliging the McCauleys might be, they were not family. Ronnie couldn't be certain the child was family either – what proof did she have? – but she knew well enough how to conduct herself. Until there was clarity in the matter no one would be able to say she hadn't been dignified in her behaviour, shown loyalty to her son.

On Wednesday morning she gave the girl a plentiful breakfast of sausages and bacon rashers. She let her fondle the dog. JP was not usually welcoming of strangers, so it was possible that he scented some Farrelly blood, but Ronnie was wary of making an inference. 'It's good that you're not scared,' she said. 'Do you have a dog at home?'

'No,' said Clemmie with a profound sigh. 'I want a dog but we haven't any room and Mummy's too busy to take him for walks.'

'You poor thing,' said Ronnie, thinking how dreadful it would be to step out of your house and see nothing but tall buildings and pavements and traffic all around. Her life wasn't easy but at least she had her own sweet air to breathe. And on a sunny day when the hedgerows were aflame with the scarlet of the fuchsia and the gold of montbretia, the sight never failed to dazzle her.

Kieran had gone out on some mysterious errand, before helping his brother-in-law with the fencing; Pat was not yet up. While Clemmie and Tom raced around the yard, throwing sticks for JP in the rain, Ronnie answered a call from Teresa Hogan.

'Teresa! I was about to ring you myself.'

'Well I have some news for you,' said Teresa. 'You remember I told you about the English doctor who was staying? And how I had an idea she might be your man's widow? Well, I checked through the press cuttings with Mary and Breda and they agree. There's no doubt at all now.'

Ronnie closed her eyes. She had no wish to relive that nightmare period but she could see it unscrolling in her brain like a reel of Technicolor film. She'd been out on the tractor because getting in the silage was a trial at the best of times and you had to seize the dry days when they came. At the sight of her neighbours' frantic semaphoring, her thoughts had flown at once to Tom. She'd supposed at first he'd been run down: some stupid feckin' drunken bastard taking the bend wide, on the wrong side of the road, would have ploughed into his skipping legs so the boy rose into the air like an angel, like he was flying.

But no: the children were on the beach. Tom had been dipping his net into rock pools, prising the green translucent shrimps from their hiding places when the tide turned and the wind got up. Back in those days, very few of the locals learned how to swim. In fact it was unlikely anyone who knew the habits of the sea would have gone after him. It would have been madness to race across the sand, shed jacket and shoes and plunge into the turbulent water, thinking only to help a child in difficulty. The madness that takes a stranger.

'Sweet Mother of God,' said Ronnie. 'Why? Why did she come?'

'Who knows? A pilgrimage into the past? Seeking closure perhaps? I wouldn't have said a word but for the fact that your Tom is here also. It's an opportunity for their paths to cross.'

Ronnie gazed out into the yard. The rain was coming down more heavily but Tom was cavorting in imitation of the dog with a wild grin on his face. A free spirit, she thought fondly. The little girl was giggling and clapping her hands and stamping in puddles.

'Are you saying we should invite her tomorrow night?' she said. 'I suppose it will be easier to meet while there's a gathering.'

'That's an excellent notion,' said Teresa. 'You'd want to be hospitable. Your boys are both such handsome fellows and don't the women always fall for Tom's charm?'

'Will you ask her then, on our behalf? It may be better for you to make the introductions.'

'I will, no problem.'

'She won't turn us down?' said Ronnie anxiously. 'Only I tried to thank her at the inquest and she looked straight through me as if I wasn't there. Or as if she hated me.'

'Sure, she's a pleasant person,' said Teresa. 'She wouldn't be the sort to bear a grudge after all this time. I'll get on to it right away. Will I ring you back when I've spoken to her?'

'Actually,' said Ronnie. 'I was thinking of calling over to you myself, in about an hour or so. If you're going to be in?'

'I'll make a point of it.'

'I have something to show you.'

Although the prospect of the Englishwoman was a little unnerving, it wasn't worth dwelling on. Ronnie couldn't imagine anything that would eclipse the appearance of Clemmie. She stood in the boot room and called for the child to come inside.

'Look at the both of you!' she exclaimed. 'All wet and bedraggled. Worse than JP.'

'We was having fun,' said Clemmie.

'I'll have to put you in the bath again. We're going out.'

She would make her as presentable as she could. She had calculated that there'd be no need to parade her around the neighbours once Teresa had been informed. She wanted their reactions under control before the child was seen at the party and Teresa would be her most efficient conduit. She'd concocted the plan last night. (And run it past Anna and Nuala who agreed, though they hadn't shown much sympathy. 'Why are you even surprised?' they'd said.)

Clemmie said, 'Is Daddy coming with us?'

Tom kicked off his shoes. His shirt was clinging to his chest and, like Clemmie's, his curls had tightened in the damp. 'No,' said Ronnie. 'He's staying here with Pat. He doesn't need to be with us.'

He cocked an eyebrow. 'What are you planning?'

'A trip to Teresa's.'

'Hah! I get you. A conspiracy of the good women of the Dingle peninsula. Head them off at the pass.'

'Tom, you have flung us into this. We have to find a way of handling tomorrow night. Teresa will help out.'

His anger flared, but she knew it would soon expire, like the striking of a match. 'It never lets up, the gossip!'

'What do you expect?'

'Kath and Sean were fine.'

A pair of hippies. 'They're nearer your generation than mine. And as it happens we've had plenty else to talk about since the money troubles began. Not just yourself.'

'And my grand little girl,' he said, tickling Clemmie under the armpits until she squealed. To make her squeal even more, he shook his hair like a dog so drops flew about in a rain burst.

Ronnie was doing her best and she wasn't certain that Tom appreciated this. She passed him a towel, wishing she could take his wet head between her hands and rub some sense into it. 'You should change into something dry before you get a chill. Why can't you take better care of yourself?' It was a question, she thought, that could apply to everything he did. Including the feckless women he went with. 'And don't be leaving Pat on his own,' she added. 'So you can go chasing after girls in boats.'

'I promise I'll look after him. And when Kieran gets back we can go out for a jar. Dad must be going stir crazy stuck in the house. He could do with meeting up with some of his mates.'

'Go easy on the drinking, the both of you.'

'Mam!' his expression was half-wounded, half-teasing. 'Don't you trust us? Anyway, it'll help him get into form for tomorrow.'

Ronnie gave up. She marched the child upstairs and dunked her in the bath. She tied fresh ribbons to her plaits, knotted the laces on her trainers and drove over to the Hogans'.

Her car wheezed and snuffled like a sick pig. The passenger windscreen wiper had snapped off so she had to drive slowly and Clemmie's view was of the rain swishing down.

Ronnie said, 'We're visiting a close friend of mine. I know you will show her what a good girl you are.'

Clemmie, sitting pert and upright, thrust forward her chin and pouted. Ronnie wondered how much of a risk she was taking.

'Well now,' said Teresa when she saw them on the doorstep, bemusement quickly turning to curiosity. 'And who have we here?'

The child didn't let Ronnie down. 'My name is Clementine Alice Beaumont,' she said in a voice that was high, clear and polite.

'Clementine indeed?' Teresa's eyes sought Ronnie's and she did a little double-take, compressing her lips, arching her brows. 'Will you come in and tell me about yourself?'

Teresa's house bristled with knick-knacks. Ronnie had never understood why you'd want to take on so much dusting, but Clemmie was enchanted. She stroked the china ornaments and admired the model boats in full sail. Her meticulous tour of the items put Ronnie in mind of Tom's homecoming routine but she soon dismissed it. 'Watch you don't break anything,' she said.

'I'll put the kettle on while you get comfortable,' said Teresa. 'Back in a moment.'

She returned with a carefully arranged tea tray: porcelain cups and saucers, a plate of biscuits, a teapot under a quirky knitted cosy. Ronnie herself had been responsible for more tea cosies than she could count.

'Will you have a chocolate biscuit?' Teresa asked Clemmie. 'A little girl like you must surely love chocolate.' Then she blushed as if she'd said the wrong thing and the plate wobbled in her hand.

'She has some colouring books,' said Ronnie. 'Sit over there, Clem, with your crayons. And maybe Teresa will put the television on for you.' The animated squawks and screeches from the children's cartoons would drown out the details of their conversation.

Teresa poured a steady stream of tea into the cups. 'So who?' she began, although there was no need for Ronnie to answer her. She completed her sentence with: 'Well, hasn't your Tom always been one for springing surprises?'

'It was as much of a shock for him,' said Ronnie.

'That seems to be the way it goes these days. Children popping out of nowhere. Has she any of his talents at all? Can she sing?'

'I've no idea. He may have been taken advantage of.'

Teresa tut-tutted. 'What do you know about the mother?'

'Almost nothing! Her name is Monique, but he says she isn't French.' (Though how you could have a name like Monique Beaumont and not be a *bit* French baffled

Ronnie.) 'She comes from London, still lives there… I don't even know how they met.'

A million questions were bouncing around her head like rubber balls; she couldn't field them all. Flapping her hands in despair she knocked a magazine off the coffee table. It fell open at an advertisement for spa treatments: seaweed wraps and hot stone massage. She'd noticed that you couldn't move these days for promises of pampering. 'Look at this!' she exclaimed. 'The self-indulgence of it. Why on earth would you want to lie around with your face dressed up as a salad? A total stranger fondling you? It's not like in our day, Teresa. People think only of themselves.'

'You're right. It's different altogether. Girls will open their legs for anyone after a few drinks. They haven't had the terror put into them by nuns.'

'Ah, the nuns. Do you remember how our embroidery had to be just as fine on the inside as on the outside?'

Teresa nodded. 'Because God sees everything.' They were both silent for a moment, contemplating the strictures of their girlhoods. Then Teresa asked, 'So what happened? Did this Monique not tell Tom she was pregnant? Why would she keep the baby a secret?'

Kieran had hinted that Tom might have let the girl down, pointing out that he wouldn't want to look bad in his version of the story. But Kieran hadn't met her, so all was supposition. 'These modern women think they can cope without a man.'

'Well you would know the truth of that. What with Pat off on his projects, leaving you to manage the farm and the kiddies.'

'I missed him though. And he was providing for us. We were doing what was necessary to survive; we weren't acting against nature.' Still, she didn't want to paint the picture too bleak. 'Maybe the mother had help from her family. I gather it's some sort of nursing she does. But she was out of work for a while. That's why she pursued him.'

'And did he help out?'

'He tried.'

Teresa whispered, 'He has acknowledged the little one then?

'Well, that's why he brought her here to meet us.'

'But they've not done the test? For the DNA?'

'I don't think so. I have to tread carefully – this is a delicate matter.'

'You don't believe she's his?'

No, Ronnie didn't. How could she? This wasn't the way you acquired a granddaughter. She'd never cooed over the new bundle and mused: who do you think she looks like? She hadn't held Clemmie in her arms as a baby; she hadn't watched her learn to crawl or toddle or caught her first words. She'd been presented with a school-age child – well behaved, which was a blessing to be sure – but one who didn't in the least resemble her son. An alien being.

'For the moment,' she said. 'We have no choice. We have to make the best of it.'

'What does Pat say?'

'Pat is glad to have his family around him. We must concentrate on getting through the week now.' She gave a wry laugh. 'Do you remember how after Conor was born, Eoin asked Anna if they could send the baby back? He didn't want it to be a permanent fixture…'

'I know exactly how you feel.'

Was that possible? Could Teresa really understand when she'd never had kiddies of her own? Ronnie could scarcely recall a time without her children, she'd started so young. She was pregnant at twenty-three with Anna, not quite ready for babies – not ready either for the terrible loss of the twins she was carrying after Nuala. It took a while for a person to get over something like that. Perhaps that was why, when Tom came along, he was so close to her heart.

'You'll be worrying about tomorrow night,' Teresa observed. 'She'll no doubt cause a stir.'

'Don't think I don't realise that!'

'But she may not be the only one.'

Teresa went over to a cupboard and extracted a box. She sat down again with it on her knee as if it were a mysterious treasure chest. Evidently she didn't want her thunder stolen. She gave Ronnie a direct look. 'She said yes by the way.'

'Who did?'

'The widow.'

'Ah...'

'I rang her after I'd spoken to you. She was pleased to hear of the invitation. Very appreciative I'd say.' She passed over a photograph cut from the *Kerryman*. 'Here she is.'

Ronnie examined the picture; recognition stirred. 'Ah yes, she had a son herself.' At the hospital, waiting for Tom to be discharged, she'd seen the woman with a little boy in her arms. Her shorn hair had been sticking up in short spikes; her eyes had dark rings around them. She was accompanied by a pair of gardai who were taking her to the hospital morgue.

'Did I not tell you? He's a solicitor. I spoke to him myself when he rang.'

'You have to take a lot of exams to become a solicitor,' said Ronnie.

'You do so. He'll be a hard worker, for certain.'

'She must be proud of him.'

'Oh, she is. He's married now – she showed me a photo – such a beautiful wife, he has. And he calls his little one Danny boy, like the song. It goes to show, doesn't it, he's been able to overcome the loss of his father.'

Ronnie smoothed the strip of newspaper and handed it back. How could you possibly tell, looking at an innocent child, how they might turn out? As a parent you could only try your best. Don't make comparisons. Be grateful. Nevertheless she felt uneasy. 'But what shall I tell Tom? How can I prepare him?'

Teresa glanced over at Clemmie. 'How did he prepare you?'

The child must have sensed the atmosphere because she turned her head and regarded them both with a grave stare. Well she may be cute enough, thought Ronnie, and Tom may be trying to do the right thing, but it's quite obvious she doesn't belong here. She could never match the image of that other family; those perfect people Teresa had conjured up.

Then Clemmie gave her such a sweet smile her heart flipped over. She would have to harden it.

PART FIVE

THURSDAY FRIDAY

22

The Fallout

Leo knew her secret. Leo knew about the bunch of cells that were dividing and multiplying inside her: not yet a person, perhaps never to be a person. And Rachael had no idea what he might do with the information. He was a loose cannon. She wished she could have sent him packing after the barbecue, along with the kids, but he'd shown no inclination to move on.

On Thursday morning Danny was in a strop because he couldn't find the book he needed. He lay on the floor and kicked his legs and refused to fetch his trainers. 'I told you, Mummy, I *promised* I would bring the frog book into class today. We're growing them. It's *important.*'

Matt intervened. 'You can't grow frogs, Danny boy,' he said cheerfully.

'Yes you can. We've got them in the tank. They start as tadpoles and then they grow legs and lose their tails and...'

'But they're the ones who do the growing, not you, don't you see? Now let's have a competition. Mummy and I will hunt for the book and you hunt for your trainers. Put them on properly and we'll see who gets to the winning post first.'

'Where's the winning post?'

'The front door. First person to touch the handle is the champion.'

Dan scrambled into action; Matt sat back, satisfied, and sipped his coffee. He might have grown up in a dysfunctional household but he had faith in his own behaviour. Rachael and Dan alike were oversensitive, affected by a change in temperature, atmosphere or setting that Matt wouldn't even notice. She worried that she transmitted her neuroses and made Danny fretful, whereas when he was with his father, he was the strong and sturdy person he wanted to be. Inevitably, she was the parent who ran up and down stairs in a panic until she found the mislaid book. Danny clutched the door handle and crowed in triumph.

Leo missed all this. Leo did not rouse himself until long after she'd returned from the school run, when, at ten o'clock, he appeared and asked for a spare front door key. 'I meant to get one off you yesterday.' (Yesterday had been spent negotiating with the garage who'd rescued the Lotus and with Nick, the car's owner.) 'You don't want to be waiting in for me.'

She was tempted to retort that no way would she do such a thing. Instead, she handed it over, suspecting this was another of his ruses. 'The lock hasn't been changed,' she said. 'In case you were thinking of making a copy.' She regretted the sentence as soon as she spoke it.

The spare key was on a worn leather fob; it was probably the one he'd used himself. She watched uneasily as he examined it, lying in his palm. His eyes could twinkle in an avuncular way one minute and freeze into marble chips the next. Luckily this was his twinkling phase. 'Oh, Raquel, why would I do that? This is your house now.' He rummaged in the large satchel he carried with him, checking phone, laptop, wallet. He thrust the key into his trouser pocket and glanced at the wall clock.

'It's fast,' Rachael said. 'Five minutes.'

'Ah.' He helped himself to a banana, stripped its skin and took a large bite. When he'd finished chewing, he said: 'The advantage of having a reputation for poor punctuality is that no one ever worries if you're late.'

'Are you meant to be somewhere?'

'The Tate. But don't worry. I'll get a cab.'

She hoped he'd be out a long while. She hoped he'd meet an old friend or colleague (not Nick, obviously) who'd invite him for a meal and then, with luck, to spend the night. What she needed, to get through the next twenty-four hours, was a period of respite. She needed to order her thoughts, to prepare what she might say to the counsellor. Then, perhaps, her dilemma could be resolved.

She should not be scared of having children. Matt had persuaded her tenderly there was nothing to be frightened of. Dan's birth had been difficult, true, but she had coped well and the second time around was sure to be easier. But the problem wasn't just the process of giving birth: Dan's entire babyhood had terrified her. Now of course she loved him to bits, a love so overwhelming it submerged her. Where was the Rachael who'd been thrilled to leave the dull small-town life of her parents and move to a city as exciting and edgy as Liverpool? What had happened to her ambition and her joie de vivre?

She *was* still ambitious, of course, but the juggling was hard and another baby would make it harder. And she couldn't say any of this to Matt because there, ahead of her, was the example of Julia: a person of supreme competence, a person who could surmount all the obstacles life threw at her. No one had ever made a comparison – Rachael knew these misgivings were in her own head – but none of her achievements as cook, wife, mother could entirely banish her childhood sense of inadequacy.

It was tricky enough to talk to Matt anyway, aware of how much he wanted to have another child and of each missed opportunity to tell him the truth. Conception had happened far too quickly and she still felt the shock of disbelief. It was blindingly obvious the timing was wrong: they had only just moved, the house needed work, Dan needed to settle in his new school. Also, she was still establishing the catering business and would struggle to keep up momentum. That was why the purchase of the Rangemaster, though it might have *seemed* spontaneous – even wilful – was so significant.

She couldn't think of a convincing excuse to cancel her regular session with Emma at the swimming pool and gym, but she powered through the water and pounded on the treadmill so their conversation was limited by gasps and grunts. She recounted the trip in the Lotus and the broken exhaust as a funny story, but she didn't mention the buying spree and she cut short lunch on a pretext.

She arrived home to find Leo sprawling on the sitting room sofa and glowering at a half bottle of whisky on the coffee table. His legs were stretched out at such an angle it was almost impossible not to fall over them. The sofa faced the fireplace and above it was a large patch of wallpaper paler than the rest. A shadow line marked where his painting, *Conflagration 2*, had once hung. It was a curious juxtaposition: the presence of the man and the absence of the work. Although Rachael was responsible for its removal, she couldn't help wondering how it might feel to him, the sense of being erased bit by bit.

'You weren't out long,' she said.

He spoke with his eyes shut. 'Long enough.'

'I'd rather Danny didn't see you drinking. Spirits, I mean, at this time of day.'

'Is he here?'

'No, not yet. But he'll be home later.'

He grabbed the neck of the bottle. 'I'll have finished it by then.'

'Please, Leo.'

With his free hand he reached for her wrist and pulled her down beside him. 'Please what?'

'Please don't.'

'You think I'm out of control?'

'No... I just don't know what you want, why you came, what you're doing here.'

'That makes two of us,' he said. But he relaxed his grip.

She withdrew her wrist and rubbed at the bone. Her leg was trembling; she couldn't stop it. They both watched her thigh jiggling up and down until he put his hand upon it and leaned towards her. She could smell the whisky on his breath. Even before this visit, she had been a little fearful of him. You never knew where you stood: whether he was joking or serious, whether he was going to offer a compliment or a put-down, whether his laughter might blast into rage. Her own family life had been quiet – Leo would probably say buttoned up – appearances had been important; deviation suppressed.

'It's all gone belly-up,' he said.

'The meeting didn't go well?'

'You could say that.'

'What happened?'

He seemed grateful for the question, for the chance to rant. 'There'd been talk of a group show from the early days of the Liverpool scene – Henri and Cockrill and so on – through my generation and beyond, but it turns out they were just stringing me along. The Walker and the Bluecoat are much better at arranging that kind of thing. Tate's too fucking precious but you can get the spin-off you see. Posters. Calendars. Fucking fridge magnets if you're lucky. Forget prestige. Money, Raquel, that's what it's about. As a subject it's crass and boring as hell. But the stuff's undeniably useful.'

'I didn't realise you were short of money.'

'That depends on whether I've had a good day at the bookies'. Sadly, art does not make the artist rich – though hangers-on are another matter. And I'm talking about art per se, rather than the art of publicity. You're a clever girl. I'm sure you recognise the difference.'

She was finding it hard to relate his present black mood to the person who had sauntered out that morning. Yet – unaccountably, given his language, drinking and general demeanour – she felt sorry for him. Perhaps it was because he had recognised her as a fellow creative. A person who knew what it was like to make something and get little recompense, to balance on a see-saw of approval/disapproval, to hanker after appreciation, to be cast down by disappointment.

'Mightn't they change their minds?'

He leaned back and gazed at the ceiling. 'Well it's still floating around as an idea. The air is full of them, floating fucking ideas. Sponsorship's the key. Sponsorship or lack of it is the hurdle we come a cropper on. Tripped up. Fucked up.' Suddenly he swivelled towards her. 'In addition, it doesn't help to discover some of one's best work has been dumped at the back of a garage, halfway to the tip.'

She said guiltily, 'They're not dumped. We're waiting for Julia to collect them.'

'Really? Julia? Another one who's avoiding me like the plague.'

She probably has her reasons, thought Rachael. 'Couldn't you go back to France? Aren't you supposed to be giving workshops all summer?'

'Yes. Well. If there are any takers. They haven't exactly been inundated with bookings.' Her attention was reviving him, drawing him out of his slump. 'Why don't you fetch yourself a glass, Raquel? Join me. Let yourself go.'

Was he remembering the effect vodka had on her? She'd only drunk it out of defiance. She would have liked to recapture some of Tuesday's recklessness, but she knew it was a bad idea. 'No, I can't.'

'It isn't so hard if you try.'

'I really shouldn't.'

'Such a good influence,' he murmured and she didn't know if he was being sarcastic.

'So what's your antidote?'

'To?'

'What shall we call it? Frustration? Bitterness? That feeling of worthlessness? The pain of self-doubt?'

She hadn't expected Leo to be tarnished with self-doubt. She began to ease away from him. This was becoming too confessional. Where would it lead? She didn't want to find herself trying to explain her hang-ups and begging him not to tell Matt. 'I generally go off and make something.'

'Something to eat, you mean? Like what?'

'Oh... it depends.'

'Why is it,' he mused, 'that one imagines a cook to be plump and mumsy? Or did they just break the mould with you?'

'Do you want me to prove it?' she said.

'What?'

'That food gives more succour than drink.'

'Throwing down the gauntlet, are you?'

'If you like.'

'Fine then,' said Leo tipping more whisky into his glass. 'I accept.'

This was her chance to escape, to retreat to her familiar lair with its herbs and spices and potions. She would make something rich and sticky like Chelsea buns. She could lose her anxieties in kneading and folding the dough, melting the butter, letting the sugar bubble into a thick glossy syrup. There was nothing more comforting, more absorbing, to her than the slow wholesome process of baking. She could picture Matt's appreciative smile, Danny licking his fingers, the sunny illusion of togetherness.

She covered the Chelsea bun mixture with cling film and carried it upstairs to the warmth of the airing cupboard. From the sitting room she could hear the racing commentary and possibly a snore. Might Leo be sleeping? She wasn't going to check. She was satisfied with the way she had dealt with him – not so different from the way Matt had dealt with Dan at breakfast – but you could never tell what would happen next and she was wary of the unpredictable. So she picked up her phone and scrolled to Bel's number.

The call rang loudly into the void but no answer came, which puzzled her. In an earlier conversation Bel had rattled on about her 'mental' journey with 'two crazy guys'. (Since she had an unerring eye for the flaky and peculiar there was nothing new in this.) Could she be out gallivanting with her new companions? What did people get up to on the western edge of the Atlantic? Rachael wouldn't dwell on it; she'd keep herself busy. She measured sugar and water and melted them together at the stove, stirring the syrup with a wooden spoon.

Then impatience got the better of her. She wiped her fingers on a damp cloth and prodded Bel's number again, speaking slowly and clearly to the voicemail. 'Hi, this is Rachael. Look, wherever you are, Bel, whatever you're doing, you need to get in touch. Leo's still here – maybe he's really keen to see you, who knows? I don't have a clue! So can you *please* ring him and find out what this is about.' She paused and added, 'Though I should leave it a couple of hours if I were you. He's a bit sulky at the moment—' A shuffle alerted her; quickly she ended the message. 'Bye now.'

She turned to see Leo leaning against the doorjamb. He didn't comment on the evidence of her industry, the bags of flour and sugar and currants. 'Find out what this is about?' he said.

'I was trying to get hold of Bel. Isn't she the reason you came here? Apart from the gallery stuff...'

'Ah, yes. My poor little fledgling pushed out of the nest.'

'Some flatmate,' muttered Rachael, returning to the stove.

'Not the flat,' said Leo. 'The family home.' He spread his arms in an expressive arc. 'All this.'

'No one's pushed her out,' said Rachael. 'She owns about a third of it.'

He looked startled, but she ignored him because her syrup was producing hot spitting noises, turning too fast to caramel, to toffee, to ruin. She seized the pan and plunged it into the sink. Things went wrong all the time in the kitchen; she was used to it. But current events were preying on her, making her more vulnerable to setbacks. She could feel tears of frustration rising.

Leo said, leaving a distinct break between each word, 'Julia. Gave. This. House. To. Matt.'

'That's where you're wrong. As it happens, she gave it to all of us.'

'All of you?'

'Yes. In exchange for our place. We had to transfer the mortgage – you can't imagine how complicated it was – but we thought it would be worth it for Danny.'

'So Bel has part-ownership?'

'Yes.'

'Julia didn't tell me,' he said.

Rachael felt something snap. 'Why the hell should she? It's nothing to do with you any more.' Then contrition made the tears spill over. They were trickling down her cheeks. She was clinging to the edge of the sink; water was still running from the tap.

Leo was at her side with a piece of paper towel he'd ripped off the roll. He dabbed at her damp face. 'Look at me,' he said. 'Jousting at windmills. Tell me, Raquel, is it simple paranoia do you think? Paranoia that a mighty art institution can't be arsed with me? That my ex-wife might be penalising her daughter for being my offspring? My bloody seed and not his.'

'But she hasn't penalised her.'

'No. As it turns out.'

She knew her voice was muffled as he continued to mop away her tears. 'Is that what you thought? That she was deliberately favouring Matt and me? I can't believe it. Nobody would be that vindictive.'

'I'm sure Julia took a great delight in letting me think the worst. But it doesn't matter. It's a misunderstanding I'll be happy to forget.'

'So that's why you came here? You were after revenge?'

'I came because there was sod-all going on in France and Dorothy Culshaw was doing my head in. I was planning to give my support to Bel, but clever Julia pulled a fast one on me.'

'That's not how it happened.'

'No?'

'No! Why do I feel like we're caught in the middle of something we don't understand between the two of you?'

'Because we're a crotchety old couple with too much history? You shouldn't berate yourself, Raquel. It's so different from my day, the atmosphere in this house. You're spreading comfort and joy.' He smoothed her hair from her brow and then stooped to inhale it. 'Oh my God, don't you smell wonderful!'

The compliment was reassuring. She often worried that she'd not quite eradicated the taint of raw garlic, onion or shellfish. Once, coming home from a function where she'd been complimented on her butterfly prawns and parcels of sushi, she'd crept up behind Matt and put her hands over his eyes. He had seized her wrist and kissed her palm. 'I'd recognise that fishy smell anywhere,' he said. She'd pulled away from him, furious.

'What does it remind me of?' Leo went on. 'Toffee perhaps? A taste of childhood. Or those big glass jars in the corner shop window, full of boiled sweets.'

She said ruefully, 'You've no idea how bitter caramel gets when it burns. I cocked it up so I'm going to have to make it all over again.'

'Is that why you're crying?'

'Of course not....'

He was stroking her hair now, letting it slide through his fingers. 'It's getting to you, isn't it, this situation you're in?'

The tears came faster. The last thing she had wanted was his sympathy; nothing was more likely to make a person succumb.

Leo said, 'In general, artists aren't judgemental you know. Too concerned with their own vision to give a fuck about other people's. But you shouldn't go through it alone. Let me drive you to the clinic tomorrow.'

'Drive me?'

'It will have to be in your car. But I won't take risks. Don't want to make things any more fraught for you.'

She mumbled, 'It's only a consultation.'

'Whatever. I'll be your immoral support.' His arm tightened around her and it was with a wave of relief that she gave in and rested her head on his shoulder.

As he steered her away from the sink, she thought she glimpsed a face peering through the window. She hesitated, but Leo took her hand, drawing her towards the door, and she dismissed the fleeting impression as fantasy.

23

The Fire

Matt was looking for a peace offering. In John Lewis, after work, he idled through displays of kitchen equipment. The way to his wife's heart, he sometimes joked, was via a new set of measuring spoons. That was bollocks of course. Sharp knives were more like it. She frequently complained her knives were too blunt and the other day had railed at Danny for using one to carve his name in a tree (Dan had denied this). But a present of knives seemed more hostile than romantic. Finding nothing that caught his eye, he took the escalator. Halfway up he got a call from Bel.

'Is there a problem with Dad?' she said. 'Only Rachael's been leaving me cryptic messages.'

'I think he's hanging on till you get back, that's all. Why don't you ring her?'

'I did, but she's not answering.'

'Probably in the garden with Danny. Pissed off because Leo's not exactly been covering himself with glory. How's it going at your end?'

'Actually we've been invited to a party tonight…'

'And?'

He was on the second floor now, wandering through chenille upholstery, Egyptian cotton bed linen and Oriental carpets. The fabrics blurred before his eyes. Bel was spinning him an extraordinary tale about coming across the boy whose life his father had saved. How Julia was going to meet him too, at some sort of local gathering. He stumbled against a heap of rugs and sat down, stroking the rich pile absently. 'Don't go,' he said.

'Why not? I mean, I wouldn't if she didn't want to, but she *does*. After all, what harm can it do?'

He found it difficult to explain his reservations. 'I just think it's a bad idea. However tempting. Like meeting the recipient of a heart or a liver or something. Too many ways it could go wrong. So if you're asking my advice—'

'Well I'm not,' said Bel. 'And it's not like he's a stranger either. I already know him. I told you, we travelled down together, got on great. When I found out who he was it freaked me a bit, but he's just a guy, Matt. Why d'you always have to do this to me, get into your Mr Solicitor mode?'

'Bel, that's ridiculous. All I'm saying…'

'Ssh, Mum's coming. Catch up with you later.'

She rang off, disgruntled. Matt thought about texting – easier to express his argument in writing than speech – but an assistant was asking if he needed help. Grateful to be distracted, he allowed the man to spread out the rugs and talk him through the different colours and patterns. He didn't really want to think about Bel and his mother and this unexpected development; he was too far away to influence their plans. He banished Bel's news from his mind and dwelt instead on an image of Rachael rolled up in one of the rugs like Cleopatra; pictured himself unfurling her, making love.

'Right, I'll take it,' he said. Rachael could put it on her side of the bed, the first thing her feet touched when she got up in the morning. She'd appreciate his thoughtfulness.

'Do you want it delivered?'

Waiting for delivery would spoil the spontaneity of his gesture. 'Can you roll it up tight so I can carry it?'

'We'll see what we can do.'

It wasn't until the purchase was rung up on the till that he realised he'd misread the price tag and mistaken a five for a three. Two hundred pounds – hell, that was quite a difference, almost double, and he wasn't a spendthrift.

'It's beautiful this one,' said the woman waiting for his card. Matronly, with very black back-combed hair, she wore glasses on a chain around her neck. 'You've chosen well.'

After all, beauty had its price and what was two hundred pounds anyway in the scheme of things: a mere blip in his weekly billing target, a couple of nights out? And he was positive Rachael would love it. He slotted his debit card into the device and entered his PIN. A fraction later the card was declined.

Fuck. He'd forgotten about the cash he'd transferred to Julia and handed over to Bel. Obviously his pay cheque hadn't cleared yet. He produced a credit card.

'Bad timing,' he apologised. 'Sorry. But this should be okay.'

He was beginning to regret the whole operation – especially when the credit card was rejected too. *Please call for assistance* read the message on the screen. In alarm he rang the call centre and after he'd navigated the security questions, the man asked, 'So you're reporting your card stolen, are you?'

Matt said, 'It isn't stolen. It's still in my possession, but someone's gone over the credit limit and it definitely wasn't me. I just want you to check to see if there's an unusual pattern of spending and if there is I want to know why you didn't alert me earlier.'

'No,' said the man.

'You mean you won't tell me?'

'I mean there's nothing suspicious. The second card-holder on the account made a large purchase yesterday.'

'She did? Oh I see.'

'Is there anything else I can help you with today?'

'No, there isn't. Thank you.' He rang off and said to the matron with the black beehive, 'My wife and I... we seem to have been at cross-purposes. Apparently she'd already bought a rug and we don't need another. I'm sorry for putting you to inconvenience.'

'No worries, love,' said the woman in a kindly tone, which made him feel like a small boy who couldn't pay for his sweets. He tried to stalk away with dignity.

Since he now had nothing to carry, his hands were free to gesticulate. He rehearsed his self-righteous interrogation all the way home.

What the fuck did you think you were doing, Rach?

How the hell do you think it made me feel?

Why didn't you run it by me?

When were you planning to let me know you'd cleared out our joint account?

There was also the possibility that her motive had been inspired in the same fashion as his. A surprise she was storing up? No, he wasn't going to give her the benefit of the doubt. She'd been sulking for days now, putting the blame first on Bel and then on Leo. It was pathetic and childish and he had to have it out with her, to clear the air.

He hadn't realised he'd been swinging his fist until somebody caught it and twisted it behind his back. He'd just turned the corner from the station when he felt the yank.

'Gotcha!' Kelly grinned. 'Strong, in't I? Hey, I didn't hurt you? Dad says I don't know me own strength.'

He was glad he hadn't yelped, though it would have been more from indignation than pain. 'What do you want?'

'Don't be grumpy. What's up with you today? Why's everyone biting me head off?'

'Everyone?'

'Like, your dad.'

'Leo?'

'Yeah. Seems like he's off his head with something. Our mam used to get like that. Y'know, the eyes go dead. It's the downers that do it. Great big pupils but she didn't really see nothing.'

'Leo's not on drugs.'

'I'm not saying they're *illegal*. Whatever, he weren't talking to us. He were talking right up close to your Rach though.'

'When? What are you on about?'

'This afternoon, like.'

'You were hanging around here? Don't you ever go to school?'

Kelly shrugged.

'Why are you telling me this anyway?' said Matt. 'Are you my spy?'

She giggled. 'Can be if you want. Like, if there's stuff you ought to know…'

The offer was disconcerting, as if he might genuinely need a spy, as if he wasn't aware of what was going on inside his own house.

Kelly hopped on and off the kerb. She filched a biro from Matt's jacket pocket and rattled it along the cast-iron railings as if testing him. Overhead the trees were spurting into leaf, bright and fresh and green: spring was full of such hope. She dropped the pen back into his pocket and hooked her arm through his, clinging to it in a contradictory combination of bravado and dependency. He'd wondered before whether becoming a father altered the signals you gave off, announcing that you were now a serious, responsible person. Someone to be trusted. Though obviously not in the case of Kelly's own useless parent, or she wouldn't be attaching herself to his elbow.

She remained attached to him as they entered the drive. The side door to the garage was open and Danny's new bike lay on the grass with its wheels spinning. Nathan was running about in manic bursts, stopping to pick up fallen twigs, freezing for a second and then darting forward again. Dan usually greeted his father with delight. Today, crouched in the doorway of the garage, he ignored him. Matt glanced over at Nathan and his curious balletic performance; did he have some special ability to keep Dan enthralled? He was an odd boy. He had the same air of insolence as his sister, but also a degree of detachment, as if he were watching things unfold from a distance. He was astonishingly attractive: long black lashes fluttered onto cheeks that were clear and rosy, whereas Kelly's streaky make-up failed to hide her spots.

'Right,' said Matt. Feeling off-kilter all the way home, plagued by the women in his life, he'd been looking forward to Dan's rush of enthusiasm, his intense absurdist chatter – none of which was forthcoming. 'Time for your friends to go, Danny boy.'

'Can't me and Nath finish our game?'

Nathan came out of one of his frozen stances and leapt across the abandoned bike. He released his pile of sticks in front of Danny and both boys began sorting through them, searching for the best weapon, Matt supposed.

'It's okay,' said Kelly. 'I'll mind them for a bit if you want to go and change, whatever.' Her phone pinged and she delved for it.

He looked at his watch. 'Fifteen minutes,' he said. 'Twenty at most. Or Rachael will be on the warpath as well as me. She knows you're here, right? No arguments. No exceptions.'

By now she was texting, but she nodded vigorously. He went indoors.

The house was quiet. Rachael was sitting at her laptop, which she closed hastily at his approach. He'd meant to lead gently into his questioning but something ungovernable took over. 'Did you think I wouldn't find out?' He blurted the words, ugly and aggressive, because he couldn't lock them in any more.

A look of panic came into her eyes. He waited for her to deny that she knew what he was talking about. 'How?' she whispered.

He pulled the credit card from his wallet and brandished it.

'Oh that,' she said, leaning back in the chair. 'I've been meaning to tell you.'

'So what stopped you?'

'I'm sorry.' A flush was creeping up her neck. 'I shouldn't have got carried away.'

'Didn't you think how it would make me look? A complete tosser.'

'It's because he's so persuasive…'

'Persuasive? Who?'

Her voice dropped. 'Leo.'

'Leo!'

'I know that sounds pathetic. But I really didn't mean to cave in.'

'Cave in?' Matt had taken off his tie. He found himself wrapping it around his knuckles like a bandage or a rope he wanted to tighten. His mind was leaping in different directions. He couldn't understand the turn the conversation had taken. He hoped he'd misheard her. He knew other men envied him. He knew Rachael caught their attention, from sidelong glances to evident desire. She carried herself regally and she had those wonderful female nurturing qualities too. Who wouldn't fall for her? Lust after her? But surely not Leo… It didn't bear thinking of…

'Christ!' he exclaimed. 'Are you saying he made a pass at you?'

'Leo?' She was instantly on the defensive. 'For goodness' sake!'

'There's nothing between you?'

'Why on earth would you think that?'

'Isn't that what you were about to tell me?'

'Honestly, Matt! What a thing to suggest! You know I don't even like him much.'

'Sometimes,' he said, his tongue swelling in his mouth, slowing his speech, 'when one person is antipathetic to another it's actually an opposite attracts thing going on. Except they're in denial. And you did say he was hard to resist: i.e. irresistible.'

Her complexion paled; she shook her head.

How did we get off the point like this? wondered Matt. Was it because Kelly had alluded to spying, hinted at mysterious goings-on he should know about? 'It's funny,' he said. 'When I was growing up I liked the fact he was different from other kids' dads. More like a reckless older brother. He was a laugh, a bit off the wall. He let us do our own thing. But now, however plausible he sounds, I can see right through him. My mother had a lot to put up with. I never blamed her for not wanting to take it any more. He's an outrageous flirt and he thinks you're gorgeous, Rach. And I... How do you *do* this?'

Her upper teeth closed on her lower lip. Her hands lay quiescent on the laptop. Rachael could do reproachful very well; she could make him feel like a shit without uttering a word. She's wrong-footed me, thought Matt in a mixture of annoyance and admiration, and I've let myself be manipulated. Well she won't win this one. 'I'm sorry we got side-tracked,' he said, going to sit in the chair by the fireplace so there was some distance between them. He crossed his legs, toyed with the credit card. 'I don't know how the hell we got onto sex. I was talking about money.'

'So was I.'

'Oh.' He was confused. 'So why bring Leo into it?'

'When we went shopping in Southport,' said Rachael, 'he made out that I could do a deal, get a bargain I couldn't refuse. It was only afterwards I realised that's his technique: he has the fun and someone else carries the can. But it's not as bad as all that. I mean it wasn't a stupid purchase and I'd just been paid for the lunch do so I reckoned the money could go towards it. I didn't realise it would cause a problem with the credit card.' She spoke with conviction but her fingers pecked jerkily at the fabric of the cushion.

'Then why didn't you mention it?'

'I haven't had a chance. I've hardly seen you.'

'What was it anyway?'

'What?'

'Whatever you bought.'

'It wasn't an indulgence! I don't buy designer shoes or dresses, do I? There wouldn't be any point. We never go out anywhere these days.'

She was doing it again, attacking him. 'All I'm asking is what you spent the money on. I'm not going to criticise. I tried to buy something today and I couldn't. That's all. I know our finances have been complicated because I had to bail out my mother – which was my fault so it's not like I'm trying to apportion blame here. But I don't think we should have secrets from each other…'

She flinched at this. 'I know. Only—'

'What?'

'Nothing. I just wanted to choose the right moment so you wouldn't blow your top.'

'When do I do that?' Matt considered himself the most reasonable person he knew.

'You're doing it now.'

'Only with provocation for fuck's sake! So tell me.'

'It's a cooker.'

'A cooker?' Deflated, he had to muster some objection. 'But we've got a cooker.'

'This is a special one. It does so many clever things.'

'You used to tell me the skill lay with the chef.'

'That's true, but this will increase my efficiency. It will make things easier. It will—'

'Fine,' said Matt. 'So this has been a storm in a teacup then?'

She swallowed. He could see her jaw contract, the fluid line of her throat. Could they really have had this whole scene about a goddam electrical appliance? Or was it masking something else? What if he pushed her to another admission? And if it was to do with Leo, would he want to know? He remembered Julia's fierce determination to take a stand, the way the divorce proceedings had gathered inevitable momentum. She couldn't have pulled back if she'd tried. Sometimes he wondered if she wished it undone, if that's why her reaction to seeing Leo in France had been so extreme.

He was formulating a question, nothing too accusatory, when Danny rushed in and he lost his chance. Dan was doing a kind of hyperactive rain dance, which came upon him, Matt had noticed, after spending time with Nathan. He was making fitful leaps from left to right, with his feet together, following some idiosyncratic pattern of his own. His hands and face were grimy and smudged and he was covered with dust.

Rachael rose, as if glad of the interruption. 'Darling, you'd better go and give yourself a good wash.'

'Do I have to?'

'Yes. How did you get so filthy anyway?'

Danny cast down his eyes and put his dirty thumb in his mouth.

'And stop sucking your thumb. It'll be covered in germs.'

'Have the others gone now?' asked Matt.

'What others?'

'Kelly and Nathan.'

His shoulders hunched up to the tips of his ears. 'Dunno.'

'What d'you mean, you don't know?' Silence. 'Danny, what have you been up to?'

'Nothing!' Dan ran out of the room. They heard a collision on the stairs and Leo's muttered curses. The child continued upwards; the curses continued; then the man loomed frantic in the doorway.

'Get help!' he yelled. 'We have to put it out.' Dishevelled and bleary-eyed as though he'd just got out of bed, he was pulling on his shirt, which billowed open and unbuttoned.

Matt's mind performed somersaults. What was Leo doing in bed in the afternoon? Like Rachael, after their day out together. Could she have been sleeping with him? Was it why she hadn't answered Bel's phone call? No, that was too ridiculous!

Leo was shouting, 'I saw it from the attic.'

'Saw what?' He wasn't going to jump into action at Leo's say-so, but he could smell something acrid and went to peer through the French windows. 'Is someone having a bonfire?'

'Call the fucking fire brigade,' said Leo, hunting for the house phone, which had been moved since his day. 'This is no time to piss about. I have to get them out.'

Rachael's hands shook as she jabbed at her mobile.

Matt said, 'Get who out?' A pall of thick smoke was squatting like a thundercloud over the garden; it gave off an unpleasant toxic odour like burning rubber. He was being slow, stupid: the realisation when it reached him was horrific. He forgot his suspicions, his differences with Rachael. 'Christ, it's coming from the garage! Do you mean those kids, Nathan and Kelly? Are they in there?'

The smoke made it hard to tell how far the fire had progressed, but they could hear a crackling, see a flame jumping. The Passat, with its full tank of petrol, was parked in the garage along with old tins of paint, flasks of white spirit and citronella oil.

'Quick! We need to set up the hosepipe. Have we got a bucket somewhere?'

Rachael was urgently giving their address to the operator. Then she said, 'The only hose we've got is *in* the garage. And it's too big to put out with a bucket.'

'Then I'd better move the car.'

'You'd be mad to go anywhere near it.'

'If the tank ignites, it'll be a whole lot worse.' He grabbed the keys.

'Matt, wait! They've said they're on their way.'

'The fire brigade? How long?'

'I'm not sure. Five, ten minutes?'

'Ten minutes!' Shit, thought Matt. A person could suffocate in that time.

Leo hadn't hung around arguing. He'd bounded outside. Matt could see him wrestling with the side door, shirt-tail flapping, refusing to be beaten back by the fumes and the heat.

'We have to move the car,' he said again. 'It'll only take a spark.'

'Matt, you're nuts. Let the firemen do it. It's what they're trained for. They have masks and stuff. If you go into the garage now it will just be pointless heroics.'

Was that a jibe at his father? He said coldly, 'I'm not aiming to be a hero. But I'm not having those kids on my conscience either.'

'Kids?' said Rachael, following him. 'Leo wasn't raving about rescuing the kids!'

Matt ignored her. From the front of the garage he couldn't see what was happening at the back. He struggled to get the key into the lock with hands that were sweaty and uncooperative. His sense of sound, smell, taste, felt deadened, cutting him off from everything but the task in front of him. Getting the car out. There was a moment's triumph when he managed to crank the doors open but it was short-lived. He should have known – it was common sense after all – that his actions would create a draught, a current of air to fan the flames. They leapt about, joyously.

24

The Party

The function room was a long single-storey extension at the back of the hotel, bedecked with bunting and fairy lights. Vince arrived as the musicians were setting up – a keyboard, a squeeze box and a couple of fiddles. His leg was mithering him again, sending shooting sensations down his calf. Cramp was his diagnosis. He wasn't going to see the quack over something so trivial, but he needed to sit rather than stand. There were no high stools at the bar – this was not an occasion to turn your back on the room – so he eased himself into a chair against the wall, not far from the band, beating tempo on his knee. The family were still at their celebration meal, in the dining suite, but Pat's friends were piling in, jostling good-naturedly to fill their glasses.

He spotted the English doctor and her daughter as they entered, with that diffident air of guests uncertain as to why they were asked and why they had come. The mother, trim but tense, was smart in trousers and a tailored shirt. She was the type of woman (erect posture; compact, agile limbs) who would do well on a horse. He couldn't picture the daughter on horseback. Her movements were unguarded. She collided with old Brian Malone and sent his Guinness sloshing over the side of his glass. Draped about in exotic colours, she hovered at her mother's side, iridescent and fragile as a dragonfly.

Vince bent to massage his calf and noted with surprise that he was wearing odd socks. He couldn't think how this had happened. Teresa paired his socks into neat rolls and stacked them side by side in his top drawer. Surely his Teresa wasn't losing her touch? Had she been distracted by her detective work? Raking up the past. He couldn't understand why she didn't let things lie, why she felt compelled to take it upon herself to broker a reunion. She hadn't even allowed the business with the little black girl – and hadn't *she* caused a fine buzz of gossip? – to deflect her.

Teresa was presently at the far side of the bar, rearranging the buffet. She had strong opinions on the capabilities of the staff (teenagers taken on for the night with no proper training). Apparently they should have established a regular sequence with the platters of sausages and drumsticks, spring rolls and sandwiches and salad trimmings – but there was no point trying to explain to people who wouldn't listen. It was easier to do things yourself.

Vince watched his wife with a mixture of admiration and contentment. She meddled, it was true, but she made life flow more easily too. The socks were an aberration – or possibly his own fault entirely. She caught his gaze as she dusted her hands together and gave an eloquent toss of her head. (She'd been earlier to the salon and a copious blast of spray ensured that not a hair faltered.) He knew this was a reproach because he wasn't circulating, so he pretended to shout across to Frankie on his accordion. Frankie had his eyes shut to the strains of the 'Black Velvet Band' and wouldn't have been able to hear anything anyway.

When Vince looked for Teresa again she had swooped down on the lady doctor. He had the distinct impression she was talking about himself and this was borne out when the daughter drifted over. She stood above him in her glowing colours like a figure stepping from a stained-glass window.

He jumped to his feet, quelling the tremor in his leg, because he wouldn't want to be thought ill-mannered.

'I'm Bel,' she said with a pretty English accent and a smile that lit up her face. 'And you're Teresa's husband. We've been very well looked after.'

'She's a capable woman,' he said, taking Bel's hand and pumping it. 'How are ye finding the place?'

'Oh the cottage is just lovely. And everyone is so friendly... I mean, you know, like inviting us tonight. You don't expect to be included in parties or whatever when you're here for such a short holiday. Although Mum was a bit apprehensive to be honest...' She paused and started to twist the ropes of beads hanging around her neck: a curious mixture of beads and feathers, in fact, that made him think of witchcraft. 'She hasn't been able to relax all day. We've been driving around the Ring of Kerry because we had to keep moving. All the way to Waterville, but we couldn't stop for more than a few minutes anywhere. We'd hop out of the car, take in the view and half a dozen photographs, hop back in again and Mum would go on driving. We came back on a deserted road through the mountains, it was *so* in the middle of nowhere, like you were totally enclosed in this vast secret valley and the whole magical place was yours. Absolutely amazing. I think the range was Macgillycuddy's Reeks. I had to learn that so I could get it right. It's such a wonderful name: Macgillycuddy.'

'You covered a lot of ground,' said Vince.

'Yes I know. Because she wouldn't *stop*. Because she's so wound-up. But I think everything will be fine. Did you know that I met Tom already? On the boat? It was through Clemmie actually. She's here somewhere, isn't she?'

It seemed to Vince that the daughter with her twirling pendants and tumbling words was more excitable than the mother, who was listening to Teresa and calmly sipping her wine. The band finished their tune and as they started up another the double doors to the dining room opened and the family began to come through. (As usual on these occasions, the timing of the meal had over-run.) The two little boys raced ahead, dipping and weaving at knee-height like puppies, while Anna chased after them with difficulty on account of the sandals, seemingly attached to her feet by a single slender thread. Pat and Ronnie, both, were being mobbed by their friends who earnestly wanted the couple to know how delighted they were and what a grand spread it was, Pat would have loads more birthdays like this one, and weren't they all having great craic and who was next in line for a drink?

The last time Vince had seen Ronnie she'd been fatigued and dishevelled like a creature at the end of its tether. Now she was magnificent in a deep crimson dress with a splendid cleavage. She was stout to be sure – you wouldn't lose *her* in a bed – but she was an imposing woman. People were saying it was her sheer determination that had kept Pat going, pulled him through such gruelling treatment. She was mightily attached to her menfolk. If she had a weakness – and didn't everybody? – it was the way she treated that son of hers. But that's how it was with parents. They didn't have the objective view.

The floor of the function room was polished parquet, good for dancing and for children to skid about in their socks. Bel was glad she was wearing flat pumps. She wouldn't want to risk another fall; tonight in itself would be enough of a balancing act. She was still aggrieved at her brother for not being more supportive. Bloody Matt, she'd cursed. Overcautious as ever. It had been the same when they were growing up. There was no point in consulting him: she had to get into a scrape *first*, then she knew he would cover for her. This afternoon she'd have welcomed some advice in handling the situation, but wimping out and telling her not to come was plain pathetic.

She was struggling to decipher Vince Hogan's country accent (which was why she'd been rabbiting on about their excursion) when Kieran approached. Vince hailed him with great enthusiasm, embracing him heartily and running through an exchange of what might have been pleasantries or insults but which defeated Bel. Kieran turned to her.

'It's good to see you here,' he said. 'I wasn't sure we'd persuaded you to come.'

'Oh no, I was keen. Honestly. We're crap in England at these multi-generational dos.'

'True enough.' He nodded towards the keyboard player. 'But do you not think the music's shite?'

When she laughed in agreement, he put his hand at her elbow and steered her towards a quieter part of the room. Vince, sinking back into his seat, was soon joined by another elderly man with a thatch of white hair and a tweedy jacket that could have been woven from bracken and peat.

Kieran leaned on the sill of the window; the panes of glass were fogged with condensation. 'Tom's been overdoing the drink,' he said. 'I wanted to warn you.'

'Is it nerves, d'you think?'

'I doubt he'd admit to it.'

'That's stupid. It would be perfectly understandable. I was totally freaked myself when I heard.' She clinked the ice in her Magners. 'But I'm going back to Coke after this.'

'Tom doesn't need much of an excuse to hit the bottle.'

She searched the crowd, but couldn't see him. 'Is it very noticeable?' she asked. 'I mean, if you were someone who'd never met him before, would you think: what a complete tosser?'

'Isn't that what you thought yourself?'

'On the boat?'

'Yes.'

'Well, in a way. But…' But she was an idiot, wasn't she? She'd been beguiled by Tom's louche demeanour, by his sudden spurts of sensitivity, his undeniable good looks. 'I guess he spiked my interest too. And he's lovely with Clemmie – she adores him, doesn't she?'

'What is it with women!' exclaimed Kieran. 'Why are they so easily fooled?'

'We're not fooled by the man,' said Bel. 'It's our hopes that are unrealistic. But you could say that of anything, couldn't you? And if you got too cynical you'd never make any improvements at all. I wouldn't expect it of you.'

'What?'

'Cynicism.'

He laughed. 'And why not? Can't I be as jaundiced a sod as the next person?'

'Well I just thought… I know the Church bangs on about hell and damnation but surely a priest needs to believe in the goodness of people. I mean I know you're not actually a priest but if you had the training and everything…'

Kieran stared at her. 'You didn't believe all that baloney?'

'Why wouldn't I?' She squirmed a little as she spoke, recalling the nonsense stories she'd told to strangers to help enliven a journey. Those people had believed her. And she had half-convinced herself. Where was the harm in trying on a new identity and parading it to someone you would never meet again? But this was different – because they *had* met again, more than once, and because the brothers had ganged up on her. The dice was unfairly loaded.

'Okay,' he said. 'I'm sorry. We shouldn't have teased you, but it wasn't a total lie. I did very briefly think of going into the Church, but I was being contrary. You see Tom was considered too good to be a farmer so I was intended to take over the reins. And this was my form of rebellion. A good Catholic, like my mother, wouldn't argue with God's calling.'

'Sounds a bit extreme!'

'I think I believed it at the time, but it didn't take me long to find out I was wrong. I'm not much better at taking decisions than my brother, am I? Fled to England and got married far too quickly.'

'Married?' Bel was finding the whole conversation topsy-turvy. She was beginning to feel hot and sticky, but she couldn't take off any layers because she didn't want to expose the savage bruising on her arm, its appearance worse today than when it happened. People would think she'd been assaulted. 'But you both told me you weren't.'

'Divorced,' he explained. 'So you see, that wasn't a lie either. I won't slag her off, I'll just say we were incompatible.'

'So do you mean...' said Bel slowly.

'What?'

'I just thought, because of the priest stuff...' Her voice tailed off. What did it matter if Kieran wasn't gay? It was Tom who had kissed her. Twice. Though, really, what was the significance of a kiss, however passionate, when shagging was as commonplace as shopping?

'Ah,' he said, 'I see one cliché following another.'

'But Tom said—'

'You don't want to pay heed to any remark of Tom's.'

'No, I realise that now.'

Kieran's thumbs were looped into his belt, his fingers tapping a rhythm in time to the music. Bel found herself staring at them for no better reason than that she didn't want to look at his face. She could feel him watching her intently. 'So,' he said after a while. 'Did you get the flowers?'

'Yes, but how...?'

'You were still sleeping and your mother didn't want to wake you. I'm not much good at these things but I do think tulips have a fine shape and yellow is a colour to cheer you up. I'm not enamoured of those elaborate, fancy contrivances they fix up with staples and raffia and God knows what, but I hope you didn't think it was sheer meanness because it wasn't...'

'*You* brought the flowers?'

'Did your mother not tell you?'

'Well yes, she did, only...'

'Only what?' He sighed in a resigned sort of way. 'Did you think I was overstepping a line? You've already a poor opinion of us, no doubt.'

Bel squirmed again. Kieran had behaved with absolute propriety from the moment he had offered her the lift. He'd shown concern for her injury. He'd made more effort than Tom to unite Clemmie with her grandparents. He was totally sound. And, foolishly, she had overlooked all this in favour of the flashy allure of his brother. 'No!' she insisted. 'I have a very high opinion of you! I feel bad because I should have thanked you from the off. My brain must be full of holes. I'm so sorry. Look, can we start again? Thank you, Kieran, for bringing me tulips. I love tulips. And you should have stayed. I wish you had.'

25

The Meeting

Julia was ill at ease, wishing she hadn't come, that she hadn't let Bel persuade her. She had managed to escape Teresa and was planning to slip out to the car park. Earlier that day she'd had another text from Leo:

The world is full of fuckers. I miss you.

Once, her instinct would have been to console him, but those times were over. She didn't know what game he was playing and she'd been debating whether to reply. A few minutes in the cool evening air, away from Bel's likely interference, might enable her to compose a message more grown-up than piss off and leave me alone. But before she could reach the door she was waylaid by a tall, striking woman draped in folds and pleats of cream silk like a Greek statue and wavering on high-heeled sandals.

'Anna Malone,' said the woman, holding out her hand.

'I'm Julia—'

In the middle of their handshake a small boy ricocheted into Anna's legs. She swept the child into her arms, fished a paper tissue from her clutch bag and wiped his nose.

Julia waited; Anna apologised. 'Sorry about this. He has the catarrh permanently.'

'Does he drink a lot of milk?'

Anna blinked in surprise. 'Well to be sure he does. We can't be giving him Coca-Cola to rot his baby teeth.'

'It can be mucous-forming, that's all,' Julia said. 'He may be having problems with his adenoids. Children usually grow out of it as the adenoids shrink.'

Why was she doing this? She'd made it a rule never to give advice unless asked and even then it would be limited to suggesting the person visit their own doctor. In effect she was stalling, stalling because she now realised who this Anna Malone was. She'd seen her emerge from the private room where the Farrelly family had been dining.

Anna set down her son and adjusted the pleated fabric that had slipped from her shoulder; her complexion gleamed under the dancing lights.

'You are the Englishwoman,' she said.

It was a neutral, irrefutable statement. Julia was relieved not to have to broach the connection herself. 'Oh goodness. Do I stick out so badly?'

'Tis only that we're not at the height of the tourist season yet. Sometimes you can hardly get by on the pavements. We have so many visitors wandering about they merge all together. And Teresa Hogan is proud to be a source of information.'

Julia wondered what was going through the woman's head, whether she felt guilt or remorse. The sisters had been in charge of their little brother that day on the beach. Was she the one who had come to the inquest?

'So you are here with your daughter,' Anna was saying. 'And would you believe it, she had already met my brother?'

Over Anna's shoulder, Julia could see Bel leaning against the wall beside a window, deep in conversation with the young man who had called around to see her yesterday. Cheap, Julia had thought at first sight of the tulips, but then amended her reaction to: simple, unshowy. There was something to be said, after all, for gestures that were understated. There were far too many people these days leaping about, yelling: Look at me! She recalled taking the flowers off him, the brush of their fingers and Bel telling her afterwards this was Tom Farrelly.

'On the ferry,' said Julia. 'Extraordinary.'

'He doesn't visit us often. Neither of them. Kieran's been in England for years too. He married a girl from Yorkshire and was settled there for a while. But the marriage fell apart as these things do. No wee ones thank goodness. But maybe your daughter has also told you about Clemmie?'

Julia could see the little girl dancing with her cousins – the children had taken over the dance floor and no adults had joined them yet.

'Yes, she said it was a difficult meeting. I can imagine.'

Bel had been quite specific on the awkwardness of the encounter. She'd also insisted it wasn't Tom's fault he only found out about his daughter after his father's cancer was diagnosed and had thus delayed the news. It wasn't a good beginning, but you had to be realistic. Julia was glad to be able to observe him from a distance, to note the thoughtful way his brow wrinkled, the gentle stroke as he stretched to touch Bel's arm, the way he made her smile.

The band could keep a tune going even while quaffing their pints (frequently replenished) and the bouncing rhythms were beginning to drive her a little mad. She tried to block out this background noise by focusing on Bel and the Farrelly boy. He was not really a boy, of course, but an adult like Matt – though there were occasions when this fact bemused her, when she'd confuse Danny with Matt at the same age. The years would contract and she'd slip though this crevice of time to find herself engaging with a solemn brown-eyed child whose desire to please was quite heart-rending.

'They seem to be getting on well.' She didn't want to say anything that might be misconstrued. She needed to meet him and shake hands formally so they could put their acquaintance on a suitable footing. Until then it was like ploughing through shifting sands. You could never quite tell where you stood.

Anna turned and followed her gaze. 'He's always been the shy one,' she said. 'I mean, within our family. We none of us lack the ability to come forward and put our point across, but Kieran, well, we used to call him the listener.'

'Kieran?' There had been a dying away of the music, a semibreve's intermission and now they were striking up again. There was no doubt she'd heard the name correctly. Besides, it was how he had introduced himself. It was only Bel, in her scattiness, who'd insisted it must have been Tom. Was it possible, Julia wondered, that she'd got the brothers confused somehow, that she didn't *know* which was which?

'So tell me, Anna,' she said, squeezing the stem of her wineglass. 'Where is your brother, Tom?'

'Ah well now...' Anna raked the room, then settled on a figure at the bar. She gave a light dry laugh. 'He's where you'd expect to find him, is he not.' She tried to attract his attention with a wave but the man she'd indicated didn't see her. With a glass held high in each hand he began to zigzag through the throng, aiming for the couple by the window. She called out but he didn't hear.

'Don't put yourself to any bother,' said Julia. 'I can go and join them.'

She'd half expected the automatic response: No bother at all, but another guest, an older man in a waistcoat with shiny buttons that gave him the look of a leprechaun, curled his arm around Anna's waist; she squealed and returned the embrace. Julia manoeuvred herself away. She wasn't quite ready to interrupt Bel. She wanted first to get a feel for the young man who had grown up with this charmed life – the life snatched back and restored.

She watched Tom reach his target and set the drinks with careful deliberation on the windowsill. Stepping away, he staggered and overbalanced. She assumed he'd slipped on some spillage on the floor. At any rate, Bel's arms shot out to save him from falling because the other brother, Kieran, had turned aside. What Julia had not expected was to see Tom, in response, crush Bel against the wall and glue his mouth to hers.

She was both shocked and astonished. Bel had sometimes, in the past, told her more than she wanted to know about her sexual adventures. Sitting cross-legged on a floor cushion, describing her night of bliss in grand passionate gestures – or storming through the hallway, banging doors, red-eyed with weeping – little was left to the imagination. Latterly she had matured. Julia recalled her assurances that she'd be taking a suitcase full of condoms to Africa (ironic in the circumstances), that there was nothing for her mother to worry about.

But not *this*, not *him*. The pair had only met a few days ago; surely, now that Bel realised his identity and the significance of it, even she, with her tendency to rush unsuspecting into trouble, would halt at this point. Then, still gazing in bewilderment, it became apparent to Julia that Tom's advances were unwelcome; Bel was trying to push him away.

She felt the tension knot along her spine. She'd wondered, fleetingly, through the years, what had happened to the boy William rescued. If diagnosing a child with a heart murmur or a potential tumour, the thought would skim across her consciousness that saving his life might only have been a temporary reprieve, that he might not even have reached adulthood. But she didn't dwell on his prospects; speculate. Yet here he was, in person, a few yards away: tousled and boorish, thrusting himself at her dismayed daughter. This was not a moment she had ever expected to reach.

Perhaps it was the contrast with the fantasy in her head – the polite greeting, the grave exchange of pleasantries – that coiled the anger so tight inside her chest she thought she would explode. She should leave; she should turn on her heel and get out of this noisy overheated place. A fine rain had been misting the air when they arrived, so soft it didn't so much fall as hang in suspension, webbing their faces like gossamer. In the mild Irish night she could breathe deeply, take stock, calm down. Her expectations had been too high: don't interfere.

Then she recalled the bruising on Bel's arm, the story about trapping it in a door. This man was the worst type of all, an irresponsible father, a bully and a drunk: sending his brother round with flowers to buy Bel's silence, and now assaulting her in public, not caring who he offended. Assault was possibly too strong a term, but Julia was not in a rational mood. She was convinced Bel was struggling to fend him off and felt an over-riding compulsion to protect her.

An image surfaced of Leo with his paramour: the girl who had delighted in being indiscreet. She could hear buttons popping and jeans unzipped, the clink of the tell-tale earrings. Her outrage swelled. She barged through a nearby knot of drinkers, squaring her shoulders for confrontation. Her voice was higher pitched than she intended.

'Whatever do you think you are doing?'

Tom was nuzzling Bel's neck and ignored the interruption. Bel said, 'For God's sake!'

Kieran moved to allow Julia access. He didn't speak. She waited.

Tom raised his head and a wide sheepish grin sliced across his face. He swayed a little.

'You looked as if you were in difficulty,' Julia told Bel. 'I was worried.'

'Not at all! You must be seeing things.'

'I think we ought to go.'

Bel rattled her bracelets. 'But we've hardly been here five minutes and you haven't even been introduced.'

Tom's linen shirt, much creased, was hanging half in and half out of his trousers. Stealing his hand from Bel's torso, he held it out. 'Tom Farrelly,' he said, in a throaty lilting voice. 'Pleased to meet you.'

'Is that so?' Julia would not be mollified. She'd spent too much of her life succumbing to hollow charms; besides, she enjoyed a fight. And, even allowing for the fact that Bel might like rough sex, the whole scene was distasteful. 'And do you think your behaviour is appropriate?'

'Excuse me?' His hand fell back to his side.

'Mum,' hissed Bel. 'Please!'

At the corner of her vision she was aware of Kieran shuffling his feet, as if about to intervene, but then deciding to back away. They were left in a triangle – Bel, Tom and Julia – while the accordion spun out its rhythms, the children skated on the parquet, and the guests balanced glasses and sandwiches and regrouped, oblivious to the three figures at the edge of the room.

'I know it's old-fashioned,' said Julia, 'the idea of decorum in a public place but I thought this man was threatening you, Bel, and somebody had to stop him.'

Tom's pupils were dark and dilated. Whether from fear or defiance, she couldn't tell.

'This wasn't what I had in mind,' she went on, 'when I heard we'd been invited here. I guess that shows how many mistakes have been made along the line.' She almost choked on her tongue and had to clutch herself tightly to stay upright.

Bel moved swiftly to her side. 'Tom's just as anxious as you are,' she whispered. 'It's a big deal for him too. That's why he's been drinking. Probably.'

'Probably?' echoed Julia.

'I don't know what you think you saw.' Bel's cheeks were stained pink. 'But there's nothing between us.'

'You were struggling.'

'No I wasn't.'

'Are we upsetting you, Bel's mother?' said Tom. 'I have terrible trouble maintaining my reputation you know, but we're getting on grand, isn't that so, Bel?'

'You should call my mother by her name: Julia.'

'Julia, will you forgive me?' He tried to clasp her hand again and this time she let him, though his fingers felt clammy and slippery as fish.

From the corner of her eye, she could see a woman in a red dress advancing. Tom rocked on his heels and Julia snatched her hand back. Could he not even stand up straight?

The woman in red, an older larger version of her daughter Anna, joined them.

Julia said to Bel, 'I think we should get our coats.'

'Surely you're not leaving!' exclaimed the woman. 'Before we've had the chance to get acquainted. I've heard so much from Teresa and I want to say how pleased we are you could join us tonight. I'm Ronnie Farrelly and – oh my goodness!' She spotted Julia's empty glass. 'Do you not have a drink now?'

'I've had enough, thank you.'

So had Ronnie, as far as she could see. She had heightened colour and a sparkle about her, courtesy of the gin and tonic fizzing in her grasp. 'Tom will get you a fresh one,' she insisted. 'White wine, was it?'

'I don't want Tom to get me anything,' said Julia.

'Ah, go on now. A mineral water at the least?'

'No, truly. I shouldn't have come in the first place.'

Unexpectedly her shoulders heaved. Ronnie put down her gin. Bel was extending her neck, flapping her hands, making clucking noises like someone trying to calm a chicken. Ronnie's perfume, floral, intense, was too close and Julia had to fight to breathe.

'What are you doing?' she said, as the other woman's arm encircled her.

Ronnie took an ungainly step back as if she were unaccustomed to wearing heels. Her brows knotted in a puzzled frown. 'I only wanted to welcome you.'

'Thank you, but I'm not sure your family is one I want to be welcomed by.'

Julia's mind was fixed on the beach at Doonshean, the negligent teenage girls and the mother who'd left them in charge of the miscreant. She saw Matt as a small boy, starting school, having to tell strangers he had no father. 'My dad was a hero,' he would say proudly. The other parents, in ignorance, assumed he was fantasising.

'I had hoped,' she admitted, since Ronnie was staring at her with her jaw slack, 'that things would have turned out better than this.'

'How do you mean, better than this?'

'I'd rather spare you the details.'

'Oh really,' said Ronnie, puffing her chest forward, her eyes blazing in a mixture of indignation and self-pity. 'How is it that you are so magnanimous towards us? Have you heard perhaps that my husband was critically ill?'

'Yes I did. And I'm sorry.' There's no dignity in pain, Julia allowed; sometimes the sufferer just needs to scream. 'But your son has been violent to my daughter and—'

'Violent? Tom?'

'Show her your arm, Bel,' said Julia.

Bel hid it behind her back. 'Look, this has nothing to do with him.'

'You told me he shut it in a door.'

'That's not exactly what happened.'

Tom's lips twitched but he didn't manage any explanation. It was the drink. Julia knew precisely how alcohol dulled the senses and the reactions. She guessed he'd been drinking when he battered Bel's arm. 'Show her,' she said again.

'I already know about it,' said Ronnie. 'He brought her to me for an ice pack.'

'That doesn't mean he didn't assault her. It's not uncommon for attackers to bring their victims to A&E and say they fell downstairs.'

'She tripped over a ladder in the barn.'

'That's not what I heard.'

'Oh, for God's sake!' exclaimed Bel. 'Stop talking about me as if I'm not here. I'm sorry I misled you, Mum. It *was* an accident. It did involve a ladder. I fell off one, as it happens. But it wasn't Tom's fault.'

'I don't suppose anything is ever Tom's fault,' said Julia. Ronnie's discomfort was palpable, but she was beyond empathy. Crushing disappointment wasn't the half of it.

It was Tom who broke the stalemate. His hand curled into a fist, which confirmed Julia's suspicions. But he didn't swing it. He made a curious strangulated sound and charged bull-like out of the room. Ronnie started after him, but her daughter Anna waylaid her.

'Leave him,' Julia heard her say. 'Let the fresh air sober him up. He'll be back when he's ready.'

'Oh, Mum, what have you done?' said Bel in anguish.

'I can't think why I ever agreed to this. Come on, we should cut our losses. Leave.'

'But that's so rude, when everyone's been so generous...'

'Sometimes things don't work out,' said Julia. 'This was one of those ideas that was misconceived from the start.'

Even so, she hesitated. If they left now they might find Tom Farrelly among the smokers in the doorway and she would do anything to avoid a second confrontation. The room was aglow with coloured disco lights and it was hard to make out another exit. As she searched for one she saw Tom return, plunge into the festive crowd and scoop Clemmie up from the dance floor. The girl was too stunned to protest but Anna called out. When he ignored her, she tried to chase after him but those high strappy sandals were treacherous and one flew off, impeding her. Tom didn't break step; with Clemmie riding high on his shoulder he swaggered into the night.

26

The Morning After

Bel woke to the sound of drumming. The insistent beat echoed the throbbing in her arm and her head. She knew what it was without opening her eyes. Rain. The Irish had so many types of rain: the soft misty drizzle that hung in the air, the wind-whipped sheets that infiltrated every garment, and the steady downpour that was pelting past her small window, stealing the light.

She wasn't ready to get up and face this new day. The events of the night before weighed heavily, raw and disagreeable like undigested food. Tom's drunken behaviour had been a nuisance, true, but nothing she hadn't dealt with before. It was her mother who had tipped everything over the edge. It made her shudder to think about it. And Tom storming off with Clemmie, as though he were taking her hostage. Bel could still see the astonished open circle of her mouth as her father hoisted her up. She'd no idea what was happening – whether this was a game, a thrill or a punishment – and he hadn't even stopped to put her shoes back on. Their last sight was of her feet waving in pink socks.

Bel and Julia had left immediately afterwards, Julia stalking ahead while Bel threw apologetic goodbyes to their hosts. Bel doubted she'd done it deliberately – sabotaging the get-together – but she couldn't help wondering whether her mother was feeling a satisfying twinge of revenge. Which was why she didn't want to get out of bed and face her. A row was almost inevitable. She toyed with the idea of ringing Matt, but that was likely to be problematic, given his warning yesterday. She didn't want to allow him the satisfaction of 'I told you so'. She eyed her phone, which lay just out of reach on the chest of drawers, then pulled the duvet over her head and burrowed beneath it. Maybe later.

The second time she woke, her mother was hovering at the end of the bed in a cagoule. 'I'm going out,' said Julia.

Bel shifted into a sitting position. 'Where? And why? It's pissing down.'

'I can't stay indoors. It's too claustrophobic.'

She couldn't help bursting out, 'So, are you going to go and apologise to the Farrellys?'

'Am I *what*?'

'We were guests, Mum, at quite a significant birthday party. And you buggered it up.'

'I broke up a fight. I didn't break up a party.'

'That's not true! Look at the way you went after Tom. And his mother. I know you think that me and Dad are the mortifying members of our family, but last night was just awful to watch. Kieran was being really sweet and considerate; okay Tom was lashed, but so what? That's what parties are for – to go a bit over the top and, yeah, act disgracefully too. You're not usually such a spoilsport. And anyway, we were the visitors; we were the ones who should have been on our best behaviour. And then, what about Clemmie? The poor kid was enjoying herself, having a whale of a time and—'

'Have you finished?' said Julia.

'Oh, Mum, please don't go all formal and doctor-knows-best on me. Can't you see it through their eyes?'

'Can't you see it through mine?'

Bel couldn't backtrack. It was a failing she recognised in herself, but once she'd launched into something, even though she knew it could be hurtful, she had to see it through. 'Last night was meant to be a celebration and we ruined it.'

'Frankly, I don't believe you and I are that important to those people.'

'Are you sure? What about the memorial stone they put up? That seems massively important to me.'

'The memorial was for William.'

'It doesn't mean you don't matter too.'

The cagoule crackled, as if static electricity were building beneath it, like the grief in Julia's voice: 'I was wrong to come here. I can agree with you about that.'

'Do you want to go back home then?' said Bel, glancing at the window. 'It's real going-home weather, isn't it?' She made the suggestion as a peace offering, but she didn't feel ready to leave. It would be a bit gross to walk out before trying to smooth things over. Like doing a midnight flit.

Julia said, 'Let me think about it. D'you want to come out with me now?'

'No thanks. I've got some calls to make. Phone calls,' she added in case Julia thought she was going to steal the car, though in fact her mother was holding the keys.

'I'll see you later then.'

Julia didn't say where she was going, but Bel guessed she would drive to the promontory overlooking the beach. She might not even get out of the driver's seat. As the windscreen wipers carried on clacking from left to right she'd gaze at the grey swell of the ocean. And weep. Bel hardened herself against this image. She knew that if Julia was going to have a crying jag she'd rather do it in private. And it was probably what she needed: a good bout of wailing the way that women in other cultures considered perfectly normal. Cathartic.

It would be up to Bel to repair the damage done to relations between the two families. As soon as she heard the car engine start, she hopped out of bed, rescued her phone and returned to her nest of sheets. She clicked onto Tom's number. It rang awhile before the answerphone kicked in but she was reluctant to leave a message or send a bald text. Mightn't he be sleeping off a hangover?

She didn't have the number of the farmhouse or she'd have rung Ronnie. It wouldn't have been an easy conversation, but Bel would have managed it because, unlike her mother, she didn't have too much pride. She wasn't sure why, exactly. But she had discovered during school and adolescence that she didn't mind making a fool of herself and that people who didn't have an inflated sense of their own dignity generally had more fun. Obviously for anyone in authority – doctors, teachers, whatever – this could be a problem, but Bel had never wished for authority of any sort.

She tried Tom again and was greeted directly by his voicemail. Perhaps, if his phone was engaged, he was at this very moment trying to call Bel herself. She liked the idea of such a neat coincidence but knew it was far-fetched. She'd no choice but to get washed and dressed and have breakfast as slowly as possible before redialling. If she didn't get hold of anyone, she was going to be marooned until her mother came back with the car.

Once parcelled into leggings and an outsize jumper, she sat at the table with a mug of steaming black coffee. The yellow tulips bowed from their vase in front of her in a sunny arc. They brought Kieran to mind and her pulse skipped a little faster. Was that a crack of blue in the sky? Could the clouds be lifting? She clicked open her phone and rang Tom a third time. A voice said, 'Hello?'

'Tom?'

'No, this is Kieran.'

'Oh, Kieran, wow, I'm so glad to get hold of you. I don't have your number but I've been trying this one for ages. I wanted to say how sorry I am about last night. I hope we didn't screw things up too much…' Suddenly she thought, why is he answering his brother's phone, what's going on? 'So where are you? Is Tom there too?

'Is that Bel?'

'Oh Lord, I should have said. Yes, it's me. I'm all over the place this morning, but you should know I didn't mean to run out on you. You mustn't think we were ratting off. I hope you were able to carry on with the party?'

'In a manner of speaking. My dad was having grand craic with his cronies and he wasn't going to be interrupted by a bit of bother between your mother and mine.'

'So what happened to Tom?'

'Well we didn't realise it until too late, but he didn't get far.'

She'd been taking a sip of coffee but it scalded her tongue and she set the cup down. 'Meaning?'

'He should have taken a taxi,' said Kieran, a weary resignation in his voice. 'He was a danger to himself and other people.'

'He didn't try to drive your car?'

'No. But it turned out he still had the keys to my mother's old crock. He'd brought her over in it and we'd planned to pick it up in the morning. It's not fit to be driven in the dark, even if you're sober. He lost control when he swerved to avoid an oncoming car and ran off the road into the ditch.'

'And... and is he all right?'

'They don't know yet.'

Bel felt a terrible chill. There had been an accident. How could she not be responsible? If she hadn't gone to the party, if Julia hadn't thought she was fighting Tom off when in fact she was just trying to calm him down, if she'd been upfront about her fall instead of trying to gloss over it, if... 'So, are you with him? I mean, if you have his phone...'

'I'm in Tralee,' said Kieran. 'The doctors are doing what they can. I'm outside the hospital having a smoke before I go over to the garda to give them a statement. They tested his blood for alcohol and they'll be getting the results shortly. And if I'm sounding tired it's because I haven't slept all night.'

She deduced from what he was saying that Tom was unconscious, his injuries not yet quantified, but if the police were gathering the evidence for a prosecution they must be expecting him to pull through. She heard the snap of a match, a sharp intake of breath and then a tinny beep.

'Either that,' he was saying, 'or the battery on this phone is going.'

'I'm stuck here right now,' Bel said, 'because Mum's gone out in the car, but when she gets back, what do you think, should we come over to the hospital? I'd like to do something useful. To help out.'

She couldn't catch his reply; the words were indistinct. She was full of remorse and self-righteousness, preparing to make amends, to spur Julia into action when she returned. Then she realised there was a question she hadn't yet asked. 'And Clemmie? You didn't say anything about Clemmie. Is she there too? Kieran…? Kieran…'

She took the mobile from her ear and shook it but it made no difference. She had lost him.

27

The Beach

Vince was responsible for frying the rashers and sausages, the black pudding and the white. He stayed in the kitchen while Teresa waited on the breakfast table, making sure the guests had coffee and toast the way they liked it. When they'd run the bar it had been the other way around. Teresa had boiled up the soup and put together the sandwiches while he had drawn the Guinness and chatted to his customers about the rugby or the racing or the hurling.

The clientele was different in a B&B, hence the role reversal. The hardest thing to adjust to was the change in the hours. They'd had to leave the Farrelly party well before it ended last night, because they were putting up a German couple who wanted to make an early start on the drive around the Ring. The morning was stormy when they set off but Vince reckoned they'd see a blade of sunshine coming in. And it was worth taking the optimistic view because nowhere was more beautiful than the lush south-westerly coast of Ireland on a sunny day.

When the beds had been stripped and the dishwasher stacked and the pans scrubbed and the perishables put back in the fridge, he drove to the post office with his wife's mail order returns. And when he came out again after a chat, there it was: a glimmer of gold fringing a cloud. You could see it moving towards you like a gift. If only the Germans hadn't been so impatient to get moving, he could have had a longer sleep and they'd have had a better view of the Skelligs.

On impulse he hopped back into the car and drove to the beach at Doonshean. You never knew what you might find, what the tide might leave behind. The chief skill required was a good eye, sharp enough to spot a glint of something unusual. He'd found a gun once. Not the shotgun you'd expect a farmer to keep, but a revolver, black and heavy. A hard man's weapon: a gangster or a terrorist. Unloaded though. He'd had a field day, joking around with it for a few hours, imagining how it had been lost. (Thrown away after a crime, was his guess, so the fingerprints were well washed off.) He'd handed it in to the garda but nothing had come of it and ever afterwards he wondered could he have made a wad of cash selling it privately.

On another occasion he uncovered a stash of Seiko watches, a whole box full, tarnished by the tide, but his hopes had risen high. Turned out they were worthless fakes. They looked the business but not one of them had been able to tell the time.

Today, he decided, he'd be happy with a fine scallop shell or a large conch. He parked in his usual spot above the bay and noticed another car nearby, with a Cork number plate. It looked familiar but he couldn't place it. He could see a moving shape on the cliff top in the distance: impossible to tell whether it was a man or a woman, only that the person wasn't riding a horse or walking a dog, but solitary.

Vince made his way down the steep channel that led to the beach and gulped lungfuls of salt air – he'd found this a tonic for a hangover. His arthritis never seemed to give him trouble either once he was strolling on the sand. His eyes roamed over the drift of seaweed, on the lookout for anything that might twinkle or a shell superior enough to add to his collection. Then he looked up and saw a figure perched on the jutting bluff above him. The solitary walker, he supposed. He waved his arms and called out. 'Stay away from the ledge! It's dangerous.'

'I know.'

He recognised the lady doctor's voice and felt compelled to greet her – especially since there were only the two of them in the world, at this of all beaches. 'Good morning to you!'

'Wait there and I'll be with you in a minute.' She vanished from sight and then re-emerged, treading carefully past strewn boulders. She was trussed up in a waterproof, but even so her hair was wet and sticking to her skull; her lashes were beaded with drops.

'That was a terrible downpour we had,' said Vince. 'You must have been caught in the heart of it.'

'I quite like the rain.'

'I do myself. Though we have an interlude at present, I'm glad to say. I hope there were no leaks in the cottage? Teresa's always on at me to check the guttering.'

'Thank you. It's watertight. Sometimes the ceiling feels a little low. Not that I bang my head or anything... I just need… I need…' She tailed off, raised her face to the wide bowl of the sky, magically clearing. 'There's so much space out here. I appreciate that.'

'It's not what you call crowded,' he agreed. 'Not like last night. Ah, but that was a grand party, wasn't it?' Her head jerked on her neck and she gave him a startled look. He pressed on. 'I'm doing a bit of idle beach-combing. It's a good time when the tide is low and the storm is over.'

'You know this beach well?'

He nodded. Was she going to bring up the husband now?

'Can you tell me then,' said Julia. 'It's been driving me to distraction. Is there a rock along here, where people try to chisel their names? Declare undying love and so on.'

'No,' said Vince.

'Really?' She looked disbelieving, as if she wanted to say: But we're surrounded by rocks! Surely one of them could have been written on? Instead she tailed off. 'Oh dear, I could have sworn I'd seen it…'

'Well now.' He didn't want to disappoint her. 'This strand isn't well known enough to attract that kind of lettering. You're likely to be thinking of Slea Head, at the tip of the peninsula.'

'Am I? Oh my God!' Her expression was so dismayed you'd have thought he'd told her they were going to erect another bloody wind farm right on the very spot where their feet were sinking into the sand.

'It's very popular, Slea Head. Grand for surfing. Good for the youngsters too.'

'Oh yes… I remember going there. My son, Matt, loved it. He was only four and the waves kept knocking him down. He'd stand up to them like a little King Canute and they'd knock him down again and he'd roar with laughter. And then, another couple of times, we came here for fishing in the rock pools and... whatever you're doing, collecting shells and so on. I must have got the two places muddled. How dreadful!'

'Well,' said Vince cautiously. 'It wouldn't be unusual, after so long.'

'Oh but you don't understand!' cried Julia. 'I know it was daft of me to be pacing up and down in search of a wretched rock – especially when I haven't even got the location right – but that's not the worst of it. The reason I was looking for it in the first place was because William, my husband, had talked about adding our names. But he was fooling, wasn't he? He couldn't have done – it was too far away.'

'Maybe he intended to. And maybe the conversation in your memory is on the hazy side itself.'

'He was coming up with all kinds of nonsense that day,' she said. 'I shouldn't be surprised if the whole story was a fabrication. But because of what happened I so wanted it to be true. I thought if I could find our names I'd feel forgiven...'

She appeared to be talking to herself, but Vince hadn't stood behind the bar for thirty years, listening to the outpourings of strangers, for nothing. He waited.

'My last words to him were angry ones,' said Julia. 'That's not an easy admission to make. Or to live with.'

'Your man wasn't angry though. Rueful, I'd say.'

She looked at him sharply. It wasn't rain glittering on her lashes, but tears; the whites of her eyes were bloodshot. The scars might be buried deep, but that didn't mean they weren't still distressing her. 'I'm sorry, but how on earth would you know?'

'I was there,' said Vince.

'Where?'

'In the bar. When you came in and sat in the snug with the little fellow. I was serving.'

'Oh my God! You were the publican at the inquest? The last person Will spoke to?'

He nodded.

'Gosh, I didn't recognise you.'

'I had hair in those days,' he said sadly, pulling at the peak of his cap. 'And in truth it wasn't myself, but Teresa who identified you. Though you haven't changed, hardly at all.'

'I have to get my head round this,' said Julia, shaking her wet hair like a dog. 'It was you who… I mean, if you were there you must have noticed we were having a row… But you didn't tell the Coroner.'

Vince's cramp was going to set in again. 'Will we walk to the other side of the strand?' he suggested. 'I seize up if I stand about too long. That's why I had to give up the pub, but I'm fine if I keep moving.'

'Cod liver oil,' she said automatically. He could picture her whipping out a prescription pad.

'I take gallons of the stuff,' he assured her. 'I'm breathing fish most days.'

She smiled then and he held out his arm like a proper gentleman so she could take it as they wandered the water's edge. Seaweed squelched beneath their feet. 'I didn't mention the argument,' he said, 'because it was trifling, as you said yourself. And because his state of mind struck me as the same as any man who's had a tiff with his wife. Not one of us wants to be browbeaten.'

Julia said in a voice so low it creaked. 'Actually I'd threatened to leave him.' There was a tension in her – he could feel it in the grip on his arm – that reminded him of a horse before a race. 'I've never been able to tell anyone before. It makes it so much worse, doesn't it?'

'Why?'

'Why does it make it worse?'

'Why would you leave him?' Vince's ideas on marriage were traditional, old-fashioned. And the man had been a good sort; a sad loss, as events had proved.

She said, 'Because he'd been offered a research fellowship in the States. My qualifications wouldn't have been accepted, which meant that I wouldn't have been able to work. Plus, Matt was about to start school and I didn't want us to be uprooted. We were living in Bristol at the time. Have you ever been?'

'The airport only.' He'd touched down on his way to the racing at Cheltenham, which was the only English town he'd ever stayed in (not that he remembered much about the accommodation).

'It's a nice city and I was enjoying living there. That was the problem basically: I wanted to stay and he wanted to go. The thing was, he sprang it on me. I'd no inkling. I think he waited on purpose till we were halfway through our holiday and I was relaxed.'

Vince was reviving the scene: the woman and child on one side of the table, the man on the other, reaching out. She had snatched back her hand. The child had sucked his lemonade noisily through a straw. There had been a sense of impasse.

'The irony,' said Julia, 'was that I'd complained of us being in a rut. In our relationship, I mean. I was very happy at work, which was why I didn't want to travel three thousand miles away. And this crazy project was Will's solution to our marriage feeling stale. I was so cross. What was he thinking of? He claimed it was a fantastic career opportunity for him, but that was the sum total of it. How could it possibly have improved anything else?'

He marvelled at her loquaciousness. This was the woman who, when asked if she'd slept well – a perfectly reasonable query from a host to a guest – had said primly, 'Yes, thank you,' as if any more information was uncalled for. Yet now he couldn't stop her: regrets gushing forth as if she were talking to a father confessor – perhaps because there were only the two of them in this expanse of sand and sea and sky. He was flattered, truth be told, to be back in his old role, as if he were still pulling the pints and wiping away flecks of foam (though he was known for never spilling a drop; his jars of Guinness had the finest, creamiest, deepest crowns in the whole locality).

'At first, when I refused to go with him, he thought I didn't mean it. That I was just being perverse. Matt hadn't actually started school, for instance, though I was very pleased with the one we'd picked… But then Will realised I wasn't going to give way. I was entrenched. I said the choice was up to him but Matt and I weren't shifting. He knew me and he knew I wasn't going to change my mind. Of course in the end we had to move anyway, because our lives went haywire.'

'He wasn't obliged to go to America,' said Vince, who'd never been keen on foreign travel. 'And I'm sure, when he stayed on in the bar after you left, he would have been reconsidering.'

'Is that the impression you got?'

He screwed up his eyes and peered at the horizon. The banner of blue was being chased by another ominous bank of cloud. 'My impression,' he said slowly, 'was of a man who knew he'd lost the first round and was reviewing his strategy.'

Julia said, 'William could put up a good front. That's part of being a medic in a way: you tamp down your emotions, balance your duty as a professional against the fears of the patient. We were both too damn controlled. I couldn't tell how much I hurt him but it must have been shattering. Oh my God, I have such a capacity for damage!' She wrapped her arms around her body as if no one else would ever do so. She certainly wasn't Vince's type, not enough to get hold of. She still looked like an adolescent boy though she couldn't have been much younger than himself and Teresa. 'I shall always feel guilty. Responsible...'

'Ah no, that's ridiculous.'

She regarded him directly. 'I was partly to blame. That's a fact. The pain isn't as raw as it was back then – so many years have passed – but it's been eating me up lately, this need to make sense of things. I used to deliberately keep myself busy, but I have plenty of time now to try and work out how and why. You get to a point in your life when old questions keep rising to the surface. Why did he come down here at all? I wanted to believe he was planning to carve our names on the rock as a romantic gesture to soften me up. But now you've told me that couldn't have been possible.'

There weren't many facts to go on, but this one was incontrovertible; he couldn't pretend otherwise. 'Maybe he'd have done that another day,' he offered. 'But he drove here first, because it was nearer, to think things over. It can have a soothing effect, can it not, the rhythm of the sea.' The repetitive suck and swill of the tide a few yards to their left bore this out, sweeping the sand smooth.

'I don't know why he didn't chase after me at once. Why he let me storm off…'

That wasn't exactly an option in Vince's recollection. 'He probably thought you needed breathing space.'

'You're positive he didn't tell you anything? When he left the bar, he didn't say where he was going?'

'No.' He'd been asked this at the inquest and the answer was the same. 'But, at a guess, I'd say he was off looking for you.'

'So, what made him come down here?'

'Because he hadn't been able to find you anywhere else?'

She nodded. 'It's a possibility. Perhaps he remembered how much fun we'd had the day before, how much Matt had enjoyed the rock pools. But he can't have been thinking straight or he'd have realised it was a heck of a way for us to get to on foot.'

She glanced up at the two parked cars, their noses pointing towards the encroaching swathe of cloud. 'I imagine him screeching down here, leaping out of the car and looking over the edge as I just did. I'd put the wind up him, hadn't I? I bet he was obsessing about losing Matt. When he saw the boy on the rocks he wouldn't have had time to check his identity. He wouldn't even have considered it. A child in danger becomes your child. Adrenalin takes over and forces the body into action.'

Vince said, 'And he was a good swimmer?' He may not have known about the riptide, but only a fool would enter the ocean if he couldn't swim.

'He was an all-round sportsman. Terribly fit. He would have raced over to that kid at the speed of light to stop him being swept away. What I don't know, what I can never know, is whether he believed he was saving his own son. And whether, when he rescued the Farrelly boy and saw that it was another child completely, it confused him. Did he turn back again because he was still searching for Matt?'

Vince had to agree the sequence of events was perplexing. Tom Farrelly had been fished from the water by his sisters. They'd been too preoccupied, fretting over him, to be able to tell whether his rescuer had been dragged under or whether he'd gone back into the waves of his own accord. The inquest had determined that William Langley must have lost his footing and struck his head. That the brief blur of unconsciousness and the force of the current overwhelmed his swimming ability, his chances of survival. The Farrelly girls had sought help, but it arrived too late. Nothing was going to change the verdict of accidental death. Why did the widow have to mortify herself all over again?

'When I first lost Will,' she said, 'I wanted to talk about him constantly, as if talking could bring him back to life. Though I wouldn't dwell on his bravery because it was his bravery that had destroyed us. Talking failed of course and, in the end, the urge atrophied. But I never told anyone what I've told you... about our difficulties. Who knows, if this hadn't happened, whether we'd have stayed together or whether we'd have separated anyway. William might have gone to America by himself and had a new family. Oh sweet Jesus – imagine that!

'It's a terrible thing to confess but it has its disadvantages, being married to a hero. It makes it hard for anyone else who comes into your life to cope with the comparison. Leo, my second husband, was completely different from Will – which was the point, of course – but I know he felt it acutely, especially when things went wrong.' She took his arm again. 'Thank you for listening.'

'We have five minutes by my reckoning,' he said, 'before the deluge.'

'Oh… right.' She didn't say any more but lengthened her stride as they approached the path leading up from the beach. He wished he could find something in the back end of his brain, some morsel or recollection that might give her comfort. She hadn't mentioned meeting Tom Farrelly at the do. Could the lad have been a disappointment to her? Is that why she had to believe her husband was after rescuing his own son?

The first drops landed. Vince was wearing his favourite flat cap but he felt the cold smack on the back of his neck. At the same moment a mobile phone began to ring. He wasn't keen on mobiles – pernicious objects of surveillance in his view – and he contrived to leave the one Teresa had bought for him at home. If he wanted to speak to his friends, he knew pretty much where to find them.

Julia pulled the instrument from her coat pocket and answered it. The expression of shock on her face deepened as she asked When, Where and How? She ended the call as they reached the cars and the rain began to patter more insistently.

'Did you know about Tom Farrelly?' she said.

'What about him?' Was she referring to his child, Clementine? For certain she had caused a stir.

'He's been in a road accident.'

'Ah no, I've heard nothing.'

She slumped against her car as if her legs couldn't support her weight, even though she was so slight. She didn't seem bothered about the drenching. 'I think that was my fault too,' she said.

PART SIX

MAY

SATURDAY

28

The Investigation

Smoke still rose from the debris of the garage. Its back section no longer existed, its contents were a heap of ash and twisted metal and most of the roof had caved in. Glass had exploded out of the window frame with the force of the heat. Half a dozen charred and ruined canvases were stacked against a wall. Matt had offered to take Friday off work (even though he had papers to clear before the bank holiday) but Rachael insisted it wasn't necessary. So it wasn't until Saturday morning that he could properly consider the position.

He used to be proud of his ability to keep things in proportion, stay sanguine, but this had waned over the past thirty-six hours. His tolerance dropped another few notches when he stumbled out of the bathroom after his morning shower, to find his wife bending to fasten the buttons of Leo's shirt, her knuckles brushing his chest. Leo stood at ease against the banisters, his arms slightly raised. Rachael's hair fell across her face as her fingers moved downwards, as she fed his belt through the loops of his jeans and struggled with the buckle.

'I can see to that,' Matt said quickly, knocking her out of the way, wanting to spare her the indignity of acting like a maidservant.

Leo couldn't do anything for himself. His hands and forearms were swathed in white gauze so they looked like the paws of a giant dog, a St Bernard, say, clumsy and shaggy. He could just about manage to drink from a cup, cushioning it between his bandages, but he couldn't manipulate smaller utensils: comb, cutlery, mobile phone. He couldn't push a button through a hole.

He was lucky to be alive. He'd been dragging the third smouldering canvas onto the lawn at almost the exact moment that Matt opened the main garage door. Within seconds of the key turning in the car's ignition had come the crackle and leap of flames – a sound like rushing water – but this hadn't stopped him dashing into the inferno again. It was too late for Matt to do anything but steer the car to a safe distance. Then he had leapt out, raced to the back of the garage and plunged after Leo.

Leo was taller, but Matt was well built, with the physical energy of a much younger man. He had seized his stepfather beneath his armpits and tussled him to the ground, rolling him on the grass until Rachael brought out a blanket. Subsequently, the firemen had both praised Matt for his bravery and admonished him for his foolhardiness.

'I could do with a shave,' Leo said now.

'I'll help you later,' said Matt, thinking that stubble had never bothered him before. 'You can wait till after breakfast, can't you?'

He needed an early dose of caffeine, an energy boost to set him up for the rest of the day. He liked his coffee dark and heaped several spoonfuls into the cafetière. Rachael joined him with Danny. Dan had been both thrilled and terrified by the scale of the fire, the arrival of the fire engine and the power of the water jets dousing the flames. He couldn't wait to go to school, to tell the story to his class, but he'd woken screaming in the night and this morning was pale and withdrawn. He had to be coaxed to eat his Shreddies.

Danny's fragile mood was eclipsed by Leo's. He shuffled into the kitchen in a pair of old moccasins and sat at the head of the table, filling the room with his bitterness. He laid his arms out in front of him and stared as if they were detachable appendages and he had no idea what to do with them. Matt poured the coffee and made a stack of toast.

Leo glowered at the toast until Rachael took the hint, spread a slice with butter and held it up for him to bite into. Matt saw her mopping the melted butter as it ran down Leo's chin and felt his anger surge again. To see his wife's compassion directed towards his son was heart-warming – but not, for pity's sake, towards Leo. He was visibly softening at the shimmer of Rachael's touch; as if in gratitude his knee jogged hers beneath the table.

Danny pushed his half-eaten cereal aside and slipped off his chair.

'Are you sure you've had enough, darling?' said Rachael.

In different circumstances Matt might have cajoled him to finish the bowl (and with more success, he suspected, than Rachael) but he watched his son trot out of the door and upstairs to the haven of his playroom, without attempting to call him back. He could still hear, in his head, Danny's agonised refrain – on and off for the past two days – 'It wasn't my fault!'

'He's a bag of nerves,' he said. 'I spent most of last night trying to explain he couldn't be held responsible.'

'Well, someone started the blaze,' said Leo sourly. 'It wasn't an accident.'

'They did warn me,' said Rachael, who had distributed her Chelsea buns to the firemen while Matt took Leo to A&E for treatment, 'that we might not get a pay-out if the insurance company think it was fraud.'

'So they're suggesting I set fire to my own paintings? Yes, I would do that, wouldn't I? Easier than trying to flog the buggers.'

Leo's paintings in their heyday had sold well: the larger ones to institutions, hotels, hospitals, banks; the smaller ones to private collectors. He'd check the auction catalogues from time to time and be pleased to find his value rising, declaring to Julia: 'I told you I'd be a good investment.' But this heyday was past and the great public art galleries had never shown much interest in him. One work, selected as a John Moores' prizewinner, was stored somewhere in the vaults of the Walker Art Gallery, but hadn't been exhibited for years.

Matt said, 'They didn't belong to you anyway. Technically the garage and everything in it is ours. We're the ones who need to get the claim in. Besides, if that were the case, why would you have nearly killed yourself trying to salvage them?'

Leo grimaced. 'You know it took years of my life to get them right? Not that anyone gives a shit about the art once it's become a fucking commodity. I shouldn't have bothered.'

No, thought Matt, you shouldn't.

'No one's accusing you,' said Rachael. 'Any more than Danny. You were upstairs in the attic. We know who struck the match. Nathan. His sister was supposed to be keeping an eye on him but she was useless, wasn't she? She even looked like she was enjoying the drama. After it was over, she actually asked if the police would want to talk to her. I couldn't decide if she was just being naïve or…'

'The girl's sharp as a tack,' said Matt.

'Then she's the one we should put pressure on. D'you know where she lives?'

'I know the street they're lodging in. She hangs around the corner waiting to waylay me when I'm coming back from the station. A couple of times now. I could try and find her, flush them out.'

'I don't see what good it will do,' muttered Leo. 'The damage is done.'

'I'll go right away,' said Matt, downing the rest of his coffee and rising to his feet. He felt galvanised, ready for action. He wanted to get out of the house.

Rachael followed him into the hallway. 'You could take Danny with you,' she said. 'Shame them into telling the truth.' She shuddered. 'Oh, Matt, imagine how awful it might have been!'

'I'd rather not,' he said. 'It'll be easier to get to the bottom of what happened if I go by myself.' He didn't need his son pulling at his sleeve and looking miserable, or sprinting ahead in a bid to win a race. Besides, he didn't want to leave Rachael alone with Leo. 'In the meantime, don't—'

'What?'

'You're not his skivvy.'

'Fuck, Matt! I wasn't the one who wanted Leo to hang on here. That was your doing!'

'Actually this is because of Bel and Julia. We just happened to get caught in the slipstream. Let's not argue about it.' He lowered his voice. 'Was there anything else you should have told me about yesterday?'

She gave a little gulp and twisted her hair around her forefinger. 'What do you mean: about yesterday?'

'When you drove him to the clinic to get his dressings changed. Which was very good of you, I thought.'

'Oh well… I don't know any more than you. I didn't go in with him, I waited outside.'

'Why take him then? He could have called a cab.'

'I hadn't anything else on.' She tugged at the twist of hair. 'And I felt responsible for making you take down his paintings. If we'd left them on the walls this might not have happened.'

This was true, but he said generously, 'If it hadn't been for the barbecue, he wouldn't have known they were in the garage in the first place.'

Danny's frail cry came from upstairs. 'Daddy, can you help me?'

'If you deal with him,' Matt said, 'I'll get going before he attaches himself to me like a rug rat.'

He grabbed the nearest jacket from a peg in the hall and marched out of the door and along the road. He felt strung-up, wrung-out, an unusual experience for an equable man. His response to most events was cautious and considered but today, despite the balmy air of the first of May, the lavish sprinkling of cherry blossom, he longed to knock the stuffing out of somebody. An empty beer can rolled at his feet and he kicked it some distance into the gutter.

He drew his phone from his pocket. He had received a text yesterday from Bel, saying only: *We've decided to stay on for a bit*. He had replied: *Good idea*, and left it at that. No point in adding to complications. She'd obviously ignored his advice not to go to the party, but he assumed the encounter had gone well. At some point he would have to tell her about the fire, about Leo's injuries, the possibility that he could never paint again. Was it worth the two of them discussing what the hell they might do with their parents? It wouldn't be the first time. Despite their age difference he and Bel had always presented a united front and agreed on parental shortcomings. But no, at this stage he couldn't face it.

He was close to tracking down his quarry. He was in a street lined with red-brick terraced houses, each with a low wall separating its narrow frontage from the neighbours and the pavement. Youths raced past him on their bikes but none were Nathan; he was such an odd, friendless boy. Wouldn't most kids his age hang out in a gang with a football or spend their free time on warring computer games? Why was he battening on to a five-year-old?

Two women stood smoking over a wheelie bin. They had a proprietary air, as if they were long-term residents. They would notice incomers.

'Hi there,' Matt addressed them. 'I'm looking for a family who moved here a week or so ago. A grandmother with two kids?'

They looked at him blankly.

'I can't remember their surname,' he went on, though he'd never been told it. 'But the girl and boy are Kelly and Nathan. Dark hair, skinny. She's about fourteen; he's ten or something.'

'Kids everywhere, love,' said one of the women as a skateboard whizzed past.

He tried again. 'Do you get a lot of comings and goings in this street? Do many of the houses belong to private landlords?'

The other woman stubbed out her cigarette with a twist of her heel. 'You could try them two at the end,' she said. 'Them bigger ones. They're in flats. Different tenants all the time.'

'Thanks, that's very helpful.'

As he walked on he heard her say defensively to her friend, 'Can't be no bailiff if he don't know their name.'

Fuck, he thought crossly. Was it because of the jacket he was wearing? Did he really look like a bailiff? The day was pleasantly warm so he took it off and slung it over his shoulder.

When he reached the dilapidated pair of carved-up semis with their peeling window frames, he was prepared to ring every one of the doorbells tacked onto the board in the porch. But he didn't need to. Kelly leaned out of a window above his head.

'I'm coming down,' she said.

She appeared on the step but didn't let him in. She shut the door behind her and sat on the brick wall, mouth in motion. He wondered if she ever stopped chewing gum.

'Were you expecting me?' he asked.

She shrugged. 'How is he?'

'Who?' For a moment he thought she meant Danny.

'Your dad.'

'Oh, not great. He might have to have a skin graft.'

'For real?'

'They don't know yet. They have to see how the burns heal. His dexterity could be affected.'

'What's that mean?'

'He might not be able to use his hands properly.'

'Why'd he do it?'

'Because he didn't want to lose his work.'

'We lost everything,' Kelly said.

Everything. He hadn't forgotten what she'd said, that first time she'd dropped in on them. It was one of the reasons he'd encouraged Dan to be generous with his toys: because Nathan had none. He'd even said to Rachael, thinking of a future sibling: 'Where's the harm? It's good for kids to learn to share.'

'I want you to tell me what happened,' he said to Kelly, 'when you used to live with your mother. Was that when you had the fire?'

'Not with Mum.' She tucked her arm into the crook of his and he didn't pull away, he didn't want to alienate her. 'It was after we moved in with Nan. It was Nan's place what went up.'

He kept his voice low, non-committal. 'Was that Nathan's doing too?'

She pushed the gum into her cheek and screwed up her nose. 'Might of been one of Nan's fag ends. Plus she had these old chairs they're not s'posed to sell any more 'cos of the stuffing. So it spread dead fast.'

'I bet she had something to say when you and your brother came back looking like scarecrows.' The fire had not threatened the children. They'd stood well back with eyes aglow as if they were celebrating Bonfire Night, unfazed by the destruction.

'She weren't in. She were on shift.'

Matt was used to dealing people who chose to be economical with the truth. They'd say, 'It's like this, mate…' and spout a long convoluted story with great gaping holes in it. And he'd point out that he could help them better if some of these holes were filled in, that he was on their side whatever, but if he was going to represent their interests it was best that he knew the facts. Not everybody came round to his way of thinking though and he suspected that Kelly had 'contrary' written all the way through her like a stick of rock.

'You do realise,' he said now, 'that what we're talking about – setting fire to things – is a serious offence.'

'Nan shouldn't smoke anyhow. It's bad for her asthma.'

'You try to keep Nathan under control, don't you? It can't be easy for you.'

'We didn't do nothing.'

'You know what an ASBO is?'

'Course I fucking do.'

'Has Nathan ever had one?'

She squirmed closer to him. 'No.'

'Well there's always a first time.'

'He in't old enough.'

'Then maybe he'll get taken into care.' He remembered her questioning him about her father's responsibilities; how he'd explained that he wasn't a family lawyer.

'They won't sort him out. No way.'

'Things must have been tough since your mum died. It would explain him going off the rails.'

'Oh no,' said Kelly blithely. 'He's always been like this. Friggin' mental. There was a doctor once, not the GP, did some tests and stuff on him. Listened to what he had to say and wrote a report. It was supposed to get him some help, but dunno what happened to it. Nath probably ripped it up.'

'How would he have got hold of it?'

She nudged him in the ribs. 'I'm kidding yous. Didn't make no difference anyhow. Soon after, we went to live with Nan and he changed schools.'

'And now you've moved again.'

'Yeah.'

'So does he go to school at all?'

'Holidays, innit?'

'You know it's not. Danny went back two weeks ago. And what about you?'

'I'm year nine, aren't I? Secondary school. It's different.'

'Where is he now?'

'It's Saturday.'

'Yes, I know that.'

'So he can be where he wants. Right?'

He wouldn't let her aggravate him. He could see she was trying to protect the boy. In his own youth he'd had that same sense of obligation; he'd looked out for Bel because she had a knack of not recognising danger.

In the summer holidays she used to go to the local adventure playground. Once, when he was sent to collect her, he found she'd strayed with a gang of kids onto the bank of the railway line. They were daring each other to swing from overhanging branches or tear up and down the tracks. Bel was performing cartwheels. Her legs scissored through the air and a shoe fell off; as it landed on the line they heard the rumble of an approaching train. She righted herself swiftly but he was close enough to see her hesitate over the fate of the shoe.

'Leave it!' he'd yelled.

Because she'd turned at the sound of his voice, she'd lost the chance to snatch back the shoe. It was crushed into a mangled strip of leather as the train rolled serenely past. 'They were new!' she'd wailed at him. 'What am I going to tell Mum?' They'd invented a tale of a friend's dog who had a habit of burying things. Bel assured Julia the shoe would reappear. She assured Matt she would in future execute handstands and cartwheels in safer places. The responsibility, the need to check on her, never entirely left him.

'You can't look out for Nathan all the time, though, can you?' he said to Kelly. 'You can't follow him everywhere. Stop him causing bother. The fact is, our garage looks like a bomb's dropped. We're going to have to get it fixed up. And someone has to pay for it.'

She pursed her lips into a whistle, drummed her heels against the wall, wouldn't make eye contact.

'We'll have to make an insurance claim. It ought to be straightforward but they may want to investigate the cause.'

'You don't need to say nothing,' said Kelly. 'Like you know who did it or whatever.'

'I don't *know* who did it,' said Matt. 'I'm guessing. But you don't seem to realise how serious this is. Somebody could have been killed. And we still don't know how much damage Leo has done to himself.'

She sniffed and withdrew her arm, which was a relief. He didn't feel comfortable with her clinging on to him like a cat. 'Your brother needs help,' he said. 'He needs to see a psychiatrist. He should have a social worker, at least. You asked me the other day what I could do, didn't you? Well I'm here now and I'd like to talk to your dad about this. Where can I find him?'

Kelly shook her head violently. 'No!' she said. 'You don't want to do that.'

'Your nan then. Some responsible adult. Otherwise things are going to get a lot worse.'

She gave him a sly sidelong glance. Was she trying to be coquettish? 'If you don't tell on us,' she said, wriggling again so her skirt rode further up her thighs, 'I got some, like, information, you might wanna hear.'

Matt had no intention of being bought off. 'Been spying again, have you? Go on then, surprise me.'

'Your dad.'

He felt himself stiffening, hoped she hadn't noticed. 'Leo. Yes?'

'It weren't, like, Nath's fault he got hurt. Me and my mate Sheba, we was talking. She goes to this happy-clappy church and she reckons it's a punishment.'

'Oh? What for?'

'It in't right what he did. It's against the law or the Bible or something. 'Cos she's your wife, in't she?'

Matt's stomach clenched.

'I seen them shagging,' said Kelly.

29

The Interview

The tide was low. The river was being sucked out to sea and the mud flats glistened, offering their booty of petrol cans, old tyres, shopping trolleys. Gulls were stalking the detritus, pecking at a misshapen piece of sacking, perching on a rusting bicycle wheel. Matt preferred the view when sailing boats skimmed the water, when it reflected the blue of the sky, when it rose and slapped against the high stone wall and the unsavoury secrets of the Mersey were hidden. He wasn't sure how he had fetched up there, thumping along the Prom. He'd been on automatic pilot since speaking to Kelly.

It was one thing to have his own doubts, to torment himself with the possibility of a sexual liaison between his wife and his stepfather, but it was quite another to have this suspicion confirmed. This must be how Julia had felt, when she was driven to instigate divorce. No, she'd had proof, actual proof. Kelly was a fantasist, almost as crazy as her brother. He needed to consider the evidence rationally.

Some things were incontrovertible: Rachael's recent behaviour had been erratic. Overemotional, secretive, hinting at guilt. Whenever he asked what the matter was, she blamed Leo; the way he'd turned up out of the blue with an apparent mission to unsettle; the way he refused to take other people's feelings into account. But she'd spent a lot of time with him all the same, and since the fire she'd nursed him almost constantly. Driving him to the clinic, going out of her way to help him eat, drink, dress. Almost as if she felt beholden.

There was *no way*, Matt reiterated, he would believe Kelly's absurd lies. Like Leo, she was one of those people who relished stirring up trouble. What groping and grinding could she possibly have seen? None. Unless she'd sneaked into the garden. Then she would have had a clear view into the sitting room, the soft squashy sofa that was easily large enough to accommodate a randy couple. No, it was bollocks. Rachael would never betray him like that. He picked up a stone and bowled it forcefully over the railings, waited for it to sink into the mud. Then he turned homewards. He'd rather confront the truth – any truth – than these painful imaginings.

When he arrived back at the house their car was no longer in the drive; he had an uninterrupted view of smoke-blackened ruins. Another vehicle, an unfamiliar Toyota, was parked outside. He wondered first, who would be visiting if Rachael were out and second, why she hadn't told him her plans. He presumed Danny was with her. He checked his phone to see if he'd missed any calls or texts. No, nothing.

Once inside the hall he closed the door quietly. Possibly the Toyota belonged to a nurse, although he'd understood

Leo was supposed to get himself to the treatment centre. Then he heard laughter. This was unexpected. Matt poked his head around the sitting room door. Sections of the Saturday newspaper lay in disarray on the coffee table, but there was no one in sight. No one in the kitchen either. Voices came from the end of the hallway: a low murmur, some barked instructions, another laugh. Female? He tensed. These people, intruders, whoever they might be, were occupying his study.

It used to be Julia's. There had been tomes of medical reference books on the shelves, a cumbersome PC on the desk and piles of reports awaiting collation. Paperwork still proliferated. Matt's slim-line laptop allowed ample space for folders, box files and bills that needed sorting. But now, when he marched into the room, he found the clutter had been moved and stacked in a corner on the floor and Leo was sitting on the top of the desk. His pose was casual but proprietorial, one leg bent, one foot spinning Matt's swivel chair back and forth. His mood could not have been more different from earlier that morning. For the first time since the fire he looked cheerful.

To his left was a young woman with a ponytail and a small black instrument Matt identified as a tape recorder. To his right was a man in a denim jacket with a large long-lens digital camera.

Matt had planned to take a strong stance. He knew it wouldn't be easy, when every room in the damned house held a memory of adolescence, of a time when Leo was the authority figure and Matt the put-upon, misunderstood teenager. But this scene, this invasion, made it easier.

'What the hell are you doing here?' he said.

The woman turned in surprise, as though he were the interloper. The photographer said, 'Chin up but don't smile. Don't want you looking too jolly. Can you raise your hands a couple of inches?' Leo's shrouded paws hovered above his lap. 'That's great. Yep. And again.' The shutter clicked rapidly.

Leo said, 'My guests are from the *Echo*. It appears that I'm newsworthy.'

Matt said, 'Well they shouldn't be in here, however newsworthy you are. This is my study.'

'Ah… *Your* study?'

Leo was trying to make him feel fifteen again, but he wasn't going to be browbeaten. 'I daresay it's hard for you to accept this, but didn't you move out five years ago? My mother's gone now too. She left behind the desk you're sitting on because it was too big for her to take. It's mine now. Like this house. So you see, you're the one who's overstepped the bloody mark.'

'*Your* study,' said Leo smoothly. '*My* painting.'

The solitary survivor; the only canvas left in the house. *Conflagration 2* used to live in the sitting room. Matt had grown up with it hanging above the mantelpiece, the swirls of its composition echoing the flames in the grate. He could tell the execution was powerful; there was a sense of drama in the brush strokes. As for the colours, he had no idea whether they were accurate or glorious or especially remarkable. (It was an irony not lost on Leo, who had tried, when he was younger, to teach him to distinguish the different tints. A mutual lack of patience had scuppered these lessons, to Matt's relief.)

'I was explaining,' he said to Matt with no hint of apology, 'that my interest lies principally in colour. I like to call myself a colourist. Regrettably, as you know, painting is rather out of fashion these days, for the powers that be. Too obvious isn't it? Squeezing a tube of acrylic, splodging it onto a canvas? Much more cutting edge to use video or sound installations. Or to be a sculptor – especially if you work in an unusual medium. Mouldy bread. Blood or piss or shit. The trouble with shit, for me at any rate, is that it's basically brown. And brown is boring. No?'

The journalist smirked as she jotted her notes. The photographer hunkered down onto his haunches and angled his impressive lens at *Conflagration 2*. (*Conflagrations 1* and *3* had been bought several years ago to face each other in the foyer of an insurance company in Leeds.)

Matt said, 'That's not the point. You should have asked before coming into this room. The material in these files is confidential. It's necessary sometimes for me to bring them home from work but it's totally outrageous that you've allowed the press to sift through them.'

'But we didn't...' the woman began.

'Leo can't use his hands,' said Matt. 'So there's no way he could have cleared my desk, is there?'

'I can assure you nothing has been disturbed. Some of the folders were obscuring the painting, so we got them out of the way. Nobody has opened a file or read a single word. I promise.'

'And I can assure *you*,' said Matt fiercely, 'there would be very serious consequences if that wasn't the case. I could get an injunction—'

'Oh my goodness!' she interrupted. 'I've just realised who you are.'

Matt immediately feared, despite her protestations, that she'd recognised a name on a folder, knew one or more of his clients. But she said in a tone of admiration: 'You're his son!'

'Whose son?'

'You saved your father's life,' she said. 'He's told us about it. How he was trying to salvage his work, how he refused to give up. He wouldn't admit it was too late. Which it was of course, and if you hadn't stopped him…'

'I'd've been toast,' said Leo.

'That's an exaggeration,' said Matt.

'I don't believe so.'

'It's a splendid human interest story,' said the journalist. 'It must have been a terrifying moment, when you had to decide whether to go after him or not, whether you'd be risking too much. Maybe you'd like to give us your take on it?'

It wasn't a decision; it was an automatic reaction. 'No, not really.'

She looked puzzled, as if she'd never met a man who didn't want to be hailed as a hero.

He added, 'And if you've got what you came for, I'd like my study back please.'

'We can take some shots out the front,' said the photographer. 'Nice scene of devastation, that.'

Nice scene of devastation? Still seething, Matt waited for them to collect their belongings and held open the door. As the trio trooped through, the journalist lifted her tape recorder invitingly. 'Sure you won't change your mind?'

'Quite sure.'

While they were outside completing the interview and photo-shoot he replaced his laptop and rows of folders on the desk. Had Leo really suggested that he'd saved his life? What a piece of nonsense. Presumably he wanted to make the whole rescue operation sound more dramatic. Matt tried to think back, to relive the scene, but it had happened too fast to be stored as a logical sequence: the onrush of air kindling the fire, his pursuit of Leo, hauling him out of the danger zone. He'd followed his instincts, that was all.

The powerful smell of smoke would linger around him for days, but no images came to mind. He could recall only the sensation of Leo's resistance, of physically grappling with him on the ground. This brought a faint echo of their play-fighting years before. In those days Leo had generally won. This time I beat him, thought Matt. I forced a man in flames to submit to my power. What kind of a victory is that?

He left the study and locked the door. He didn't like the idea of locked rooms, the implication he had something to hide, but these were exceptional circumstances. Sometime in the future – he couldn't see it clearly yet – the dust would settle. Leo would leave, Rachael would explain Kelly's gossip was the result of an absurd misunderstanding and the three of them would be able to get on with family life, undisturbed. He was beside the fridge in the kitchen, wrenching the top off a beer bottle, when Leo loped back indoors.

'Excellent idea,' he said, with a nod towards the San Miguel. 'Can you open one for me?'

'How are you going to drink it?' Usually Leo closed his fist round a bottle and necked it with gusto.

'Your kid had the right idea. Got me a straw. Just the answer for cold drinks.' He settled himself in a chair in his usual lordly manner. 'Lovely girl,' he said, closing his lips on the straw Matt provided, closing his eyes in pleasure as he drank.

Matt remained standing. 'Who?'

'Jean… Janette… Janine… The one who was here from the paper. Given me hope, God bless her. Something I could do with right now.'

'You certainly spun her a line.'

'Don't knock yourself, Matt. Respect where it's due. I may still be fucking furious that years of my life have gone up in smoke, that I'm in constant mind-numbing pain, but I'm not going to take your grand gesture away from you.'

'It wasn't a gesture!'

'Didn't mean to sound patronising. You got to me in the nick of time and like I told you, I am grateful.'

'Then you can do something for me.'

'Shoot.'

'I want you to leave Rachael alone.'

'What?'

'I'm not having my wife running around being your nursemaid or whatever.'

'Raquel and I have an agreement,' said Leo levelly. 'She doesn't do anything she doesn't want to.'

What the fuck did that mean? Matt longed to dissect the remark, to demand clarification, but he resisted. 'Then how did the press get here? You can't even make a phone call. Where did that invitation come from?'

'Oh, I contacted the paper yesterday. Got the nurse who was changing the dressings to dial and put me through.

They called me back this morning. Turned out they were really interested. No pressure on Raquel. The last thing I'd want to do is cause her any grief.'

'I hope you mean that. She can be too obliging for her own good sometimes.'

'Too obliging?'

Christ, the innuendo! The words unsaid were suffocating him. But he had to stay calm; an accusation could misfire. Leo took pleasure in winding people up, in baiting his victims. 'Look, we never invited you to stay in the first place. You swanned in with no warning, which pissed us both off I can tell you. And then you go and get yourself into a mess like this and expect the whole world to take notice.'

'Matthew,' said Leo with an air of enormous patience. 'You know perfectly well I came to see your sister because I'd been worried about her. No doubt Julia summoned her overseas to spite me. But I don't see why I should become the scapegoat. I shouldn't have to remind you that I am not the person who set fire to your fucking garage. Nor am I the person who left valuable works of art casually lying about in it.'

'No, that was Rachael,' said Matt, for the pleasure of seeing Leo crestfallen.

'Not your mother?'

'No.'

'Oh.'

'Anyway I'm not talking about the fire.'

'I don't see how you can avoid it—' he waved his arms in the air '—when this is the consequence. A few days of TLC and I should be on my feet again.'

'There was another reason you came here, wasn't there? Tell me about it.'

Leo said, 'I know I have a reputation as a troublemaker, but your mother can give as good as she gets. I don't understand why she's being so difficult. I didn't want things to go so badly between us.'

You should have thought of that a few years back, swore Matt silently. Kept your fucking dick in your pants. Aloud he said, 'You can hardly blame her.'

'It seemed an extreme form of punishment.'

'What did?'

'Nothing for you to worry about. Julia may have misled me, but your Raquel has set me right. All sorted now.'

He was talking in riddles. Matt would have liked to throw his empty beer bottle at Leo's head. Instead he thumped it on the table in frustration. 'About my wife,' he said. 'I don't know why she had to "set you right", but here's the thing. Like I told you, you're not to bother her any more.'

'Bother her!' exclaimed Leo with a pained expression.

'Rach has already had to deal with one invalid in the house. She needs a break. In fact we would both like some time together.' He kept his voice steady. 'I'm off work now till Tuesday so if you have to stay here till then and you need help dressing, making phone calls et cetera... I'm prepared to do it for you. But that's the limit. Okay? I don't want her involved.'

'Hands off?' said Leo, holding them up as if Matt were pointing a pistol at him.

'That's right. You'll keep to yourself and do as I say as long as you're in our house.'

There, he'd done it, made it clear: *our* house, *my* wife. He'd drawn a line Leo was forbidden to cross.

'I understand.'

'Do you? Really?'

At that moment he caught the familiar sound of Rachael's return: the car revving through the gateposts, then jolting to a halt because she'd taken her foot off the clutch and pulled on the handbrake too soon. He heard the engine stall, the clang of the passenger door as Danny slammed it shut, the electronic beep of the central locking system.

Leo heard it too. 'This is your territory,' he agreed. 'I have no intention of coming between the two of you. I shall make myself scarce. Any chance of another San Miguel before I start on my trip back to Colditz?'

Matt snapped open a second bottle and held it out.

'Don't worry. I shan't ask you for anything else,' said Leo a little grumpily as he stowed the beer under his arm. His movements were slow and shuffling and he bumped into Rachael on his way out of the kitchen. Her face flushed a deep pink as she squeezed past him and saw the guarded way Matt was appraising her.

He said, 'Where the hell have you been?'

'Dan had a swimming lesson. We went back to Emma's after. I could say the same to you. I mean, you scooted off ages ago to look for that wretched girl – at least, that's what you said—'

'You could have texted me.'

'You could have texted *me*.'

'Children,' said Leo from the doorway. 'Please.'

Matt scowled until he moved off and they could hear the creak of the stairs under his tread.

Danny was bouncing his swimming bag on his back. 'Can I have an ice cream?'

Usually his parents would both jump to attention when he made a request, but on this occasion they ignored him. Matt was aware of his son wavering, then crossing the room to the freezer, opening a box of Cornettos and selecting one, half expecting with each advance to be told No! grazing is bad for you. Dan, becoming bolder, dropped the Cornetto wrapper in the bin and sauntered through the gap between his parents, even though he knew well Rachael's rule about not eating in front of the television. If he expected a veto, none came. Matt watched him go, waited.

Rachael hadn't lost her high colour; her eyes seemed magnified and he understood why when a tear spilled down her cheek.

'Rach, what is it? What's the matter?'

'Oh, Matt... I'm sorry, there's something I should have told you.'

30

The Hospital

The road swooped away from the coast, dipped beneath an arching tunnel of hawthorn, rose to cross the hills to Tralee. This trip had not been on the agenda. Bel and her mother should have been packing up today, dropping off the hire car and taking the ferry home – that was their original plan. But yesterday morning, when Julia had squelched back into the cottage and changed out of her wet clothes and dried her hair, Bel had confronted her.

'We can't just leave,' she'd said. 'Not until we know if Tom and Clemmie are going to be all right. We've nothing to get back for and it's a bank holiday on Monday anyway. I'm sure Teresa will let us stay. She's no one else coming in. So you must see, Mum, that we can't run out now.'

Julia hadn't argued. She'd been surprisingly meek, shivering so much that Bel had added more peat to the fire and thought briefly how the tables had turned and how *she* was the person in good health for a change. It didn't make up for the horror of the accident, but it enabled her to take command while Julia put on an extra cardigan and nursed her mug of tea, staring at the curls of smoke as if they were spelling out messages from another world.

Julia had drawn the line at going to Tralee herself. 'Can't you find someone else to take you, darling?'

Bel understood completely that her mother would find it hard to visit Tom as a patient, or to refrain from asking the staff technical questions. But it turned out this wasn't the stumbling block.

'It must seem absurd,' she'd said, 'for a doctor to have difficulty entering a hospital. It's just that particular hospital…' there came a long pause '…was where they took William… Where I had to identify him.'

'Oh God, Mum, I'm so sorry. How stupid of me. I wasn't thinking.'

And so it was arranged that Kieran would drive her; he was going himself anyway.

He picked her up at the top of the track with a sombre expression on his face, and they travelled for several miles in silence. Beyond the car windscreen, clouds danced on the hilltops and everything sparkled – the sun on the ocean, the dew on the clover – but Kieran's hands were clenched on the wheel and his shoulders were hunched under an invisible weight. It was exactly a week, Bel realised, since she'd travelled down to Kerry with the Farrelly brothers. A different Saturday. A different journey. There'd been some fraught moments, true, but they'd made it more intriguing for her, whetted her appetite. It had been fun. The four of them had laughed a lot. One week on there was nothing to laugh about.

Against her nature, she was forcing herself not to ask questions – there wouldn't be answers to half of them anyhow – but she couldn't keep quiet for the *entire* journey and after a while she ventured: 'Will your mother be there?'

Kieran seemed to be relieved she'd spoken, as if it eased the atmosphere. 'Probably, yes. She stayed last night with a friend. She was in the habit of it when my dad used to have to go in regularly for treatment.'

'Oh Lord, I'd forgotten that. She's not going to want to see me though, is she? She must think I'm nothing but a nuisance.'

'Well,' he said with a shrug that brought his shoulders even higher around his ears. 'It's true she sometimes has a problem seeing things in proportion. She's unlikely to think any girl good enough for our Tom.'

'And you too?'

'I'm not sure she has the same expectations.'

'Well if *my* mother had never come here,' she muttered, 'you can't deny you'd have been a lot better off.'

She was surprised when Kieran turned his head – he'd been fixed on the road in front of them until now. 'I'm glad she did,' he said.

'For real? After all that's happened?'

He was closing on an ambling tractor. He revved and overtook it deftly. A carrion crow lay squashed on the tarmac, one black wing raised stiffly in salute; he sailed over its corpse. 'We're in a terrible mess,' he said. 'Tom has taken too many chances, too often. All I'm saying is I'm glad I met you. None of this is your fault.'

This caused a brief flutter of pleasure, then a pang of guilt. 'That's not true.'

'Sure it is.'

'I spoke to my brother,' she said. 'The day of the party. He warned me it was a bad idea and I should have listened to him. I made out that Mum was keen, but actually she wasn't. She was really apprehensive. I had to persuade her to come, that we would all benefit. Except the opposite happened. So you see, it *is* my fault.'

'We're adults,' said Kieran. 'We can make up our own minds. You can't be taking the blame for other people behaving badly.'

Adults perhaps, thought Bel, but it was a child who was caught in the crossfire. 'So tell me,' she said, as he swept around a treacherous bend. 'How is Clemmie doing?'

She'd already learned that they were keeping the child under observation, but she was afraid the information might be incomplete. She knew that was what Julia did sometimes. There were patients who couldn't take in everything at once. You had to lead them gently forwards, building up a worst-case scenario. As the brain processed each grim morsel, it was better equipped to take in the next piece of bad news.

'They think she'll be fine,' said Kieran. 'She has nothing broken, no serious injuries. Tom had strapped her in so she was well protected. Shame he didn't do the same for himself.'

'He wasn't wearing a seatbelt?'

'Feckin' eejit. At least the airbag worked and cushioned the impact, but it couldn't prevent the head injury. God knows what he was thinking and I doubt he'll ever be able to tell us.'

Bile rose in her gullet. 'He'll come out of the coma, won't he?'

'We hope so, of course. But if and when he does come round he's not likely to recall a thing, one way or the other. The crash would have taken place in seconds.'

Bel had had plenty of time recently to ponder the fragility of life, the speed with which it could be put under threat. For weeks she'd been saying to herself: when this is over, when I get back on my feet. Now she wondered whether there wasn't always going to be some lurking disaster waiting to unfold. Why worry about not having any money or love life or work when it was a major achievement just to stay alive?

When Kieran finally pulled into the hospital car park and cut the engine he didn't seem to be able to detach himself from the steering wheel. He leaned across it, taking deep breaths. Tentatively Bel touched his arm. He roused himself and gave her an enigmatic look. 'Ready then?'

'Yes. I'm ready.'

'You know they might not let us see him?'

'I'm here for Clemmie too,' said Bel. 'Poor little thing. I really ought to get her something.' They were passing the shop at the entrance and she dived inside. She should have thought of a gift before – although most of the fruit she'd been given during her own convalescence had gone mouldy; the bouquets had withered.

Kieran waited while she bought a box of Maltesers, but she stumbled on her way out of the shop and he grabbed her elbow to steady her. The bruising was not as painful as it had been, but she couldn't control a wince. He snatched his hand back and shifted away from her before she could explain the reason. My arm still hurts, was all she'd needed to say, but now it was too late and he was striding ahead.

He'd said he was glad that he'd met her, hadn't he? Which was a lovely thing to hear. And he'd given her flowers. He must think she was so ungrateful. Oh why did she always have to cock things up?

He noticed she was dawdling and stopped. 'Having second thoughts?' he said.

'I am a bit... yeah.' He was giving her a let-out. And there was no denying an association of dread. Like school. Like the dentist. Like that very scary little aeroplane in which she'd flown from Khartoum.

'You don't have to come. No one will think the worse of you.'

'I'm fine. I mean, grand. I'm coming.'

Tom lay like a creature in an experiment, connected to drips, tubes and monitors. His left leg was in plaster under a protective scaffold. A patch of curls had been shorn so fluid could be drained to reduce the swelling in his brain. He presented a grotesque figure, yet his face was serene. His lips parted slightly as he breathed (on his own, which was a good sign). His eyes were closed. The fine bones of jaw, cheek and brow, the shape of nose and mouth were undamaged. He could have been a beautifully chiselled effigy.

But his spark of wickedness wasn't visible any more: the devilish light behind the eyes, which made people do things they'd probably regret later. Had that been the main attraction? Had that been what she'd seen in him – an invitation to go off the rails?

'He thought he could get out of anything,' she said. 'When we were stuck on top of the haystack he bragged he had nine lives.'

'He has a temper on him,' said Kieran. 'And he'd had too much to drink. He knew perfectly well he shouldn't have got in the car. There are laws here just as in the UK, even if we may not be so good at enforcing them. Don't you be making excuses for him.'

She guessed that Kieran had a temper himself and was reining it in. She could feel the tension building beside her, his whole body stiffening. He was gripping the end of the bed, with its clipboard of indecipherable notes and charts. 'As you see,' he said. 'I'm finding it awfully hard to forgive him.'

'It doesn't stop the two of you being close though, does it?'

'No,' he agreed. 'And that's another twist of the knife.'

Neither of them made a move to sit down, although chairs were available. Bel wished she could speak to Tom, but she didn't think the sound of her voice would be familiar enough to have any effect. And what could she say? Apologise over and over again: I'm sorry. We should never have come. I didn't know my mother was going to erupt like that or I would have kept her away from you. I'm sorry… so sorry…

Kieran said, 'Will we stay, do you think, or will we go and find Clemmie? We can come back here later. You never know when there might be news and I get the feeling this is troubling you.'

She nodded mutely.

'I'll take you to Clemmie,' he went on. 'Then I'm going to look for my mother. You have my number now so you can text me if you need me, okay?'

He left her at the entrance to the children's ward – off for a smoke, she suspected. Her own craving for cigarettes had dwindled practically to nothing. Perhaps there could be some good results from bad experiences; surely Tom would never drink and drive again?

The ward was bright, busy and colourful but she picked Clemmie out right away. She was perched on her high bedstead, the only child fully dressed. A nurse was with her, listening and laughing as Clemmie chattered, intent on the tale she was telling.

The nurse said, 'A visitor for you.' And then, slightly puzzled. 'You're not her mum, are you?'

Bel was disconcerted. She'd supposed that the status of parenthood changed a person in some way, gave them an indefinable aura of maturity. She knew, realistically, this was nonsense – but she still couldn't believe anyone would imagine her fit to be in charge of another human being; her or Tom Farrelly.

'Bel!' crowed Clemmie, holding out her arms for a hug.

'I've brought you some Maltesers.' She passed them over and said, a little awkwardly to the nurse, 'I'm a friend of the family. How is she?'

Clemmie rattled the box with satisfaction and then rolled up her sleeve to show a discoloured area of her smooth dark skin. 'I've a bruise just like you! And on my legs too.'

'She had mild concussion,' said the nurse, 'which is why we've been keeping her under observation. But the doctor has said she can be discharged now, so we're waiting for her mother.'

'Do you mean her grandmother?'

'We understood her mother was coming to collect her and take her home.'

Bel saw a small suitcase was standing next to the bed. 'To England?'

'I'm not sure.' The nurse patted Clemmie's braids and blew her a kiss. 'See you later cherub.'

Bel sat down, processing the information. Clemmie's mother. Well, naturally she would come. What parent wouldn't rush to their child's bedside after an accident? She'd've cut short her holiday, or maybe she was back home and waiting for her daughter to be returned. Clemmie had been so much part of Bel's visit, so much a part of Tom, that she hadn't given any thought to the woman who'd actually brought her up. She couldn't decide how she felt about meeting her – although she had to admit she was insanely curious.

'Will you draw me a picture, Bel?'

It was good to have a diversion. She pulled out a fresh sketchbook. 'Right then. Why don't I draw you being a heroine? Would you like that?'

The little girl nodded solemnly. 'Because my daddy did a bad thing.'

'Well…'

'He took me away from the party and I didn't want to go. It's not fair.'

So that rankled more than the car crash? Bel said, 'And you've been very brave, haven't you? It must have been ever so scary, that accident.'

'The car was stuck in a ditch!'

'You poor lamb.'

'Will you draw it in the ditch?'

'Are you sure that's what you want me to do?' Mightn't this be a tad traumatic? She wished Julia were around so she could consult her.

'Yes,' said Clemmie, as emphatic as ever. 'Proper stuck. My daddy was stuck too and he couldn't speak. I couldn't get out. I couldn't open the door. But I didn't want to walk in the road anyway because it was wet and I hadn't got my shoes on.'

Bel was sketching the two waving feet she'd seen leaving the party, but now they were behind the car window. She tried to stop her fingers shaking as she shaded in the socks. Maybe she could treat this as therapy. Maybe she could give Clemmie a positive story with a happy ending.

'Now,' she said. 'I have to draw the person from the other car who sees you waving and calls the ambulance for you. Who was that?'

Clemmie dug her fingers into the weave of the cotton coverlet, ruminating. 'A man in a hat,' she said at length.

'What sort of a hat shall I give him?' She didn't want to be too literal in case Clemmie became upset. She recalled a guest at the party who'd worn a yellow waistcoat with shiny buttons. 'Shall I make him a leprechaun?'

'What's a leprechaun?'

'Oh my goodness, did no one tell you? Ireland's full of them. Helpful little people. A bit like Santa's elves, only all year round. You must have seen some toy ones in the shops. They bring you luck, like four-leaf clover. So you were very lucky indeed to be rescued by a leprechaun. I've got no crayons with me so you have to imagine his hat is green and he has bandy legs, like this…'

'And a mobile phone.'

'Sure. Right. He'd have to be able to call the ambulance for your daddy, wouldn't he?' She began to sketch an outsize phone in the little man's hand.

'He looks like a dwarf,' said Clemmie. 'Like Dopey or Sneezy.'

'Well then, we must give him a name. What do you reckon?'

'Matey.'

'Okay, that's good. Matey it is.'

She held her pencil more firmly. Kieran had told her how the other vehicle, quite unscathed, had stopped to investigate. It contained a group of Americans on a golf tour; they'd hired a local caddy to drive them and he had raised the alarm at once. Luckily, although trapped in a terrifying situation with an unconscious father, Clemmie hadn't had time to become lonely or frightened. The delay had not been in getting the casualties to hospital so much as alerting the next-of-kin to the accident.

Because the two of them were bending their heads so close together over the drawing, they didn't notice the arrival of another person. The ward was noisy in any case: the clang of metal trolleys, the high querulous voices of sick children, the hum of DVDs playing.

Bel raised her eyes before Clemmie did, to see a statuesque woman, an ebony goddess with sleek hair and chandelier earrings, wearing high heels, orange jeans and a purple jacket (colours she favoured herself). The goddess ignored her totally.

'Clementine,' she said in a husky voice.

Clemmie bolted upright, bolted into her mother's arms. Bel's sketchpad fell onto the floor and her pencil rolled after it. Scrabbling to pick them up, she understood why the child was so self-assured.

'Who are you?' the woman asked, when she had finished covering her daughter's face with kisses.

'She's Bel,' said Clemmie.

'I'm a friend of the family.'

'His family?'

'Er… yes…' It wasn't strictly true and perhaps it was unwise. Should she have distanced herself from the Farrellys?

Clemmie's mother picked up the suitcase; her earrings bobbed and swung. 'I knew it would be a mistake to let her come. Are you ready, sugar?'

It would be useless, Bel thought, to try to defend Tom. She could see quite clearly why he would have fallen for the goddess, equally clearly why she would have despaired of him. But she hated standing there like a spare part unable to stop Clemmie leaving the hospital, leaving Ireland, walking out on her new-found relatives without saying goodbye. She had to do something.

'Before you go,' she said, 'I have some pictures I drew for Clemmie. Not just now, I mean…' The surreal images of the nose-diving car, the legs without a torso, the dwarf with the phone lay uppermost on the bed. Clemmie's mother looked disdainful. 'Let me find the others,' Bel went on. 'Somewhere in my bag.'

She turned her back and pretended to hunt, while sending a swift text to Kieran. 'You remember when we were on the boat, Clem? When I told you about the magic dust the volcano spewed out? And how you grew wings and were able to fly? Well here you are! You can take it.' She handed over the notebook.

'It isn't finished,' Clemmie objected, flicking through the pages.

'What did you say your name was? Bel? I'm sorry, but I'm in a hurry. We have to leave now.'

'You don't want to see… him… at all?'

Her expression told Bel all she needed to know. Why would she waste time on a man who ran out on his obligations? Why would she want to weep over an inert intubated body that might never regain consciousness? She'd come to rescue her daughter from a dreadful experience and she wasn't going to hang about.

'Okay then,' said Bel. 'Give me your address and I'll finish the story off myself and post it to you. How about that?'

She deliberately pressed too hard on her pencil point so that the lead snapped and she had to find another. She kept writing down the postcode wrong. Covertly she resent her text. But her delaying tactics finally ran out. 'You really can't stay another minute?' she said, hugging Clemmie goodbye.

'I'm afraid not.'

With the rhythm of the righteous, the mother swayed out of the ward on her perilous heels; the daughter trotted happily beside her. Bel, her hands hanging at her sides, stood and watched them go.

31

The Patient

Ronnie had no idea how long she'd been asleep. She was surprised she'd dozed off at all, upright in a narrow chair, but that was the way of it: the brain shutting down, shutting out clamour and chaos. That was what Tom's brain had done, that was why he was lying peacefully beneath the gentle rise and fall of the sheet while a jagged line scribbled its way across the monitor screen.

So many times she'd been in this hospital: for the births of her children and then Anna's; for the miscarriage of the twins; for friends with breakages and removals and investigative procedures; for Nuala with her appendix and Kieran with his tonsils. And then the past few months with Pat and the treatment they hoped had finished. She'd never have guessed, after months of visiting oncology, she'd back so soon.

Tom had been a healthy child; not a day's illness, she used to say proudly. There was the odd patching-up – stitches for cuts, bandages for sprains, a dislocated shoulder – but it was nearly thirty years since she'd sat beside his bed all night and thanked God for his survival. In the faint blue light of the ward, he'd been a frail ghost of the gleeful four-year-old swinging his bucket for the beach. She'd practically been able to see through his flesh to the bony skeleton beneath. Just like the shrimps he'd sought in the rock pools.

There was a different cast to things now and she suspected God was playing games with her: holding out two fists and asking her to guess which held the prize. She always picked the wrong one. She reckoned even if He turned over his palm and she caught a fleeting glimpse of joy, it would be snatched away. She'd be left staring at emptiness again.

It had been wonderful to have Pat restored to her and their sons coming home, how could she have imagined the pleasure would be so short-lived? Though there were clues: the girl, Clementine, for a start. The shock had knocked the breath out of her. She'd struggled with indignation and disbelief, but she'd kept her reservations quiet for Tom's sake. Now she was seeing things differently, seeing the child as a gremlin come to upset the structure of her family, the plans she had coveted for them.

She was suffering pins and needles in her leg from sitting too long in the same position. She'd have to walk about to get her circulation back. She heaved herself out of the chair. Her knitting bag lay on the floor beside it, abandoned because her fingers were becoming tangled in the wool, even though she could generally operate by touch alone. There were magazines abandoned too; she'd kept being drawn to tales of loss or betrayal or acts of desperate courage that made her start crying or want to rip out the pages. Either way it was an unhappy experience and unhappy experiences were something she could do without.

At least the magazines contained words she could read. The monitor told her nothing except that Tom was still alive and she could see that for herself. She moved towards the bed. Should she take his hand? Little chance he'd let her do so when he was awake and alert. He might dance around her, hug her, whisper nonsense in her ear – but it would be on his terms only. In the past, if she'd tried to comfort him with a squeeze or a cuddle, he would pull away. He couldn't pull away now.

She bent nearer to the pillow and ran her thumb softly over his chin, feeling the rasp of stubble that didn't stop growing just because the mind was absent. Was that a tremor in his cheek? An involuntary response to her touch? Or a protest? Did his lip twitch? A sign, that was all she was waiting for, a very small sign.

She straightened her spine and took a step back, colliding with another person whose shape was familiar. For a second, no – less, she imagined Tom was playing tricks, rising from the bed to taunt her. But it was Kieran, with his jacket collar turned up and a closer shave and a better colour than his brother. He cocked a hopeful eyebrow.

'No change,' said Ronnie. 'Not yet.'

'I know. I came to see if you wanted a ride back with us.'

'Us?'

'I have Bel with me. We called in before to see Tom.'

The clumsy English girl, was how Ronnie thought of her. Couldn't make her way through a farmyard without tripping over. She had a pleasant enough manner, though there was also the question of her mother. She had tried to thank the woman once. A true irony, considering how all these years later she'd despatched Tom to this twilight zone and he might never come out of it. 'When was that? I didn't see you.'

'Did you go out for a bite maybe?'

'I went for a sandwich, yes, but that was ages ago. I've been sleeping since.'

'Well it can only have been a catnap if you came back after we left.'

'A catnap!' She'd felt as if she was being dredged up from the bowels of the earth, it had taken her so long to surface. 'Would you believe it?'

'Anyway,' he said patiently and she had to allow that Kieran was a patient man. 'Will you be needing a lift?'

For a moment she wavered. This wasn't a world she could ever be useful in. She should be at home with Pat and the grandsons who loved and appreciated her. 'But what if Tom wakes up, alone in this room?' He wouldn't know where he was; he'd be totally disorientated. He'd already lost two days of his life. 'I can't let that happen.'

'Mam, you can't stay here forever. Aren't they talking of moving him to Cork? Then what will you do?'

She set her jaw, didn't answer.

He said, 'Perhaps it's you who shouldn't be alone.'

'Why? Do you think I'm not up to it? That I'm not used to a little adversity? I've had plenty of practice.'

She shouldn't be shouting at Kieran. None of this was his fault. He'd done exactly what she'd asked, back in March: he'd brought his brother home. The English girl, the black child, the car accident, they were none of his doing. He waited with his hand in his pocket. She could hear the chink of loose change.

'I can spend another night with Carmel,' she said. 'It's no problem.'

'I shall have to leave tomorrow,' he said. 'I've changed the date of the crossing once already and I can't delay any longer. I have to get back to work and Tom won't be coming with me, whatever.'

They both looked gravely at his body. Ronnie wished she'd been able to keep her children close. She had long ago recognised the boys' need to escape but it didn't stop her missing them. Usually it was a latent niggle, like a toothache, though it could grow to enormous proportions if she stopped to think about it. That was the great compensation of keeping herself busy: less time to think.

'I'll get Bernie or someone to bring your dad over in the morning and fetch me back. He'll be wanting to see Tom anyway. But if there are developments, or any change overnight I ought to be here. You do understand?'

'Yeah, sure.'

'Then I'll be home tomorrow and we'll cook up a fine roast dinner before you set off. Are you getting the night boat?'

'No. I'll stay over in Dun Laoghaire, at Ned's place. Leave the next day.'

Was she imagining it or did he seem relieved to have made his plans to go? He was turning away from her and pulling out his phone. 'I have a message from Bel.' He frowned. 'Urgent, she says.'

Urgent? Ronnie could no longer imagine any circumstances in which she would need to hurry. Could that be the one and only mitigation for having her son in a coma? Anything and everything from now on would happen very slowly. Recuperation. Rehabilitation. There was some pleasure in the thought. She had noticed, as she aged, how fast the days slipped by and wished she could slow them down. Perhaps this was a twisted granting of her wish. If Kieran's claim that she could only have slept for a matter of minutes was true, so what? It hardly mattered.

'Where is she?'

'She wanted to see Clemmie. I guess she's still with her.' (Ronnie was, of course, mightily relieved that Clemmie was unscathed by the accident.) He added. 'Did you get in touch with...'

She pursed her lips. 'The mother? Yes, Nuala rang her. I believe she's on her way.'

'You mean Monique.'

'Whatever her foreign name is.'

'You didn't speak to her yourself?'

'There was no necessity.'

'That's an awfully high horse you've climbed onto,' said Kieran.

'Nuala's good at that type of thing,' insisted Ronnie. 'Dealing with difficult customers. I might have said something I regretted. You know how I get when my tether's frayed.'

In truth she didn't want to be put on the defensive by a woman she disapproved of, a woman who went around having children out of wedlock and finding some unfortunate man to pin them on.

'You might regret *not* speaking to her. Don't cut off your nose to spite your face. That's what you always used to tell us when we were young, remember?'

She stroked the limp hand lying on the sheet. 'Leave me be, Kieran. I can only deal with one thing at a time right now.'

'You realise Tom loves that kid?' said Kieran. 'He may not have been much good at taking care of her, but I'm pretty certain he carried her off because he didn't want to leave her somewhere she might be rejected.'

'She was never rejected! We made her welcome, you know we did. I wouldn't have a child suffer for the misdeeds of its parents.'

There came another beep; they were in thrall to their phones, her children. Kieran wasn't even looking in her direction. 'She's sent it again,' he said. 'I wonder what the matter is…' He was edging towards the door.

Ronnie decided to be magnanimous. 'You'd better go and find out.'

'Are you sure you'll be all right?'

'I'll be fine.'

'I'll probably take her back to Dingle after.'

'I'll see you tomorrow then,' she said. 'And we'll have a proper goodbye.'

But once he'd gone, retreating down the corridor, she felt a horrible sense of isolation. He had taken with him a warm vibrancy, an animal energy and she was left with the sad pallid scent of sickness and inertia. She returned to her chair and picked up her bag. She was knitting a collection of toy ducks. A family of six, she had decided, with plump yellow bodies and red felt beaks. The parents were already complete and she was going down a size for the little ones. She was on the second to last duckling (she'd started at the tail and was pleased with the way it curled into a point) and she didn't need a pattern any more. If she could only make the effort, the rhythm of her movements might soothe her.

It was no good; within moments her fingers and the yellow wool were in knots. She was trying to untie them when a nurse entered the room and nodded to her. He picked up the chart at the end of the bed, adjusted the IV drip and then stayed longer than she would have expected, gazing at Tom's face.

Ronnie dropped the duckling. 'Is something wrong?'

The nurse bent closer and murmured in a low coaxing tone. He said to Ronnie, 'I think he may be coming round.'

Her heart thumped so hard against her ribs she feared it would break them. 'How can you tell?'

'I'll see if I can get the doctor to verify it.'

Ronnie stumbled over to the bed as the nurse left. Could this be possible? She hadn't waited in vain? 'Oh, Tom,' she said. 'Tom, my darling. Will you open your eyes? So blue they were when you were little, like pieces of sky.' A summer sky, clear and sharp. They could pierce her like no one else's.

Hope swam inside her, the first real hope since the accident. It made her giddy. And now, instead of time stretching and looping like skeins of wool into infinity, it concertinaed. There was a distinct speeding up of activity (even though it was a Saturday) – a second nurse, a registrar, a doctor she hadn't seen before, an auxiliary with a cup of tea. Some noises were issuing from Tom's throat, although you couldn't call them words. His eyes did eventually flicker, though his gaze was unfocused, you couldn't call it sharp.

'It's looking hopeful,' the doctor said. 'We may need to perform some more tests. Why don't you go out for some fresh air, Mrs Farrelly? This has been an awful strain on you and you could do with a break. You could ring your husband with the good news.'

'It is good news? Definitely? I couldn't bear it if there'd been a mistake.'

'It's early days,' conceded the doctor. 'But your son is on his way back to us. The coma is partly a defence mechanism of the body…'

'Yes, I know.'

'And we never expected him to be in it for long; the trauma was not so great—'

'That's not what you told me before.'

'Well now, Mrs Farrelly, it's hard to judge these things and it's better to err on the cautious side.'

'So he's going to be all right?'

'We mustn't rush. Why don't come back in half an hour? The nurses will sort him out, try to make him comfortable. You'll be better off seeing him when he's more composed.'

Half an hour? That didn't give her time to get over to Carmel's. Anyway, she wouldn't want to leave the hospital site with Tom so near to recovery. And why was your man talking about fresh air? What was there on offer but a car park full of petrol fumes? Then she remembered Clemmie. She ought to check on the poor little mite. She'd be going home soon and maybe it wasn't her fault entirely that Tom had been distracted from his driving. All kiddies were attention-seeking.

Ronnie headed through the labyrinth of corridors towards the children's ward, a positive bounce in her step. It was extraordinary how different everything looked once you had some good news. She pictured Clemmie's animated face, the endearing gap in her teeth, her pink satiny ribbons; she was brimming with good intentions as she buzzed for entry.

'Clementine Beaumont?' said the ward sister. 'I'm sorry, Mrs Farrelly, she's been discharged.'

'Are you certain? When?'

'Let me see.' She consulted a chart. 'Not long ago, in point of fact. Her mother came to collect her.'

Her mother? Well, she was expected, as she'd told Kieran, but to appear and disappear so quickly into thin air; to leave without a word? Had she not even wanted to know how Tom was doing? Ronnie couldn't credit it. Surely there'd been a mistake? She strode into the middle of the ward and nobody stopped her. She gyrated her bulk slowly, taking in every occupied bed, every pale complexion. One bed was stripped, she saw, awaiting a new patient. There was no lively black face giggling up at her.

The realisation was like a plunge into icy water: it was Tom's giggle the girl had inherited – how could she not have spotted it before? She could hear it, mischievous and unmistakeable, but in her imagination only. Not in real life.

PART SEVEN

SUNDAY MONDAY

32

The Leave-taking

In retrospect, Pat's birthday dinner was a high spot. Ronnie had no idea when it might happen again: the chance to have the full complement of Farrellys around the table. Now they were back in the familiar groove with Anna and her husband bringing their children over and Nuala absent because she was working. But she wanted to give Kieran a good send-off so the rib of beef was magnificent and there were more than enough potatoes, boiled, mashed and roast, for the seven of them. Their spirits were high too, everyone talking at once. The little boys, Eoin and Conor, were bashing the table legs rowdily but nobody much cared. Least of all Ronnie, who was feeling reckless and half drunk – although there was only one bottle of wine between them on account of Kieran setting off for Dublin.

In fact it was Anna who'd organised the meal, according to her mother's instructions. Most of the morning Ronnie had been in the hospital, clasping Tom's hand as if she would never let it go. (She worried that she should have been at Mass, giving thanks, but the moments were too precious so she promised God she'd go in the evening when events had quietened down.)

'Don't you dare run out on us again!' she'd told Tom over and over, not bothering to mop up her tears. She had him where she wanted him for once because he was too feeble to taunt her or answer back. He lay, propped at a slight angle, almost as white as the pillows and as contrite as they come, his words emerging in feeble spluttering croaks.

Pat, who'd arrived soon after breakfast, had observed wryly, 'You were supposed to come home to celebrate me getting out of this festering place. Not end up in it yourself, you eejit. You know the garda are onto you?'

'I don't remember anything,' Tom mumbled.

'Don't be worrying about the red tape,' said Ronnie. 'The important thing is to get well. You'll be on crutches for a while. You'll have to let me take care of you.'

He'd given her a look of such utter helplessness she thought maybe she'd be able to take him in hand after all and maybe for the first time she'd make some headway. She was a realist though. She was keeping her hopes pinned down.

'I'm sorry we can't bring you home with us right away,' she said, 'but they'll let you out soon enough. We will see Kieran off and then I'll be back again tomorrow.'

'Clemmie?' Tom had said, as if he hardly dared voice her name. 'She's okay?'

'She is. She's gone home with her mother.' It was where the child belonged, but the manner of her departure rankled. Ronnie's relationship with Clemmie was unfinished, undefined, and this troubled her. 'At least the two of you have no lasting damage. Yet again you escaped by the skin of your teeth. So how many layers have you left, Tom Farrelly?' She shouldn't hound him. Surely, in any man's life there comes a point where he has learned his lesson?

It had been hard to tear herself away and Pat had to put the pressure on to get them back in time for Anna's lunch. They'd eaten very well and were now sitting around a clutter of empty plates, congealing gravy and cooling vegetable dishes.

Eoin and Conor slid down from their chairs. There was a litter of new kittens in one of the outbuildings they were eager to inspect. 'Don't you be tormenting them,' warned Anna. 'You have to wait until their eyes are open at least.'

Their father went with them and Ronnie moved on to the topic the family had been evading throughout the meal. 'I don't know what we should be doing with him,' she said.

'Nothing,' said Anna. 'He's a grown man, he has to face his own mistakes.'

'He'll not be going anywhere soon. He'll need crutches for weeks.'

'Bones mend fast when you're young,' said Pat.

'It's incredible that he's never broken anything before.'

'He can settle himself in the invalid's chair,' said Kieran. 'The one Dad's been keeping warm for him. He'll have the two of you running around like blue-arsed flies.'

'Not me,' said Pat. 'No chance.'

'The true blessing,' said Ronnie, 'is that Clemmie didn't have a mark on her. I don't know how he would have coped if he'd done her any injury.'

'So instead,' said Anna, 'all he has to think about is himself. What's new?'

'Ah no, he's taken a proper beating. Don't be so hard on him.'

'It's not me being hard! It's you being soft. You've always been too soft. That's the problem.'

'Well, Anna, my love, I think you haven't fared badly yourself. No one can say we've not done right by our children.'

'That isn't the point, Mam. You put him in a different category from the rest of us and much good has it done him.'

Ronnie bridled. 'So I've been overprotective? It's what happens, you know, when your child's been under threat; you'd be doing the same.'

'There's nothing *special* about him though, is there? Nothing to mark him out. I know we wanted to believe the other feller's sacrifice was worthwhile, but the accident was a simple freak. God hadn't anything to do with it. You need to see Tom for what he really is.'

'Anna! I don't know how you can say these things.' She looked around the table for support. Pat was toying with a knife, but Kieran's gaze was steady and uncompromising.

'She's right,' he said. 'Take the way he handled the kid. Whatever his motives, you can't call that responsible.'

'Sure, he was in a state at the time.'

'Isn't that just the point!' said Anna in exasperation.

Kieran said, 'Not that it matters. You're unlikely to be meeting Clem again anyway.'

'I don't see why not.' The fact was, she'd felt an emptiness just under her ribs (at least that's where she imagined it) ever since she'd seen the vacant bed in the ward. She could have done with a while longer to get to know her granddaughter.

'Because he's blown it with Monique, that's why. She wasn't fussed on letting him bring Clemmie over in the first place. So what makes you think she'll trust him again?'

'She might give him another chance if she sees he's reformed.'

'You plan to work on him, do you?'

'I like a challenge,' said Ronnie sharply. Their criticism had got her hackles up. 'And I'll have him where I want him. While he's hobbling around over the next few weeks he can make himself useful, play with his nephews, practise some parenting. I'll sort him out – you wait and see. He'll be better off away from London. It must be a dreadfully corrupting place.'

Kieran and Anna roared at this but Ronnie wouldn't be fazed. There were advantages to being a stubborn old matriarch. She knew how to deal with calamity: stay resolute.

'The magistrates may take a tougher view,' mused Pat. 'Put him away. For all we know he could go up before someone who's been wanting to get even for years.'

'I daresay we could find out who's to judge him,' said Ronnie. 'But I, for one, shan't complain if he loses his licence.'

'You do realise,' said Kieran, 'that he'll be driven mad by frustration, hanging around here.'

'Well I won't stop him leaving when he's ready to go.'

'It'll have to be under his own steam. Don't expect me to come back and fetch him.'

'As if I would!'

Kieran lolled in his chair. He didn't seem to be in any hurry and Ronnie wasn't going to chivvy him. Let him relax before his journey, there'd not been much chance of that for any of them. And it would be a lonely drive without Tom to accompany him. She wouldn't relish so many hours of silence herself. She spread her elbows on the table and rested her chin in her hands. Anna rose and began to collect the empty plates and stack them in the dishwasher.

They were startled when the doorbell rang. Nobody they knew ever came to the front door. Friends and neighbours tended to walk in through the scullery, kicking off muddy boots if necessary, calling out a greeting. A delivery might arrive from a courier who wasn't one of their regulars, but this was a rare event – so rare that it took Ronnie a while to recognise the peal of the bell.

Anna, on her feet, was quicker to react. 'I'll see who it is.' In fact the front hallway was used as a handy storage space, full of cardboard boxes, and she had to shout through the letter box to tell the visitors to go round the side. They heard the rasp of the dog's bark and the sound of clipped voices.

Kieran leapt up. 'It's Bel.'

'Well now,' said Ronnie, thinking there was no harm in some light ribbing at the girl's expense. 'Let's hope she makes it through the door without falling over.'

Bel entered the kitchen hesitantly. She was wheeling a floral suitcase and wearing jeans so tight the wind whistled through the gap in her legs. 'Hey, I hope I haven't come at the wrong time. I'm not disturbing you? Only Mum needs to get going. She has to drive to Cork for her flight.'

'No,' said Kieran, too quick, too tender. 'Not at all.'

Her eyes were bright and bold. 'It's brilliant news about Tom, isn't it? I was so delighted when I heard.'

'Yes,' said Ronnie. 'It's a relief to us all.'

'I'm sorry I shan't be able to see him before we go, but I hoped you'd give him my... our best wishes. Speedy recovery and so on.' She turned to Kieran. 'So here I am.'

He said, 'The boys are messing with some new kittens. D'you want to take a look too?'

He'll do anything, thought Ronnie, to get her out of my orbit. I'm not going to bite her for goodness' sake. 'Can you spare the time?' she said. 'I thought you had to be off.'

Anna interrupted. 'It's Bel's mother who's in a hurry. I've put her in the sitting room.'

The widow was here too? Ronnie nearly burst out: Why couldn't she join the rest of us? Why does she have to be given special treatment? Why is she sitting like the queen on my best suite? Instead, she said. 'Can we offer you something? You've had your dinner, Bel? You're not hungry? I could make you a sandwich. We've plenty of beef left over.'

The girl glanced in horror at the remains of the succulent rib. 'We're fine. Honestly.'

'A drink then. Coffee? Tea? A glass of brandy?'

'Julia wants to speak to you,' said Anna.

'To me?' said Ronnie, staring at Bel who met her gaze with round, innocent eyes.

'That's what she said. We'll clear up in here, the rest of us. You get along now, Mam.'

'She wants to apologise,' said Bel so quietly Ronnie was uncertain if she had heard her correctly.

She left them to it. In the front room the three-piece suite had been newly recovered in a pale sophisticated linen that looked as grand as a picture in a magazine (although they had to keep the door closed against the dog and his long moulting hairs). Julia wasn't sitting on it; when Ronnie came in she was standing by the window as if a budding fuchsia hedge were the most interesting sight in the world.

The women had met only twice before, in crowded public places. This was the first occasion they had faced each other without an audience.

'Hello,' said Julia – Ronnie could see the contraction of her throat as she swallowed. 'I hope you don't mind my… dropping in?'

She held out her hand so Ronnie was obliged to take it. 'I can't say I'd expected you. But you're welcome, naturally.'

'You welcomed me to your party too,' Julia said. 'And I behaved unforgivably. I wanted you to know how sorry I am.'

Ronnie wouldn't forget her manners, but she was not in any hurry to accept an apology, however abject. The widow may have suffered in the past, but that didn't stop her being culpable now. In addition, Ronnie was piqued by the way Clemmie had been stolen from under her nose. In her mind, Monique Beaumont and Julia Wentworth metamorphosed into a single adversary.

She eased herself into one of the chairs and indicated Julia should take the other. Julia sat in the same neat, decided manner with which she'd proffered her handshake. She bore herself with a composure very different from that of her daughter. She reminded Ronnie of a sleek well-behaved dog, a pointer or a greyhound.

'I heard that Tom is out of danger,' she said. 'That he's recovered consciousness. I'm so glad. And the child…'

'We have lost the child,' said Ronnie.

It was gratifying to see Julia's face drain white. 'Oh but surely... I thought she wasn't hurt!'

Ronnie said, 'The situation was difficult for all of us. We had never met her before. My son was doing his best, but it put him very much on edge. You know the result.' She waited a beat. 'And now Clemmie's back in England with her mother and there's an end to it. Do you have a granddaughter?'

'No,' said Julia. 'Not yet. I mean... one hopes.'

'One hopes indeed.'

They both fell silent. Ronnie wasn't used to her hands being idle. She wished she had her knitting with her, the rhythmic clack of the needles to counter the hush. Julia's fingers were playing a tune in her lap, a barely perceptible betrayal of her nerves. Eventually she spoke.

'It was kind of you to invite me to your party. But it was stupid of me to accept. It wasn't going to achieve anything... Except, I suppose, curiosity satisfied. Curiosity can be dangerous. I should have known that. I shouldn't have put either of us through it.'

Ronnie nodded. How many times in the past three days had she wished the invitation retracted, Teresa's meddling undone?

'I jumped to the wrong conclusion,' said Julia. 'And I lost my temper. We ought to have better control of ourselves in adulthood, but sometimes we just revert, don't we? That's the risk of bottling things up: you can crack under the strain. It must have been awkward for Tom, too.'

Tom had known well enough who the widow was, the significance of her. Ronnie had spelt it out to him and he'd taken it in his stride – at least she'd thought he had. He said he liked the girl; he'd be happy to meet the mother. But he must have been putting on a show for her sake. She reflected on the way he laughed everything off. Pretended he didn't care. About the voice, the music, the lack of career, the disappointments in his life. That painful gap between potential and achievement.

'Tom's inclined to be impulsive,' she said. 'The sort who'll act first and think later. But he's a good man. A bit of a tease sometimes, nothing worse.' She stopped. What was she doing, making excuses? She should be keeping her mouth shut.

Julia said, 'In my case, there's been all sorts lately, boiling away under the surface. My ex got the brunt of it. I'd been so worried about Bel, you see. Did she tell you she'd had malaria? It's easily treatable – as long as you're swift enough with the antidote. But it's made her vulnerable. That's why I over-reacted when I met Tom.' Her chest began to heave. She picked up her bag from the floor and hunted in it for a tissue. 'I was misreading the situation. I know that now. But I never intended to cause harm to anyone. I'm so sorry.'

Ronnie had satisfaction, did she not? The woman who had disrupted her family was begging for forgiveness. There were people round about who could bear a grudge for decades, but Ronnie wasn't one of them. She couldn't see a person weep without wanting to console them. She forgot that Julia had shaken her off when she'd tried to embrace her at the party. She went to perch on the arm of the other woman's chair and patted her shoulder.

'When a child's been saved you see them differently,' she said. 'As a boy, Tom played up something shocking, the tinker, because he knew he could get away with it. Maybe he'll have finally learned better now. He's had a jolt – we all have – and it gives you a new perspective.'

Julia tilted her head so that she was looking up at Ronnie and because the shape of her face, the cropped hairstyle, the dark eyes had scarcely changed, Ronnie was back in the Coroner's Court again, reliving the grim formalities of the inquest. Evidence as slippery as the rocks. Nothing to hold on to, but a man gone, a boy who was supposed to have a fine future in front of him.

Julia's voice was husky, as if the unshed tears were collecting at the back of her throat. 'In a job like mine you can spend a lifetime reassuring other people. Don't worry, he'll grow out of it – that sort of thing. Not always of course; sometimes you have to reach into your own reserves, offer what relief you can. I thought I was strong, because I'd coped with tragedy before. I could handle things. But actually, in practice, I'm just as frightened as the next person… Loss isn't less painful a second time around.'

Ronnie's hand was still resting on her shoulder; she placed her own on top; their fingers interlaced. 'It seems to be easier to admit these things to a stranger. I bumped into Vince Hogan on Doonshean beach a couple of days ago.'

Ronnie was confused. What did Vince have to do with anything?

'I discovered he'd been behind the bar when William and I went in for a drink. Will's last drink. We'd quarrelled you see and Vince saw it first hand: the damage my bad temper could do…' She paused, as if remembering, and then continued. 'We were still on the beach when Bel rang with news of Tom's accident. My fault again. That's why

I'm here. I shouldn't have been so angry with him. I'm not proud of myself.'

Ronnie held her tongue. Julia was constructing a fragile peace and she didn't want to say the wrong thing and spoil it. The living room, being little used and thickly carpeted, felt disconnected from the rest of the activities in the farmhouse. They were in a sealed bubble and the silence – no clock, no radio, no TV – was almost overpowering.

Then Julia said guardedly, 'There's another reason I wanted to see you. The memorial stone. When I came across it, it totally flummoxed me... It was so unexpected.'

'Ah,' said Ronnie, thinking it was safe now to return to her own chair, letting the cushions sigh at her back. 'We knew it could have been Tom buried the other side of the wall. It was a small enough gesture, to thank your husband. We had no other way of doing so once you had disappeared back to England. At the inquest I did try to speak to you.'

'I'm afraid I was too numb to take anything in.'

'We put the plaque up when the land was ours. Then the parish started running out of space for burials so we sold them a couple of fields. Now your husband has company and other visitors to remember him. That's good, is it not?'

'Oh yes, it's wonderful.' She hesitated. 'I have to admit when I first saw it my emotions were all over the place. But it's the most moving tribute I could have imagined. We scattered Will's ashes, Matt and I, so there's nowhere else...'

A pity, thought Ronnie. Everyone should have a place to mourn.

Julia continued with an effort. 'Matt's very like his father actually. Both in appearance and in temperament. He has a strong sense of fair play, keen to do the right thing. He's the same age as William was when he died, so every year from now on I'll be getting a glimpse of what might have been. How he might have grown old.' She shivered and narrowed her eyes, as if imagining an alternative future.

Ronnie saw Pat pass outside the window, whistling to JP. His clothes hung loose on him, the neck rising from his collar was scrawny. He was no longer the beefcake who'd roared up to the top of the Conor Pass with Ronnie riding pillion. Their first bike trip was the best part of fifty years ago, but she'd never forget the thrill of the perilous mountain road. She'd wrapped her arms around his waist and laid her cheek against his leather jacket and the screams had been whipped from her mouth by the speed of their dramatic switchback descent. There'd been long absences and tough times since, but they were still together. She knew she was lucky.

Julia rose. 'I couldn't have left without coming to see you. It wouldn't have been right. I don't know what drove me to Dingle exactly, or what I thought I would find. It was one of those inexplicable spur-of-the-moment decisions. But the memorial has been a huge comfort.'

'I'm glad to hear it.' As Ronnie got up and padded to the door, the atmosphere between the two women recalibrated itself. No more apologies, no more confessions. 'Will you take some refreshment? A cup of tea?'

Julia glanced at her wristwatch. 'I'd better get going. Your Mr O'Leary doesn't like his passengers to be late and it's a two-hour drive, isn't it? I'll just say goodbye to Bel.'

As she led the way to the outbuilding where the kittens tumbled in the straw Ronnie said, puzzled. 'Is she staying on in the cottage then? Is she not going with you?'

'She can't,' said Julia. 'She didn't bring her passport because you don't need it on the ferry, only on the plane. I didn't know if I'd be able to get a flight back, but I grabbed at the chance because, for various reasons, I want to get home quickly – I've been away a long time.'

'I see,' said Ronnie, who didn't quite.

The kittens were suckling. The mother cat lay stretched out and resigned as the small silky bodies scrambled over each other and plundered her teats. Eoin and Conor sat astride ancient tricycles pretending they were horses.

'Where's your daddy?' said Ronnie. 'Or your uncle Kieran?'

Eoin slapped his steed's flanks with a cane and trundled across the yard, waving the make-believe riding crop at the barn opposite. Bel was leaning back against it. Kieran, facing her, had one hand resting on the stonework just above her shoulder. They were close in conversation, but when Julia called out they sprang apart.

'Mum, are you going?' Bel darted forward to embrace her.

'It's very good of you to offer her a lift,' Julia said to Kieran. 'By all accounts the train journey can be tedious.'

A lift? He'd be carrying a passenger from Dingle to Dublin and he hadn't said a word. Ronnie opened her mouth to speak, but thought better of it. She tried to catch her son's eye; he avoided hers altogether.

33

The Stopover

The goodbyes were extravagant and heartfelt. Bel stood aside as Kieran was passed from brother-in-law to sister to father to mother in a leave-taking of epic proportions. (Her own mother had left quietly, a good hour earlier.) Ronnie was extracting a promise that he'd be back in the summer. 'A weekend's easy enough now the planes are flying again. We can pick you up from Farranfore.'

'Sure I'll come,' said Kieran, inching away from his family, whirling one of his nephews into the air like a shield, indicating that Bel should get into the car.

But Bel had to be embraced by everybody too and Ronnie insisted on fetching a hand-knitted scarf to wrap around her neck in case it got breezy on the boat.

Chased by the dog, they rumbled down the lane away from the farmhouse. It no longer looked as bleak as on her first visit because the sun was shining. The fields fanning out behind them in shades of green were tipped with bronze and gold, as iridescent as the ocean. Inside the Renault the atmosphere lightened. They were both in high spirits. 'Well,' said Kieran, taking his eyes from the road to flash her a smile. 'We've made our escape.'

'Don't you like being with your family?'

'They drive me mad, that's all. Probably because I'm the youngest.'

'Me too! I hadn't realised you were.'

'There's only eighteen months between me and Tom. People often get us the wrong way around.' Nevertheless, his tone sounded reproving, as if she should have known better. As if he'd expected her to be in a different league from those who saw the brothers as interchangeable, or worse: Kieran blighted forever by Tom's shadow. 'You're not worried, are you?' he added, accelerating.

'What about?'

'What you're going to find when you get home?'

Matt had rung her the night before with the news of the fire. 'Well it took my brother two whole days to tell us anything, so it can't be too dreadful, can it? It's only a garage.'

'It wasn't why your mother decided to fly?'

'No, I think she'd just had enough. She's been away much longer than I have.'

It had crossed her mind that Matt was playing down the gravity of the event, particularly in relation to her father. Second-degree burns, he'd said. Bel didn't know what this meant. Her mother had said it would be too early to predict the prognosis, but Bel could see she was apprehensive. They both knew there was nothing more important to Leo than his work.

Kieran's hand left the wheel and squeezed hers, lying in her lap. 'Hey. It's been a heavy week. Let's try and enjoy what's left of it.' She squeezed back. 'Right then,' he said. We're away.'

They bowled along lanes and highways and onto the motorway. As the countryside sped past, Bel could see crumbling stone towers, deserted ruins garlanded with ivy, lime-washed cottages under a crop of thatch, meadows studded with spring flowers. Such a lyrical romantic landscape, she thought. How tempting to hide yourself away in it with a lover. Maybe, if she ever got the chance to come back…

The sun was streaming from the west, from the counties they were leaving behind. It was sinking too, sliding beneath a trail of light cloud on the horizon, turning its edges pink.

Kieran said, 'Now, about tonight. You'll need a place to stay.'

She fidgeted in her seat. 'Oh don't worry about me. I can find a room somewhere and get myself to the ferry.'

'I'm not going to abandon you! I'm driving you home.'

'To Liverpool? But it's out of your way and I have the train ticket.'

'Don't you want me to?'

'Well yes, but only if it's no trouble.'

'It's no trouble.'

'Okay then. Thanks.'

'Grand, we'll head for Ned's house. It's where we often stop off.'

'He won't mind?'

'No, but I should warn you, it's a bit of a tip. If you'd rather somewhere civilised we could look for a hotel.'

She liked the idea of meeting his friend; hotels were impersonal and besides, she had scarcely any money left. 'Oh no, I'm not bothered. I can crash anywhere.'

The light was fading when they turned into a narrow side street in Dun Laoghaire. The blue door at the top of a flight of steps was faded too, its paint flaking, battered by the salt-laden winds. Most of the neighbouring houses had gleaming brass numbers screwed to freshly varnished doors; some had bay trees in pots.

Kieran ran up and rang the bell. When no one answered he patted the pockets of his jacket. 'I should have the key here.'

'You're going to let yourself into the guy's house?'

'It's fine. He's expecting me. Why d'you think I have the key in the first place?'

As he pulled it out another object clattered onto the steps: a disposable orange cigarette lighter. 'I remember this!' she exclaimed. 'It's the one I thought you'd dropped on deck and tried to give back to you. Only it was Tom who—'

'It's empty. I should have thrown it away.'

'But you didn't?'

He turned the key and pushed open the blue door. 'No, I didn't.'

She followed him into a sitting room in splendid disarray. Silver discs were scattered like giant coins amid piles of empty CD cases, a guitar was balanced in a corner, a mug of coffee dregs stood on the mantelpiece beside an Arabic dictionary, an iPod dock, a bottle of Bushmills and a giant conch shell. A sagging sofa crouched under a faded throw, which might have been woven in the Middle East; dog-eared magazines surfed along it.

'Are you sure he was expecting you?'

'Ned's place is always like this. I did warn you.'

'It seems like quite a smart area.'

'Oh it is. Comes with a high price tag too.'

'So how can he afford it, your mate?'

'Actually he's my cousin. Through my dad's sister. She lives in Boston now with her second husband. Ned's meant to be keeping the place warm for when she comes back over. Not very often, as you might imagine. He persuaded her to hang on to it when she wanted to sell, which was a wise move. Otherwise he'd be out in one of those housing estates builders threw up when money was cheap and planners thought the best thing you could do with a fine green belt was swamp it with identikit concrete boxes.'

She'd noticed the suburban sprawl replacing quaint picture-book Ireland the closer they'd got to Dublin. She was a little uneasy about being in this stranger's house. 'Where is he then?'

'I'll text him. Shall we fetch the bags indoors?'

After they'd dumped their cases in the hallway they progressed into the kitchen, which also had the look of a sinking ship hastily abandoned. Kieran opened the fridge and she peered over his shoulder at a dozen beer bottles and a lonely piece of cheese. She didn't regard herself as fastidious, especially in comparison with Rachael and Julia, but even she baulked at the growth of blue fuzz. 'Oh my God, it's got hair!'

He took out two of the bottles and nipped off their tops. 'Thirsty?'

'A bit.' She would drink from the bottle. As a rule, to her mother's dismay, she was casual about hygiene, but it had been drummed into her that she shouldn't take any more risks. Her immune system was weak; if bacteria or viral infection took hold, it could set her health backsliding again.

'D'you want to eat? A lot of places are shut on Sundays but we could find somewhere for a pizza.'

'Only if you let me pay.' She reckoned she could run to pizza, even if the cash she'd be using was Matt's.

'Sure, if you insist.'

'I do.'

His hand rested lightly in the small of her back as they descended into the street again. Once in the pizzeria she discovered that she was ravenous, ended up gobbling too fast to speak. He was less hungry – on account of his enormous lunch, he claimed – and apologised for the time he was spending checking emails on his phone.

Watching him as she ate, the swift typing, the methodical clicking, the occasional expressive arch of the brow, she realised that when she was with Kieran she felt no manic compulsion to make conversation. As the quiet member of a voluble clan, he could focus with calm intent – and this was catching. Were they not, the two of them, in perfect harmony? Mellow and relaxed?

She murmured, as she placed her knife and fork together, 'I suppose he might be back now.'

'Who?'

'Your cousin.'

'Ned? Ah no, he won't be coming back.'

'Why not?'

'He's in Kabul.'

'What!' She recalled the detritus littering the house. 'But it looked like he'd just popped out for a packet of fags. How can he be halfway across the world?'

In the restaurant the lighting was low but Kieran's eyes glinted with amusement. 'He's a foreign correspondent so he often has to drop everything and scoot off at short notice. At least, that's his excuse. Basically he's a slob.'

'Did you know that he wasn't going to be there? Is that why you had the key?'

'I often stay over. And Tom too. When I first asked him about tonight, he came back to me saying yeah, cool. He didn't happen to mention he wasn't going to be around.' His thumb skimmed the surface of his phone; he held it up to show her the recent text. 'He's only just let me know he's in Kabul. Typical. Does it bother you?'

'Of course not,' she said emphatically. 'Don't be daft.'

'It can't enhance your opinion of the Farrellys.'

'I should think it's wildly glamorous, being a foreign correspondent.'

He snapped the phone shut and consigned it to his pocket. 'It's like a lot of things: the image is a bit different from the reality. But you know what, I'd like to show you we're not all hopeless feckin' eejits. You can see for yourself, if you ever visit my place... It was a wreck when I bought it but I'm pleased with what I've done.'

'Tom said you were good at DIY, that you can bang a nail straight.'

'My ambassador,' said Kieran with a spark of sarcasm.

'Oh no... I always say the wrong thing.' She reached across the table till their hands met. 'I'd love to see your house. Do you live alone?'

He gave her a probing look. 'I do at present, yes. But it's through choice, not because I have unsavoury habits.'

'Like cultivating hair on rancid bits of cheddar?'

He laughed. 'Can you face going back there?'

Perhaps she'd been too quick to turn down his suggestion of a hotel: the prospect of white Egyptian cotton and spotless sanitary ware was now more appealing. But comfortable as she was in his company, she still didn't know quite where she stood. And the money business could be tricky. She made a point of opening her wallet and counting out her last euros for their dinner bill. 'It's no problem. Honest.'

A faint chill permeated the dark night air. As they left the restaurant, Bel wrapped Ronnie's scarf around her neck and slipped her arm through Kieran's. It seemed a natural enough thing to do. It was only a short walk back to the house which, under the street lamps, blended with its neighbours. When they got inside and Kieran switched on the lights (not every bulb had a shade), the disorder was brutally and vividly illuminated.

He started up the stairs. 'Trust me: the spare room at the top isn't too bad. But we'll need to find you some clean sheets.'

He rummaged in the linen press on the landing. Bel peered through open doors. The one to Ned's bedroom was wedged ajar with boxes full of books; a second room, also book-crammed, was apparently used as a study. Up a further flight, under the eaves, the third bedroom was refreshingly sparse. It contained only a double bed, a chest and a chair and seemed an oasis of tranquillity. The sheet billowed between them like a sail as they laid it over the mattress. Bel stuffed pillows into cases; Kieran shook out the duvet. She colonised the chair with her bag and jacket, couldn't suppress a yawn.

He said, 'You're right. It's been a long day so I'd better leave you to it.'

She wasn't sure what to make of this. 'What about you? Are you going to sleep in Ned's room?'

'No, I'll take the couch downstairs.'

'Oh, you can't do that!'

'Why not? I've done it before.'

'I bet you woke up black and blue.'

'Actually I slept okay.'

'Couldn't you stay up here?' said Bel. 'I've had enough of being stowed away in the attic all alone like Rapunzel. God, that sounds awful, like I'm not grateful to you. What I mean is…' butterflies beat their wings against her stomach wall; her intestines tied themselves into bows '…please will you sleep with me?'

He was standing on the threshold, half in and half out of the small room. In a trice he could be leaping down the stairs away from her. She waited.

He said, 'Sleep with you?'

She said, 'Look, I just meant… this is a big bed, so we could share it. I often do that when I stay over at friends'. I'm not coming on to you or anything.'

'You're not?' His voice was neutral, giving nothing away.

She kicked off her boots and lay back on one half of the mattress. 'See?'

'You want me to join you?'

'Yes please.'

She was curious to see what he would do, although she worried about her tactics too. Had she come across as hopelessly needy, like a child who was afraid of the dark?

Or a young woman desperate to be held by another human being?

Kieran took off his shoes as she had done and stretched himself out beside her.

'Plenty of room, isn't there?'

He turned, propping himself on his elbow, and regarded her until she felt exposed beneath his scrutiny. She raised her hand to push him away, but he caught her wrist and held it. Within an instant, this simple move had ripened into an embrace that was nothing like the farewell hugs she'd exchanged with the other Farrellys (or that brief lustful flirtation with Tom). She closed her eyes and Kieran kissed her lids, her ear, her throat before meeting her lips. This is well worth waiting for, she thought.

Tentatively he began to slide her top from her shoulders and she wriggled to make it easier for him. She fumbled with the buttons on his shirt and the buckle of his belt. Thus, by degrees, they undressed each other on Cousin Ned's only respectable bed, peeling off socks, jeans, underwear, letting the garments tumble onto the bare boards of the floor.

Take it slowly for God's sake, Bel told herself. To Kieran, as she removed his boxer shorts, she said, 'Now, will you lie on your back? Make a shape like a da Vinci man.'

'*What*?'

'You know.' She spread her limbs in demonstration. 'Leonardo Da Vinci's drawing of a man inside a circle, the really famous one.'

He gave her a wry look. 'Am I going to like this game?'

'Chill out! I'm not going to tie you up or anything. But you have to keep still. This is important. I want to draw you. Like, get to know you.'

She knelt between the V of his legs and traced a path along his neck and pectoral muscles, the underside of his arms. She smoothed her fingertips over his ribs, over his hips, thighs, calves and ankles, down to the soles of his feet and very slowly upwards again. He clenched his jaw, making an effort not to quiver at her touch.

'Hey, you're good,' she said. 'What self-control!' But she could see his erection growing as she completed her body map. When she reached his penis it was satisfyingly sensitive to each stroke of her palm. 'Now I feel like I've got magic powers.'

Kieran pulled her towards him as if he'd had enough. His heartbeat throbbed against hers. 'Jaysus, Bel!' he said. 'You shouldn't have to look far, to get an idea of your powers all right.'

'Oh no,' she said, burrowing her face into the hollow of his shoulder, inhaling the scent of him. 'Not me. Rachael, my sister-in-law, is the one to give guys wet dreams. She's the beauty in our house.'

'Don't be putting yourself down all the time.'

He wasn't interested in hearing about Rachael. He was taking his turn, his hands exploring the curves and crevices of her anatomy – though she was short on curves and she bemoaned the way her bones poked through her skin, the sharp jut of pelvis and clavicle. 'I've lost a lot of weight,' she said in apology for her small breasts, but he seemed hungry for them. When he fastened his mouth on hers again she couldn't say anything else, which was just as well because it would probably be something stupid that she'd regret later. Magic powers! It could have been Clemmie talking. And then, with a swoop and a plunge, he was inside her.

The bed was groaning and they were making love and the foolishness and disappointment of previous weeks were completely unimportant. Didn't matter a bit.

She lay afterwards in the crook of his arm, their bodies close and slick with sweat. 'We'll have to get up early to wash the sheets,' she said.

'I'll set the alarm on my phone.'

'I don't know if I can sleep.' Her limbs felt drowsy, true, but her mind was in overdrive, churning with excitement. 'I never imagined this would happen. I was so slow on the uptake. I mean, when you brought me the flowers I did get a little clue, but you were so damn courteous and well behaved, I wasn't certain...' She prodded him gently. 'Why didn't you push yourself forward more, like Tom?'

'There's your answer,' he said. 'Plus, I was wary of your mother.'

'My mother?' This was a surprise. 'I know she helped fuck things up for Tom, but what on earth did she do to you?'

'It was more what I did to her.' He hesitated. 'I don't know whether I should tell you this, Bel.'

'You've started, so you can't stop now. Tell me what?'

He brushed her hair away from her face. 'About what happened at Doonshean.'

'You mean the beach where they have the riptide? She took me there. It's beautiful.'

'Sure it is, and in general fatalities are rare. You have to have an unlucky combination of circumstances. But it's at low tide, when the strand looks so peaceful, that the current is at its most savage. Anyhow...' He sighed.

'What are you trying to say?'

'Just… I was responsible for setting that particular chain in motion.'

'You? In what way?'

'I don't actually remember any of it. Only what the girls told me.'

'Go on then.'

'Well, the story goes that Tom had been collecting shrimps and shells and what have you, during the afternoon. We were supposed to share them out but I had some kind of tussle with him – you know how little kids get into a strop – and spilled the bucket. Everything drained back into the sea. At this point, apparently, I became inconsolable so he went off to gather some more. That's why he was clambering over the rocks again when the wave got him – it was for my benefit. And my sisters were too busy trying to stop me wailing to notice he'd gone too far.'

'So how old were you?'

'Two. And maybe a half.'

'A toddler! You're not telling me you've been feeling guilty ever since?'

'Certainly not.' He tightened his grip around her waist. 'Like I said, I don't even remember the bucket – though the drama: the ambulance siren, the wailing and the panic, they made an impression, they're lodged in my memory somewhere. I was only a bit player; my part was insignificant compared with Tom's. I'm not beating myself up over it. I wasn't even going to mention it, but…'

'You can go too far with cause and effect,' she said.

'True enough.'

'It was a terrible tragedy, Kieran, but you do realise that if it hadn't happened I – me, myself – wouldn't be here? Isabel Wentworth wouldn't exist.'

She let the thought sink in, then rolled on top of him. She gazed down at his face, the clear steady eyes and the smile that was no longer so rare and fleeting. She could feel his cock stirring to life again. 'We're onto new beginnings now,' she said. 'You don't really want to sleep, do you?'

Later they did doze, fitfully. There was no blind at the window so Bel surfaced with the dawn. Kieran was facing away from her, his body spread-eagled in a spent, loose sprawl, the duvet cast off. She reviewed all the other mornings in her life when she'd woken beside a new man. The blue of the sky beyond the glass was intensifying. Perhaps those volcanic particles were still airborne, adding depth and a third dimension. Perhaps this time things would be different.

34

The Bicycle

Rachael lay soaking in the bath, a supreme indulgence on a Monday morning (even if it was a bank holiday). She'd opened the sash window to let out steam and the air that entered in return was fragrant with lilac. She dipped her head backwards and let her hair float around her in fronds. She was alone in the house. Matt had got up early to give Danny breakfast so she could sleep in and now he'd taken him down to the Prom on his bike.

She surfaced above the water again and let it ripple along the length of her body. She laid one hand on her abdomen, smooth, flat and unmarred. In the end it had been so simple. She had picked up her phone and cancelled the appointment with the Pregnancy Advisory Service. She didn't need to consult anybody: her decision was made.

The fire had been horrific – Dan wasn't the only one to have nightmares – but it had profoundly altered her perceptions. The sight of Matt going after Leo, the fear of losing him, made the worries that had loomed so large for her seem trifling and irrational. Matt's affection, his support, his indestructible self-belief – all these helped to make her a better person. She couldn't betray him. She loved her husband and she wanted to have his children.

It had occurred to her, on Friday, that Leo might remark on the fact that he'd offered to drive her to the clinic and now it was the other way around. But no, he was in mourning for his work and Rachael's problems were irrelevant, erased from his memory. However, he let her run around after him and she was keen for Matt to see she was making an effort. She had also finally confided in Emma, who'd advised her to keep her reservations to herself. 'Matt doesn't need to know you had a wobble,' she said. 'Everybody wobbles. Just give him the good news. It's what he's been waiting for, isn't it?'

Which was why, when she'd arrived home from Emma's, it had been disturbing to find Matt so hard and alien. He wore no trace of his usual boyishness, but an air of suppressed wrath. Deep grooves were scored between his eyebrows and down either side of his nose.

'Where the hell have you been?' His tone was so aggressive she'd almost burst into tears on the spot.

She managed to contain herself until Leo left the room and then she'd confessed. The frown lines vanished. Matt's eyes shone behind his glasses and his face split into a smile. 'Oh my God!' he exclaimed. 'I never imagined...'

'Didn't you? Why not? I thought you wanted more kids.'

'Sure I did. But we'd only just started trying. And they said it might take ages...' Then the frown hovered again as if he were computing something. 'So, what date?'

'New Year's Day. Do you reckon that's a good omen?'

'Definitely! When did you find out?'

This was where she had fudged her answer. 'Well, I thought I might be pregnant a couple of weeks ago, but I didn't want to take the test too soon. Emma had a spare kit so she let me use it today when we went back to hers after swimming.'

Matt had gathered her into his arms. 'You're not scared this time, are you?'

The feel of him, the thick brushed cotton of his shirt, the firm space between his neck and shoulder where she could lay her head – all these were infinitely consoling. 'A bit.'

'It'll be fine. My mother will help out.'

'Julia? Really?'

'She was working when Dan was born. She has more freedom these days.'

'Oh yes, I suppose she does.' She added, 'I'm sorry if I've been flaky and irritable lately, about Bel being here and then Leo. I didn't mean to knock your family. You think I've been intolerant, don't you? Put it down to the hormones.'

She couldn't see his face but she felt him stiffen. 'No,' he said softly. 'I think you've been a paragon of patience. Leo's enough to drive anyone up the wall. Worse in his old age, without Julia to rein him in.'

'I don't want to kick him out,' Rachael said. 'Well, not until Bel gets back and needs the room.' In truth, she was grateful to Leo. He'd taken her work seriously and encouraged her to see herself as an artist with a valuable talent. He had boosted her self-belief.

'Frankly I can't wait for him to go,' Matt said, which had surprised her– but didn't give her quite so much pleasure as his next pronouncement.

She lathered her limbs with soap and rinsed it off again. She reached for a towel with a thick deep pile and pulled out the bath plug. Above the gurgle of water draining she heard the slam of a door, Dan's excited voice and Matt's lower tones. They were back. Wrapped in the towel she leant across the basin and tweezered stray hairs from her brows. She massaged moisturiser into her face and body lotion into her legs. She needed to look after herself, Matt had insisted. He'd also said they could go ahead with the new kitchen.

'Do you mean that? No kidding?'

'Yeah, if we get onto it right away you'll be able to use your new cooker for all those summer parties.'

All those summer parties was an exaggeration but she could pitch for more. And a revamped kitchen would make a big difference. 'But what about the cost? Can we afford it?'

'We can use the insurance pay-out.'

'You mean for the garage?'

'It won't do the car any harm to stand outside at this time of year.'

'What if they decide the fire was deliberate?'

'We were the victims,' he said. 'And there's not much anyone can do about Nathan because he's under the age of criminal responsibility. He's only nine.'

'You know that for a fact?'

'Yes, I checked with Kelly.' His voice thickened. 'We won't be seeing those two again.'

'That's a relief.'

She folded the damp towel and hung it on the rail. Tomorrow she would pick up some paint charts, contact a joiner, make the house fit to bring up her family in. As she fastened her bra she noticed that her breasts were already feeling tender. She chose a button-through dress from her wardrobe, one that was not restrictive but made her feel as if she could waft through fields of wheat and barley like a girl in a shampoo advert.

When she went downstairs and into the kitchen she was pleased to find Danny slathering peanut butter on a slice of bread. Some years ago a health visitor had commented that he seemed under-nourished and Rachael had been mortified. Matt and Julia had both tried to reassure her: the health visitor was old school, traditional, insensitive; Danny was perfectly healthy, there was nothing wrong with his diet. But Rachael knew he was picky. He would leave vegetables at the side of his plate because he didn't like the shape of them. He was much reedier than Caleb, Emma's little boy. So the calorific peanut butter was an encouraging sight. So was the flush of colour in his cheeks.

'Darling, you're quite pink!' she said.

'So are you.'

'That's because I've been in the bath. Yours is a better sort of pink because it comes from being in the fresh air. How did it go?'

Immense pride infused every syllable: 'Daddy says we can take the stabilisers off.'

'That's fantastic! Well done.' She had visions of a bike toppling over, the front wheel spinning and a small boy trapped and wailing beneath the frame. She dismissed it.

'He did great,' said Matt. 'He's really gaining confidence.'

Rachael joined them at the table, picking grapes from the fruit bowl, watching with satisfaction as Danny demolished his sandwich. 'Is Leo still around?'

'No,' said Matt. 'He called a cab about the same time we went out. He's gone to visit friends I think.'

'I'm surprised he's got any left.' She wondered as soon as the words were out how Matt would take this, but he laughed.

'I think it helps to have an ego the size of a mountain. Since they re-did his dressings and he can use his fingers again, he must have rung round his contacts until he found someone prepared to listen to him.'

'So it's just the three of us,' said Rachael, the sweet grape juice bursting in her mouth. 'What a treat.' A family, chilling in their own home, without uninvited guests; a tranquil afternoon spread out before them, no commitments, no pressure, no conflict. 'I thought I'd make a cake. Red velvet. You'd enjoy that, Dan, wouldn't you? You can help me break the eggs and add the colouring while Daddy's sorting out your bike.'

Like Rachael, Dan was enthralled by the way the magic of chemistry could transform a disparate heap of ingredients into a stunning centrepiece (although he ran off as soon as the layers were put in the oven). When everything came together it was as though the planets had aligned in her favour. This was what she could do; this was what she was good at. She beat the icing vigorously, energised and even a little excited about her future. Covering the icing bowl with cling film and leaving the cake to cool, she wandered outside.

Unfortunately Matt was having less success. Sweaty and cursing on the front driveway, he was still struggling to unscrew the nuts on the bike's stabilisers. Danny was hopping up and down in impatience. As the spanner slipped and clattered to the ground for the nth time, a Renault Megane drew up and parked outside. Bel got out of the passenger seat and hoisted her luggage from the boot.

It gave Rachael a shock to recognise her own suitcase. She'd forgotten she'd lent it and she was sure she spotted a streak of black grime where none had been before. But she wouldn't make a fuss; she wouldn't allow a scrap of dirt to destroy her mood. As Bel approached, Danny launched himself at her knees and began telling her excitedly about his riding prowess. The car's driver followed close behind.

'This is Kieran Farrelly,' said Bel, introducing the Irishman. 'He's been ace, brought me all the way from Dingle. Have you heard from Mum?'

'She called us this morning,' Matt said. 'Said she got back last night. She's coming over later. I think she wants to check up on Leo.'

'Isn't he here?'

'Not right now.'

Rachael said, 'You're looking really well, Bel. The holiday must have done you good.'

'Yeah, some bits were brill... others, not so. Like your week, I guess. Is that what's left of the garage?'

Rachael refrained from saying: it was that loopy boy you let in who burned it down, because she didn't want to sound accusing in front of the stranger, Kieran. 'Afraid so, bit of a disaster isn't it?'

'The problem,' said Matt. 'is that we can't store stuff in it any more. We're going to have to keep Danny's bike indoors.'

Bel peered at his hands, covered in grease. 'What are you doing to it?'

'I'm trying to get the damn stabilisers off but I think the nuts have rusted.'

'Have you any WD40?' said Kieran. 'The miracle solution?'

Matt looked at Rachael. 'Have we?'

'I don't know. Possibly in the garage?'

'Worth a try.'

While Matt and Kieran picked their way through the debris, Bel said, 'Were Dad's paintings the only valuable things left in there?'

'Well, Matt got the car out and we were already using the garden furniture, so yes.'

'Matt downplayed it when he rang,' said Bel. 'Like he didn't tell me how badly Dad had been injured.'

'He didn't want to worry you.'

'Amazingly, Dad seems okay about it.'

'Have you spoken to him?'

'He phoned me when we on the hydrofoil. On the open deck at the back. The seagulls were chasing our wake – it's quite mesmerising, all that white froth – and suddenly Leo rings. It was surreal.'

'He was massively pissed off at first,' said Rachael. 'When he realised what damage he'd done to himself. How crazy he'd been. But he cheered up a bit when the *Echo* asked for an interview.'

'He's done better than that now,' said Bel. 'He's got his dealer on the case, setting up all sorts of PR. He's asked me to go back to London with him.'

'And will you?'

Bel's eyes were following the men shifting tins and cans from the collapsed shelves in the wrecked garage. Puffs of dust and ash rose and settled again. Their shoulders looked as though they were speckled with dandruff. 'Yeah,' she said. 'I might as well. He has room for me and he needs looking after. Whereas I'm, like, fully okay now. I'll have a better chance of finding work in London and I can go to Birmingham at weekends.'

Rachael felt she must have missed something. 'What's in Birmingham?'

'Oh… Kieran. He lives there. And if I manage to get any web design contracts he can help me with the technical stuff.'

'Right. I see.' She wanted to say: Don't be hasty, Bel; but what was the point? That was precisely Bel's character. She didn't weigh things up at length like her brother. Anyway the guy wasn't one of her usual lame-duck misfits. He looked a promising choice. Competent. Reliable. He was coming towards them armed with a spray can and an adjustable spanner. It barely took him five minutes to detach the stabilisers from the rear bicycle wheel and line them up at the foot of the steps.

'Well done, mate,' said Matt.

'Come on now, Danny boy,' said Bel. 'You have to give us a demonstration.'

The street was quiet. It had a sleepy bank holiday torpor. Fair-weather gardeners were planting out marigolds, clipping their hedges or strimming their patches of grass. Traffic was minimal. Only two other cars had passed by since Kieran's. Even so Rachael was nervous. She wanted to protest that perhaps it was too soon, perhaps he wasn't quite ready after all, but she was clearly outnumbered.

She clasped her hands tightly in front of her and could only peep sideways through her lashes as Danny set off. Matt jogged alongside him. The bike wobbled at first and she was convinced he would overbalance. She nearly reached out to clutch at Bel, but Bel had moved within the shelter of Kieran's arm so Rachael was on her own. What would Dan do if a car suddenly backed out of a drive, or a football shot across the road? But as the bike gathered speed his balance grew more assured. He was gripping the handlebars as if he would never let go, but he was managing to ride in a straight line – at least until he turned the corner and disappeared from sight.

'Hey, Rach,' said Bel. 'I bet you're proud of him. God, I can't tell you how many times I fell off my bike when I was learning. Down this very street in fact. Imagine!'

A fraught ninety seconds later Dan came back up the road, pedalling fiercely, expressions of triumph and terror jostling on his face.

'Oh my God,' said Rachael as he sailed past them. 'I hope he can stop. Suppose he can't brake without falling off?'

'He'll be fine,' said Bel. 'Matt's keeping pace anyway.'

Father and son disappeared on another circuit of the immediate neighbourhood: Matt red-faced, wiping the sweat from his hairline, Danny becoming more relaxed with each lap completed. Finally he shot into the driveway – Kieran grabbed the handlebars and steadied the frame – and Rachael was able to relax.

She flooded him with extravagant praise, but as she picked up the bike to help him bring it into the house, she thought she glimpsed the boy, Nathan, with his odd lurching gait. Had he been watching and waiting to intercept Danny when no one was around? He'd probably be envious, even though the bike was far too small for him. But the figure was distant still so she told herself she'd made a mistake.

35

The Homecoming

Julia parked outside her former home in the spot vacated by Kieran; Bel let her in. She didn't need to ask how her journey had gone. Bel, glowing for the first time since her illness, was full of it – especially the little house in Dun Laoghaire.

'Cousin Ned?' said Julia. 'Good Lord! He sounds like someone in a Victorian novel.'

'Oh but he's a real person. Quite high-powered I think. I'm sorry I didn't meet him. We stayed up in his attic because the rest of the place was such a tip. If you lifted the skylight and poked your head out you could see the harbour and the masts of all the yachts. Ace.'

'Sweetheart, we spent the past week by the sea! Dingle's full of boats.'

Bel nodded. 'Yeah, absolutely… But he's a dark horse, Kieran. I didn't feel I got to know him till we travelled alone together. He went out of his way to bring me home. You only just missed him, but he had to get back.'

Julia recalled the tulips she'd left on the table at Dolphin Cottage, their petals forming perfect cups, vibrant with life and delicate colour.

'And you should know, Mum, that I've decided to go too. I've been here long enough. I've agreed to get the train to London tomorrow with Dad. See how dutiful I am?'

'Are you sure you feel up to it?'

'Oh yes, honestly. Terrific!'

Julia was used to Bel's enthusiasms, to her spurts of passion, her complete enthralment to her newest idea or latest romance. She itched to warn her at each headlong turn that she should prepare herself for pain and disappointment. But it had been something far more arbitrary and unforeseen that had sabotaged her, so she wasn't going to deflate her hopes now – even if they did rest on a Farrelly.

Besides, Bel wasn't the only person to have a different aura about her. While they talked in the sitting room, Rachael was gliding about with new poise, offering them tea and slices of red velvet cake. She used to undermine her stately presence with submerged tension like an oversensitive racehorse; not any more. There was a fullness to her face too, which Julia didn't comment on, although she suspected she knew the cause.

'Matt will be down in a minute,' Rachael was saying. 'He has to finish the game he and Dan are playing on the Wii. Danny's full of himself today because he's learned to ride his bike. He'll probably want to show you after supper. You are going to stay and eat with us, aren't you? I've no idea when Leo's coming back but there's plenty of food and if it's not a problem for you...' She broke off.

Julia said, 'No problem. There are things we need to sort out and I'm sure we can be civilised.'

Rachael said, 'I don't fucking believe it.' She had crossed to the bay window that overlooked the front drive. She leant her forehead against the pane, her shoulders slumped and the back of her neck, exposed by her upswept hair, looked frail and vulnerable.

'Whatever is it?' said Julia.

'Matt said he'd seen them off. He *promised*.'

Bel leapt up. 'Who?'

'I feel like they're stalking me. Wherever I look, there they are, casting an evil eye or something.'

'That's just bullshit, Rach,' said Bel.

Julia went to join them in the bay. She could see a boy and girl on the opposite side of the road. The girl was chewing gum, texting on her phone, bending to fiddle with her shoes, cuffing the boy when he spun around and knocked into her. She had put some thought into her outfit. It didn't flatter her, but it showed that she followed celebrity style – short, tight and glitzy. The boy's T-shirt was far too big for him and he was rocking from one foot to another in a manner that seemed familiar. Julia tried to focus on his features, though they were not close enough to see clearly. 'Who are they?' she said.

'He's the kid who nearly burned us alive.'

'Whoa…' said Bel. 'That's a bit extreme. Plus you told me it was a good thing. You're going to get a new kitchen out of it.'

'A new kitchen?' said Julia.

'Well, it's just, with all the cooking I do…'

'Heavens, Rachael, I'm not offended! I've been remodelling yours after all.' It had been a delight to walk into the flat last night and find a clean uncluttered space with polished flooring, shining tiles and a smell of new paint: a pleasure worth waiting for. 'Leo may be a professional painter but he was a pretty amateur carpenter. That old kitchen needs ripping out. I should never have let him loose on it.' She ran her finger along the windowsill. 'He started the fire, did you say?'

'Not Leo, Mum. Nathan.'

'Nathan Carter! Of course.'

'Do you *know* him?'

Julia had avoided thinking about work since the day she left, paperwork complete, handover smoothly effected. She'd concentrated on moving house, on initiating the changes she'd planned. And from the moment she'd begun her holiday – the innocuous trip to France that had turned into something quite different – she hadn't wasted a single second wondering what had become of her patients. 'Yes,' she said. 'I do.'

'Really?'

'I remember him quite well. He was referred to me by the school because he was so disruptive. I wrote the report a while ago. There's a whole dossier on him somewhere. It needs to be pulled into a statement.'

'I don't think he goes to school at the moment,' said Rachael. 'They're in temporary accommodation because their own house—'

'Burned down!' said Bel triumphantly. 'He's a pyromaniac!'

'He's on the autistic spectrum,' said Julia. 'Relatively high-functioning, but still with a significant impairment. There are parents who try to claim their kids have a disorder when in practice they just lack boundaries, but Nathan isn't like that. He genuinely can't help himself.'

'Oh my God! And Danny thought he was so wonderful.'

'He was probably thrilled that someone older would allow him to tag along. They wouldn't have actually played with each other. A boy like Nathan doesn't share.'

'He'd ignore me totally,' said Rachael. 'Like, whatever I said was completely unimportant. Almost as if I wasn't there.'

'He wasn't being disobedient on purpose. He has problems processing information, understanding cause and effect.'

'Even so.' Rachael was defensive. 'You do see why we can't let them in? He's done enough damage and we don't know what he might get up to next.'

'What he needs is proper intervention and someone to look after his interests. His sister shouldn't be minding him; it's too much to expect.'

'So how…?'

This is nothing to do with me, thought Julia. I don't have to conduct any more investigations and write them up. I don't have to nag social workers and psychologists. I don't have to fill in any more tedious forms. I am retired. I can do what I choose.

Across the road Nathan had unfurled a yo-yo. He'd looped it around his middle finger and was letting it drop and rise with sustained dexterity. His sister was gabbling into her phone. Nevertheless, the pair of them looked utterly forlorn.

'I'll chase it up tomorrow,' Julia said. 'What's happening to the case, I mean. It's hard to believe no one's taken any action. I thought they were going to transfer him to a pupil referral unit. And he should be getting one-to-one support. There was a question mark over his hyperactivity too. I did prescribe some medication, but I don't know whether he took it. It was only temporary anyway, till we sorted out the cause. I had a bit of difficulty pinpointing his diagnosis because there'd been some trauma in the family, which could have clouded the issue. I've forgotten what…'

'Their mother died,' said Bel. 'Overdosed. She was schizophrenic or bipolar or something. I never know whether to believe Kelly – she comes out with such outrageous stuff. They are living with the grandmother though, so it's probably true.'

'People slip through the net all the time. And I expect the school was glad to be rid of him. It isn't the kid's fault, but that family have been through hell.' She sighed, but there was an element of relish in it. 'I'm not going to make a habit of nagging my successor, but I'll check tomorrow what the social worker's doing and why my report's been shelved. We can't have you being harassed, Rachael, especially not now.'

Kelly finished her call and pulled at Nathan's sleeve, which made him lose his rhythm. The yo-yo flew about on the end of its string like a stunned blackbird. She stuffed the phone in her pocket and shouted at him. The three women watching at the window couldn't hear the words, but the tone of impatience was clear enough. Nathan kicked the garden wall; he kicked a stone into the gutter; he wheeled the yo-yo around his head like a lasso and made whooping cries. As a taxi grumbled slowly down the street he shouted at that, too, and then, finally, chased after his sister.

Rachael was staring at Julia in astonishment. 'Did Matt tell you?'

'Tell you what?' said Bel.

'Remember, I haven't seen you for nearly a month,' Julia said. 'And I'm attuned to these things, so I'm more likely to notice the difference in you.'

'What difference?' said Bel.

Nathan and Kelly were out of sight, but the taxi had stopped in front of the gateposts. Leo got out and trustingly handed over his wallet. The cab driver took his fare and handed it back. Leo, coming up the path, waved cheerily at the faces in the window.

'Damn,' said Julia. 'He thinks we've been waiting for him. I'm going to go and see what Danny's up to. I have missed him, you know.' She withdrew and started up the stairs as Rachael went to open the door.

She hadn't seen her grandson for a month either and at his age children changed so rapidly. Dan had the same earnest brown eyes as Matt, and William before him, and she loved the serious way he would confide in her. It was a knack worth having, she believed: persuading your listener that nothing and nobody was as important as this moment you shared. Especially when the information came with such child-like certainty.

From the landing she could hear the greetings and exclamations below – most of the excitement coming from Bel. She peeped into the room full of Lego and train sets and pirate ships and inter-galactic adventurers, but Dan wasn't there. Nor was the Wii. He and Matt must be playing on it somewhere else. She climbed another flight of stairs to check the attic, calling his name aloud, but those rooms were empty too. She opened a window to let in the scents of the garden. She had a fine view of the spreading pear tree, the last of its snowy blossom falling.

As she stood in contemplation, the floor creaked and another person entered the room. Matt, she presumed, sent to fetch her, but before she could turn, Leo said, 'Hello, Julia.'

'Leo!'

He never looked any different. His hair was still abundant, if greying, his frame still rangy; he was wearing jeans and one of those soft cotton chambray shirts that he favoured – but at each encounter he was a little more rumpled than the last (and she'd wanted to take an iron to him from the beginning). Today he came with the addition of white gauze bandages. He was holding up his arms as if for inspection.

You mustn't think I can fix everything, she used to say to Matt and Bel when, as children, they'd had such faith in her ability to mend broken toys or treat cuts and grazes. She would do her best, but she would never make false promises. Things did not always turn out fine in the end.

'So,' she said to Leo. 'How bad was it? Have they told you? Is there any damage to nerve endings?'

He let his arms fall to his sides. 'They think not.'

'You'll be able to paint again?'

'Try and stop me. They say there'll be superficial scarring, but I don't care about the scars.' She could believe this. He had a fine specimen at his temple, mostly hidden by hair, from an incident before they had met. He wasn't vain. 'The pain can be a bit grisly, especially at night, but I'm moving my fingers now. Which is a good thing, isn't it?'

'It sounds as though you'll be all right. But it could take a while and the skin will be thin for ages so you'll have to be very careful which is not—'

'In my nature. Yes, I know.'

'Why on earth did you do it? Rushing into a burning building! I mean, you must have known...'

'Because I thought I had a chance. The flames weren't too bad initially. It was when Matt opened the doors – not that I'm blaming him. He didn't want the petrol tank to explode. But what would anyone else in my position do? Christ knows, I'm not overprotective. I don't follow the life of every painting I've ever produced, checking auction catalogues obsessively like some people do. But I couldn't stand aside. It was deflating enough to find you'd bundled them into the garage in the first place.'

'I don't want another argument,' said Julia.

'I'm not arguing.'

'Anyway it wasn't me who put them there. I'd left them on the walls. There wasn't any point in my rehanging them until the decorating was finished, but I wasn't abandoning them. I may not want to live with you any more, Leo, but I still believe in your work.'

'You do?'

'Yes.'

When this room had been his studio it had been ablaze with colour, the floor thick with hardened spills of acrylic. He'd also kept a huge sofa to sprawl on because he was one of those lucky people who could catnap and wake refreshed. Sometimes in the evening, when the children were sleeping in their beds below, Julia and Leo would make passionate love on it. The rampant chaos of the studio gave them a sense of escaping from domesticity and humdrum family life.

His affair had tarnished those memories, so the first thing she'd done after their separation was sand the floorboards and repaint the walls. She'd thrown out the old sagging sofa and replaced it with a spare bed – which Rachael had dressed with white linen. Now, apart from a scatter of Bel's possessions, the ambience was almost monastic.

He took a step towards her. 'You ran out on me,' he said.

As if she'd been a teenager having a tiff with a boyfriend. 'For goodness' sake! Okay, I'm sorry I flew off the handle. Blame Dorothy. She hadn't given me any warning that you'd be there.'

'So I come with a warning now do I?'

'You always did, Leo.' He was looking so shaggy and sorry for himself, she had to bite her lip to stop a bubble of laughter escaping – though really there was nothing funny about his situation. 'Look, I know it wasn't your fault Bel hadn't got herself to a doctor earlier. I just got an awful fright because malaria's such a killer and that's why, I suppose, I took it out on you. I'm sorry about that.' My God, she thought. My second apology in twenty-four hours. I am eating humble pie. 'But why did you keep badgering me when I was in Ireland?'

'I wanted to know when you were coming back.'

'Why?'

'Because of the house.'

'This house, you mean? It's no use to me. The kids are welcome to it.'

'If you remember,' he said quietly, 'I got the impression you'd given it to Matt and Rachael, deliberately excluding

Bel – which in any view was grossly unfair – and I wanted to sort it out with you.'

She did remember. They'd been in the converted barn, across the courtyard from the farmhouse, far enough from their hosts for raised voices not to travel. Leo had been drinking – too much cheap red wine, from a flagon on the bench – and when their row escalated, he had tried to patch it up, as in the old days, but his caress had been clumsy and inept. She had shaken off his touch at once, saying bitterly, 'You can't even look after your own feckless daughter. Thank God Matt's prepared to take her in.' There was more, but she had chosen to blank it out.

A glimmer of pain passed across Leo's features and his left arm twitched. 'God,' he said. 'It's unbearable sometimes, the throbbing, the monstrous urge to itch. I want to rip off these bloody dressings and—'

'Don't,' said Julia.

'Doctor knows best,' he mocked. He sank into the window seat and patted the space beside him as if inviting her to sit. She refused, preferring to lean against the wall; she liked being taller.

Leo said, 'Of course I never got the full story because we ended up…'

'I know how we ended up,' said Julia. 'With you accusing me of favouritism.'

'Because I thought you were taking it out on Bel for being my kid. Not… his.'

'Which simply isn't true.' For all his faults – those lost hours either spent carousing or staring at the ceiling in search of inspiration – she hadn't loved Leo any less than William. But he had the disadvantage of still being around to aggravate and make demands. 'Please don't turn everything into a competition. I try very hard to be even-handed with Matt and Bel. It's just that she tends to attract trouble more often...'

'Like me I suppose?'

This was hard to deny. 'Well look at you! How can I help but worry about you?'

'Is that all?'

'What do you mean?'

'You don't feel anything else for me?'

'Stop fishing, Leo. We had twenty sometimes terrific years together but we've gone way beyond sentiment now. I told you before, I have faith in your work, but – let's be honest – I've had quite enough of being a long-suffering wife.'

He gave her the lopsided grin which, despite herself, she still found endearing. 'I do miss you, you know. Couldn't you hack being a man's long-suffering friend?'

'I thought that's what we'd already agreed.'

'Yeah, but you didn't keep your part of the bargain.'

'*I* didn't?' She stopped short; she shouldn't let him goad her. 'Sorry, what I meant to say was—'

'How about a truce?'

She smiled. 'Yes. Exactly.'

He saw her glance at his bag leaning against the chest of drawers, a small holdall because he'd expected his visit to be brief. 'So,' he said. 'I'm off tomorrow.'

'And Bel's going with you?'

'She needs a place to stay. I need someone who can wield bottle opener and corkscrew so we should get along fine.'

'You mean she's going to be taking care of you this time?'

'No doubt she'll make a better fist of it than I did with her. And I've managed to set up a few things, interviews, meetings and so forth. You know what they say about publicity and I'm going to milk this, Julia, for all it's worth. Till I can pick up a brush again. What about you?'

'Me?' They stretched in front of her: the weeks, months and years to spend exactly as she pleased. But first there was Nathan Carter to deal with. 'Ah, well, I have a few phone calls to make, some casework that needs tidying up. I might do more consultancy actually. There are too many Nathans out there, falling through the cracks. And then of course there are the grandchildren. I want to be able to help out when the next one arrives. And enjoy it.'

As she spoke, a cry floated up through the warm still air, entering the open window. 'Danny! Where are you?'

Looking down, they saw Rachael stumble into the garden, closely followed by Matt. Bel was outside, leaning against the trunk of the pear tree, petals dusting her shoulders like confetti.

'Have you seen Dan?' they heard Rachael say. 'I thought he was with Matt in the study, but he's lost him.'

'I didn't *lose* him,' Matt protested. 'He wanted another ride on his bike and I told him he'd have to wait so he went dashing off...'

'His bike's there,' said Bel, pointing towards the hedge. 'So he can't have gone out on it.' There was a mischievous gurgle at the back of her throat, which Julia noticed at once.

Leo nudged her arm. 'Look.' The leaves shivered in the tree. 'Clever little bugger,' he said. 'He's been wanting to get up there all week, though I reckon Bel must have given him a helping hand.'

Six feet off the ground, a small pair of trainers were just visible, also two round knees gripping the thick branch as if astride a horse.

'Darling…' said Rachael faintly. Matt clapped.

Danny's face, framed by blossom, was a picture of delight.

36

The Letter

4th June 2010
Dear Bel,

I am enclosing a letter from Clemmie. She says she would like to see you again and as you are in London, I expect something can be arranged. You say you are in touch with her father's family through his brother. You will understand the difficulty I have in trusting Tom, but if her grandmother chooses to make the journey from Ireland, I wouldn't stop them meeting. Clemmie is very precious to me as you can imagine and I want her to be happy.

Yours truly,
Monique Beaumont

Dear Bel,
Thank you for sending me the story about the volcano. I reely liked it. Will you send me anuver one? My gran-

ny on the farm sent me sum nitted ducks. They are cool.
She mite cum to see me. It wud be reely nice to see you
and unkle Keeron too.
I hope you are well.

Love from
Clementine Alice Beaumont xxxx

Acknowledgements

I am deeply indebted to my agent, Laura Longrigg, for her guidance in the initial shaping of this book; to my editors, Lucy Gilmour and Laura Palmer, for insight into character development and polishing the final draft; and to the team at Aria for their commitment and attention to detail. This is a story about families, so many thanks are also due to the families I know best: Cross, Brovender, Carmody, Ryan and, of course, all the Feenys.

About the Author

Penny Feeny grew up in Cambridge, but has been settled in Liverpool for most of her adult life. She has worked in a gallery in Rome and in publishing in London, and has been an arts administrator, editor and radio presenter. She is married with two sons and three daughters. Her short fiction has been widely published and broadcast and won several awards. She is the author of three previous novels and her debut, *That Summer in Ischia*, was one of the summer of 2011's bestselling titles.

Hello from Aria

We hope you enjoyed this book! Let us know, we'd love to hear from you.

We are Aria, a dynamic digital-first fiction imprint from award-winning independent publishers Head of Zeus. At heart, we're avid readers committed to publishing exactly the kind of books we love to read – from romance and sagas to crime, thrillers and historical adventures. Visit us online and discover a community of like-minded fiction fans!

We're also on the look out for tomorrow's superstar authors. So, if you're a budding writer looking for a publisher, we'd love to hear from you. You can submit your book online at ariafiction.com/ we-want-read-your-book

You can find us at:
Email: aria@headofzeus.com
Website: www.ariafiction.com
Submissions: www.ariafiction.com/
we-want-read-your-book
Facebook: @ariafiction
Twitter: @Aria_Fiction
Instagram: @ariafiction

46326531R00235

Printed in Poland
by Amazon Fulfillment
Poland Sp. z o.o., Wrocław